# HE WAS THE ONLY MAN
## SHE EVER WANTED . . .

"Who do you think you are, Trefyn Connor?"

He smiled, showing a flash of white teeth. "Your lord and master," he said, as she stood again confronting him, "King of your own wild heart. Your lover, maybe—when you learn what love is all about—" A laugh escaped him; the comforting sound she'd known as a child. He took her hand lightly. "Off with you now, or like the devil they'll be after me."

She pulled her hand away and lifted it with the other to his face, bringing it down to hers. For a moment he did not respond; then warmly, as her lips touched his, the pressure of his mouth was on her own, hot and demanding, draining, it seemed, all the sweetness that was in her to himself.

Then it was over. He let her go abruptly, controlling with an effort the trembling of his limbs. "And don't come this way again until you've learned your manners!"

# THE PROUD HUNTER

*Marianne Harvey*

A DELL BOOK

Published by
Dell Publishing Co., Inc.
1 Dag Hammarskjold Plaza
New York, New York 10017

This work was first published in Great Britain
by Futura Publications Ltd.

Dell ® TM 681510, Dell Publishing Co., Inc.

ISBM: 0-440-17098-2

Printed in the United States of America
First U.S.A. printing—April 1981

# THE PROUD HUNTER

# INTRODUCTION
## 1900

She sat in the heather, with her hands clasped over her chest, face lifted toward the autumn sky. Her small chin was set, her clear gray eyes brilliant with emotion and all the changing light of the afternoon.

"Don't let me hate my mother," her lips murmured presently, almost soundlessly; "please make me like her. . . ." What she prayed to was uncertain. But at the moment her young form could have been resurrected from some far ancient past of pagan gods and ritual. The moorland winds blew fresh and strong about the standing stones above, whirling through furze and undergrowth, and stunted sparse trees, whipping the glowing hair from her forehead in a flying cloud of streaked russet. Her cheeks glowed scarlet from the stinging air, and very slowly her red lips relaxed into a secret smile. There on the wild heights of Rosebuzzan she felt free and could really be herself. It was her own place. Nicholas and Donna Trevarvas, her parents, had no right to send her away.

Yet tomorrow morning, early, she was being packed off to boarding school in Bristol, just because her mother said so. She could have got round her father, she knew it. Nicholas adored her. And that was the trouble, she told herself with uncanny insight for a ten-year-old. Donna was jealous. Well—perhaps not *exactly* that, but annoyed because Nicholas made such a fuss of her. It was so unfair. After all, her mother had *her* favorite—Jason, Juliet's youngest brother who was just fourteen. Jason, unlike the rest of them, was fair like Donna's own mother had been, with bright blue eyes and stubborn as a mule when he set his mind on anything. He was already determined to be a sculptor. Andrew, three years older than Jason, was the adventurous one, and had caused a commotion in the family by running away from Rugby to join the Army.

When he'd returned from the Boer War, wounded, Nicholas had "damned" a good deal and called him a young scoundrel and fool, but from the look in Nicholas's eyes Juliet had known he was secretly proud.

William, a man now at eighteen, had his father's passion for tin mining and land development. Of all her brothers she felt she knew him least. He was a strong, withdrawn character who generally got what he wanted in the end through mere dogged persistence and avoiding any family arguments wherever possible. Rather dull, though, Juliet thought musingly. After all, what did dark, dead, old mines matter? She'd much rather be like Trefyn Connor who lived with his mother and sister Jet on the farm below the curve of Rosebuzzan hill.

Trefyn loved growing things and all wild creatures. He was tall and slim, black-haired, with gleaming dark eyes and strong as any man, though he was only fifteen. One day, Juliet told herself, not for the first time, she would marry Trefyn and he could take her away to a new home, safe from Donna's interfering bossy influence and Trefyn's own mother Elinor, too. She disliked Elinor even more than Donna, because she acted as though everyone but her own family were dirt.

"Keep away from her," Donna had told her daughter sharply more than once. "I won't have you mixing with the Connors, or laying yourself open to that woman's insults. She's an unstable, wild character or she'd never have got herself into such a mess with a man like Dirke."

"Now Donna," her husband had said with a glint of amusement mingling with irritation in his eyes and voice, "best leave the past alone, don't you think? Elinor did what she wanted, like most women worth their salt. She was probably quite content."

"Oh, rubbish, Nicholas," Donna had snapped. "A mere *groom*."

Juliet had listened avidly to this conversation, hoping to hear further details of the scandalous elopement years ago of Sir Paul Gentry's daughter Elinor with his half-Gypsy servant and horse breeder. She'd been disappointed. Nicholas had suddenly laughed, taken Donna's chin in his hand, and planted a kiss on her lips with that ardent, certain look in his eyes which never failed to annoy his young daughter. It was always that way. However much her father loved her, Juliet thought reminiscently, sitting in the heather that afternoon, Donna meant the most to him.

*Donna!* who tomorrow was sending her off to school.

It was *cruel* of her, and unfair.

Instinctively her eyes turned left to the valley where one wall of the Connor farmstead jutted out from the base of the hill. She wondered what Trefyn was doing, and if Elinor was about, or safely occupied in the kitchen. Since Dirke's death from a fall on a horse a year ago, Elinor had become a more hardened and embittered woman than ever, and far more possessive of her children. Juliet had gathered this, not only from Trefyn whom she met occasionally in secret but from William's remarks concerning Connor land. He wanted desperately to get a hand on a few acres of it so he could reopen an ancient mine that had been left derelict for fifty years. In William's judgment there was still copper there to be worked—new lodes that might be rich, even with tin.

But Elinor would not sell.

All she had she meant to retain. Society might cut her off, and herself and her husband be ignored by her own kind, but she remained a Gentry—proud, hard, and sufficiently independent financially to defy the ambitions of any greedy Trevarvas. Without realizing it herself, Nicholas Trevarvas's wealth and thriving estate had become a symbol to her of all she had lost. Marriage to Dirke, however passionately rewarding at the outset, had proved a frustrating, sour business once the novelty had worn off. The small, dark, horsy man with the winning smile and fiery black eyes had recognized no laws but his own, and he made no attempt to suit his life to hers.

Two things had mattered to him—horses and sex. In that order. Of the latter he'd claimed what he wanted of Elinor, and when on occasion she'd felt repugnance, he had not noticed. He'd been fond of his children when they came, and had taken a whimsical natural pleasure in demonstrating to them the ways of small wild creatures. He could whistle like a bird himself, and had even trained an adder to circle his palm without striking. But domestically he'd had no manners, nor had he tried, and this, perhaps more than anything else, had driven Elinor into a shell of hatred and reserve.

His death, possibly, had been opportune, for her. But for Trefyn and Jet it had been a tragedy. They'd loved Dirke, and in some way felt Elinor had been to blame, although Trefyn kept his thoughts to himself. He was an enigma to his mother; something intimidating in the glance of his dark, slightly tilted eyes under slanting brows frequently silenced her when a hot remark was on her lips. A mysterious quality in his personality evaded her. He fitted into no definite category or type, possessing a certain amount of his father's wildness combined with an inborn cultural sensitivity that proved wildly disturbing.

With Jet it was different. Jet was inherently unprincipled, dark-haired and olive-skinned, with a wild, free beauty and grace of movement derived entirely from the Connors. Elinor was strict with her, and from her earliest childhood Jet had learned to fear her anger.

Nevertheless, despite their varying temperaments, they stuck together as a unit, presenting a combined front against the Trevarvas stronghold.

Juliet thought it a great nuisance and shame that the two families had to be such enemies. In her childlike but passionate way she loved Trefyn, and before she was packed off to boarding school the next day she knew she had to make him understand, so that he wouldn't let some other stupid girl capture him in her absence.

No one—*no* one but she must marry Trefyn.

This was her secret childish ambition—to live with him always near the open moorlands of Rosebuzzan hill, helping him tame the young colts, and keep their land free for the animals and wild things that lived there. What right had William, her eldest brother, to open that ugly old mine again, spoiling the heather slopes with smoke and slag, blackening the yellow gorse and hidden dells of bluebells and thyme?

Once she'd watched with glee as Dirke had taken his gun and shooed huntsmen away. Trefyn, who was only thirteen then, had caught the fox and carried it to the farm for safety. Elinor had found Juliet at the door and told her sharply to take herself off home. "You keep to your family," she'd said, "and leave mine to me." She was a large woman, with a gaunt face that had once been good-looking in a hard way, with thick yellow hair scraped from high cheekbones to an untidy knot on her neck. Her blue eyes had blazed so coldly that the little girl, frightened, had run away.

But Elinor Connor didn't frighten her anymore. After Dirke's death something had happened to her physically. She could no longer move easily, and although her temper was still violent, it was easy to avoid her hand and find a quick hiding place.

So that early September afternoon—her last before the dreaded journey to school—Juliet braved the thought of Trefyn's mother and jumped up suddenly to run quickly down the narrow sheep track toward the farm.

The wind blew fresh and keen against her, brushing her hair with a few driven leaves from the lean branches of a bent tree. As she rounded the bend, the farm itself could be seen, fenced in an acre of its land with stables to the back. The house was of gray granite, L-shaped, enclosing a yard and sheds for the few cattle. The front portion was flat-walled with square windows on either side of the porch, beneath two rows of smaller ones. A hundred yards or so along the valley was a water mill by a stream, and beyond that stood a half-ruined stamp house. The ancient mine stack projected from a clump of furze and grasping undergrowth some distance up the hill. It was this piece of land in particular that William wanted. Juliet thought it was rather silly of him. After all, her father had three proper mines still working near Penjust, and she knew he didn't really agree with her brother's determination to get the ruined one going again. But William was like that—always wanting what he couldn't get. And of course Donna backed him up, simply because she was so against the Connors.

Why? *Why?* Juliet wondered, as she stopped running, near the farm gate. If Donna were friendly, everything could be so different. She and Trefyn wouldn't have to see each other secretly. Even Elinor might soften. Of course if Trefyn's mother *would* sell, that would help too. The Connors would have more money, which would mean that when she, Juliet, was old enough, Trefyn would be considered more her equal by her family.

It all seemed suddenly stuffy and stupid, and certainly not worth pondering over when she was about to be parted from Trefyn for such a long time.

The thought saddened her. Her vivid face clouded, bringing a glimmer of tears to her gray eyes. At that moment Trefyn appeared from the stables. Though slender, he was tall and strong, with a golden glow catching his black curls and clear skin from the slanting sunlight. Seeing her, he walked briskly to the gate. His tilted mouth smiled above the cleft chin, but his dark, rather almond-shaped eyes were slightly wary.

"Well, what are *you* doing here?" he asked.

"Oh, Trefyn, it's the last time I'll see you for *ages*. Tomorrow I'm going to that awful place—the school. Unless—" a wild idea occurred to her—"unless you'd keep me here and hide me. You *could,* couldn't you?"

The slanted brows came abruptly together in a frown.

"Don't be silly," he said.

"Silly?" Her lower lip trembled, and something in her face then mildly disturbed him—something mature beyond her years that was neither child, sprite, nor yet woman, but something of all three.

"Yes, daft," he reiterated, taking her hand. "How would I hide you? Why? *Where?* And what would I do with you?"

Her head drooped. "I don't know. I thought—"

"You didn't think at all," he told her firmly. "And that's why they're sending you to school—to teach you sense."

In a flash she rounded on him. "I don't *want* to be sensible, I don't, I don't. I want to stay here with you—forever and ever."

"Well, you can't do that and you know it." His voice was hard. "You shouldn't be here now, either. If your ma knew, there'd be trouble. So run away now. I've had enough trouble already with your stuck-up family—" He turned to go back to the farm. She ran after him, catching his arm.

"Trefyn—"

He spun around, staring directly down into her clear eyes. Strange eyes, he thought, like moorland pools with the sun on them. And he was instantly troubled and irritated with himself for thinking so.

"Yes?" His voice was sharp.

"When I come back for good—when I'm older, grown-up I mean—couldn't we be married?" The words tumbled out in little gasps. Her face was suddenly wildly red.

He stared at her, too astonished at first to speak. Then he said, "You 'n' *me*? A Trevarvas and a Connor? Don't make me laugh, Juliet."

"I don't want to. There's nothing funny in it. But if *you* think so—all right, *laugh*. And I'll hate you, Trefyn, I'll hate you all my life—"

She'd have rushed away but he pulled her back and turned her round fiercely to face him again.

"Now you just listen to me Juliet Trevarvas, I'm not promising marriage to any girl unless *I* do the asking, least of all—a—a kid of —ten, is it?"

She nodded mutely.

"So you just behave yourself, go to school and do what you're told for a change. Then, when you come back with your hair up, knowing how to act like a proper woman—well, maybe we'll think about it."

"Maybe?"

"Yes. And that means, p'raps—p'raps not. I don't know yet whether I'm the marrying kind. Anyway, I thought you were all for being an actress?"

"I've changed my mind. They wouldn't let me, anyway."

"Neither would they let you marry me."

"If you—"

"Stop it," he said, "don't argue. Run away now. Here's my dear mother on the warpath."

Juliet cast a quick glance toward the porch. Elinor's figure looked square and forbidding standing motionless on the path. Her face was in shadow, but Juliet well knew the hard set of her mouth and dead stare of her cold eyes.

"You like me, Trefyn, don't you?" the child said quickly, pleadingly, "you *do* like me—a bit?"

"Quite a lot," he told her.

She turned and started to run, as Elinor shouted, "Trefyn—Trefyn—send that sly puss off. At once, do you hear?"

A look of dislike, almost hate crossed his face. He waited until Juliet's small form had reached the bend of the hill. She glanced back, waving, and he lifted his hand once before turning and ambling lazily toward his mother. She was quite mad, he thought; one day she'd have a second stroke, and it would kill her. Always at such times he tried to feel compassion for the thwarted outcast, but it was difficult when no vestige of feminine charm remained.

"You shouldn't get so upset," he told her. "The girl's all right—what are you afraid of, eh?"

"She's a forward hussy, too old for her years by half, and not an ounce of breeding behind her," Elinor said, as the mottled color began to fade from her heavy face. "*You*—you're different. A Gentry."

"*Gentry?*" Trefyn laughed. "*Me?* Oh no, mother

dear. Make no mistake about it—*I'm* no gentry. Now, do you want me to help you to your chair?" Muttering, she allowed him to lead her to the parlor where a fire burned in the grate. All anger suddenly faded from her eyes, leaving them dull and listless. When Trefyn left, closing the door behind him, she was staring into the flames, remembering. Remembering what life had been before Dirke Connor disrupted her existence.

She saw herself as a bold girl, proud, willful, and Dirke's teasing glance as he restrained a recalcitrant colt momentarily beyond her own control. From the first moment his strange narrow eyes gleamed down on her, her destiny had been settled. A destiny that too soon had become her tribulation.

As she sat there, bitterness intensified in her. Only one thing in her life now remained—to see that Trefyn and Jet kept to themselves, holding on to what was their own.

Outside the sun spread a sudden streaking flash of rosy gold above the distant horizon before it dipped quickly below the rim of the high moors, leaving only a shadowed film behind.

Trefyn, after leading a white goat and her kid to their shed for the night, paused and stood briefly glancing across the valley toward the roofs and towers of Polbreath, the Trevarvas home. It was not a beautiful house, having been added to through different periods of the centuries. Its main towers, though majestic, were too ornate to be in good taste. But in the fading light the place ruled darkly as a symbol of power and prestige.

Poor little rich girl, he thought, remembering the

wild pleading of Juliet's eyes. But perhaps, after all, she didn't have to be pitied. She knew what she wanted, or thought she did.

As for him? His mind had no clear ideas for the future, only feelings and a sense of mysterious belonging and unity with the wild Cornish earth that had become his heritage.

## 1

On an autumn day in 1907, Juliet, daughter of Nicholas and Donna Trevarvas, gave an irritable little shriek as a pin pierced her thigh near the waist.

"That hurt," she said. "What a nuisance this is."

The dressmaker, a dark-haired, thin, bespectacled little woman, glanced up sharply like a bright-eyed bird, and when she'd taken several pins from between her teeth said briskly, "All in a good cause, Miss Juliet, there must be not the slightest tuck in the wrong place. I do not wish to prick you. But if you *will* wriggle—Ah! *mon Dieu!* what an impatient one you are! and how your dear mama will scold if we do not have you *parfaitement*—quite exquisite for your party—" She looked down again and once more started upon the tortuous business of fitting Juliet's new dress. It was of green shimmering silk, cut low on the shoulders and tight-waisted, falling in fitted slender lines over the hips to a circular full hemline brushing the floor. Silk embroidery in a butterfly design had been

handworked from just below the knees, and at each
movement of the graceful young body it swirled entic-
ingly above the lace petticoats beneath. Juliet knew
that eventually the gown would, indeed, be lovely.
But the business of having to stand still for so long,
being pushed and prodded and pricked, annoyed her.
And why on earth did this gushing little Miss West
put on such stupid airs, using French words when she
came from Falmouth and had been born the daughter
of a maid (employed by Lady St. Clarryn) who'd married a Cornish fisherman?

That black dress she wore, too—so dreary and depressing with her yellowish skin and black hair.
Donna, Juliet's mother, thought her very smart because of the St. Clarryn connection, of course, and un-
failingly took her advice on fashion. Even before Juliet went to boarding school—which she'd left now for
good, thank goodness—there'd been endless sessions
whenever a new dress or coat was needed, of being
measured and turning, of standing this way and then
that. While the scissors snipped and the tape measure
pulled, Miss West grimaced, revealing white teeth far
too large for her small face that made her look, Juliet
always thought, like a dressed-up monkey.

Today the fitting seemed longer and more tiring
than it had ever been, with Donna coming in at intervals to fuss round and criticize. "The neckline a *little*
higher perhaps, Miss West?" she'd suggested the last
time. "My daughter, after all, is only seventeen—*just.*"

"Ah!" Miss West had said, raising her hands in a foreign gesture, with a flutter of her eyes at Donna.
"How right you are. Sweet seventeen with all life before her. We must not be too sophisticated—no." And
her hands had tugged the bodice more fiercely than

was strictly necessary toward the young neck. Juliet
had wriggled her shoulders protestingly. She'd seen
the expression on the little woman's face and it had
not been pleasant. Criticism from Donna was hard to
accept. But "madam" had to be satisfied, because she
was a valuable customer, and after a moment the ingratiating smile was back again. Juliet generally had
to pay for such indignities by suffering a series of
more painful tugs and jerking at her stays, maybe an
extra prick on her breast or thigh. She knew Miss West
disliked her, resenting her youth and beauty and the
luxuries denied to the less privileged. Sometimes even
she was sorry for the poor, plain little creature. The
trouble was it was hard to be really kind to anyone so
completely without charm.

Today of all days the dressmaking session was a
bore and a profound irritation. The sun was shining
outside, washing the autumn landscape to gold. Gorse
still flamed on the moorland hills, and the air was
heady with the tangy nostalgic scent of woodsmoke,
heather, and the pungent odor of fallen leaves on the
damp earth. A drift of it filtered through the sewing-
room window, which was open a few inches at the
top, and Juliet instinctively thought of Trefyn Connor.
Was he working at the farm that afternoon, she wondered, or trying out a half-broken-in colt somewhere?
She'd not seen him to talk to since she'd returned from
boarding school the previous week. Donna had been
too concerned with her over her birthday party which
was to take place the following Saturday, and her eyes
far too watchful for her daughter to slip off unseen.
Such a nuisance. And how unfair it was that Trefyn
wouldn't be invited to the celebrations. He was the
only friend she wanted to be there. The rest, men-

tioned approvingly by Donna, would be the most awful bores—the Court boys and their parents who had
estates near the Lizard and in Ireland and were very
rich; Major Carne, not so wealthy but well connected,
with his children, Geoffrey and Charlotte; and Sir
Hawtrey Boltham, a middle-aged but eligible bache-
lor who'd made a fortune in cotton. He'd bought up
Traskiss Castle, near Helston, where he lived with his
sister Florence. They had even acquired a coat-of-
arms and a crest which was embossed on their note
papers. Juliet thought him a silly little snob, although
he was certainly very kind. But Donna said that as
new "gentry" and so extremely wealthy they should
not be ignored.

Then Sir James and Lady Penverrys. They would
be present, naturally, Juliet thought, as Miss West
fumbled with pins round her hemline. Their niece too,
Rosina, who, according to gossip, had once been in
love with her father, Nicholas. A little giggle escaped
her when she thought of it—Rosina was such a large,
lumpy woman now; it really did seem ridiculous that
Donna could ever have been jealous of her. But then
her mother had a proud and haughty temper. Beautiful she still was, with her orange eyes and luxuriant
dark hair as yet untouched with gray, but difficult to
live with. Only Nicholas could really manage her,
which was, Juliet thought idly, the reason she was still
so obviously in love with him. When it came to a crisis
he remained master in his own house, though he generally managed, these days, to avoid scenes. Sometimes Juliet wished he'd be firmer with his impetuous,
strong-willed wife. Jason, for instance, still couldn't do
a thing wrong in Donna's eyes, and because of it her
father was allowing this fair, handsome youngest

brother of hers to do just what he liked with his life, had even said he'd consider allowing him to study art in London or Paris if he proved he had a gift for it.

Juliet didn't begrudge Jason his charm or talent, but she *did* resent Donna's attitude toward *her*, and the ruthless way she'd been packed off to that awful, strict "academy for young ladies" at Bristol, run by the Misses Smart. Yes, the last year really *had* been awful. Getting up at six o'clock each morning to wash in cold water before going downstairs to practice scales on the piano. The music room had been cold, and her fingers had been stiff. The woolen combinations she had to wear under the constricting underwear of tight stays and flannel drawers had itched and brought goose pimples up on her cold skin. The long, navy serge skirt and high-necked navy woolen blouse had smothered her. Then the awful breakfast of lumpy porridge and thick soggy toast!—the endless prayers afterward and hymn-singing conducted by Miss Lucy Smart, who could be vicious with her cane if any girl dared to be late or absent without leave. Their morning lessons had commenced at nine and continued until twelve-thirty, when all pupils would march in pairs behind Miss Arabella, who took them on a scheduled walk for half an hour before the midday meal. Miss Maud was in the rear to see that no girl stepped out of line, and it was forbidden to look to the right or left. Lunch was boiled mutton on Sundays, followed by mutton stew on Mondays, and dumplings with a liberal amount of boiled cabbage on Tuesdays. Wednesdays were hash days, Thursdays cold ham or rabbit pie, and Fridays—the worst of all—boiled fish and soggy, damp potatoes. Saturdays, naturally, meant fish cakes.

Juliet had made the mistake at the beginning of her first term of complaining in a letter to her father, not knowing that every letter was steamed open and perused before posting. The result had been three strokes of Miss Lucy's cane across her palm and a polite letter written at the "tyrant's" direction, telling "dear papa" and "mama" she was happy at Fairgates, learning her catechism as she was told, and in every way trying to become the young lady they wished her to be. She had added that she was studying history and arithmetic, and was enjoying her music and painting lessons.

She had hoped wildly that Nicholas would not believe she could have become such a paragon of virtue in so short a time and that he would come rushing to Bristol to rescue her from hell.

But no such miracle had happened. So eventually she'd learned to endure her fate and discovered there *were* bright moments after all—including the midnight feasts when bread and drippings smuggled from the kitchen by one of the maids was eaten surreptitiously half under bedclothes in the dormitory. Such caution was necessary in case Miss Lucy heard the slightest sound and came to investigate.

There had been carefully concealed nudges and smiles too, when they had passed boys from a nearby college walking in formation with their tutor. And somehow, despite the privations and disadvantages, Juliet, like her companions, had thrived, put on weight in the right places, and emerged at the end of her seven-year Fairgate period as an elegant young lady, well equipped to move in approved social circles. To catch a husband, naturally, or rather—in more polite terms—to make "a good match."

Juliet shuddered inwardly. Her mother's ideas of a good match were so dull. Obviously *her* first choice was for one of the Court boys—Desmond or Ralphe; Desmond preferably, because he was the elder and would one day inherit Castle Clamourne and all the Irish lands that went with it. Desmond was one of the reasons for the party, but if Des didn't come up to scratch or *she* didn't, then Ralphe would be a good second best; failing either, there remained Geoffrey Carne who at least had "family" behind him—or even Sir Hawtrey, despite the fact that he was three inches shorter than herself and old enough to be her father. Oh, yes, Juliet was fully aware of her mother's plans. In a friendly way, of course, she *was* quite fond of Desmond and Ralphe. They were fun to be with, and during the school holidays she'd seen a good deal of them. They both had a sense of humor and shared her love of riding. Both were quick-witted and, like herself, knew what Donna had in mind.

But *marriage!*

Because Juliet saw the prospect as such an immense joke, they pretended to do the same, although at last half-term break she *had* fancied Desmond's eyes had a new warm look in them when he glanced at her. Well, she'd soon have to disillusion him over any serious ideas brewing there, she thought idly, surveying herself with satisfaction at last through the long sewing-room mirror. Funny little Miss West had certainly made an expert job of the gown so far; the whole effect really was elegant, and when her russet hair was taken in a roll off her face as she'd seen in photographs of the Gaiety Girls and famous beauties like Lily Elsie, she knew she'd make an impression at the forthcoming party. Not that she cared much about fashion generally. If Trefyn Connor had been coming to it, she'd have been wildly thrilled. It seemed a waste to look so attractive and have only old men or youths to admire her. Still, as she had to go through with the boring business she'd get the most out of it she could, and if she broke anyone's heart, it would be her mother's fault and not hers.

The fitting—the last one, thank heaven—was finally over, and after Donna had given her seal of approval, Miss West was taken downstairs, given a cup of tea, and later departed in the Trevarvas chaise for her rooms in Penzance, taking the gown with her to finish.

Juliet sighed heavily as the door closed, stretched her arms, yawned, and reached for her blue alpaca everyday dress to step into. Then, on impulse, she gathered it up under her arm and, wearing only her white petticoat over her bloomers and stays, slipped out and made a dash for her own room further along the landing.

Donna unexpectedly appeared round a corner of the stairs. "Whatever are you doing, rushing about like that?" she queried sharply. "Supposing your brothers were to see you—"

"Oh, mama, don't be so *stuffy*!" Juliet exclaimed. "Suppose they did? They've seen me in far less than this before."

"That's not the point," Donna retorted. "I thought at least that expensive boarding school might have taught you a *little* restraint. Now go and get dressed immediately."

Juliet glared.

"I'm sorry, mama, I'm not wearing this thing anymore. It chokes at the neck. Anyway, I'm going out."

"Out? Where?"

"Riding," Juliet answered. "It's a lovely day, and I want to try the new colt out properly, the one papa's got specially for me—Firebrand."

Donna was going to protest, and then she thought better of it, fully aware that if it came to an argument concerning his daughter, Nicholas would be sure to stick up for Juliet.

"Very well," she said shortly. "Only don't be too long, and for the sake of your good name and your father's peace of mind keep well away from the Connor farm. Elinor died six weeks ago, and Trefyn's got a girl working there now—some distant connection from London they say, a wild character from what I hear—"

Juliet let the dress slip from her arm to the floor.

"A *girl?*"

"He'll probably marry her," Donna told her in remote cool tones. "Why not? Like generally links up with like in the end. Oh, I know you were fond of Trefyn as a child, Juliet—" her voice had softened, "but *don't*, please don't give him another thought. He's not your *kind*—none of the Connors are. You've grown up now, and belong to different worlds—"

Juliet said nothing. She reached down for the fallen dress, and pushed past her mother with a riot of mixed feelings churning her thoughts.

Trefyn and a girl! a wild girl from London. She didn't believe it—not about marrying her anyway. He'd have waited to see her, Juliet, first. Or *would* he? A niggle of discomfort quickly changing to acute anxiety seized her. For several long years she and Trefyn had managed merely brief glimpses of each other during the holidays, and in the whole time had exchanged only a few words due to the vigilance of her own family and Elinor.

The last time Juliet had seen Trefyn's mother she'd looked quite mad, standing at the gate waving a thorn stick with her yellow hair gone gray and tumbled about her shoulders. Juliet had heard she'd had a stroke and made the excuse of calling to inquire about her health. But when Trefyn appeared he motioned her to leave and took his mother's arm, leading her slowly and laboriously back into the farmhouse.

Now Elinor was dead.

Juliet didn't pretend to herself she was sorry. How could she be, when Elinor had hated her so much? But to have another, younger woman step into her place so quickly was intolerable to think about, especially following Donna's pointed remarks.

So there was only one thing left to do about it—ride over to the farm and find out for herself how things were.

She changed into her dark blue velvet riding habit quickly, and was mildly shocked to find the coat was slightly tight at the front. Good heaven, she thought, taking a keen look at herself through the long, beveled mirror; her shape was changing. Last holidays, when the habit was new, she'd been slim all over; now, though her waist was if anything thinner than it had been, her breasts were distinctly fuller, tilting upward under the soft material, and prickling with a delicious, desirous feeling when she thought of Trefyn.

She laid a hand briefly over the soft curves, longing to be free of the constricting bodice and to race as she had so often when a child, wild and unrestrained through the heady autumn air.

Race into Trefyn's arms.

Her heart nearly stopped beating when she thought of it. Trefyn, Trefyn. Suddenly her pulses were dancing again. She twirled round once, to see if her coat lay properly at the back, straightened the jabot at her neck, and with her hair conventionally pinned and netted in case Donna saw her leaving the house, placed the shining hat on her gleaming russet hair.

Then, looking considerably more the young lady of breeding and conventional proprieties than she felt, she walked gracefully with assumed dignity downstairs, knowing that Donna would probably be on the watch in the hall.

Donna, in fact, was engaged in a heated argument with Nicholas as Juliet went through the hall and out a side door to the stables.

Nicholas had just had a letter.

His daughter Ianthe, Juliet's older half sister who'd been estranged from her father and stepmother since her marriage six years previously to the elderly, extremely rich debauchee, Robertson Wycksley, wanted to return on a visit.

"Dearest papa," she'd written, from her elegant London address,

"I know very well what worry and sadness I caused you by marrying Robertson, and believe me there are times when I have suffered very much because of it. I do not ask you to forgive me—but I *am* your daughter, papa, and if I do not have a little peace from this dreadful life inflicted on me I don't know what may happen to me. So please—*please* let me see you again, if only for a little time.

If I don't hear to the contrary, I shall take the

train from Euston one day next week and have a
cab from Penzance.

Your devoted daughter,
Ianthe.

"The *nerve* of it!" Donna exclaimed, with her orange eyes flaming. "After all this time—and *next
week*! Do you realize it doesn't give us a chance to
stop her—and talking like that, about the dreadful life
*inflicted* on her. She brought it on *herself*—and you
know very well her reputation's a perfect scandal. One
love affair after another—and that dreadful play she
was in last. I won't have her Nicholas—I simply *won't*.
Juliet's at an impressionable age. Ianthe's influence
would be wicked. You must *do* something. Stop her in
any way you like—but I won't have that woman in my
house. Why, for all we know Wycksley may have
turned her out, and be divorcing her. *Him*! imagine
it—"

She broke off with her breasts heaving, the wild
color rich in her lovely face. She was wearing a dark
olive-green dress cut tightly on the gently swelling
hips from where it flared in voluminous folds to the
tips of her high-heeled shoes. Never had she appeared
more sensually desirable.

Nicholas waited a moment, then he said in controlled, even tones, "Have you quite finished?"

"No." Donna answered quickly, "I haven't. There's
just this—if Ianthe comes here, *I* go, and take Juliet
with me until she's packed off again."

"Is that your last word?"

"Yes."

"Then here's mine. This is my house, and if Ianthe

wishes to come home, she'll do so. As for leaving and taking Juliet with you, you'll do nothing of the sort. So don't threaten me with running away my love. We had enough of that kind of thing in the past. I thought by now you'd have learned more sense—" he sighed. "*Really*, Donna. You're acting like a child yourself. Has it ever occurred to you that if you'd been a little more generous to Ianthe in the past, she might never have thrown herself away on that old reprobate?"

"What a thing to say!" Donna exclaimed, genuinely outraged. "I tried harder than you even to stop her. Why, if you remember, I wouldn't receive him at Polbreath at all—" She broke off, lost for words.

"No. If you had, probably things would have turned out differently," Nicholas said drily. "You were too hard on her Donna, you always were. Sometimes I think the same thing's happening with Juliet."

"What do you mean?"

He flung her a dark, shrewd glance. "Young Connor. She'll see him you know, whatever either of us say. And if you pull the reins too hard, she'll jib."

"*Must* you refer to women as though they were horses?" Donna said tartly.

"Most are." Nicholas answered, adding after a short pause, "excluding you, of course."

Donna felt the warm color staining her cheeks. Even after twenty-five years of marriage Nicholas's compliments spoken in a certain way never failed to stir and excite her. Even at that moment, despite her indignation, she could feel her pulses quicken. She turned away and walked erectly with a brave attempt at dignity to the parlor table. Late chrysanthemums blazed in a glory of bronze and gold from a cut-glass bowl, filling her nostrils with their pungent, earthy scent. She lifted a flower on the pretense of rearrangement, and a moment later felt Nicholas's arm enclosing her waist. She turned her head, glancing up at him, and against her will smiled. He looked so handsome and virile still, as he had been a quarter of a century earlier. The hair was still black and luxuriant, with only a slight graying at the temples. His figure, if a trifle heavier, showed no sign of portliness, and though the lines were more deeply etched on either side of the strongly carved nose, the dominant chin and well-formed lips were as clearly defined as they had ever been—the deeply set dark eyes as magnetic and compelling.

He let his mouth brush her cheek momentarily before saying, "You'll behave, won't you, love?"

*"Behave? Me?"*

He pulled her to him, seeking her lips. She closed her eyes briefly. Then as he released her she heard him saying cajolingly, "with Ianthe—for *my* sake."

"Oh, Nicholas." Her sigh was desperate. "You spoil her, just like Juliet—"

"As you spoil Jason."

She jerked herself away. "What's *Jason* got to do with it?"

Nicholas regarded her speculatively. "What's sauce for the goose is sauce for the gander. It's time that young man put his mind and energies to something useful. All this talk of art and sculpture and going to Paris—"

"You're trying to *blackmail* me," Donna protested.

"If there's no other way, I've got to," Nicholas protested. "Ianthe's coming home, and peace with my womenfolk I will have. You *do* understand, don't you?"

"You've made it quite clear," Donna said. "But don't expect me to be warm and gushing, and 'oh how *lovely* to see you Ianthe' sort of thing. I couldn't do it, Nicholas. I still think she behaved despicably to you, and I always shall."

A quirk of amusement touched his lips as she lifted her head haughtily, went to the mirror, and trying to repress a renewed flare of temper, tidied a few strands of rebellious black hair from her forehead. Nicholas had won, as usual, she thought. In the end, when it came to a clash of wills, she knew he always would. The thought of Ianthe's intrusion again into life at Polbreath already set her nerves on edge and mildly depressed her; not only on her daughter Juliet's behalf—Juliet was already showing signs of being beyond her control—but because of the distasteful reminder that at one time another woman had lain in Nicholas's arms and borne his children.

Yes, she could still be jealous when the occasion arose, although she knew there was no need to be; Nicholas loved her as much as she loved him. But there were times when she wished irrationally all other memories except those of herself could be wiped clean from his mind and heart. She was fully aware of her own shortcomings—the possessive, deeply rooted passion that still remained for the man, her husband, who'd so arrogantly swept her off her feet those years before. Something of the rebellious girl she'd been then still lingered within her. Juliet had a good deal of the same quality—a single-mindedness that could be dangerous. Very often, though she would not have admitted it, Donna resented her daughter's youth—the wild sweet years ahead of her, which she sensed were Juliet's inevitable destiny. She loved her, of course she did, she assured herself frequently; Juliet was her child—she'd borne her. But a secret niggle of envy persisted. Whatever richness the aging years might bring, youth had a glory, a color to it, that could never be recaptured. At certain moments a queer sadness filled her, a melancholy awareness of time passing, of which Nicholas was quite unaware—her Celtic, Penroze heritage. At such moments she had to steel her will to reality and force memories of the past to the back of her mind—of William, her father, who had fought so hard and idealistically for his workers and the mine, Wheal Faith, and was now gone; the house, her old home on the Cornish cliffs destroyed by fire, her brother Luke taken by the sea; and his wife Jessica, the brash beauty who'd inveigled him into bigamous marriage, slain by the ruthless murderer, Silas Flint. Donna would never forget the day she'd been found broken and twisted in all her finery at the bottom of the cliff, with the mad, glazed eyes of Silas, her former husband, staring at her, his arm over her blood-stained breast.

Sometimes, very occasionally, Donna had nightmares that she was staring down on the two dead faces upturned from the wild cold beach under the leaden sky. There'd be a shrill high sound—the whinny of an animal—and Donna with her heart pounding wildly would be suddenly astride her horse, Saladin, galloping madly away toward the sullen horizon, hooves thundering through the rising clouds black with smoke, and the crimson, hungry tongues of leaping flame. She'd ride and ride, till the ground was far beneath them and Saladin would rear, terrified, throwing her. Below was nothing anymore but a vortex of evil darkness filled with grasping claws and the hungry shrieking of demons and witches, all bearing the features of Silas Flint. She'd scream and scream, and wake screaming.

Then, mercifully, as her senses calmed and registered she'd find only Nicholas's eyes staring down at her, hear only his voice saying with concern, "My love, wake up. It's only a dream. Donna, Donna—" and the nearness and warmth of him would bring comfort and peace.

"I'm so sorry," she'd murmur, "I've woken you. Oh, Nicholas, don't leave me."

Those were the times when he'd soothe her like a child, asking nothing of her except the knowledge that she needed him.

So her concern for Juliet and her determination to steer her to security and a settled life were not entirely selfish. In Trefyn Connor she sensed a mysterious, unpredictable quality that baffled and almost frightened her.

Juliet, she told herself stubbornly, would find no peace with him. Apart from his uncertain mixed background he had a mocking self-assurance not only exceedingly irritating but intimidating.

She never spoke or acknowledged him when they met by chance in a lane or horse riding on the moors, but the glance in his narrowed almond eyes glinted generally with half-concealed amusement. She sensed, irrationally, that in some way he felt superior. His looks were striking, his carriage and way of holding himself proud and independent. Unlike his sister Jet, whose olive skin and black eyes were dark as any

Gypsy's, his own complexion, though warmed and glowing from his open-air life, was smooth and clear; his features finely carved, derived obviously from his Gentry ancestry. This strange mixture of male strength combined with almost poetic good looks seemed calculated to strike havoc into the heart of any impressionable young girl. He was, as well, a hard worker, and Donna had heard from kitchen quarters that he was already extending the farm and stables and was planning to take on a couple of men. But what of the other, untamed side—the subtle, wayward quality that, like his father, could charm wild creatures by a whistle or touch of the hand?

As a child Juliet had been enchanted; and Trefyn now was a far more dangerous threat, insolently determined to go his own way, defying even William's quite reasonable determination to retrieve the old mine, Wheal Blair, which in her great-grandfather's day had been part of her family's estate—Trencobban's.

Until the copper began to pinch out, making the mine unprofitable, none but a Penroze had owned it. Later, at a period when so many Cornish mines were closing and workers taking off to America, those few acres had been sold with a couple of granite cottages to a small-holder possessing more gold in his pocket at that time than wisdom in his head. Most of the gold had disappeared with his luck in the bar of the hilltop pub, The Wandering Woman. The farm had failed and the buildings become half derelict. Before Dirke's time, distant relatives of the previous owner had taken over when the man died. The last—an old woman who kept a few pigs and goats—had been prevailed upon to sell to the Connors, much to William's chagrin.

The whole affair had been very badly managed, Donna thought. She had never trusted Dirke, and she trusted Trefyn far less because of his Gentry ancestry.

Where Juliet was concerned, her only hope was that she could see her satisfactorily married or at least engaged before the worrying association started up again. The forthcoming birthday party would be a beginning. If she could keep Juliet sufficiently diverted by young people of her own kind until the novelty of Trefyn Connor's nearby presence had worn off, there might be a chance her wayward daughter would see sense for herself. It was not as though Trefyn had money. He hadn't—yet. And Juliet had always liked her little luxuries and pretty clothes when she felt like it. So perhaps after all it was a blessing in disguise that Elinor Gentry's stubborn son had refused Nicholas's ridiculous financial offer for the land William wanted.

With her mind planning this way and that, Donna forgot for the moment that Juliet was already out on her own, riding somewhere over the moors, most probably in Trefyn's direction. The niggling distasteful thought of Ianthe's impending return was a further distraction. She would not put it past that young woman to do all she could to lure Juliet away for a taste of her own shameful life in town, just for spite. Juliet, characteristically had always had a youthful yearning for the theater, and Donna mistrusted her ability to withstand the glamor of her half-sister's charm if she cared to exert it. But perhaps her profligate years as the wife of Robertson Wycksley had coarsened and aged her. It was to be hoped so. Not only for Juliet's sake but for Nicholas's. When he once realized how low in social esteem his elder daughter

must have fallen, he might send her packing at the
first available opportunity.

Oh dear! how complicated life was; and with dear
Jason so dependent on her to get round his father concerning the Paris venture, her hands *were* uncomfortably tied.

Her mind was warmly relaxing at the thought of Jason, her best-loved child, when he came into the
room, looking very handsome as usual. He was wearing a green velvet jacket, cream shirt, bow tie, and
striped drain-pipe trousers. His fair hair waved naturally back from a wide and intellectual forehead. He
had sideburns and the faint suggestion of a newly acquired beard. Donna did not agree with the latter,
and had told him so, knowing that Nicholas would
disapprove. But Jason, having his fair share of family
stubbornness, went his own way. Being partially responsible for keeping estate accounts, he spent three
hours daily dealing with the boring task, and had obviously just concluded a session. He had books and
files under one arm, and looked tired.

"How long is this going on, mama?" he asked
slightly pettish. "I've been God knows how long
working on these blasted books, when I should have
been finishing that carving I promised the Penverryses. Is my father going to stump up for France or
isn't he?"

Donna went toward him and placed a hand on his
shoulder. "You must be *patient*, Jason," she said win-
ningly, "I can't make miracles. If you'd only—"

"Yes, mama?" he queried with a glint in his blue
eyes.

"If you could—well, perhaps be a bit more *like*
him," she said tentatively. "I mean—that *beard*. Have

you *got* to have one Jason? Without it you look so much more a Trevarvas—"

"And why should I want to be a Trevarvas particularly?" He said quickly. "You've always said I was the image of your mother. Well, haven't you?"

"Yes." Donna said shortly, "in features perhaps. But that's beside the point. You happen to be your father's son, and should be proud of it."

Jason sighed. "This family pride business is a bit 'old hat' now, you know. Democracy and individualism's coming in. Look at art—Gauguin, for instance— the Expressionists and French Impressionists—everything's changing."

"And you, too, it seems," Donna said pointedly. "If you talk that way, your father naturally won't understand."

Jason suddenly relaxed and smiled. "Oh, all right, I'll be good and watch my manners, pretend to be the dutiful son. If *you* do your part."

"What do you mean?"

He planted a kiss on her forehead. "You know very well. One flutter of your eyelashes, one seductive smile and he'll be clay in your hands."

She was pleased, but her voice was ironic when she said, "You overestimate my powers. I'll do what I can, but I can promise nothing. Another thing—"

"Yes?"

"You've no conscience, Jason. Sometimes I wonder where on earth you got your scheming mind—"

"From you, mama, of course," he said lightly. "I'm sure you could outwit any man you wanted, if you tried."

He picked up his books again and went to the door. "By the way," he remarked before going out, "what's happening over the prodigal daughter, Ianthe? Are you receiving her with loving stepmotherly courtesy when she turns up?"

"I shall be politely formal, no more," Donna answered. "Under the circumstances, for *your* sake, remember, it's better not to annoy your father."

"Good." He gave her a whimsical glance and departed. It was only sometime later that Donna's thoughts turned again to Juliet, and the worrying problem of how to intercept any assignation of hers with young Connor. Deep down she doubted that she could.

And she was quite right.

At the very time of Donna's brief conversation with Jason, Juliet, holding Firebrand by the reins, was in conversation with Trefyn at the gate of the farm. His eyes, shrewd and contemplative, had a warm glint in them as he noted the slender, budding lines of her young figure in the velvet habit—the swelling breasts above the incredibly slim waist, and rounding thighs that even the full skirt could not entirely disguise. She held her absurd, tall hat under her arm, with the riding crop in her hand. Her hair, in the afternoon light, shone bright and glossy as sunlight on beech leaves. Her clear eyes, so childishly frank when they stared up at him, held nevertheless a new secret awareness that against his will set his senses alight and a stiffening through his whole frame. But he was damned if he was going to let her know it; she was too intriguing by half, and he knew that if he gave her a chance she'd have him by the nose in no time.

"You're looking quite grownup," he was saying in the manner of one talking to a child. "Home for the holidays?"

She flushed.

"I've left. I'm not going back."

"Have you now! I didn't know they let them out so young."

"I'm seventeen," she reminded him.

"Seventeen. Quite an age."

She frowned. "What's the matter, Trefyn? Why are you acting so . . . so funnily?"

"*Acting?* I'm not."

"You mean you don't want to talk to me? You're not really pleased to see me at all? Very well. If that's how you feel—" she swung herself with a rush of anger and disappointment on to the colt's back, and would have been away if Trefyn hadn't grabbed the reins. Firebrand reared, but quieted at a touch of his hand.

"Get down, Juliet, and stop playing the spoiled young madam."

She gaped. "Who do you think you are, Trefyn Connor?"

He smiled, showing a flash of white teeth.

"Your lord and master," he said, as she stood again confronting him, "king of your own wild world and heart. Your lover, maybe—when you learn what love is all about—" A laugh escaped him; the comforting sound she'd known as a child. He took her hand lightly. "Off with you now, or like the divil they'll be after me."

She pulled her hand away and lifted it with the other to his face, bringing it down to hers. For a moment he did not respond; then warmly, as her lips touched his, the pressure of his mouth was on her own, hot and demanding, draining, it seemed, all the sweetness that was in her to himself.

His body pulsed with the urgency of any lusty young male finding his mate. For a brief interim the world spun to darkness.

Then it was over.

He let her go abruptly, controlling with an effort the trembling of his limbs. "And don't come this way again until you've learned your manners."

She laughed, turned, mounted Firebrand, and with a wave of her hat galloped away at an ever-increasing speed toward Polbreath. Her flying hair streaked from brown to red in the wind, her heart sang. If Donna had seen her at that moment, fears for Juliet would have increased a hundredfold.

Trefyn, meanwhile, watched until the flying figure was out of sight. Then he made his way slowly to the house, knowing he would one day have the wayward nymph as his own, and on whatever terms he chose.

It was only when she reached Polbreath that Juliet realized she'd quite forgotten to ask Trefyn about the girl who was supposed to be working for him.

## 2

For the next few days before the party Polbreath was a hive of activity, which William avoided as much as possible by taking himself off to Penjust. There was indication at one of the Trevarvas mines of tin veins beneath the copper, which had temporarily diverted his attention and chagrin from the thwarting problem of acquiring Connor land. The feminine flutter caused by Juliet's return from boarding school and Ianthe's impending visit bored him to distraction.

He was also in need of sexual diversion, and knew just where to find it.

Hannah Marne, the daughter of a Cornish farmer and a tinker mother, lived halfway along the cliffs to Penjust in a remote spot just above the coast. She still farmed the few fields and patch of moor belonging to the huddled granite house, although her mother had run away with a "traveler" when she was a small child, leaving her to the harsh mercies of the disillusioned husband. Until she was sixteen Jake Marne had

alternately used, bullied, spoiled, and beaten her,
taught her to work like a man, observe the Bible in
public on Sundays, and drink in private. For all that,
she had grown up strong and handsome with a full-
blooded pride about her that kept men at bay.

Shortly before her nineteenth birthday Jake had
been gored by a bull, which had left him maimed and
useless for life. Their roles then had been reversed.
Hannah was mistress, running the small farm herself
with the help of a shepherd boy, Matt James, leaving
Jake a useless invalid, immobile and disgruntled, sitting in the kitchen or front porch. Hannah had little
affection for him, but because he was her father she
gave what care she could to his needs.

And there was William.

If she loved anything or anyone in the world it was
William Trevarvas, though she knew he would never
marry her. Neither did she wish it. She'd seen enough
of marriage as a young child to know what hell it
could be. Besides, freedom was in her blood. Who
could tell?—one day she might want to break the tie
herself and walk out just as her mother had done. But
that would not be until the old tyrant was dead. In
the meantime her body was her own, and Williams's
when he wanted it. Their mutual need was rhythmical
and instinctive as the rising and ebbing of the tides.
When the urge rose strong in her, she'd know he'd
soon appear to assuage it, and she'd be waiting.
There'd be no delicacy or modesty between them.
William was not a man of words. He'd just look at her,
with an odd, twisted little half-smile on his mouth and
a glow in his dark eyes, before slipping the clothes
from her and taking in full what she so willingly gave,
savoring with sensual gratification every facet of her

rich womanhood, his lips hot and hungry on her own. His hands would be hard and fierce on her flesh, then soft and gentle as the climax flowered between them. For a time, afterward, they'd lie at peace—hands clasped, limbs relaxed and apart. He might take her again that day, or not, depending on circumstance.

Their lovemaking could be anywhere—upstairs in her room, or during summer in some hidden hollow, remote from humanity and sheltered by furze and heather. Sometimes even they'd lie supine in a secret cove with the sleek forms of seals grouped gray and shining about the smooth rocks of the shore below. Hannah's naked body would be whiter than the silver cream of their young, her hair a shroud of silken black over the pale sand. William would arch over her, and their union would be swift and strong, holding the force of the breaking tide and wanton fire of sun and wind and stinging rain.

When passion was appeased she'd sit up, lift her arms toward the sky, with a secret smile on her lips. Her nipples would be buds of flame from his ravishing, her eyes dark wells of sensual knowledge. He'd watch her lazily for a moment, then laugh, get up, and dress.

Presently he'd walk away casually, with a touch of regret—until he remembered the mines and the work he had to do. His speed would quicken then, and she'd know with a touch of wry sadness that although she mattered, his ambitions and work would always come first.

The day before the party William arrived about five, later than usual, following an unsatisfactory confrontation with Trefyn, whom he'd met by chance in the lane below Rozebuzzan. Jake Marne was seated in

the small kitchen by the fire; his legs, almost useless
now through injury and inactivity, were drawn up at
right angles to his terribly scarred side and stomach,
feet resting on a stool. He had a mug of gruel in his
hand and a glass of home-brewed ale on the table,
waiting. Since the bull's savage onslaught, he could
only take liquids which were quick to pass through
him. So the seat of the chair was a roughly contrived
commode, made by his daughter with the help of
Matt.

Hannah found his presence there distasteful and
much preferred him upstairs in his own room. But
pity kept her irritation in check. In return, Jake put up
with William's occasional appearances unprotestingly,
though his eyes glowered, increasing the macabre expression of his face which was scarred and twisted
down one side.

That day Hannah had glimpsed William approaching from the window, and was already outside when
he arrived.

He sensed immediately that there was something
different about her. Although her glance was warm,
her physical presence seemed more withdrawn. Desire
was in her eyes but her voice was guarded when she
said, "Come along, better get away from here—"

He was surprised. "Of course, isn't that the idea?"
His hand touched her buttocks insinuatingly. She
pushed it away. "Be careful now. Matt's about."

"Oh! *Matt.*"

"We don't want any talk. That's what you've always
said—no talk, no show of things, just you an' me keep-
in' what's ours to ourselves." She walked with a
swing of the hips down the narrow path leading to the
cliffs and their favorite meeting place. It was in a

sheltered hollow, almost a grove, encircled by thick gorse and twisted elder. He swung after her, frowning.

"What's the matter, Hannah?"

"Nuthen," she said, with a toss of her black hair. "Just . . . there's goin' to be changes round here."

"What do you mean?"

She didn't answer.

"Go on," he insisted, "explain."

"Later."

When they reached the hollow he didn't make love to her immediately, as usual, but sat half-pensively with his arm round her shoulders, staring at the smooth contours of her cheek and temple from where the dusky hair flowed back over her shoulder. In profile she looked younger, more vulnerable. For the first time passion rose quietly in him, and was richer in fulfillment.

When it was over and she eased herself up to adjust her clothes and tie her hair with a scrap of ribbon, he said, watching her closely, "Now perhaps you'll tell me what you meant . . . what you were talking about?"

She hesitated, searching through her mind for the right words while one hand fumbled at the back of her neck trying to fasten a button. Quite gently, William assisted her, noting with reawakening desire the soft sheen of glossy hair tumbling in a coil to her waist.

"About a change," he insisted. "What is it?"

She turned away so he should not see the softening of her eyes, the faint tremble of the lips before replying overcasually,

"Oh that. Yes, it's true. From now on, we won't be seeing each other so much—mebbe not at all."

He jerked himself up. "What? What the hell do you mean?"

She tugged a twig of heather from a nearby clump, held it to her nostrils for a second, then turned to him and said, "I've got to have more help, William; so my cousin Pete's comin' to join me. He'll live in, an' won't be wantin' other men about."

"I *see*," he said, only half-comprehending. "Your cousin Pete's coming so you won't be requiring my services. How very convenient for you."

Her cheeks flamed. "You needn't take that tone with me, William Trevarvas. From the beginnin' we had things clear, didn't we? No ties, no duty involved—nuthen to make things awkward, 'specially for *you*! Right from the start I warned you I'd be off one day, and it suited you fine. You didn't want to marry me, did you? Or is that what's troublin' you?"

He flushed.

"Now look here, Hannah—"

"Oh, I know. I know. You *would* if it was possible, but it isn't, not with your fine stuck-up family. Well, *I* don't want it neither an' I've always told you. But that doesn't mean to say there's not other things—"

"What do you mean?"

She shook her head slowly before answering.

"Sometimes I think you're not so clever after all. Sometimes I think you're nuthen, but a blind, blunderin' great, great fool William. I'm havin' a child, that's what I mean; *yours*. And there'll be work needin' to be done that I'm sure you won't want to be botherin' about. Well? Isn't that right?"

He stared at her, gaping and shocked, suddenly on

guard as desire faded into self-contempt and fear. A sad, ironic smile twisted her lips. "Don't worry, William. You won't suffer. No one'll know."

"But I don't see—"

She jumped up. "Oh, for God's sake don't say you don't know how it happened. You've had me enough times to give a whole brood. Just . . . just—" her voice calmed, "let things end pleasantly so we can remember the best until . . . until we don't have to think of it at all—"

"Hannah—"

"Stop it," she said, as his hand touched her cheek, "don't go soft on me, William. And don't pretend. You know as well as me that you'll be damn grateful to be let off so easy."

He was silent. A little wind shivered through the undergrowth, stirring the hair from her forehead, chilling her flesh with its autumn breath. From the headland beyond, the boom of the sea echoed mournfully against the rocks. She got up. "Come on, let's go."

As they started to walk back he said, "How will you manage?"

"As I always have, I'm that sort. Pete'll be a help. He's big, strong, used to work in a fair. They're all the same, my mother's lot. And later—" her voice quivered slightly—"there'll be the boy, when he's grown."

"How do you know it'll be a boy?"

"Or a girl, it don't matter. I'll see she's taught to be useful."

"I shall send you something regularly," he said after a pause, "that's only right."

"Right? I reckon right and wrong don't enter into it. But a present when it's born would help, if you insist.

Nuthen after." Her tones were final, just as though any idea of future contact between them was distasteful, he thought morosely. Well, if that was the case, so much the better. Although he'd wanted her, he hadn't meant to father her child, and for that matter didn't wish to set eyes on it. Maybe when Jake Marne was gone, which couldn't be too long ahead, she'd take off with her cousin Pete and that would be the end of the matter. William was no hero or gallant respecter of blood ties. A bastard was a bastard and could never be anything else. Any accepted son of his loins must be a Trevarvas born in wedlock. He realized for the first time he'd been reckless where Hannah was concerned, and as they stood in the shelter of a stone wall before parting, the situation seemed suddenly incongruous. Something must have shown in his face. She laughed unexpectedly, tossing the mane of black hair back over her shoulders.

"Don't you fret, William," she said brightly, hoping he'd not sense the hurt misery behind the words. "There's plenty of fish in the sea for you as well as me. We'll get through, both of us—"

She turned sharply to go. He caught at her arm. "Hannah—"

"Aw! get on with you. Go on, now. It's been good, William, an' I won't forget you. But believe me, I'll bloody well try."

A moment later she'd torn herself away and was speeding up the moor toward the cottage, a streak of flying scarlet and black against the brown and gold autumn landscape. William turned and cut down to the cliffs, taking the path along the coast that led up abruptly past Wheal Jakke, one of the Trevarvas mines. Jakke was drained by the large adit of Penmartin, with two other mines, one of which was idle—Wheal Flower. It was William's conviction that with further shaft-sinking Wheal Flower also could be made productive again, although the operation could be a tricky and expensive one, involving the building of a dam to stem surplus water. Nicholas considered the scheme far too dangerous and had so far been uncooperative, but frustrated as he was by Trefyn Connor's refusal to meet him over the Wheal Blair project, the reopening of Wheal Flower had become an added obsession to William.

Mining was his life. More than it had ever been his father's. What was the point of working for ore at all, unless you were going to exploit the land's potential to its limit? he asked himself continuously. If life wasn't an adventure, a continual struggle, it was nothing.

The argument started up in his mind again that late afternoon as he strode westward following his parting from Hannah. Reactions had set in and the sight of miners plodding over the moors to their homes from the day shift gave him a queer sense of satisfaction and achievement. A maiden or two, neat in their white aprons, trudged wearily toward the upper lane, their shoulders tired and drooping from a long day's tin dressing and sorting. Yet they were singing, their voices a muted, youthful echo on the freshening evening air. William, with a stab of conscience and irritation, recalled the cause of his sudden earlier visit to Hannah: the tittle-tattle and vanity of stupid feminine gossip going on at that very moment at Polbreath; his mother's—Donna's—determined devious plans to ensnare a worthy suitor for Juliet at her forthcoming party; and the ridiculous extravagance entailed, when so many miners' families found it impossible to live decently with sufficient food to keep them going.

Heaven forbid that Juliet should get entangled in a liaison with Trefyn Connor, whom he mistrusted and disliked with every nerve in his body. But Desmond Court was little more than a rich dilettante—of the half-Irish absentee-landlord breed with no brains to speak of and not an original thought in his head; nothing to commend him at all but his romantic looks, his air of breeding, and fine manners. As for Geoffrey Carne or Hawtrey Boltham—*Sir* Hawtrey Boltham—poor Juliet, William thought wryly—one a stuffed shirt, the other a jumped up, elderly opportunist out to found a dynasty! The whole affair was a farce, and he was annoyed with his father for being involved in the affair at all, if he was. The only bright spot ahead was the prospect of Ianthe's unwelcome visit. If what he'd heard of her was correct, she could be relied on to provide considerable diversion.

She did.

Ianthe arrived, days earlier than had been anticipated, in the middle of the after-dinner-party concert, when Sir Hawtrey was giving an impassioned rendering in his light tenor voice of a pathetic ballad, "Parted," accompanied on the grand piano by Rosina Penverrys. She was a commanding figure in black satin, seated straight-backed on a slender-legged stool that appeared too frail for her. Her dark hair, untouched by gray, was swept up from her ears and forehead in a roll, from which ostrich feathers curved outward like immense antennae. Occasionally she allowed her eyes to stray approvingly from the keys toward the correctly dressed yet undistinguished figure of Sir Hawtrey. It was obvious to William, who'd entered the proceedings glumly at the last moment, that the middle-aged curvaceous Miss Penverrys had ambitions in that direction not entirely musical. Juliet, bored but dutifully trying to conceal the fact, was sitting between Donna and Desmond Court whose hand at intervals wandered to hers. At such moments her fingers generally located a handkerchief or found her fan, which was the same shade as her dress—pale shimmering green dotted with brilliants. She was looking very beautiful and knew it.

From the other side of the room, Nicholas, standing with Major Carne, regarded her indulgently. His shrewd eye had not missed the jealous glance of Lady Penverrys, the yearning expression in young Geoffrey's eyes, or Desmond's covetous admiration. Every male present, in fact, was impressed and probably indulging fancies of having her in his arms. Not that he considered a single one worthy of his daughter. *Let her wait a bit,* he thought. One day a man worth his salt, and with more than money to offer her would come along, and he'd see her wed with pride to someone she could love and trust to sire his grandchildren. He knew very well Donna was anxious to have her off her hands, and although at times the knowledge irritated him, he was mostly amused. Their relationship as man and wife was as passionate as it had ever been, and there was a streak of jealousy in her he'd long since learned was untameable. But one thing was certain; he was not having her drive or inveigle Juliet into a marriage the girl herself did not want. That was hardly likely in any case. Juliet was every bit as strong-willed as her mother, for which heaven be praised.

He only wished Jason had half her spirit and pluck. Jason was a concern to him. Look at him that evening, for instance—lounging near the large palm in the corner, wearing that absurd fair beard, which, with his velvet jacket and cigar dangling ostentatiously from his mouth, gave him such an arty, foreign look! Why couldn't he wear normal evening dress like the rest of them? And why couldn't he behave decently to that poor girl Charlotte sitting on her own just in front. She might not be a beauty—none of the Carnes were; but, damn it all, she had a pleasant face, if a bit plumpish, and fine eyes.

From Jason, he glanced at William in the doorway, and the look between them spoke volumes. Both were bored, both had the impulse to yawn or take off to the smoking room. Hawtrey's woeful voice droned on and on, and when it was over, following dutiful applause, Rosina herself had to give a full-blooded rendering of two Indian Love Lyrics. This was followed by Major Carne's reciting, "The Green Eye of the Yellow God," and two of Rudyard Kipling's "Barrack-Room Ballads."

The drawing room was becoming exceedingly stuffy. Because of the women's low-cut gowns, no window was open behind the rose-pink brocade curtains, and the scent of perfume was becoming nauseatingly oversweet.

Donna got up to open the adjoining door to the conservatory. A breath of pungent steamy air, heavy with the odor of potted plants and ferns, crept in to merge with the rest.

It was at that moment Ianthe entered from the hall.

Instantly all other sounds and voices ceased. She stood for a moment, poised like a queen, or the actress she was, about to make her début in the doorway. Her dress of scarlet silk was both outré and seductive, cut extremely low at the bosom and suggestively draped tightly round buttocks and thighs, from where it flowed in a sudden swirl from the knees to the points of her glittering shoes. Her luxurious black hair, liberally curled, was swept up high and caught by jeweled combs. She wore white kid gloves covering the elbows. One hand held an enormous fan, the other was delicately poised on a hip. On the left side of her bodice was pinned a large white artificial poppy flower near enough to a breast for a petal to touch the creamy skin. Two long ropes of pearls hung almost to her navel.

Donna was aghast.

"*Ianthe—*" She stood with a slow-rising anger mounting her skin in a wave of deepening crimson. Before a spate of words could leave her lips, Nicholas had gone quickly forward.

"We didn't expect you quite so soon," he said, offering his hand to her. "However, as it's your sister's birthday party, you're welcome. You know Major Carne, of course. And Geoffrey and Charlotte—let me introduce you to our other friends—"

The rest of the proceedings were a nightmare to Donna, who could hardly control her indignation at the intrusion of her wayward, flamboyant step-daughter. At a moment when Nicholas was introducing "Mrs. Robertson Wycksley, my daughter, Ianthe," to Sir Hawtrey, she left quietly to question the servants concerning Ianthe's arrival.

They were all taken aback. Beth, now housekeeper at Polbreath, who had remained in service and loyal to Donna since the early stormy days of marriage when Nicholas and his headstrong young wife had parted for a time, was upset and a little indignant at the emotional attack.

"How could I stop Miss Ianthe—Mrs. Wycksley— from coming in?" She demanded. "She simply told the cabby to dump her valise and bags, paid him off, and walked upstairs to her old room. So I called the boy and got him to take the luggage up to her. I was going to tell you, but she said I mustn't worry you. Well, there *was* rather a noise, and the party was on. It didn't seem the time to make more fuss than was necessary."

"No," Donna agreed grudgingly, calming down. "I suppose not."

"And I certainly didn't expect her to burst in on you."

"She didn't burst in exactly," Donna said. "She entered regally, like a queen, or some celebrated actress making a stage entrance. It was embarrassing."

"As I said, I'm sorry."

Donna shrugged, softened, and touched the other woman's shoulder briefly. "It wasn't your fault, Beth. Of course not. I suppose—" glancing toward the door of Beth's comfortable small sitting room, "the servants know all about it."

The kitchens adjoining were humming with the sound of subdued chatter and laughter intermingled with the ring of cutlery and glasses. "You couldn't expect them not to, Mrs. Trevarvas, Ma'am. Miss Ianthe—I mean, Mrs. Wycksley—made quite a flurry, and seemed in high spirits. She's—she's changed."

Donna's expression darkened. "Has she? She appeared very much what I expected. Still, we must make the best of things while she's here."

"Will it be long, do you know?" Beth queried, trying not to appear too curious.

"I hope not," Donna answered. "I don't want more responsibility piled on you, and my stepdaughter, as you know, was never very considerate. You must tell me if any difficulties arise."

A fleeting indulgent smile crossed Beth Paynter's face. "Don't you worry on my account. I'm lucky to be here. It would be funny to leave Polbreath now."

Donna didn't reply, but her mind went back in a flash to the dreadful scene that had driven her years ago from Nicholas in a fury of distress and temper to her old home, Trencobban, where she'd stayed for months before William's birth. Beth had proved a stalwart and loyal friend then, and through the dark period following when fire had destroyed the house. Nothing remained of the Penroze estate now but stretches of wild moorland and the granite monument marking the spot where Trencobban had stood, and which Donna herself had suggested to commemorate the memory of her father and of the workers of the family mine Wheal Faith, now defunct.

That had been in 1882; and in the past twenty-five years Beth had changed little except for the gray liberally streaking the dark hair, and the small tell-tale lines round her eyes and mouth.

Donna knew she'd feel lost without her.

"Well," she said, "you've made me feel better, as usual. I wish I could stay, but someone would be sure to notice, so I'd better get back."

Actually Donna's presence had not been missed at all. When she returned to the drawing room she found, to her chagrin, all the menfolk except Jason gathered in a little crowd round Ianthe—even Nicholas, who was standing on the fringe of it with a quizzical, faintly ironic look on his face. Rosina was at the piano, making a pretense of studying musical scores. Charlotte Carne, in a pink dress that did not suit her gingerish hair, was trying ineffectually to catch the attention of Ralphe Court who, like his brother Desmond, appeared completely entranced by Ianthe.

Old Major Carne, well fortified by port and good brandy, was making sly, suggestive innuendos to Sir John Penverrys. His wife, obviously disgruntled, was trying desperately to engage Sir Hawtrey Boltham in conversation.

Two girls, twins, the daughters of a neighboring "gentleman farmer," who'd been invited at the last moment as a gesture and to even out the numbers, were standing awkwardly aloof, hoping Jason or William might notice them. Andrew, much to Donna's annoyance was absent, on the pretext that he had business to attend to concerning a tenant farmer.

"What use would I be at a party, with this gammy leg?" he'd said an hour before, giving her one of his most charming smiles. "Forgive me, mother dear, I'm sure you'll get along very well without me. Father would agree. When he made me manager—so to speak—of the estate, it was providing I put the job of work before pleasure."

"If Jason can find time to be here with all that bookkeeping of his, I'm sure you can," Donna had snapped. "The trouble is you think of nothing but horse talk and playing the young squire to farmers and yokels. Ever since you left the Army, it's been the same—"

"I didn't *leave* the Army, I was pushed," Andrew had reminded her significantly, "because of *this*—"

touching the lame limb. "And it's because of *this* I've no intention yet of getting bedded with one of your eligible fillies—if ever."

"Andrew!"

"Well, that's the idea of it all, isn't it? The fun and games, I mean? A cunning little plot to get your progeny successfully settled in life?"

"How unfair of you to suggest such a thing. And on your own sister's birthday!"

Andrew had taken his mother's chin in his hand, smiling disarmingly. "Come along now, Mrs. Trevarvas. You know it's true. Cheer up, though. Find me some gorgeous creature with pots of money and no parents, who'll leave me to live my own life, and I may consider marrying one day. But only maybe."

He limped away, leaving Donna not only irritated but saddened, because beneath his banter she recognized the hurt and bitterness. Following the war, Andrew's natural exuberance, which had thrived for a time from excitement, and the adulation naturally accorded to a wounded hero had gradually faded, leaving him increasingly aware of his own physical deficiencies. He'd seen, too soon and too young, things no man should experience. The glory of war could be, superficially, a gallant façade. But the reality to him had become, now, shame. This was something he kept to himself. So while he drank his pints with tenants and farmers in pubs, attended gatherings of various country functions, and was generally acclaimed as a jolly good fellow, his mind was aloof, determining "never again." No more wars, no more killing. No more slaughter of man by man. Should the challenge ever arise again, he'd denounce it, if necessary, with his last breath.

Neither Donna nor Nicholas had the slightest idea how fiercely he felt on this one point, although Nicholas frequently sensed about him a defensiveness impossible to penetrate; harder than granite, cold as steel. He could smile and joke with anyone when necessary, but the blue eyes that crinkled with laughter one moment could be frozen and blank as ice the next. He was the enigma of the family, neither all Trevarvas nor Penroze but a unique blend of both. Of the three brothers, however, Juliet loved him best, and wished he was at her party. She didn't blame him for his absence because she understood. He thought the whole thing was a stuffy bore. So did she.

If Trefyn had been there . . . ! The thought of Trefyn quickened her heart. She had a sudden urge to be outside, with the cool night air blowing fresh from the hills on her face, away from the inane chatter and conversation, the admiring glances from the Court boys and that funny little Sir Hawtrey who meant nothing to her.

On impulse, while Donna was busily trying to placate Lady Penverrys who was fanning her face vigorously to soothe her outrage concerning Ianthe's impudent scene-stealing, Juliet hastily left the room and ran down the hall through the front door. She stood for a moment letting the wind ruffle her hair, turning her head toward the humped dark shape of Rosenbuzzan hill, thinking of Trefyn, wondering what he was doing and if Donna had really told her the truth about another girl living at the farm.

She was staring pensively over the valley when a man's dark shape appeared down a side drive, as though he'd come from the stables. The rising moon was a full golden ball in the sky, throwing elongated shadows across the grass. As her eyes grew accustomed to the fitful light she saw that the figure limped, and that it was Andrew.

She hurried down the terrace steps and was with him in a few moments. He looked surprised and took her hand.

"Juliet. What are you doing here? Shouldn't you be at your party?"

She nodded. "Yes. But it's all right. Ianthe's come. They won't miss me for a minute—"

"Ianthe?"

"A week early. Poor mama! she's furious, and Lady Penverrys is simply *raging*. Because of Rosina, of course." A giggle escaped her.

"You'd better get back," Andrew said, "or you'll have Desmond and Ralphe after you. Not to mention our esteemed parents."

Juliet shrugged. "They're *much* too occupied. Ianthe's really the limit—all scarlet silk and pearls, and such red lips. I think there'll be a scene later. Well, it will liven things up a bit."

"Things don't need livening with you about." Andrew said drily. "By the way, Juliet—I'm sorry not to've come. If you like, I'll go and change now, just to put in an appearance."

She glanced down, shaking her head. "No. It's all right. *I* didn't want the stuffy party anyway. I know how you felt. Really, Andrew." She paused, then looking up at him asked, "Where did you go? Did you have to see someone? The business meeting, I mean?"

"Briefly. Old man James. It didn't take long. And as I was in St. Figgans, I—hold your breathe—I went to church."

"*Church?*" she gasped. "But surely there was no service? And it's *Catholic*."

"It didn't matter. There was no one there. I just wanted the feel of it . . . the peace. You know how it is sometimes . . . you get a longing for something and you're suddenly acting completely unexpectedly. Or perhaps you don't. You're too young yet, thank God—"

"No, I'm not. I feel like you exactly, often. I'm not a child."

He squeezed her hand. "You're not supposed to be, after tonight. This party's your launching into the marriage market, remember." His voice had changed again, become dry, ironic.

"I'm not marrying anyone," she said, "unless it's . . . someone I love. Someone . . ." her voice faded.

"Trefyn Connor?" he questioned lightly, "Well, if you feel that way, cling on to it, Juliet. He's not a bad young fellow in his way. Got guts. Only don't be rash. Give yourself time."

Just then, lights flickered from the doorway. There was a stirring of shadows and forms emerging.

"Oh, heaven," Andrew said, "they're on the scent already. Off with you, Juliet, I'll cut in by the side door."

They separated and Juliet turned, hurrying back to the terrace, with her skirts lifted in two hands, the narrow tip of evening slippers glittering gold in the moonlight. She could have been some Cinderella of the fairy tale or a giant butterfly flitting against the velvet night sky.

Nicholas was standing at the top of the steps with Desmond Court by his side. Both were smoking cigars.

"So there you are," Nicholas said. "You'd better tidy yourself. Your mother's looking for you."

He didn't ask where she'd been. *He wouldn't, he is a dear*, Juliet thought. She wished all men were as nice.

As she hurried into the hall she heard Desmond calling after her,. "I say, Juliet, I hear there's going to be dancing in the large lounge. May I have the first one?"

She turned, smiling dutifully. "If you like, Desmond. But not if it's a waltz. I hate waltzes, they're so slow."

She was running upstairs when Donna appeared on the landing above, accompanied by Charlotte Carne and Lady Penverrys.

"Oh, Juliet, where *have* you been hiding yourself?" she asked almost petulantly, "I relied on you to look after your guests, and you know what we arranged about the powder room."

"Sorry, mama," Juliet answered, not sounding sorry in the least. "I was feeling a bit funny, and went out for air."

"Funny? What do you mean? Ill?"

"Oh, not exactly. Just flurried and hot. It was seeing Ianthe, I suppose."

The last remark was a clever one, well calculated and succeeding in silencing Donna. Juliet took the last two stairs at one bound, and was halfway to her own room before any comment could be made.

Five minutes later when she went down, the dancing had started. Desmond was waiting for her at the foot of the stairs near a marble statue of Aphrodite holding an electric light bulb. His boyishly handsome face was flushed with excitement, anticipation, and the very good wine he'd drunk.

"The next dance is a polka and ours I think," he said, glancing from her clear gray eyes to the subtle shadow between the upthrust young breasts. Juliet had loosened the neckline a little through cunningly snipping a stretch of ribboned binding. The effect through the mirror had stimulated her; she felt adventurous and a little wicked—sufficiently so not to be outdone or intimidated by Ianthe.

"I say!" Desmond said, lightly touching her gloved hand. "You look absolutely ravishing. Or did I say that before?"

"I don't think so," Juliet answered.

"Well, I should have. You're quite the loveliest girl I know."

His arm slid to her waist. She pushed it away.

"Oh, Des, don't be sloppy. Come along if we're going to dance, let's."

The trio engaged for the occasion—pianist, cellist, and violinist—were already tuning up when Juliet and Desmond entered the large lounge. Rugs had been taken up, and the furniture pushed to one side. Under the row of arched windows facing the garden, potted palms had been placed, and along the opposite wall chairs arranged for nondancers. Lady Penverrys was seated there with her husband near the marble fireplace. The rest of the gathering were partnered and waiting for the first chords of *See Me Dance the Polka!* to be struck.

Then it came.

Donna and Nicholas took the floor first, followed by William and Rosina, Ralphe Court and Charlotte Carne, Sir Hawtrey Boltham with his arm gallantly half-round Rosina's waist. Jason from a sense of duty had succumbed to one of the twins' imploring glances, and Major Carne, obviously infatuated by Ianthe, was one-two-three-hopping with her at a speed quite unsuited to his heart and lungs.

"Just look at them," Juliet whispered in Desmond's ear as they flung themselves with youthful gusto into the whirling scene.

"I can only look at you." Desmond whispered, letting his lips brush her hair.

"Stop it, silly," Juliet said. "If you don't, I won't . . . well, I won't go on. I said *look*—"

Desmond lifted his head. "What at?"

"Them, the parents."

Desmond saw what she meant. Nicholas's eyes were burning so bright on Donna's face—hers so limpid, as she yearned toward him, so filled with longing that it seemed for a brief interim of time that no one else existed in the world for either of them.

A moment later the graceful neck suddenly arched back, and laughter rippled from Donna's throat as Nicholas swung her off her feet and down again.

"I love you—" he whispered. "My wife, my darling," and then, with his voice rising to the refrain, "See me dance the polka, see me twizzle around, watch my coat tails flying—"

Juliet suddenly turned her head away and slackened.

"What's the matter?" Desmond asked.

"I'm tired. This is boring. Do you mind, Desmond? I'm going for a lemonade. I'm thirsty."

"Oh. I'll come with you."

"No, dance with that girl—the twin. Her name's Honey something. Honey Blake, that's it. It must be horrible having to watch with the Dragon—Lady Pen-verrys. *Please*, Desmond."

"Oh, all right," he answered grudgingly, "so long as you come back again."

"I will. I've got to, haven't I? It's my party."

Juliet wandered to the dining room where drinks and refreshments were still arranged on the long buffet table. Only a parlor maid, Elise, was standing there. The man Boulter, who'd earlier served as butler, had returned to the kitchens.

"Can I hand you anything, Miss Juliet?" the girl asked.

"No thanks," Juliet murmured. "I'll pour it myself. Just a lemonade."

She took a glass, half-filled it with lemon, and added a liberal amount of soda water.

"Have you ever been in love, Elise?" she said on the spur of the moment.

The girl shook her head. "Can't say I have. Not much chance in these parts for one of my sort. I'm pertickler."

Juliet stared. "What a thing to say."

"Well, I mean it's true, isn't it? There are good sorts about—miners an' farm laborers, you know what I mean. But I'm not going to marry one of them—I've seen too much of poverty in my family. So I don't let my thoughts wander. Of course I'm not talkin' of the *gentry*, Miss Juliet, not those like Mr. William or Mr. Andrew. But none of them's for servant girls like me. A soldier, perhaps now, if some fine sergeant came along—" she broke off with a giggle. "But I'm running on too fast. If madam heard, there'd be trouble."

"Madam won't," Juliet assured her briskly. "She's

swirling round in my father's arms as though . . . as though she'd never danced before. *Fancy* at her age."

Elise flung her a shrewd look. "She's not that old, Miss Juliet. And I must say I've never seen anyone quite so beautiful—"

"Not even Ianthe?"

Elsie shrugged. "Oh, well, Mrs. Wycksley's different. Sort of worldly, like all actresses."

"Her lips are painted, I think," Juliet said. "It must be exciting being on the stage."

"Maybe," the parlor maid agreed dryly. "But why's she left it so sudden then? Her husband I suppose. They say he could be her grandfather. Fancy marrying an old man. It wouldn't be my choice, I can tell you."

"No. Nor mine," Juliet agreed, thinking of Trefyn.

"Hadn't you be getting back, Miss Juliet? The music's stopped and they'll be missing you."

"Oh, I suppose so."

Juliet was about to leave when Major Carne appeared with Ianthe. Both looked slightly tipsy. Ianthe moved unsteadily on her high-heeled shoes toward the buffet.

"Hullo, little sister," she said in mocking tones. "All alone at this time of night?"

"Any champagne left?" the Major queried. "Bless my soul! All gone? Claret cup? What do you say, dear lady?"

"I'm lost for words," Ianthe told him sweetly, "in your company."

Juliet rushed from the room feeling mildly disgusted, and almost bumped into her father.

"What's the matter?" Nicholas asked, taking her arm. "Why the hurry?"

"I don't know, I'm—I wish it was over," Juliet confessed. "It's lovely giving me the party, but I can't stand the heat and the noise and the—the silly *people*. Desmond's so sloppy, and Major Carne in there with Ianthe! He just *oozes* drink. Oh, I'm sorry. It's awful of me, but—"

Nicholas's arm went round her shoulders comfortingly. "You've had enough? So have I. We'll get rid of them presently. Only don't upset your mother. She's tried hard to make the party a success. And don't be too hard on Desmond. He's fond of you. Had his eye on you all evening."

"*And* Ianthe," Juliet said. "When she came in he looked quite gaga."

"Ah, yes. Well, Ianthe does have that gift," Nicholas agreed wryly. "And she's another problem I've to face, for your mother's sake."

"Will you let her stay?" Juliet couldn't help herself asking.

"She's your sister," Nicholas said more abruptly, "and my daughter. Remember that, young lady, and no more questions."

By the time another hour had passed, the carriages and guests had left. It was already twelve o'clock when Nicholas found Ianthe in the conservatory.

Juliet was lingering on the stairs, her ears pricking, as Donna appeared on the landing most inopportunely and prevented her from overhearing anything but an irate "What the devil do you think you're doing?" from Nicholas.

"Come along," Donna said, "time you were in bed," and Juliet, knowing it was useless to argue, obeyed.

Ianthe, in fact, was doing what was becoming the rage in certain circles of sophisticated society at that period. She was smoking a cigarette, from a long jade holder.

"Put that thing out immediately," Nicholas said in a cold hard voice that belied the heat in his eyes. Ianthe stood for a moment defiantly facing him, then answered "I'm not a child, papa."

"Mores the pity," he told her grimly. "I knew how to deal with you then. And if your husband was a younger man and had the guts, he'd 've put you over his knee long ago."

Ianthe flushed. "I've left my husband—forever."

"We'll talk about that in the morning," Nicholas said. "Meanwhile, try and behave." He snatched the holder from her hand, took the cigarette out, and ground it under his foot. "I don't allow nicotine in here, or any womenfolk to smoke in my presence at Polbreath. And also, since you *have* come back, see you dress decently in future. You look like a—"

"Yes, Papa?" Ianthe's tones were sweet but edgy.

"Not my daughter," Nicholas replied bluntly.

"I don't seem to 've been that for a long time," she said, looking away, and adding with a catch in her voice, "a very, *very* long time."

Nicholas stared at her broodingly, hurt more than he'd admit even to himself, to find the wayward lovely girl he remembered become the disillusioned, flamboyant woman confronting him. Now that the first excitement had passed her eyes showed the dark rings under them. Her mouth drooped, and the makeup on her face was obvious. She was only thirty, but at that moment she looked ten years older. He noticed also that her hand trembled, and he wondered how long she'd been drinking, inwardly cursing the lascivious old reprobate who'd driven her to it. Nicho-

las had heard from time to time of her notorious reputation, her numerous lovers and theatrical first nights.
But the truth—the reality and effect—had not properly
registered until then. Now he was shocked. "I think
you should get some rest now, Ianthe," he heard himself saying more gently. "It's getting late. We can discuss things tomorrow."

"All right." Ianthe picked up her gauzy shawl and
fan. "I suppose I shouldn't have come back. It must be
distressing for you and Donna. Tell her I won't incon-
venience her long."

Nicholas patted her arm. "I'll do no such thing.
Your stepmother's not an ogress. You'll stay as long as
necessary or as you wish. But no putting wild ideas
into Juliet's head; remember that."

"Of course. Donna's daughter."

Nicholas winced. "And mine."

"You love her very much, don't you?"

"Naturally. I love you, too, or I'd have sent you
packing the moment you arrived."

Ianthe shook her head. "Oh no you wouldn't, papa.
Not to cause a scene." She walked to the door, stum-
bling slightly as the toe of one shoe caught a step.

"Steady, Ianthe. And don't come down in the morning until you're quite recovered."

"I won't," Ianthe told him. "Don't worry." Her smile
before she turned was mildly cynical, but her dark
eyes were haunted, condemning.

It was only when she'd gone that Nicholas realized
with a stab of compunction he'd not even kissed her.

No one was up when Juliet went down to breakfast
the next day. She felt fresh as a daisy and looked it.

"I thought you'd sleep late," Beth said, meeting her
in the hall. "I was sending a tray up."

Juliet laughed. "Not for me. I'll go to the kitchen and grab something. Just an apple or toast. I'm not really hungry, and the morning's gorgeous."

"What are you up to, Miss Juliet?" Beth asked suspiciously.

"Me? Nothing," Juliet answered, with her gray eyes widening innocently. She was wearing a soft blue dress that contrasted becomingly with her russet hair. "Where are the others?"

"In bed," Beth said, "except for Mr. William. He's gone to Penjust. Some business or other to do with a mine."

"Trust William; well, I don't blame him—for going out, I mean. I'm off for a walk myself."

"A walk?"

"Yes. So if anyone comes fussing about where I am or what I'm doing, tell them I'll be back sometime."

Beth shook her head slowly as Juliet, without waiting for a reply, pushed by and went to the kitchen. Five minutes later, wearing a navy cape and carrying a scarf in her hand, the girl's slender figure could be glimpsed half-running down the drive toward the lane. It was easy to guess where she was going, and though Beth understood Donna's misgivings, she had sympathy also with Juliet.

Juliet was running not only from high spirits but to reach Trefyn's place in the least possible time. It would take her almost an hour to get there and back, and she wanted time to talk with Trefyn without having to face an argument when she returned home. The air was heady and invigorating with autumn freshness. A frail mist silvered the fields and moors, draping the hedges with networked cobwebs in the early light. Behind the filmed horizon the first sunlight was climbing the sky. Soon the landscape would be brilliantly clear; but for the moment all was softened to mystery, holding the muted sounds of birds chortling and the rhythmic murmur of the brook tumbling over the stones.

By the time Juliet reached the track, threading sharply to the left, past the old stamp house, the light had lifted considerably and the farm was visible round the bend. Most of the building was still shadowed, but the front wall shone mellowed above the lane. Juliet's heart leaped. There was someone moving by the stables, and she guessed it was Trefyn. But it wasn't. The figure striding toward the gate was a woman's, and as she drew nearer, Juliet realized she was pushing something and was wearing queer baggy knickers that looked like bloomers. Her blouse was red flannel with long sleeves, and she had a checkered tam-o'-shanter on her red hair.

A *cyclist*. Juliet stared. Was this the wild girl Donna had described? She didn't look wild at all, just cheeky and comical, and rather fun. The two girls were face to face when the stranger said, "Hullo. I say, do you mind holding this a sec while I hoist myself on?" Juliet took the handlebars obligingly while the other girl bent forward and with one leg on one pedal swung the other over. She had a flat box strapped over her shoulder.

"I'm off sketching," she said, "my name's Judy. I'm staying here. Thanks a lot."

There was a swerve and a sudden lurch of the machine to the other side of the lane before balance was properly established. A moment or two later the cycle and its rider were disappearing in an almost straight course toward the main road.

Juliet turned and reached the farm a minute later.

As she went through the gate, Jet came out of the house with a bucket in her hand. She wore an apron, and her black hair fell loose on her shoulders, covering her forehead in a fringe above the smouldering dark eyes. She didn't smile. Her voice was a little resentful when she said, "I suppose you're looking for Trefyn?"

"Yes," Juliet answered.

"I thought so."

"Is he about?"

Jet waved toward the stables. "A mare foaled late last night, so he's top of the world. Go on up if you like. You'll find him at the stables."

Juliet hesitated before saying, "I met a girl down the lane on a bicycle. She said she was staying here."

Jet frowned. "Oh, *her*. Yes, she's a sort of guest. At least that's what she calls herself. But she doesn't pay. She's supposed to help. *Help* I ask you! Just apple picking and that sort of thing. Most of the time she's off painting, or trying to. You should just see her work—it's awful. I can't see anything in it. A child could do better. But of course Trefyn admires it."

"Why?" Juliet asked sharply.

The girl shrugged. "He's a funny one, that's why. As you should know. I only hope he doesn't fall for her. If he did, I'd be off like a shot."

"Why should he fall for her?" Juliet spoke lightly, but jealousy gnawed at her.

"She's something new, that's why. And such a talker, too. Of course that's coming from London. All about those new women—the suffragettes—you know, the ones who want the vote and throw eggs at Lloyd George. Mind you, Trefyn wouldn't agree with *that*.

He's a boss man at heart and says women should keep to their proper place in life. That's why *I* do all the housework and anything else he wants to put on me. So beware."

She smiled briefly, and the gesture turned her suddenly from a cross, Gypsy-looking creature, into a tantalizing fawn of a girl.

Juliet managed a smile. "I'll go then. I'd like to see the foal."

When she reached the stables Trefyn was already leaving. He came toward her, slowly, and her whole frame stiffened, though her pulses quickened like leaping fire through her veins.

"Hullo, Trefyn," she said.

"You're out early," he remarked, studying her with the deep, strange look in his eyes she found so oddly exciting.

"Yes. That's when I like it—all fresh and dewy."

"Like you."

"Oh, Trefyn—" she said impulsively, "I wished you were at the party last night. It was so dull."

"I'm sure you had plenty of admirers."

"Yes, I did," she lifted her chin defiantly. "Desmond Court wants to marry me, you know."

"No, I didn't." He paused before asking casually, "Have you said yes?"

"Of *course* not. Why should I?"

"He'd be a very good match. He's rich and I'm sure wouldn't beat you."

"Neither would you," she said pointedly.

"Oh, I might. And I'm not rich either."

Juliet's head drooped momentarily. "Don't tease me Trefyn," she said in a low voice. "You're the only person I could possibly—possibly—"

"Marry?"

She nodded. "Yes, really."

He took her hand. "Juliet . . . you haven't the first idea what marriage means. Good God! If I thought there was the slightest chance of making a go of things together, do you think I wouldn't carry you off right away? We'd elope, make a dash for it, and be damned to your parents and the rest. I'm mad about you, more fool me, everything you've got—your looks, your spirit, your wild-cat little temper, the bold way you go for what you want. But as a *wife*, I just can't see you scrubbing floors or cooking, washing babies' diapers and churning butter—and that's the way any woman of mine would have to be."

"I could do anything for you, Trefyn," she said impulsively. "Anything. But I wouldn't have to scrub, because—"

"Because what?"

"We could pay for a helper. Especially if you sold that land to William. He's so *keen* on starting that old mine, Trefyn, and you'd get an awful lot of money for it if you managed him properly. We could do the farm up and make things attractive. The parents would be easier then. Don't you see, it's so simple really?"

He dropped her hand abruptly. "Stop it, Juliet. You're talking nonsense. Or has that brother of yours sent you to bribe me?" His mouth was hard, his jaw set.

"How nasty of you to say that."

"Oh, I wouldn't put it past him or you either."

"You mean you don't believe me when I tell you I—"

He relaxed suddenly. "I don't know what I believe.

And this isn't the time for talking. The boy's about and there's work to do. Would you like to see the foal?"

Juliet nodded. "Please."

He took her hand again and led her to the box where the large mare, a fine shire horse, was fondling her son, a chestnut sired by Trefyn's champion stallion, Red King.

A gasp of surprise, almost of awe, caught Juliet by the throat. "Oh, but he's *lovely*. And look! He's getting up." As the small creature struggled to its still wobbly legs, the proud mother came to the stable door and pushed her nose out affectionately to Trefyn's hand. She was a magnificent mare, nearly twenty hands high, which was considerable even for a shire horse. Trefyn told Juliet that she had Brabant-Belgian blood in her, and that he hoped eventually to breed the best of her type in the country.

Juliet, whose knowledge of horses was confined to hunters, said sweetly, "That would be wonderful for you. You probably will, too, if you set your mind to it. But I suppose you'll need money, won't you, for more stables and stock? My father always said breeding was a fool's game except for millionaires."

"Well, I certainly won't ever be a millionaire," Trefyn said, "but I shan't need Trevarvas money, and I'm not a fool." His arm went to her waist, lingered, and then tightened. Her body thrilled to his touch. She could feel his hand traveling upward to her breast under the cape. His breath was warm against her ear, his lips hot against her neck. She turned impulsively until their bodies were close; even through her thick dress she felt the male hardness of him, the urgency of his need for her as strong as her own pulsing desire. The smell of hay and steamy animal scents were warm and vibrant in the air. Her arms went upward as her spine and neck arched back under his. He lifted her up. Her long skirt fell away, and his grasp was warm and trembling against the cotton underwear, quivering with contact from buttocks, thighs, and her urgent, anguished love cry of "Trefyn—Trefyn—have me, take me—I love you so much."

For a heady second or two, reason deserted him. He was aware of nothing but sweetness and desire and the rash impulse to take in abandon what he'd known one day must be inevitable—her surrender to his need, subjection to the deepest, most primitive and spiritual hunger of his being.

They were both victims, he as much as she, to the proud hunter—that deepest instinct of the human race: love. For a second, awareness quivered between them; then it was over, broken by a boy's whistle from the yard.

He dropped her abruptly as his senses registered, leaving him shaken and drenched with sweat. She stood, trembling, eyes bright with knowledge, a deep joy intermingled with frustration.

"Trefyn—"

"Look out," he said mechanically; "the boy's coming. Tidy yourself."

She smoothed her hair and stroked the folds of her skirt and cape into shape. By the time the lad reached the stables they were both leaning over the door of the box, eyes riveted on the mare and foal.

A little later Trefyn walked with Juliet to the lane.

"What do we do now?" she said.

"Go on as we are, for as long as we can," he told her. "You're a menace, Juliet."

"Say 'darling'—say it just once," she pleaded.

"No," he answered. "Witch—that's what you are—a witch."

She caught a falling leaf from a tree and tickled his neck with it. He put up a hand, brought it down, and gave her a slap.

"Behave yourself."

"I can't. I'm not that kind, Trefyn."

"No." He stood a moment studying her intensely. "If you were, maybe I wouldn't want you so much. All the same—"

"Yes?"

"One day you'll be sorry."

"What for?"

He shrugged. "This hour, this day; for growing up perhaps. Nothing can ever be the same between us. You know that, don't you?"

"Oh, yes, I told you, I'm a woman, Trefyn. I know what I want."

He didn't speak again until they reached the track facing the Polbreath estate. Beyond the trees, the roofs and towers of the house glittered bright in the sunlight. To their far right the Atlantic was calm and still as blue glass under a cloudless sky. Behind them, Rozebuzzan's summit rose starkly, brown-tipped by the primitive standing stones of prehistoric times. A different world, yet symbolic somehow of hers and Trefyn's.

Before parting, she lifted her face to his, but he did not kiss her.

"Hurry now," he said, "or you'll be in trouble."

"As if I cared."

"I do—for you."

"When shall we see each other?"

"Sometime," he answered ambiguously. As he turned she caught his arm. "Trefyn—"

"Yes?"

"Is that girl nice? The one who's staying with you?"

He looked taken aback before answering. "How did you know about her?"

"I met her. She looked odd in those knickers, but she seemed . . . fun."

"Yes, she is, so long as you laugh at her and nothing else."

Relief surged through her. "Is that how it is with you, Trefyn?"

"Asking a question like that makes me want to beat you," he told her.

"Oh, I know, I know." She laid her head briefly against his shoulder. His lips touched her hair, then he turned suddenly and was striding up the hill without looking back.

Very slowly she made her way to Polbreath.

The world was suddenly colder and more lonely. Even the sun seemed to have lost its warmth. It was funny, she thought, how loving could hurt.

Three weeks passed; a restless interlude at Polbreath, filled with uneasy silences from Donna, and arguments between Ianthe and Nicholas, which, although meant to be private, cast an atmosphere of ill temper over the household. Andrew absented himself as much as possible; Jason, concerned with his own affairs, was constantly worrying his mother over the art venture. Nicholas refused to discuss the matter, for which Jason blamed Ianthe entirely. She, for her part, was resentful of her half-brothers, especially William, whose concern for mining business took Nicholas away to Penjust for days at a time. William's fanatical zeal for work had increased since his parting with Hannah. The physical urge that had formerly driven him to her was now concentrated with tremendous energy into the possible reopening of the two defunct mines, Wheal Flower and Wheal Blair. Especially the latter, if he could get his hand on it.

"Leave Connor's land alone," Nicholas told him one

day sharply. "We've enough on our hands without spending money on a skeleton. It could be a complete white elephant with nothing to work at all. The Penrozes would have hung on to it in the first place, if the ore was there. And it's quite clear Connor's not selling. The more you bribe or try to bargain, the more stubborn he'll be. He's a fighter, William, which you should know by now."

"So am I," William said doggedly, "and if I can't reason with him, I'll break him." His dark eyes smouldered. Nicholas didn't like the set of his jaw or the thrust of head from his broad shoulders.

"And just how will you do that?" he asked dryly. "Fight him with fists in a drunken brawl at The Wandering Woman, or set his stables alight? Now you watch yourself and see you don't bring Polbreath into disrepute or you'll find yourself out on your ear without a penny of mine."

It was very seldom the two men came to open conflict, but William was astute enough to know that his father meant what he said.

"I'm not a fool," William said with an angry gleam in his eye.

"Aren't you?" Nicholas paused before adding, "I've been hearing a few things lately. Watch your step. Let a certain woman alone and find yourself a wife, that's my advice."

He turned sharply and walked away, leaving his son pondering. William's handsome face glowered, with eyes sullen beneath the frowning brows, the full, well-carved lips set stubbornly above the cleft chin. He drew a hand irritably through his black, crisply curling hair. So something was known of his affair with Hannah, he thought morosely. He hadn't been as clever as he'd imagined. He hadn't been clever at all—just wanting and taking what was natural for any man of his age and health and normal instincts. He should have been more careful where he conducted his little amours. You could never be certain some peeping Tom wasn't about.

A wife. Nicholas was probably right. But acceptable ones didn't grow on bushes; they were either social outcasts like Hannah, or well-bred young ladies with too many strings attached. He had never been imaginative or glib with words. Romanticism was not in his nature. But quite clearly, with things as they now were, he had a good deal of thinking to do. Marriage would be a safeguard. He knew he could trust Hannah to keep her mouth shut concerning the coming child. The fact remained, however, that a lawful family of his own would stabilize his position at Polbreath.

His mind wandered reflectively over the girls he knew: the twins who'd been invited at the last minute to Juliet's party; Dorothy Venn, a remote relation of the Penverryses who'd been unable to attend because she'd developed chicken pox; and Charlotte Carne, of course. There were one or two others, but the selection was very limited, and he didn't travel or get round the country except for purely business reasons. London bored him. He had a contempt for wily dowagers with feather-headed debutantes well-primed for the marriage market. Donna, during the past two years, had produced one or two at occasional intervals—hopeful aspirants whom he'd unchivalrously ignored, much to Nicholas's secret amusement and his mother's chagrin. William was quite aware of his immediate impact on the opposite sex, but it was a fleet-

ing one which was soon diverted to Jason, or, more
often, to Andrew, who had the gallant capacity to
soothe and restore wounded feminine dignity.

Probably the likeliest candidate as a wife at the
moment was Charlotte. The thought of bedding her
was unexciting but possible. She was no beauty, but
on the other hand she had a pleasant face and a good
figure with full, firm hips that were promising for
childbearing. Having no money to speak of, and with
very little dowry forthcoming, she'd accept her duties
as a wife with no fancy ambitions. Her background
was good, and she could appreciate a joke. He could
do worse, he decided.

The question of being in love or not didn't enter
into it. His heart was in mining. A mate in bed was all
that mattered otherwise, and it was quite possible that
Charlotte's body would be rewarding under the
sheets. Courting her would be no problem. The Major's house was only a few miles away, on the outskirts
of St. Figgan, and Charlotte had already shown evidence that she more than liked him.

Once he'd set his mind to a project, William was
quick to act, and in mid-November he announced
that he and Charlotte Carne were engaged and would
be married shortly after Christmas.

Donna was pleased, Nicholas speculative and skep-
tical.

"I hope you know what you're doing," he said, "and
will give the girl a fair deal."

"I'm marrying her, aren't I?"

"That's not what I meant," Nicholas said sharply.
"The whole business seems a bit quick on top of your
other little indulgence. I heard, by the way, that Hannah Marne's pregnant."

William's eyebrows shot up. "Oh? I haven't seen her lately, and I don't listen to gossip."

"There's a man living there, I understand," Nicholas continued, with his eyes unblinkingly on his son's expressionless face. "That's lucky for you, isn't it?"

William turned abruptly. "I don't know what the hell you're talking about."

"Oh, yes you do. Damn well you do," Nicholas said. "And another thing—don't think for one moment I condone your behavior. If it wasn't for your mother, I'd have a good deal more to say—and do. But she thinks a lot of you, so we'll keep things to ourselves. But just you see you do the right thing by Charlotte. She'll make a good wife, and good wives deserve faithfulness and respect. I hope you'll keep that in mind."

"I'm hardly likely to forget," William retorted acidly. "It seems strange, though, that you should be so concerned with my morals and welfare when you can be so shortsighted over your two daughters. I would have thought you had enough to occupy you with Ianthe's carryings on, and Juliet—"

"What about Juliet?" Nicholas interrupted quickly.

William shrugged. "Oh, nothing in particular. She's all right herself. I've always been fond of her. But so are others—that blasted Trefyn Connor. If he was off that land, it would be better for all of us. Especially Juliet."

With this parting shot William went out of the room, leaving Nicholas to his own reflections. He agreed with his son about getting Trefyn away but saw little chance of it. Young Connor had dug his heels in and was proving a menace not only to his own peace of mind, and Juliet's future, but to the local hunt and other organizations that, in the past, before the Connors' time, had had free access to the land. He was a crank, there was no question of that, and a dangerous one, possessing all the wayward whimsical charm of his father's forebears, with the pride and astuteness of the Gentrys.

For some time Nicholas had been aware of his daughter's increasing inclinations for riding toward the farm. He knew she and Trefyn met occasionally, and had tried to ignore the fact, not wishing to play the heavy father. But Donna was becoming increasingly worried.

"You should talk to her," she'd said several times. "If you'd only put your foot down, she'd have to listen."

"Not if she's like you," Nicholas had thought, though he'd held his tongue. A heated argument with Donna on top of coping with Ianthe and the problem of Juliet was not to his taste at the moment, especially with Jason's immediate future to settle.

Ianthe, of all his children, irritated him the most. Although she insisted on remaining at Polbreath, her restless moods and flashes of temper over nothing made it increasingly clear she was far from satisfied with remote Cornwall. Yet for weeks she'd refused to confide the exact circumstances of her flight from Wycksley and her whirlwind London existence. How much he believed the stories of her scandalous social life or theatrical successes he could not make up his mind. He did know she was hiding something. When one afternoon he asked her if Robertson had ill-treated her, she merely said, "*Him?* Ill-treat me? He's an old man."

"Then why? What happened? You wouldn't run away for nothing."

"I'll explain sometime," she said. "And don't think I'm not grateful, papa. You're the only person in the world I mind about. That's why I wanted to come back."

"Not much good is it," he said, "if we don't talk."

"How *can* we talk, with always someone here? William or Andrew or Jason, and Juliet rushing in and out. As for Donna . . . you know she's always hated me."

"I know nothing of the sort, and I wish you'd get that idea out of your head. Why can't you try and be civil to her? Fit in with the household better. You could do a good deal to help if you behaved like a grown-up woman instead of a resentful child. Do you realize, Ianthe, that you're—"

"Thirty years old, disillusioned and heading for a disastrous future? Yes, I know," Ianthe replied. "But so are lots of us. Life's changing, feminine suffrage is coming in, values aren't the same anymore. Some people even think there's war ahead—"

"Not while Edward's on the throne."

"He won't be . . . forever," Ianthe said cryptically, "And then what? Oh, I'm not interested in politics or women's rights, I don't want to throw myself under traffic or set fire to the Houses of Parliament. I'm not that kind of person. But I want something. I want to *live*, before it's too late. You get the feeling everywhere, in town. There's that American jazz and rag-time, and—"

"Smoking and slit skirts and no faith in anything. Is that your trouble, Ianthe?" Nicholas's eyes were worried, his voice more gentle.

She smiled wryly, then remarked, "I've made my bed, I must lie on it, isn't that what you said when I married Robertson Wycksley? Well, I've done it—for quite some time, and it's a very cold bed."

"You knew his reputation."

"It isn't his reputation that worries me, papa. It's the bloody hypocrisy of it. Oh, I'm sorry, you didn't know I swore, did you? But you know now, just as I drink, and have lovers, and do all the things no nice woman does. Why? Because Robertson's nothing to give me but money and notoriety. *Nothing*. Do you understand? Can you imagine for one moment what it's like being pawed over by a lascivious, lusting impotent old rake who thinks he's bought you body and soul for his filthy lucre?"

There was a pause. Then Nicholas said, "Why didn't you come home before?"

"Because those things matter to me," Ianthe replied, with cold frankness, "I've grown used to them—the wealth and being able to spend and have what I want at any time I choose. It's like an appetite. Once you've tasted certain things you find it difficult to do without them."

"Is that what you've been trying to do since you returned? Do without?"

Ianthe faced, him unswervingly. "Of course."

"Then why—?"

"Why did I come back?"

"Exactly."

"Robertson's going to divorce me," she answered flatly. "But that wasn't the only reason. No—*no*. Believe me, I *did* want to see you again; I suppose I was looking for comfort of some sort—to belong, like I used to; *that* wasn't pretense. Please—" her voice broke and faded.

Nicholas's first anger at hearing the news softened, in spite of a lingering sense of outrage. He put his hand on Ianthe's shoulder and with an effort said calmly, "We'll see about that. If I know anything about the law, the boot could easily be on the other foot."

"No." Her voice was bitter. "Robertson has allies everywhere. When you're rich like he is you can always find witnesses and liars to support you. Oh, I know, I've seen enough of it. And he can be very—bland, when he chooses to be. Respectability?" She gave a hard little laugh that jarred him. "It's a cloak. Didn't you know? A very protective cloak that can be bought by anyone wealthy enough to pay for it. There's hardly a business venture in town that Wycksley isn't concerned with. His body's soft, but his mind isn't—"

"Neither is mine," Nicholas told her. "And I'm not lacking the wherewithal."

"I know that. But—"

"I take it his evidence has a certain foundation?" he interrupted.

She had the grace to turn her head away. Her voice dropped when she admitted, "Yes. You must have heard enough to know that. It just happens that Robertson's got a grudge against Lester and means to break him."

"Lester?"

"Lester Hereford. Need I spell it out? He's in politics. Some think he's got a brilliant future. But any scandal like—like divorce!—well, don't you see what a weapon it is?"

"Does he love you?"

"Dear papa! How trusting of you. *Love?* In such conditions, in *our* little social set? Oh, no. Lester's just as keen to be rid of me now as Wycksley is."

Fury was beginning to mount in Nicholas again. He recalled Ianthe as she'd been when a child: warm, impetuous, rebellious often, but loving-hearted. Gall filled him that she could have landed herself in such a despicable predicament. His marriage to Donna, of course, had started it all. He'd been caught between them—by his young wife's possessiveness and Ianthe's passionate devotion. Through the years Donna's attitude had softened, but mostly because of his wayward daughter's departure; Ianthe knew this, had always known it, and he recognized bitterness in her had cut deep.

Perhaps he'd been selfish. If his life had taken a different course . . . but a man in his prime couldn't be expected to sacrifice his future to a young girl's whim. On the other hand he could, perhaps, have taken a firmer line with Donna.

William's affairs and forthcoming marriage, combined with the problem of Jason's future and Ianthe's troubles, temporarily obscured any niggling fears concerning Juliet and Trefyn Connor. Later, when Ianthe had gone to her room to write what she called a "stinker" to Wycksley, he set off for a sharp walk in the direction of Penmartin, hoping to clear his head and somehow restore a less gloomy view of things.

Donna, who'd been shopping in Penzance, alighted from the carriage by the steps as he went through the front door. She was wearing a rust-red outfit with a long full skirt, a three-quarter-length waisted coat, and a wide-brimmed hat trimmed with a ridiculous-looking bird on her highly dressed swept-up hair. One hand was enclosed with a fur muff, the other held her skirt to reveal the tip of a high-heeled shoe. She had a long feather boa twisted round her neck that dangled snakelike over an arm almost to her knee.

So very fashionable, Nicholas thought indulgently, although slightly overdone for the place and occasion. On any other woman the effect might have been slightly ostentatious, but Donna had the capacity and style to look ravishing in everything, and following the years of her youth, when her father William Penroze had been so financially pressed to keep his estate Trencobban and the mine Wheal Faith going, he didn't grudge her little extravagances.

"Oh, Nicholas," she exclaimed when she saw him, "surely you're not off now? Charlotte's coming for the evening, remember, and—"

"Just a leg stretch, my dear," Nicholas said before she could finish, "and I'm sure you and William can deal very well with Charlotte for an hour without me."

Donna pouted, then shrugged. "Where's Ianthe?" she asked pointedly.

"Oh, I've no idea now," Nicholas answered. "But I can assure you you won't find her troublesome. We've had a little chat, which should have relieved her repressions."

Donna eyed him suspiciously. "What about?"

Nicholas's face hardened. "Now stop the questions, Donna. If Charlotte's coming, I'm sure you'll want to change."

"Why? Don't you like my outfit?"

"My love, you look extremely smart. But hardly right for receiving your future daughter-in-law, which you well know. Now please, I've things to do."

He gave her a brief smile, and started walking sharply from the drive to his right, where a path led to a side gate and the moors.

Donna sighed, and turned sharply to the man who was standing patiently a few yards away with parcels under both arms.

"Take them through to the hall please, Peters," she said, "and leave them there. I'll have Mary sort them out."

Peters went ahead of her up the dozen steps leading to the handsome Georgian front door, leaving Donna to follow at her leisure.

Nicholas's mind meanwhile was far from Polbreath and its household affairs. As he walked sharply seaward, toward the largest of his mines, Penmartin, his thoughts strayed unwittingly again to the unsatisfactory interlude with Ianthe. *Blast that old villain Wycksley*, he thought with his first anger returning, intensified. *Blast him for stealing my daughter and turning her into a strumpet. And with her background and breeding, too!*

It was not often he thought of Belinda, his aristocratic first wife. But he did so then, with a kind of torture mounting in him. Incompatible as they'd been, and failures in their relationship to each other, the children, Jonathan and Ianthe, had deserved better things. Jonathan was all right, doing well in the Army. But Ianthe!—the willful and beautiful—the girl who'd once meant so much to him. God! how could she have landed herself in such a mess, at the mercy of such a lascivious old reprobate? And the threat of divorce!

*Divorce* by *him*; it was unthinkable. Despicable. To-morrow, Nicholas decided, he'd take a trip to Truro and see his solicitor Blakerley. Charles Blakerley was an astute man. When he heard the facts he'd be able to advise what action to take if Wycksley fulfilled his threat. A lawyer would be needed if they fought any possible case, and Blakerley would know the best man. It would cost more than the proverbial "pretty penny," but thank God he, Nicholas, could afford it, and more. If the whole sordid business had to come into the light, he'd see that Ianthe emerged in the best possible colors, and Wycksley with such shame no de-cent club would allow him inside. But then Robertson Wycksley had no use for decency. That was the irony of it. Only his damned filthy lucre that could buy up practically everything else.

With this gloomy truth churning his brain, Nicholas reached the bend in the cliff path, which abruptly cut a little inland from there to Penmartin half a mile away. The pumping rod was clearly visible against the gray winter sky, moving rhythmically as a symbol of power and man's inventive energy—undefeated by slumps or failing lodes. *A monarch of mines,* he thought, relaxing into a more cheerful mood. He slowed his pace a little, and paused momentarily to glance seaward, where the cliffs were starkly outlined against the Atlantic. In the distance he saw a woman move from a fold in the moors where the Marne farm crouched. At first she was only a dark shape mingling with the brown and black of the leafless under-growth. Then, as she drew nearer, he saw it was Han-nah with a basket on her arm. She passed by quite close to him. He gave a slight inclination of his head, and fancied uncomfortably she gave a faint ironic

smile. A handsome young woman, he thought resentfully when she'd gone, wild looking but nothing slat-
ternly. He could understand William wanting her, but
why couldn't he have sown his wild oats further
afield? For such a hardheaded, down-to-earth character, the young fool had shown little common sense.

Poor Charlotte. Although she'd be welcome as a
daughter-in-law, he didn't envy her lot with William.
Still, she was a sturdy, sensible creature, and with
luck might have a restraining influence on Juliet,
though he doubted it.

When he reached Penmartin, Nicholas found Fred
Couch the bookkeeper in the counting house. His father and grandfather before him had been captains of
the mine, and much of Penmartin's continuing working success, at a time when rumors of closure and failing lodes were so widespread, was due very largely to
his faith in the mine, an unerring, inherent knowledge,
and his unfailing perseverance.

Fred now was beyond the age of normal retirement,
but preferred to keep working with the aid of several
trustworthy and diplomatic agents.

"Well, Fred," Nicholas said, "how are things?"

"Normal, surr, good," Couch answered. "Dividend's
up, an' the new levels promisin' rich. But then you
know that, don't you?"

"It's my business to know these things, Fred."

Couch stroked his chin thoughtfully, as a wary
frown creased his gray thick brows. He was a small
man, lean-featured, with an assessing quality in his
shrewd eyes that had proved competent in the past in
successfully handling many tricky mining situations.

"By the way, Mr. Trevarvas, surr," he said after a
short pause, "there's a furriner 'bout these parts. Did

you know? A rough kind of fellow come to the Marne place."

"I'd heard, yes."

"Pity it's that woman's property an' not yours," Fred continued.

"Why?"

"He could be a nuisance. Last night in the pub there was a bit of trouble; he an' Rick Brodie got into an argument. Could've been a punch-out if Bob Pengelly hadn't stepped in."

"Brodie?" Nicholas was surprised. Rick to his knowledge was one of the most reliable and even-tempered workers at Penmartin.

"Yes. An' that's proof itself, isn't it? Rick isn't an easy one to rouse."

"What was the argument about?"

"Nothing in particular . . . well, I s'pose you could say women," Couch answered. "Of course the fellow was well in his cups, Hannah's man, I mean. But it doesn't look good."

"No, it's a pity," Nicholas agreed. "But probably it will blow over all right. Still, I know you'll keep your eye on things, Fred. Let me know if anything else arises. I'm not having my own men upset over nothing. Another thing—"

"Yes, surr?"

"Be a bit careful how you refer to Hannah in public. I know you're not one for gossip, but words have a habit of slipping from most of us sometimes that would have been better not said. In the past Marne's daughter's kept pretty much to herself, and the man I understand is her cousin, come to help her work the place."

"Oh, I see. Yes, I understand." But Couch's tones

were doubtful. Whether he'd heard anything of the
girl's association with William, Nicholas could not
make out, but he firmly intended to impress on his
son the additional necessity of keeping well away in
future. He was not only irritated and annoyed by William's obtuseness in ever blundering into an affair
with Hannah, but inwardly affronted to think any
child of Trevarvas blood should be bred in such unsavory circumstances. And William seemed to be taking
the matter so lightly, blast him. There was no doubt
at all in Nicholas's mind that he was responsible. Hannah's offspring therefore would be his own grandchild, unacknowledged and deprived of any decent
place in society.

My God! Nicholas thought as he strode back to Polbreath, William needed a good horsewhipping, and if
he'd been younger he'd have got it. All his sons had
been spoiled because of Donna's indulgence, except
perhaps Andrew, who in some ways appeared so much
older than his years. Lately, especially, he'd seemed
curiously withdrawn from the family, as though some
inward conflict which had nothing to do with his
lame leg was worrying him. Yet tenant farmers and
workers liked him. He did his job adequately. Of all
his children by Donna, Andrew gave least to worry
about outwardly. But there was no rapport between
them. No understanding.

At the moment Nicholas reached Polbreath, Andrew was approaching from the other direction. He'd
been waiting by the lane leading to Rosebuzzan valley, hoping Juliet would appear. She was the only one
he felt he could talk to when he'd anything on his
mind, and he'd watched her earlier, cantering left toward the Connor farmstead on her mare Firebrand.

After half an hour he'd given up his vigil, realizing she might easily have taken another route back round the opposite side of the moors, skirting the coast.

Juliet, in fact, was with Trefyn.

They were lying in the old barn less than a hundred yards from the stables, with the soft sweetness of hay about them, his tilted eyes warmly glowing on her up-turned face, his lips pressed against her cheek, neck, and curve of her throat, where a little pulse beat, leaping with a joyous life of its own to meet the fiery hunger of his embrace. The riding jacket lay care-lessly thrown aside; her thighs and buttocks and full young breasts throbbed with a consuming desire that was a terrible sweetness, burdened with pain while his hands pushed up the constricting skirt that bound her, enclosing the soft warm flesh.

"Love me, Trefyn," she urged, arching closer to-ward him, "oh, love me, love me—" her voice was thick with emotion and unshed tears so choked with longing they could not fall. His hands were every-where—soft and gentle one moment, cruel the next, to which the life in her responded like the juice of a ripe young fruit about to be squeezed dry.

"Oh, Trefyn, Trefyn—" Her arms were about his neck, fierce and strong as coiled ropes. Against her she could feel him hard upon her. And then, suddenly, streaming with sweat and self-torture, he gave a groan and sprang from her.

"Get up," he said harshly. "Get up and go, for God's sake—"

She stared at him blankly, trembling and dazed with disappointment and the wild anguish of love's re-jection. Her skirt was still hoisted above her knees; one nipple bared above the embroidered cotton chemise. Her face was white, blank with pain and slowly gathering anger. He had his back to her and was adjusting his trousers with fingers that were bruised and stiff. When he turned she was standing up, automatically buttoning her bodice. The hair fell like dulled fire over her shoulders. Her gray eyes appeared darkened coals with the light gone from them.

"So you don't love me," she said in cold, unnatural tones. "You've never loved me. It was a lie, wasn't it?"

He shook his head slowly.

"I adore you, Juliet. That's why . . . I won't have it this way. Don't you understand?" He went forward and grabbed her hands, enclosing them with the force of steel.

"No," she said clearly and coldly. "You led me on and let me think you felt the same as I, and then you pushed me off like a—like some bundle of rubbish to be dumped in a bin. What do you think I am, Trefyn Connor? Who? What? D'you mind telling me?"

"Listen, Juliet!"—his grasp went from her wrists to her shoulders, "I know what you are, and I know what you want, what we both want. But it's not going to be in the hay like any whore or village girl wanting a mate. When we come together it will be legally with a ring on your finger and no sly games in barns—"

"Then marry me, Trefyn, marry me," she cried, "You know that's all I want. There's been no one else ever . . . even at that awful school you were all I thought of; and you promised—"

"And what do you think your parents would say? And how do you think you'd like being the wife of a poor man with no means to keep you properly—"

"But you could, you could," she insisted, staring up

at him pleasantly. "If you sold that land to William . . ."

He jumped away from her and when she saw the sudden relentless set of his face, her heart felt suddenly leaden.

"*William!* William's land. So in the end it all comes down to that, doesn't it? Power for William and his precious family."

"No, *no*. You know that's not true. I love you. I—"

"Maybe," he said, "in your own way. But it's not quite mine, Juliet. I've told you before, you'd never stick with it. You haven't the first idea of what life with me would mean. Why, you're not even grownup yet, you're a child—"

"A child? Me?" She rushed at him, and brought her fist sharply against his chest. "You know I'm not. It's just an excuse. I hate you—hate you."

"And that proves it, doesn't it?" he said. "You need a sound walloping."

Against her will, the tears came flooding from her eyes. She turned away, burying her face in her hands. Her whole body was racked with stormy, ungovernable sobs. Grief and humiliation drowned her, taking both body and spirit into a dark well of loneliness and loss.

Then she felt his arm round her waist, and the gentle pressure of his touch against one breast.

"Don't, Juliet; please, love—don't," he begged. "We'll talk about things later. For heaven's sake, don't carry on—"

Presently she allowed herself to be comforted, and although nothing was settled concerning a future meeting, she knew as she rode away on Firebrand ten

minutes later that all was not over between them.
Sometime, however far ahead, the issue would arise
again, and then she'd manage things better.

To regain composure she didn't return home immediately, but continued down the valley lane, cantering
past Polbreath's gates, up the hill that presently met
the high moorland road. From there she took her left-
hand turn leading westward to Penjust and Land's
End. On the right, small stone-walled fields and
patches of rough moorland sloped to the coast, which
clawed with jagged granite fingers into the sea. Black
against the horizon the stark shape of a ruined mine
stack stood, bleakly reminiscent of the past. To the
left, the brown hills rose in an undulating line broken
only by occasional cromlechs, boulders, and, further
on, a half circle of standing stones—relics of Druid
days.

The road was empty that day. No sign of a farm
cart even to disturb the complete peace and quietness;
only the clip-clop of Firebrand's hooves through the
solitude, and the sudden shrill crying of a gull disturbed. At intervals, thin smoke spiraled upward from
small cottages crouched in folds of land, half-hidden
by furze and clumps of twisted elder and thorn; but
further ahead, nearing Wheal Jakke, the air was
thicker with distant smoke and steam, denoting man's
industry and several mines still thriving in spite of the
nineteenth-century depression. Two of these—situated
halfway between Polbreath and Penjust—were owned
by Nicholas, providing not only a considerable income
to shareholders and "adventurers," but ensuring regular wages to a large number of other workers. As Juliet neared the small hamlet of Zavorna, a man in miners' clothes—an underground captain obviously, still

wearing his white coat and miners' hat—lifted his hand in respectful greeting. A little further on, a woman and child smiled.

From seeing Juliet about in the past, during her school holidays, they'd learned to know and like her. There was nothing snooty about the master's young daughter, they said, not like that other one who'd been so difficult and haughty in her youth, Miss Ianthe. It was already common knowledge that she was back again at Polbreath, more shame to her. Although Cornwall was still comparatively cut off from the rest of the country, news—especially of the wild and sensational order—was quick to travel, and to all decent-living countryfolk, Ianthe's reputation was a scandal and affront to the Almighty. In the old days if she'd been anyone but Nicholas Trevarvas's daughter, she'd have been stoned and beaten, whatever the Good Book said about forgiveness and offering the other cheek.

But there it was. There was one law for the rich and one for the poor. And all things considered, most natives of the district considered themselves lucky to be working for a man like Trevarvas, even though in the past there'd been a bit of gossip about his life with his first wife.

Still, all that was forgotten now. On the whole he'd done well for them. Even provided a fine new row of workers' cottages for a number of those he employed. Small but granite-built; nothing grand to look at but with proper sewerage and outdoor lavatories instead of the smelly cesspits that the authorities said had been responsible for outbreaks of typhoid, cholera, and smallpox in days gone by.

Juliet was well aware of the benefits bestowed by

her father, and as she drove past that day a sense of pride and well-being filled her, partially dispelling the tormenting restlessness following her emotional interlude with Trefyn. *If only he wasn't so stubborn,* she thought impatiently. He said he loved her, and she believed he did; she knew it. Then why couldn't he be reasonable and let William have the patch of land he so desperately wanted. Of course Trefyn was right in one way: a mine working would spoil the upper part of the valley, but Connor land stretched seaward too; the stables and farm could be extended in that direction. Surely for her sake he could eventually be made to see sense. If he was cooperative she might even induce Nicholas to include him somehow in working the family estate. It would be a tussle for both of them, including a process of give-and-take. But if she and Trefyn made it quite clear they were going to be married, she felt certain she could gain Nicholas's support when he realized how strongly she felt.

The trouble was it would take time. And Juliet didn't want to wait. Why should she? Why should either of them waste a delicious moment of loving and living together just because of a stuffy argument about land and old-fashioned ideas about not marrying "beneath her."

*Beneath!* What a funny word to use in that way. Involuntarily a smile touched her lips, and she was inwardly thrilled again, remembering how she'd lain with Trefyn's body on top of her, longing for him. Longing and longing so desperately she'd thought she'd die. If anything had happened—properly—she might have had a baby, and then everything would have been settled. For one moment she wished it had,

and was angry that Trefyn hadn't let it. Then, just as
quickly, her mood changed and she knew he was
right. He'd been looking after her, that was all. It
would have been terrible anyway to hurt her father
by having to have a shotgun wedding. None of the
family would have liked Trefyn after that, and it was
very important that they should. To be left as his
mother Elinor had been, outcast and embittered with
no friends or acquaintances of her own, was almost
unthinkable. So long as she had Trefyn, of course, she
could put up with it; but beneath her passion for him
a lurking streak of common sense told her she'd miss
some of the things she'd been used to. Especially Nicholas. And Andrew, too. So she'd try to be more patient, get her family gradually used to the idea of her
marrying a Connor, and in time they'd have to give in.

Her mood had quieted and she was more reflective
when she headed to her left, leaving the high road for
a track that climbed sharply for a bit then dropped
abruptly into a thickly wooded valley of stunted trees
and bushes interspersed with larch, willow, and sloes.
Leafless thorn trees were tangled into the undergrowth. It was a lonely district, seldom used except by
tinkers and Gypsies.

In a dip at the side of the track a shabby-looking
caravan stood, with a lean pony nibbling grass
nearby. A woman smoking a clay pipe came out as
Firebrand cantered by at a leisurely trot. She was
dark-skinned, lean-featured, with the tips of gilt rings
glinting through her tumbled black hair. Her small
eyes were shrewd and watchful. Juliet knew the family by sight. The menfolk had a bad reputation for
poaching and stealing, but they were mostly left alone
because of a canny habit of producing witnesses in

their favor should any question of their honesty arise. The woman's stare was unblinking. Juliet gave a slight nod and smile, but there was no response. Round the bend, which eventually took her by a different route back to Polbreath, a large man, carrying two bundles of sticks under his arms, appeared. He wore a woollen jersey and trousers caught in at the ankles by string. His face was hard, large, and angular under a tweed cap pushed to the side near one eye. Instinctively, Juliet's hold tightened on the reins, but dropping the wood, he sprang with the speed of a panther and had them hard under his own fist. Firebrand reared, with his hooves pounding the air. Juliet raised her crop.

"How dare you! Get off—" He laughed contemptuously, ducked his head, looked up, spat, and said, "You listen to me, young madam, or you'll get sum-then' you're not reckonin' on. You jus' tell that lustin' brother of yours—that William—to kip away from my place, see? Pete Hearne's my name, an' I'm not havin' any fancy feller sniffen' after *my* women. Got it?"

Breathing quickly, both furious and frightened, Juliet shouted, "I don't know you. I've never seen you before in my life. Let me go or I'll . . . I'll—"

"Have the law on me? Is that it? Ho ho! Missie, you watch yourself or I'll—" before the foul word left his lips, Juliet brought the whip hard against his cheek. Firebrand snorted, whinnied, and reared again. The man swore and dropped the reins, lifting a hand to his face where a trickle of blood oozed from temple to chin.

A moment later the colt was off at a smart gallop. Juliet was aware faintly of a string of oaths following her. Her heart was beating so heavily she felt sick, but she didn't slow the pace until the walls of Polbreath were clearly in view and the dark lane well behind her. William was chatting to the groom when she took Firebrand to the stables. Though color had returned to her cheeks, she was still breathless, her eyes scared and mouth strained.

"What's the matter?" he asked. "Had a fright?"

"Yes."

As they walked toward the house she told William of her encounter with Pete Hearne.

"What did he mean, William?" she said, noting the angry color mounting his face. "About you? And his women. I thought he was one of the Gypsies, at first. But he wasn't, was he?"

"No," William told her grudgingly. "He's Hannah Marne's cousin. The woman with that small farm near the coast. Her father's the one who was gored by the bull. Remember? No, of course you don't. You weren't here."

She looked puzzled. "Gored? By a bull? How horrible. But I still don't . . . I still don't see where you come into it."

"I used to chat with her occasionally when I passed that way," William said noncommittally. "I suppose he resents it. These rough types get funny ideas sometimes."

"He wasn't at all funny," Juliet said shortly. "He nearly attacked me. I shall tell my father and get him to evict them."

"You can't do that," William's voice was curt, hard. "The farm's their own—Jake's. Better let things rest, Juliet. Steer clear of that lane and that particular district. For heaven's sake, don't begin trouble for father.

He's enough on his hands with Ianthe and Jason to worry about." There was a short pause before he nodded meaningfully, "and you."

"Why me?"

"Trefyn Connor, of course. Don't you realize you're getting talked about?"

Juliet lifted her head defiantly. "Who's talking? And why should I care if they do? Anyway . . ." her voice sweetened, became quietly wheedling, "I'm trying to help you, William."

"What are you talking about?"

"That land you want—the Wheal Blair part. In the end maybe you'll get it, if you're patient."

"Is this bribery?" William sounded incredulous.

A mischievous smile dimpled her cheeks. Her face was suddenly radiant, her eyes dancing. "Perhaps. You see I—I love Trefyn. One day we'll be married."

"You and *him*? But he's a working small-holder, a laborer almost. You'd be a *peasant's* wife, an outcast like his mother."

"No, I won't. We shall have a nice home, and you'll get your land. Everything will be all right in the end. You just wait, William. I know what I'm doing."

William was uneasy. His conscience told him he should inform Nicholas himself of his sister's unpleasant experience with Pete. On the other hand, with his marriage to Charlotte drawing nearer the last thing he wanted was for his unsavory history concerning Hannah to be resurrected. The Carnes were proud. He knew he could trust Charlotte to overlook any past indiscretion; she was eager to be married, had been sweet on him for years; but her old man could make things unpleasant, and William had neither the taste or time for personal arguments and antagonisms.

Therefore it was important, in the words of the old adage, to let sleeping dogs lie.

"Well, what do you say?" he heard Juliet asking wheedlingly. "About Trefyn and me? Don't be stuffy, William. And I promise you I won't poke my nose in about that Marne woman."

"You're a sly chit and no mistake," William said, giving her a sidelong look. "And you ought to be spanked."

Juliet laughed. "That's what Trefyn said."

"Then he's got more sense than I thought. If he does marry you, I hope he starts early enough."

"There, you see?" Her eyes were brilliant.

"What?"

"If he marries you. That's what you said. You've already accepted it. The possibility, I mean."

Knowing himself to be beaten, William let the matter drop. Simpler to keep out of things, he told himself; he was enough involved as it was.

Toward the end of the week everyone was surprised when Ianthe came downstairs one morning fully dressed for traveling, wearing a plum-colored velvet pelisse over a fur-trimmed costume of the same shade, with a wide-brimmed hat extravagantly heaped with velvet flowers and feathers perched high at a sideways angle on her black, curled hair. She had one hand in a muff, from the other was suspended a silver chain bag. Her cheeks were slightly rouged, her dark eyes brilliant. There was a defiant lift to her chin and a secret triumphant smile on her lips. The overall effect was startling, and Elise, who came down the hall unexpectedly, almost dropped the bowl of flowers she was carrying.

"Mrs. Wycksley, ma'am . . . why . . ."

She didn't finish because just at that moment Nicholas came out of the library. He stopped, frowning. "Where are you off to?" he said. "A shopping spree somewhere?"

Ianthe shook her head. "I'm going home papa. If I could have the carriage to take me to the station, I'd be grateful."

"*Home?* To Wycksley, you mean?"

She nodded.

"But damnit, Ianthe, I had an interview with Charles only yesterday about the divorce tangle you've got yourself into. And now this! What does it mean? Do you mind explaining—"

For a second or two Ianthe's hard veneer crumpled. Her face softened. "I'm sorry, *really* I am, for all the trouble I've caused. But . . . I had a letter yesterday, from Robertson, I should have told you, I know. But I had to think about it. He wants me back, you see. And I . . . I think it's best."

Nicholas regarded her sternly before asking, "May I see the letter?"

Ianthe fumbled in her bag and produced the note. It was brief, and to the point, without sentiment or any pretense of affection.

Madam,

If you would return forthwith I would be obliged. On second thoughts I have decided to disregard your indiscretions, providing you behave sensibly in future. Vincent French has told me in no uncertain terms he will not consider appearing in "Uneasy Virtue" unless you play opposite to him. This production, as you know, is important to me. I have sunk considerable capital into the venture, which I'm not prepared to lose due to a woman's whims. The play is not a good one, but would command a large public with Vincent's name on the program. And yours, of course. No doubt I could find as adequate—perhaps a better—actress than you. But Vincent has stated his terms, and they are his final word. So I shall expect to see you at your earliest convenience.

Rehearsals start on Monday.

I remain

Your husband, Robertson Wycksley.

P.S. If I do not see you within two days, I shall myself take a trip to Cornwall to ensure my legal rights are restored.

For a moment or two Nicholas stared blankly at the offensive note, his face grim and pale. Then, with a rush of color, his temper flared, and he had a violent impulse to set off that very day for a confrontation, physical if necessary, with Wycksley.

"The damned old swine," he said explosively at last. "I'll see him dead before he gets away with it—treating a daughter of mine like any . . . any . . . My God, I'll—"

"No, papa," Ianthe's voice cut in, coldly, but very calmly and sweetly. "You'll do nothing. I'm returning to London because I want to. If you must know, these last few days here have been deadly boring. I've never acted with Vincent French. It's an honor, don't you understand? I can't afford to miss the chance."

"An honor?" Nicholas queried, "under such terms? What *are* you, Ianthe? Isn't a shred of decency or pride left in you?"

Ianthe shook her head slowly. "Not your kind, I don't think so. Donna killed that years ago, when she—"

Nicholas brought his hand sharply across her cheek. "Don't talk in that way of my wife, do you hear? I won't have it in my house—or out of it, in my hearing. If you feel that way, it's perhaps better you should leave immediately."

"Yes," a cold feminine voice said just behind them, "I agree. Not for my sake, but Juliet's."

Both turned sharply. Unknown to them both, Donna had come out of the parlor and was standing with a bitter smile on her pale lovely face. The orange eyes glowed. Both hands were clenched tightly at her sides. A beam of light from the half-window caught her luxurious hair, giving it a temporary glitter of gold.

Ianthe said nothing, but a contemptuous half-smile touched her lips.

"Don't interfere, Donna." Nicholas said in controlled tones. "Leave us if you don't mind. This is a matter for Ianthe and me."

"I think my name was mentioned," Donna said acidly.

"Nevertheless, you heard what I said."

"Oh, very well."

Angry to be put in her place in front of Ianthe, Donna lifted her head proudly to return to the parlor. Ianthe was still smiling; the sting of Nicholas's palm showed in a red flush on her cheek.

He was struck by sudden compunction. "I'm sorry. I didn't mean to strike you," he said.

"It doesn't matter. Words can hurt far more," she replied coldly, "and attitudes. Oh, don't try and reason with me, papa. Don't pretend. You never did. And I'm not pretending to you either. It's time I left. I've only been an embarrassment. In London at least I have a place. However unspeakable Robertson may be, he has his uses. We know where we stand too; that's something!"

"I never thought to hear you say such things," Nicholas said heavily, "or see you so—"

"Dolled up? Depraved?"

"I didn't say that."

She shrugged. "You didn't have to. Your eyes told enough. And perhaps it's true. But life changes . . . the pattern of it. Values. Except here perhaps." Her glance wandered wistfully round the familiar surroundings: the furniture she'd known since babyhood, hall table, antique chest, and massive grandfather clock ticking away in its recess. Tick tock! tick tock! Time slipping, and so much still to savor and experience, even perhaps enjoy. No use getting sentimental and soft. What was the point in trying to identify herself with Polbreath when any real contact had been cut so many years ago.

Nicholas himself sensed the futility of further effort and reasoning on his daughter's behalf. After another brief conversation, when she promised to contact him if any necessity arose, he said with no show of emotion, "Very well, Ianthe, obviously you've made up your mind. I'll see the carriage is brought to the front in ten minutes. Meanwhile, you'd better say your goodbyes while your luggage is brought down."

Relieved at the prospect of Ianthe's departure, Donna's farewell was comparatively congenial. "I can't say I'm sorry to see you go," she said frankly. "For our sake and certainly your own I'm sure it's for the best.

I've heard various reports of your stage career, some very complimentary. If you give your full attention to it, I'm sure—"

Ianthe interrupted with a laugh. "I'm no dedicated actress," she said with equal frankness. "It's just fun, and I do it because I like admiration and nice things. Well, what more is there in this old life after all?" Her eyes were hard as they contemplated the orange glow of Donna's. For some unfathomable reason, Donna felt discomforted.

"Good-bye then, Ianthe. There's no point in us talking. There never has been. But I wish you every success."

At that moment, Peters came downstairs, carrying two of Ianthe's bags. From outside the sound of carriage wheels and horses' hooves clattered along from the stables. Ianthe went out by the side door for a last look at the garden, and saw Juliet hurrying down a path to meet her.

"I'm sorry you're going, Ianthe," she exclaimed. "And that's really true. You've been fun. I wish things could have been different. Are you sure you're . . ." Her voice faltered on the phrase "doing the right thing," because her half-sister looked so completely self-possessed, so very much a lady of fashion.

Ianthe smiled with mechanical, brittle sweetness.

"I know what you were going to say. Yes, I'm quite sure." She paused before adding, "If ever things get too much for you at Polbreath, you can always pay me a visit. Here—" she took a card from her bag and thrust it quickly into Juliet's hand. "You'd better hide it and keep it safe, or I'm sure your precious mama would confiscate it. Don't let them bully you. And if you can't be good, be thoroughly bad, darling. Believe me, the world has no use for half measures."

A few minutes later the carriage was rattling down the drive toward Penzance. The sky was sullen and cold, leaden as though snow might soon fall. From a window Juliet watched the vehicle disappear round a bend, with a queer, unpredictable sadness mounting in her. However lively and nonchalant Ianthe had appeared to be, Juliet knew she was inwardly unhappy. But then who wouldn't be, married to an old man like Robertson Wycksley? And why couldn't anyone as beautiful as Ianthe have found a young husband? There must have been plenty in London to choose from. Obviously, from brief remarks overheard during school holidays, Juliet had gathered Donna was somehow held responsible. There had been arguments between her and Nicholas from time to time, which were common knowledge to the household, including the servants.

She was sorry for her father. Once he must have loved Ianthe very much.

She hoped that when she married Trefyn, Donna wouldn't make too much of a fuss. Juliet hated hurting people—especially Nicholas. But even her father's feelings counted for little against her heart's deepest need. If Nicholas refused to understand, he'd have to suffer. It would be terrible cutting herself off, but Trefyn came first. He always would. There were moments when she wished she could be like others girls and accept love more lightly. At school she'd had friends who'd passed from one affair to another, emerging completely unscathed when romance faded. To her this was incomprehensible. It was fun, of course, to go to parties sometimes, and dance.

But loving! That was quite different: a dark tide and all-consuming passion for just the one person in the whole world who could give warmth and meaning to the most ordinary things, bringing a sense of wonder and thrilling awareness, to every new day that came.

Trefyn Connor.

If she lost him, she thought, she'd want to die.

## 4

Christmas brought the usual traditional festivities and the unexpected arrival of Jonathan, Nicholas's eldest son, who was on leave from the east. He spent over a week at Polbreath, then left for a stay in Gloucestershire with his great-aunt Belinda on his mother's side.

Like Ianthe, he had never entirely accepted Donna, although he managed to hide his feelings under a veneer of politeness that deceived no one, certainly not Nicholas.

Most of the family resented his presence: William, because of a certain air of condescension about his handsome half-brother, his seniority in age, and the fact that he assumed a subtle but proprietary manner concerning the estate; Jason, because he had unknowingly diverted and thwarted Donna's promise to win Nicholas's approval for his art career; and Andrew, because he detested army talk, and predictions of war ahead. Only Juliet found Jonathan interesting. She was fascinated by his stories of India, although she had a mind of her own where racial problems were concerned; she did not accept that Britons were in any way superior to natives, and believed they had no right to steal the Indians' country from them.

Jonathan, surprised and faintly patronizing, told her that if she were older and more experienced she'd see things differently. Juliet lifted her chin proudly, and with her clear gray eyes very straight upon him, said, "I think you must be a very conventional person, Jonathan. History was my best subject at school, and I learned quite a lot there. Of course they tried to din their own ideas into me—the teachers, I mean—but you could always think what you wanted, thank heaven."

He shook his head slowly, thinking how lovely she was, and what a waste she should be incarcerated at Polbreath.

"I didn't realize I had a revolutionary for a sister," he said ironically.

"Half-sister," she pointed out.

He gave a slight bow. "I stand corrected."

She laughed. "Really, I'm not," she said.

"What?"

"A revolutionary—one of the new women. I think men should be responsible for looking after and adoring their wives. Women should be beautiful and ravishing and get their husbands and lovers to do just what they want, but not in a bossy way, very subtly of course."

"Rather one-sided," Jonathan observed.

"Yes, if they're clever."

"And are you?"

She didn't answer for a moment, then she said, "I

don't suppose so. It's hard to be subtle when you love anyone, isn't it?"

"I've never loved anyone so I can't judge," Jonathan said.

"Do you mean you—"

"Oh, I've been in love," he interrupted, "the whole lot. *Women!*—black, brown, white—I've had hundreds of 'em. In the dark they're all alike."

His eyes were amused, waiting for her reaction.

"I think that's extremely cynical," she retorted quickly, "and rather vulgar. I don't believe it anyway."

He touched her hand lightly. "You're not meant to. But don't get too serious over anyone, Juliet. I can see you're the suffering kind, and I wouldn't want things to go wrong for you."

"They won't," she told him. "I shan't let them."

"So there is someone?"

She didn't answer. But he knew from her expression he'd hit on the truth.

Jonathan left for the New Year. Everyone except Juliet was inwardly relieved, including Nicholas who more than once had felt intimidated and out of touch with the assured Army officer of aristocratic and sardonic manner who, except for name, bore no outward resemblance to the Trevarvas family.

With Juliet it was different. In many ways Jonathan reminded her of Andrew, not in looks but by his capacity to view things objectively. In days past she and Andrew had been able to talk on equal terms; but lately their companionship had diminished, mostly because her brother had become so withdrawn and concerned with spiritual and philosophical matters. Several times she'd alluded to Trefyn, hoping to exchange confidences in the old way. But Andrew, though polite, had appeared remote and almost unaware of what she was saying. More than once she'd seen him walking back from St. Figgans, and had guessed—rightly—that he'd been visiting Father Strawn. She'd said nothing, feeling it was not her business. This in itself proved they were drawing apart. They'd been so close in the old days. Jonathan, therefore, had filled a gap briefly, and his departure left no one at all for her to confide in about her emotional life. There were times when she felt desperately in need of assurance. Trefyn, loving one moment, could so easily be casual the next, making her uncertain of herself and his need of her.

Their opportunities for meeting were limited, and once when she'd again tactlessly brought up the possibility of a compromise over Wheal Blair with her family, he'd said firmly, "Whatever our future is together, remember this, Juliet—I'm no servant or plaything of yours. On my own land I'm master. And I shan't change, even for you. Do you understand?"

Her mouth had set mutinously before she replied, "Do you realize how old-fashioned you sound? Master. Boss man. That's what Jet said."

"Then perhaps you should listen to Jet," he'd told her, "and it might be better if we didn't meet for a time, just to get things straight between us."

"You mean you don't want to see me any more?"

"I mean I want you to know exactly where you stand," he'd told her, with molten sparks glinting in his narrowed, dark eyes. "Because once we're married—if we marry—there'll be no throwing of fancy airs and tantrums in my face. I've a way with horses—and with women too, if necessary."

"Women!" she'd exclaimed hotly, "How many?"

He'd smiled then, and touched her lightly under the chin. "Just one. I could hardly manage two of you. But you remember what I've said; I'm not aiming to marry a shrew."

She'd stared at him defiantly for a moment, then softened because of that certain look on his face that never failed to thrill her.

They'd parted amicably enough, but she'd recognized that until matters were settled properly between them she'd have to tread more warily where Trefyn was concerned.

One day, by chance, when she was walking home after a disappointed stroll toward the farm she met Judy in the lane. She had no cycle with her this time, and instead of knickers was wearing a long navy skirt under a checkered cape with the same tam-o'-shanter on her loose red curls. She was carrying a thick sketching pad, and her nose and cheeks were flushed bright pink from the cold.

"Hullo," she said, "how are you?"

"I'm all right, thank you," Juliet replied. "Can I see your painting?"

"No, you can't. It's not a painting, just a drawing and anyway you wouldn't understand it."

"How do you know?"

The girl grinned. "I don't myself. No one's supposed to. It's Futuristic."

"What's that?"

The girl shrugged. "Oh, golly! You are inquisitive."

"Perhaps," Juliet agreed. "I've got a brother who wants to be an artist, you see. Jason. He's probably going to Paris."

The round eyes became rounder. "Paris? *Ooh.*

Lucky him. I wish we could've met. But I'm leaving tomorrow."

"Oh, why?"

"No cash," the girl said. "None of my work's sold. I thought it just *might*—in Saint Inta, at one of the exhibitions you know. But they're terribly conventional there. Haven't heard a thing about Braque or Picasso or Cubisim . . . or . . . or any of the *new* things. It's all traditional . . . they haven't crawled out of the Rossetti period yet." She paused, then continued. "I think I could have liked you if we'd had time together. If you ever come to London, just look in. I'm mostly there."

"Where?" Juliet asked.

"Oh!" With a little laugh the girl took a scrap of paper and pencil from a pocket, placed it on the pad, and wrote an address. "It's not an elegant neighborhood," she said, "rather gray and dusty—small houses and big shabby old ones all huddled up together. But somehow it's got a feeling. Of course most people like me—with ideas, I mean—*creative* people, choose Chelsea or Bloomsbury, if they can afford it. But I can't. So we muck in all together."

"Who?"

Judy gave her characteristic shrug again, "Poets, writers, *would*-be-writers and artists, women and men. It's a kind of experiment. It may sound unrespectable, but it isn't. Anyway, what's respectability?" Her laugh was so lively and infectious that Juliet laughed too.

"I shall keep this," she said after glancing at a Camden Town address. "One day you may see me. You never know."

"I hope so. I'm sure you're far too intelligent to be stuck here forever. Oh, I love Cornwall—in bits. And

of course if you've a family and other interests—" she
broke off significantly, with a knowing look in her
eyes. "Trefyn, I mean," she added before Juliet could
speak, "you've got a pash on him, haven't you?"

With the warm blood mounting her cheeks, Juliet
said haughtily, "Pash? What a ridiculous word."

"Well, I didn't mean it like that, but it's obvious
you're sweet on each other. I don't blame you. He's
attractive. But you should take care."

"What do you mean?"

"He's the possessive kind. Bossy. Once you got
hitched up he'd take the reins and whip, and if you
didn't behave . . . oh my! I just daren't think of it.
Still, maybe you've a liking for wife-beaters and he-
donists. Lots of women are like that. But not me. I'm
all for female rights and equality."

"So am I—with my brain," Juliet admitted grudgingly. "But not in *feelings*. That's what's so difficult—
bringing the two together. Once all I wanted was to
be an actress. . . . Can you imagine it? But then
when I grew up—"

"You changed because of Trefyn," Judy interrupted.

"No. He'd always counted most, deep down. I just
gave in . . . *apparently*," Juliet admitted, adding
quickly, "and you don't know him as well as I do. He's
a gentle sort of person really. Calling him a wife-
beater type's just silly. As for hedonist—that's stupid
too. He works hard. He has ambitions for the right
things . . ."

The other girl shrugged. "Oh, well, they say love's
blind. To me it seems just balmy. Anyway, good luck
to you." She offered her hand, gave Juliet's a squeeze,
and the next moment was swinging along the track to
the farm.

When Juliet reached Polbreath she found Charlotte
embroiled in an argument with Donna about the wedding, which had been fixed for March the second at
St. Mary's Church in Penzance. Donna was trying to
insist there should be five attendants led by Juliet as
trainbearer. Charlotte was proving to be unexpectedly
awkward over the number, saying neither she nor William wanted a large gathering. They preferred a quiet
ceremony with Juliet as the one bridesmaid.

"But that's not sufficient," Donna was protesting as
Juliet entered the drawing room. "You're marrying my
eldest son. Everything should be as elegant as possible with a trainbearer and—"

"Oh, I don't want a train," Charlotte interrupted
quickly. "I haven't got the figure for it. And white
doesn't suit me. My skin's too dark. I should feel quite
wrong somehow. Peach or a goldish tone suits me so
much better. And I thought a small hat with just a
few flowers on it—"

"You mean no orange blossoms?" Donna's voice was
coldly incredulous.

"Is it important?" Charlotte asked quietly.

"I should have thought so, at your wedding," Donna
answered. "Most girls consider it the one great day in
their lives."

"I think Charlotte's right though," Juliet said tactlessly. "She wants to look her best, and she's not the
fair fussy type to wear white."

Donna sighed. "Do you mind keeping out of things,
Juliet? This is between Charlotte and myself."

"And me. If Charlotte wears peach I could be in
green. Green suits me. And it will be spring. We could
have daffodils for bouquets. All green and gold—"

"You make it appear like a pagan feast."

"Well . . . " Juliet smiled mischievously. "I think that sounds rather nice."

Donna turned abruptly and went to the door. "I can see there's no point in discussing it at the moment," she said. "But tomorrow Miss West's coming, and I want to give her an idea of the styles and materials necessary for the dresses. We have to have a scheme. I hope you understand, Charlotte, and, when you've thought things out properly, will agree with me. I'm not going to quarrel with you over the bridesmaids if you're determined to have only Juliet. But it would be a gesture to ask Winifred Rose, Lady St. Clarry's goddaughter, and the two Blake girls. I know they're not great friends of yours. But now that you're marrying William you'll find it a help to be on good terms with local society. I don't want to sound snobbish or too conventional. But really, dear—" she broke off, suddenly at a loss, and discomforted by the direct stares of the two young women confronting her: Juliet, with her mouth serious, had a contradictory imp of devilment dancing in her large smoky-rimmed gray eyes; and Charlotte, so stolid and reliable looking, yet in her direct way unexpectedly stubborn and set in her opinions.

She'd given in over one major issue, it was true. The question of living quarters. Charlotte had wanted a home of her own for the start of married life; but in the end had agreed to wait for this until a house in the vicinity was available, or one could be built suitable for her and William's needs. William, dedicated to the mines, and appreciative of the domestic comforts he already had, had supported Donna's suggestion of independent living quarters being converted for them at Polbreath.

"What about my father though?" Charlotte had said. "I've looked after him ever since my mother died. I rather hoped to have him with us."

Major Carne, luckily, had dismissed the suggestion of trespassing on the future privacy of the young married couple, and had even appeared to enjoy the prospect of being his "own master," as he put it. "I'm no decrepit invalid, damnit," he'd said, with staunch joviality. "Smithy and I will get along as we've always done. Smithy will look after me. Like old times it will be, with no interfering busybody of a woman to tell me how much I should drink and what hour I should go to bed. I'll stay on at Whitebrook so don't you fret yourselves. Just get on with your lives, and you girl—" to Charlotte "see you provide me with a grandson by the end of a year or I'll think your honeymoon backfired."

Charlotte had blushed, but she'd known then the problem had been solved for her. Smithy, who'd been the Major's right hand man during the years of active service, was loyally devoted to him and, although a wizened sixty-year-old, was agile as a monkey, a good cook, and competent about the house, treating the treasured relics of his master's army career with reverence and fanatical care.

Many times when Charlotte had put aside certain mementos to be taken to the thrift shop, she had found them back in their accustomed places an hour or two later; a brass, ornate Buddha placed upon the too-crammed mantelshelf; a hideous ornate vase back on the table; knickknacks of Eastern ornaments cluttering the chest as dust gatherers; and half-threadbare pieces of embroidered silk covering the backs of carved chairs. There were certain things of course

she'd known were there for good, such as the tigerskin
rugs, ancient swords hung on walls, and an assortment
of paper knives and ivory figurines. How many more
would be fished out from chests and the lumber room
when she left, she couldn't guess. But it was her father's life, she told herself, and so long as he was well
and contented, no one had a right to interfere.

Eventually Donna complied with as good grace as
possible to Charlotte's wish for a quiet ceremony.

Spring came early that year, and on the wedding
day an air of well-being filled Polbreath, a mellow
contentment intensified by the weather, which was
uncharacteristically mild for March with pale sunlight
sprinkling the moors and distant sea with gold, and no
sign of winds or hovering storm ahead. Everything
was extremely well-organized. The church was full,
and most well-known families of the district were rep-
resented.

The Major, who gave his daughter away, was a little flushed, and wearing his regimental uniform and
medals. Otherwise the menfolk, including Andrew
who was best man, were in morning dress.

Charlotte made a comely enough bride in a peach-
colored gown designed to flatter her figure and bring
a little color to her rather pale face. The small feathered hat with discreet veiling added a touch of romance. Her bouquet was of cream roses and maidenhair
fern lavishly tied with gold satin ribbon. As Jason remarked privately to Juliet later, "She didn't look half-
bad for such a homely creature."

It was Juliet, however, who stole most of the attention and secret admiration. In the pale green chiffon
dress and small embroidered cap set intriguingly on
her dark russet hair, she had the air of some legendary

character from a fairy tale. As she walked up the aisle behind the bride, a beam of light from a stained-glass window caught her slender figure with sudden radiance, lighting the daffodils to a splash of quivering gold. She was smiling faintly. Her gray eyes were misted by inner longing for Trefyn. Oh, she thought, how wonderful if he could be there, waiting at the altar for her instead of William for Charlotte.

The reception following the ceremony was held at Polbreath. The bride and groom were staying the first night there before leaving for London and Paris the next day. Not unlike the occasion a quarter of a century ago, Donna thought, when she and Nicholas were being toasted by the household. But in one way so different. She and Nicholas had been so wildly in love, and she doubted that William her first-born knew the meaning of the word. He was the most handsome and virile of her sons, but curiously lacking in imagination except for mining, and Charlotte was hardly the type of girl to stimulate any lurking capacity for romantic affection. The knowledge mildly saddened her. She hoped the marriage wouldn't fall too flat, or fail altogether.

She need not have worried.

Behind the closed doors of the bridal suite Charlotte was quick enough to shed maidenly restraint and use what female attributes she possessed to full advantage. She had, William discovered, an unexpected knack of stimulating the male libido, which came as a pleasant surprise. He had meant to impress on her from the very beginning the nature and extent of her wifely duties. No shilly-shallying, no mock modesty or going cold on him; no denial of sexual obligations.

Eyeing her appraisingly as she sat on the gilt stool brushing her long thick hair before the dressing-table mirror, with the firm lines of her back clearly defined through the thin negligee, he thought, *Better get on with it; now's the time. And if there's going to be trouble, the soon it's over with the better.*

But there was no trouble.

As he touched her shoulder, letting his hand stray insidiously to the shadowed curve just above the plump buttocks, she turned abruptly, and stood up.

The flimsy wrap fell to the floor. She stood smiling at him pleasantly, naked and inviting. His heart jerked and quickened. He swallowed, noting the full breasts and spreading hips, the luscious curves of thighs, and shadowed mystery below rounded navel. In the subtle light of shaded candelabras, her features were softened and less plain. Her hair fell in a thick cloak to her waist.

"Well, William?" she said. Her voice was encouraging, faintly husky.

Hardly aware of his actions, he lifted her up, excitement mounting as he felt the warmth of her, the strong pumping of her heart against his own, and quickened breathing beneath the thrusting breasts. He laid her on the bed, and her legs were round him, her arms outstretched as he plunged and took her, savoring with closed eyes the hungry flood of her desire.

Fulfillment was complete and mutual. They lay together and mated several times that night, and following each occasion were at peace. There was no troublesome questioning of "Do you love me, William?" No senseless demands for promises of eternal faithfulness or romantic adoration. Charlotte, who'd been a virgin, had found release and gratification in abandoning such an unrewarding state of being.

William had no subtlety or fine words, but he was all man. And she—well, she was no longer Miss Charlotte Carne the Major's daughter, but Mrs. William Trevarvas who, though she did not know it, on her first night of marriage had conceived a child.

## 5

The new domestic arrangement at Polbreath commenced, to everyone's relief, with surprising harmony.
Although Donna, privately, considered Charlotte
somewhat dull, she had a pacifying influence and was
helpful in many ways without being assertive.

The married couple's quarters were on the eastern
side of the house with windows overlooking the drive
and the seaside of Rosebuzzan hill. They had a parlor,
three bedrooms, and a dressing room with a bathroom
attached, and a small kitchen to be converted properly in the future. William insisted there was no
hurry for the latter. He didn't wish his wife to be immersed in cooking and too many household chores.
Charlotte for her part was agreeable to taking her
meals with the rest of the family for the time being.
William was a hearty eater used to a variety of menus,
which was a professional cook's business, and in spite
of her homely exterior Charlotte had no wish or intention of becoming a slave to his needs. Their parlor and

one bedroom were on the ground floor. The rest of
their suite had a side stairway leading from the far
end of the main hall next to Beth's apartment and the
kitchens.

One afternoon at the end of May when William was
about to set off for Wheal Flower, there was a knock
on the door, followed by the entrance of Elise who
informed him there was a woman at the door wanting
to see him. He frowned, looking puzzled.

"A woman? What woman? Did she give her name?"

"It's that—it's that farmer's daughter, the Marne
girl," Elise said doubtfully. "I'd have sent her away,
but she says it's important." She paused, while William
recovered from the shock, then continued, "She's got a
baby with her." William got up, steeling himself for
the interview.

"Very well, I'll come along now. Is she still outside?"

"Oh, yes, surr. I didn't ask her in. I thought—"

"Then do so immediately," Charlotte told her before
William was at the door. "You say she's carrying a
child. It must be tiring for her."

"But Charlotte, this is hardly the place—" William
began.

His wife smiled with placid sweetness. "Oh yes,
dear, I think so. I'll go upstairs, and she can talk comfortably. We must be polite."

William's frown became a scowl. He was about to
start an argument when something in Charlotte's
steady glance stopped him. He turned away abruptly,
both hands in his pockets, and walked to the window
where he stood with his back to the two women,
shoulders squared and stubborn-looking.

"Please go and tell her," Charlotte insisted to the girl in a voice that though gentle was quite firm.

Elise gave a grudging bob of an acknowledgment, and left quickly, shutting the door behind her a smarter snap than usual.

William turned. His face was red, eyes blazing.

"What the devil do you think you're doing," he said, "defying and contradicting me in front of a servant? The sooner you learn your proper place, the better. Never do that again, Charlotte, do you hear?"

"Yes, dear. You're speaking very loudly," Charlotte answered. "But please calm down. We mustn't appear to be arguing must we? So unseemly in our first days together."

With difficulty William controlled his chagrin, though inwardly he was in a turmoil.

A moment or two later Hannah was ushered into the room.

Charlotte picked up the needlework she'd been doing, and went to the door. Before she left she offered her hand, then paused briefly to take a close look at the tiny face in the hand-knitted shawl. "What a *lovely* little boy," she said glancing from Hannah to William. "Such dark eyes. It *is* a boy, isn't it?"

"Oh, yes, ma'am," Hannah answered. "Matthew."

"And how old?"

"Only two weeks, nearly three," came the answer. "I had to bring him along, because there's no one to mind him, you see. My father died yesterday and—"

William started, as the red flush drained from his face, leaving a curious grayish pallor round the cheekbones, and nostrils of the finely carved nose. Automatically he heard Charlotte saying, "Oh, I'm so sorry.

And you've walked all this way. I shall tell Elise to bring tea—"

"Charlotte—"

"And you must rest here for a time," the quiet voice went on relentlessly. "Don't think it's any trouble at all. I've things to do upstairs, so you and my husband can have as long as you wish to discuss your business."

Hannah's dark eyes widened, staring at her wonderingly. Either this new wife of William's didn't know a thing, and didn't even guess about the old association, she thought, or she was just being clever. Maybe it wasn't even that. Perhaps she was one of those saintly creatures you heard of in history that she'd never believed existed before.

"Well?" William said, when Charlotte had gone closing the door and latching it firmly. "What is it? I thought it was understood that you were never to visit my house."

A curious bitter half-smile touched Hannah's lips. "And I thought maybe you had a bit o' heart in you," she replied. "You heard what I said, I suppose? Dad died yesterday."

With a twinge of guilt, he looked away because the sight of her face, so much thinner and more strained than when he'd last seen her, troubled him. "I'm sorry about that," he said uncomfortably, "but perhaps it's for the best. His life wasn't much use to him; you'll find things easier now, I hope."

"Shall I?"

He faced her again quickly. "You've got Pete, haven't you? And the . . . the child . . ."

"Yes. Want to look at him?"

"No." William retorted resolutely. "You know very

well how we arranged things. And I still don't know why you've come. You know I've not long been married. The whole business is extremely embarrassing . . . for me."

"For you? Yes." Her tone was soft but condemning.

"What do you mean?"

"Do you remember what you said about . . . a present, William? For Matthew?"

"Matthew?"

"That's his name. After my granddad."

Realization with a flood of light broke over him.

"Oh, I *see*. That's it . . . money."

She nodded. "Only what you promised though; a present for your . . . son."

He looked round furtively. "For God's sake, Hannah, stop reminding me, and stop calling me William. As for the . . . the child . . . I didn't even know he was born. Well?" His glance was hard. "How much do you want? What's the sum to buy your silence?"

Her figure and face seemed to crumple up. She dropped into a chair, with the baby's face pressed against her breasts. "My God, you're a cold one," she whispered after a pause. "Do you have to insult me? I've got my pride, I wouldn't harm you, I've kept my word. But so soon as I can manage it, I'm off, me and the little 'un."

"Off? Where? Leaving, do you mean?"

"That's right. Up country . . . to an aunt of mine. But I haven't got anythin' for the way; Pete's had it all. Every bloody penny, William. All I scraped and worked for these years. So that gift you talked of would be useful."

He forced his eyes to her face. There was no hint of bitterness there anymore. Only a contemptuous kind of sadness that filled him momentarily with shame. Her luscious looks had diminished during the last ten months, but in a strange way, beauty was still there, etherealized and more unapproachable. He had the grace to say, "I'm sorry about the way thing's have turned out for you, Hannah. I'll help you, of course." He went to his desk, took out a wad of notes, counted them, and said, "Fifty there. You can have them for the boy, and yourself, of course. What are you doing about the farm?"

"Let Pete arrange that. There's been nothin' this last year but debts. He can shoulder them."

"But Hannah—"

She stood up. "I'm through with everythin' round here. After Dad's buried you'll see nothin' of either of us any more."

"When is the funeral?"

"Tomorrow."

"I—"

"No one'll be there but me. That's what he wanted, that's what he'll get. Good-bye then . . ." she held out a hand. He took it automatically. It was very cold. Just then the baby started to cry. She opened the shawl and put her lips to one small ear. "Sh!" she murmured. "Be quiet. There's a good boy, then."

Against all inclinations, William glanced down. Something in the baby's face startled him. There could be no resemblance, and yet—just for a second—a likeness of Nicholas seemed to concentrate into awareness and recognition. Without meaning to, he put out a hand and wiggled a finger against a flushed cheek. Matthew's dark eyes widened in surprise, then suddenly he let forth a lusty scream. Elise knocked at the same moment and entered with tea on a tray.

William glanced at Hannah indecisively. She shook her head. "Thank you, no," she said to the girl, "I'm late. I have to be gettin' back."

"Put it down," Nicholas told Elise. "And you needn't wait. I'll see Mrs. Marne out."

Keeping her expression blank but annoyed at her dismissal, the maid returned to the kitchen where she expressed her opinion that there was something up between Mr. William and Jake's daughter.

"Called her *Mrs.* Marne, too, he did," she said. "When everyone knows she's not married and the child's a—"

"Hold your tongue, Elise," Beth said, entering unexpectedly. "I won't have other people's business discussed in that way. No one here knows anything about that poor man and his family. It's quite likely she *is* Mrs. Marne. For all we know, she and her cousin could be legal man and wife. If I hear any more unpleasant gossip there'll be trouble. You understand?"

"I didn't mean anything," Elise said grudgingly.

"Well, watch your words, that's all."

Elise, huffed but silenced, lifted her head and with a haughty air marched into the dairy.

William said good-bye to Hannah at the side door. "I didn't mean to sound unfeeling," he said in an undertone, touching her hand lightly. "If you're ever in need or distress, write to my attorney . . ." He took a card from his pocket and handed it to her, "You can always contact me at this address."

She glanced down, and pushed his hand away. "No, thank you, I don't need that. I'm no scrounger, an' I don't want your charity. You've given enough already.

A kid and a handful of notes into the bargain. That's a damn good gift, I'd say."

Resenting her sarcasm, William remarked coldly, "Very well. There's nothing more to be said except good-bye and good luck."

"Good-bye."

She drew the shawl more closely round the baby's head, turned, went down the step into the drive and, without another glance back, walked sharply away toward the lane that cut through the valley toward the sea. For a time the air was quiet and motionless, sheltered by thick rhododendrons and lush undergrowth from freshening moorland winds. But when she reached the high road turning sharply in the direction of Penjust, a gust of salty air, tangy with heather and gorse and distant brine, swept with refreshing vigor over the wide track of open moors. She went on for a while then crossed the lane and took a path to her left. For a hundred yards, perhaps more, it cut straight and clearly through heathered clumps and pale, curled heads of tall, young bracken. Then the track narrowed, winding this way and that between twisted stumps of windswept bushes, large boulders, and clutching thorn. Bluebells were already out, sprinkled with the purple pinkness of a few early foxgloves. Occasionally a bird sang joyously before it mounted the air with a flap of silvered sunlit wings. Primroses peered thick and glistening yellow in clumps from the springy turf. Gorse flamed.

Young summer was rich everywhere, yet Hannah's heart was heavy with loneliness and a dull, mounting anger. Matthew was his son—William's—yet he'd hardly noticed him. He should not have been born, she thought resentfully. Better the child had never lived at all than to have come into such an unfeeling world. She'd do the best she could for him. It was her duty. He was hers. But he'd have a chill welcome from her aunt, and his future would be hard. Poor little devil!

It was true what they said: one law for the rich and one for the poor. Blast William. Blast Pete. Blast all men. Anger, despite her tiredness, seethed in her, and by the time she came into view of the farm, any trace of sentiment in her had completely died. The hours she'd relived countless times—remembering the closeness of William's arms round her, his tongue seeking hers, dark eyes burning into her own, pulsing hard limbs drawing her to nature's final culmination—no longer held any comfort or meaning. If he'd come running after her now, she'd have spit in his face, lashing him with fury and derisive contempt.

In such a mood she saw Pete's figure waiting for her by the gate of one of their small fields. Once it had been well tilled, providing greens and potatoes sufficient for their needs with some left over to sell at a profit in Penzance and Penjust. In her father's day, broccoli had thrived and had been despatched to London. Now grass and weeds had been allowed to thrive. Their pigs and few cows had been sold. Much of the ground was stony and unproductive. Pete, who'd worked like a laborer at Fairs, had proved uninterested and comparatively useless about the land, demoralizing the lad who'd been a promising worker before. Any small gain they'd had, had replenished his own pocket and gone to swell the landlord's at The Wandering Woman, or the pub near Wheal Jakke. And yet he had the affrontery to resent her taking a stroll when she wished. And his jealousy was not only unfair, but unwarranted. Since William, no man had touched her, and no man, if she had anything to do with it, ever would. She'd made this quite clear to Pete when he first came. Often, she knew, he'd lusted after her; she'd recognized only too well the desire hot in his eyes, the lascivious, hungry glance as she turned after laying his meal on the table. Once or twice he'd caught at her skirt as she passed, and her hand had been hard and sharp on his face.

"You watch your ways, Pete Marne," she'd snapped, "and keep to yourself. You have your place, I have mine. An' don't you go forgettin' it, or you'll be out in no time."

He'd been sullen but kept the ugly words back. A day would soon come, he'd told himself in the past, when the sick old bag o' bones upstairs would shuffle off, and then the boot would be on the other foot. She'd do his bidding the hard way if necessary. Once her father had gone and her fine body was free of the bastard she carried, he'd assert his rights, even if a belt was needed.

He was filled with hatred now as she approached up the path with the child. He didn't have to guess where she'd been; he knew from the weary look of her, the fiery pain of her eyes that had never given him a second friendly glance.

"Well?" he sneered, standing full in her way, a massive giant of a man, six-feet-two and broad, with a dark brooding face under a thatch of black hair. "An' how is he? That fancy feller of yours?"

She was about to push by when something in his expression deterred her. She hesitated, lifted her head, and said in controlled cold tones, "Let me by, Pete. Get out of my way."

"Get out of my way," he mimicked. "Always the same, isn't it? Get out of my way—off to your barn, your kennel, like a bloody great dog—" he was breathing heavily. Through the summer air his breath was strong, like a hot wind. It was clear to her he'd been drinking heavily. She waited for a moment; then, before he realized her intention, she made a sudden dive forward, pushing under his arm with a force that shook him.

She stumbled along the short hall to the narrow flight of stone steps leading to the upper floor. If she could reach her room, she thought wildly, she'd be safe. Pete was in an ugly mood. Once he'd killed a man in a fight, and she wouldn't put it past him to kill again. She felt sick. Sick and frightened, and revolted by the situation—with her father a corpse waiting for burial and only herself to protect the child. Her red skirt was long, and halfway up the stairs her boot caught it. She tripped. The baby started to scream. Pete's hand clutched an ankle, but she freed herself and went on. At the top he sprang in front and caught her before she could turn along the landing. A great hand clutched a breast, swinging her round. She gasped and spit, and bared her teeth. "Get off, you. Damn you—" a leg went out and caught his shin. He muttered an oath and his arm was round her, tearing at her waist, so the material slipped in torn, jagged lines round her thighs. She fell to her knees, laying the baby down, and as he lugged her to her feet again she brought one knee up against his pelvis.

There was a yell of pain followed by a flow of curses. She stared at his maddened face, gasping for breath, then turned. But she was too late. Like a great bear he had her, struggling and panting and screaming. The stony surface of the top step was slippery from dampness. Below, the hall was a well of darkness from shadow and the failing light.

Suddenly, as she bit his hand, he released her abruptly, and it was then she toppled and fell. He stood watching her, sucking the salty taste of blood from his bitten fist; hearing, through the pain of lust and rage and creeping terror, each thud of her head as it hit the hard steps; watching her body rolling like a sack of potatoes or weighted rubbish, over and over, down and down, until it reached the bottom and lay there twisted and still.

For a minute or more he did not move. All was silent with the silence of death except for his own rasping breathing. Even the baby had stopped his wailing.

When he crept down slowly and saw her face, her eyes wide and staring, tongue protruding slightly from her teeth, the dark hair matted with blood half-covering a cut and bruised temple, he knew, without having to be told, that she was dead. A shudder of fear swept through him, bringing streams of sweat to his body and a convulsive trembling to his limbs. He couldn't bear to touch her, nor even speak her name.

Presently, when the power to move returned, he let himself out by the door behind him, not even locking or closing it properly. He looked round furtively to see if the boy was about. There was no one in sight. With the speed of a panther he raced, head down, to the small barn allotted to him where he'd slept on hay for the past nine months. In a box hidden beneath earth and stones, he took what notes and gold he'd hoarded from Hannah's gains, pulled a coat and scarf from a nail on the wall, and grabbed a bottle of whiskey lying near a pillow. Then, after a cautious look round, he set off, and made his way toward the high road and the moors beyond.

The light was quickly fading to a misted spring dusk that offered protection and assurance. After a tentative, groping beginning, he walked more sharply and had soon reached the stretch of wild land leading eventually cross-country to the opposite coast. Once he got to Penzance, he thought, he might find a boat ready to take him on with the crew—a trader bound for the east, or for some other destination far from any connection with Hannah and what had happened. If not that, maybe there'd be a Fair in the locality. Strong men like him who knew their job were always wanted.

But as things turned out he had no choice.

Near a slope skirting an ancient mine stack, the ground under his feet suddenly lurched and fell away. He hadn't noticed the yawning gap below him—the deadly deserted shaft so deceptively covered by brambles and tangled weed. He had not time to extricate himself or even cry for help before the black hole claimed him, echoing moments later with a mournful thud and plop of water when his body reached the bottom.

No one heard his belated scream. No human eye glimpsed the clawing shape of a hand outthrust before it disappeared forever. A solitary gull circled and cried plaintively overhead. From the bushes a wild thing, disturbed, scurried to safety.

Then all was still.

In time, perhaps centuries later, his bones might be discovered with a handful of coins scattered about him.

But by then the name of Pete Marne would be forgotten except as a no-good brute who'd murdered his cousin and had taken off somewhere to die unknown and unregretted.

Only the gold would have value for collectors, and it was highly unlikely even this would be found. Nature had a devious way of retaining its secrets, and a queer, uncanny way of having its own revenge.

Jim Curnow, a worker from Wheal Jakke, was the first to pass the vicinity of the Marne small-holding early next morning on his return home from night shift. He was a middle-aged man who'd worked in the mines since youth. His hearing was keen, accustomed to listening for any danger signal when crouching and making his way along long, dark levels in search of new copper lodes. There had been times when he'd alerted his comrades to the seeping of water where water should not have been. He'd learned to suspect every faint creaking of timber in places where the earth was slimy and linked with old workings.

His fears had frequently proved groundless, and then his mates had put them down to the "Buccas"— the spirits of the old Jews who, according to legend, had crucified Christ. But on the whole he was respected and his words taken seriously. He'd lived so long on his own without a woman or kin about him it was said he'd the peace and time to hear things others didn't.

So it wasn't surprising that, as he cut below the Marne small-holding before taking the track onward to the road, he detected a sound unfamiliar at that hour of the morning in such a lonely spot. There was a wind getting up, ruffling the waves below the cliffs to driving force, booming with monotonous rhythm against the rocks. A few gulls wheeled overhead, crying thinly as they dipped and rose again to the lifting sky. Out at sea a ship's siren sounded mournfully. But the sound that stopped him in his walk was something quite different: the chilling, intermittent cry of a human being—an infant if he wasn't mistaken, in distress and possible pain. He stood quite still for a few moments, staring up at the Marne place which had a curiously empty look about it, standing bleak and dark in its dip, despite the rising light of a summer morning, with no sign of activity about the yard or patch of land, and with the door open, swinging on its hinges.

A sense of foreboding filled him.

He moved abruptly and cut up to the building, apprehensive yet prepared for something his bones and instinct told him was wrong.

"Hannah," he called at the door, "are you all right? Is anyone there?"

When there was no response except the fitful wailing that ended suddenly in a drawn-out scream, he pushed the wood wider and went in. Then he stopped, horrified. Hannah's body had stiffened through the night hours, and the blood was congealed on the bluish face. He bent down, took one hard look at her glazed eyes, felt the lifeless pulse, got up and searched for something to cover her body. There was a coat hanging from a peg. He took it down and laid it over her carefully, hiding the distorted features from view. Then he glanced up the stairs as the baby started whimpering again. He went up, two steps at a time, and found the child shivering on the stone floor

where Hannah had laid him the previous evening.
"God in heaven," Jim murmured. "What am I goin' to
do with 'ee?"

He lifted Matthew up, held him against his chest
for a minute, rocking him to and fro. The face was
bluish red with cold, the small limbs icy to the touch.
Presently, when a little of the man's warmth had penetrated the child's body and the crying died again into
a mere whimper, Jim carried him to the kitchen. It
was an untidy place with a broken beer bottle on the
table, by an unwashed, greasy plate. A drop of milk
had been left in a jug on the dresser. There was no
fire or stove to warm it on, but a teaspoon had fallen
to the floor, and with the aid of it the miner managed
to get most of it through the child's lips. After that he
took off his own coat and wrapped the infant in it.
There was only one more thing he could do. He had
to get the baby to the nearest house as quickly as possible. Polbreath was quite a way, but it was a large
place with folk living there who'd know how to care
for it.

Once the decision was made, Jim wasted no more
time but set off at a smart pace toward the Trevarvas
estate.

The butler and kitchen maid were already about.
But it was Charlotte, back from an early-morning
stroll, who after the first brief explanation took the
child in her arms and carried him upstairs. William
was dressing. "What's that you've got?" he asked in astonishment. "What the devil are you carrying?"

Charlotte gave him a very straight look. Something
in her expression unnerved him—something deadened
and cold.

"A baby, William," she said calmly. "I'm not quite

sure whose, but I think he's your son. There's a man downstairs, a miner. If you go and see him, he'll explain."

From furious red, William's face blanched to greenish white. How had she guessed? What did she know?

"You must be mad," he said, as he pulled on his coat and strode to the door.

Charlotte shook her head. "Don't worry, William, I won't desert you." The emotionless, flat quality of her voice was in itself abnormal, almost frightening.

There was a slam and the sound of receding footsteps down the stairs. She stood quite motionlessly for moments, shocked, yet still calm, a set, unfathomable expression on her face. Then, lifting her head resolutely, she went to the mirror and took off her cape. There'd be a fuss of course. William wouldn't admit anything. He'd want to find foster parents or some orphanage for the poor little thing. But she had other plans, which she fully intended he'd comply with, if he wished their marriage to survive.

It was really quite surprising what a great deal she'd learned of her husband's character during the short time they'd been together.

## 6

When the first shock of the Marne tragedy had passed, and police inquiries concerning Pete's disappearance were well under way, Charlotte provided further dismay at Polbreath by stating that she and William wished to adopt the little boy. The baby had been allowed to remain there while the authorities decided what should be done with the child. But no one except William's new wife had faintly contemplated providing a permanent home.

"But Charlotte, dear," Donna protested, forcing herself to sound reasonable, "it would hardly do, would it? *Adoption?* That's a very legal responsibility, and you and William have been married such a short time. Of course, we're all very sorry for the poor little thing. Who wouldn't be? But there are many childless people wanting to adopt these days—people who can't have children of their own. It isn't as if the baby wouldn't have a good home somewhere . . ."

"How do you know?" Charlotte said with equal

calmness. "He might be unfortunate. He might even be sent to an orphanage."

"I've heard some of them are extremely good these days," Donna retorted more sharply. "Apart from that, it doesn't seem fair to William."

"I think William quite agrees with me," Charlotte persisted with the quiet stubbornness that was beginning to jar Donna's nerves. "Don't you, William?"

"It's up to you," he answered grudgingly, trying not to show the smoldering anger beneath the words. "If you want to saddle yourself with an unwanted—" the word "bastard" failed on his lips. Donna supplied it for him.

"Bastard. That's what you were going to say, isn't it? And that's what he is. Hannah Marne had no breeding, no shadow of principles or morals about her. No one knows who the father was—he could have been some tramp or thief, or that low creature she called her cousin. *Cousin!* I don't believe it, and I won't allow that child of hers to remain in my house."

Nicholas, who'd remained silent until then at the back of the parlor, spoke up suddenly. "I must remind you the house is mine! and I'm surprised at you for taking such a tone. A certain incident in your own family history apparently hasn't taught you as much as I thought. What about Luke and Jessica?"

Donna flushed. Bitterness at the reminder of her own brother's wasted and ignominious youth, especially in front of Charlotte, filled her with an urge to lash out, as she had in the past, with wild words and condemnation. But she managed to say calmly, "I'm not going to argue. As you point out, it's your house, Nicholas. If you wish to harbor any ill-bred waif or stray that's thrust upon us, you'll do so."

His eyes on her were hard. "Exactly." Then he turned to William. "I can see you've no strong objection taking responsibility for the boy," he said with a cold, inscrutable look in his narrowed dark eyes.

"I think it's far too soon to decide anything either way," William answered doggedly. "Charlotte and I will talk about things tonight." His glance at his wife held a dangerous, cold anger, but Charlotte seemed unconcerned. "Naturally we'll have to discuss it more," she said pleasantly, "a thing like adoption can't be settled in half an hour—"

"Adoption? What's all this about?" Unknown to them the door had opened quietly, revealing Juliet standing there with an excited, anticipatory look on her face, her cheeks flushed from a moorland canter on Firebrand. When no one spoke, at once she continued. "Were you talking about the baby? Hannah Marne's? Oh, mama, is it true? Are we going to keep him? I think that really would be marvelous. To give a child a chance who—"

"Please, Juliet," Donna said, "don't jump to conclusions. "It's certainly not my idea, and I have nothing to do with the suggestion. So try and curb your enthusiasm and keep your thoughts to yourself."

"Your mother's right," Nicholas told her, "this affair's between Charlotte and William. And you had no right to be listening at keyholes."

Juliet shrugged. Her eyes flashed when she said, "As if I would. And please don't treat me like a child. I see things for myself; I know more than you think I do about what's going on round here."

"What are you suggesting?" Donna queried icily.

"Nothing," Juliet retorted before flouncing out. "It's a statement of fact."

The door slammed. Donna sighed. Nicholas touched her arm lightly. "Come along. I didn't mean to snap at you just now. Take no notice of any of us. We're all wound up."

"Except Charlotte," Donna couldn't help saying, and turning to her daughter-in-law added, "You seem to have very strong ideas of your own Charlotte."

Charlotte's plump face relaxed into a disarming smile. "I suppose living with papa so long made me think for myself. He was always rather vague, and there was no one else but Smithy to talk to. But you must never think I want to inflict my opinions."

Later, as Donna and Nicholas were undressing for bed, Donna, referring to her brief conversation with Charlotte said, "That's just what she *is* doing though— forcing her ideas on the household. I'm rather disappointed in her. She seemed so . . . so amenable before her marriage, and now here she is already determined to go ahead with her ridiculous plan for adopting that baby—"

"It seems the prerogative of women to be self-willed," Nicholas said, with a wry glance at the beautiful, half-naked back of his wife. She was trying rather laboriously to unfasten a clip of her petticoat at the waist, one creamy arm twisted provocatively below her shoulders.

"Allow me," Nicholas said, letting his hand linger against the soft flesh above the fallen bodice. Contact excited her. She lifted her head, and something in her face aroused the old desire in him. His arm tightened. A slow sweet smile curved her lips.

"Oh, Nicholas, you're such a bully," she whispered as the male thrust of his body pressed hard against her.

"And you, my sweet, are so damned adorable," he whispered against her ear. "Child . . . woman . . . temptress all in one. Sometimes I wonder—"

"What? What Nicholas?"

"Why I haven't tamed you better—"

"But you did, you did, Nicholas," she murmured, with a spurt of subdued laughter. "Do you remember the time when—"

"I put you over my knee and spanked your beautiful bottom?" Nicholas interrupted. "My dear love, it was the highlight of my career."

"You're a great brute, you know," she said as he lifted her up. "And I love you so very much—in spite of it."

He lay astride of her on the bed for a few moments, staring down into her eyes. So unfathomable they were—clear gold changing to glowing orange, as his warm mouth sought hers. The plunge of love was rich and strong as it had ever been. Their flesh and senses united in a flood of sweeping exhilaration mounting to a wild culmination. When at last it was over and they lay side by side, throbbing and breathless, she took his hand and said, "I'm afraid the children would be rather affronted."

Nicholas rolled over and kissed her again.

"The children be damned," he said softly. "They've caused too many arguments between us lately. Let them go to the devil if they must. You tell Jason as soon as you like he can have the cash for Paris, and as for William—well, one more mouth to feed or not doesn't matter. The baby business is his problem. Let him learn how to handle Madam Charlotte the hard way. It's his own business."

"Oh, darling . . . do you mean it? About Jason, I mean?"

"Of course. If you must know, I've been resigned to it for quite some time."

She gave a sigh of deep sensual pleasure. Her thighs cool against his with the dewy satin smoothness of a flower waking to a summer morning, opened to receive him. This time their lovemaking was quieter and more prolonged with all the richness, knowledge, and passionate interludes of their life together revitalized and concentrated in the one act of physical and spiritual unification.

Sleep came at last, easily and filled with a deep peace.

But at the other end of Polbreath in the east wing, matters were very different.

William and Charlotte lay back to back, following a drawn-out argument concerning the baby, Matthew. William had told his wife in no uncertain terms that he had no intention of taking the child into his home as his son. Charlotte had proved equally insistent that he should, ending with a statement that had shattered him mentally with the impact of a pistol shot.

"Well, he *is*, isn't he, William?"

"What?"

"Your child."

"You must be mad," he'd said after a drawn-out pause.

"Oh, no. I'm very clear-headed. You see, things get about. I'd heard rumors in the past. You can't keep matters of that sort secret forever. And when I saw that little face I *knew*. The likeness was . . . remarkable."

"If you think—"

"I think nothing, William," she'd said in a spurt of energy, sitting upright with an uncharacteristic fierce look on her face. "I've told you, I *know*. And we shall keep the boy, whatever you say. He'll have your name and you'll do your duty by him. You see, I hate lies and deception and unfairness. If you'd told me in the beginning about Hannah, I'd have understood and married you just the same. But you hadn't the courage. You think you're so strong, William, such a *man* . . . so dedicated to the mines and the family name. Well . . . I despise you for the way you've behaved—" his hand closed on her firm rounded shoulder, bruising it.

"Don't you talk to me that way Charlotte—"

"And don't you dare touch me, William—"

"Touch you, you need a horsewhip—"

She laughed. "Take your hand off or I'll scream . . . I'll shout the truth. . . ."

"You wouldn't dare."

"Of course I would. I'm not afraid of men—any man, especially you. I've been brought up with them, remember?"

He fell back astonished against the pillows while she adjusted her nightdress. The closeness and sight of her plump comely body inflamed him to an irrational, unwarranted show of male passion. Despite the lunging of her knees against him, the clenched fists and frenzied attempt to push him off, he had her in one swift act of sexual frenzy that left her smarting and hurt, moaning fitfully with her face buried in the pillow.

"Charlotte—" a hand went tentatively to her shoulder. Shame seared him. "Oh, Charlotte, I didn't mean it—"

"Don't touch me," she said. "Don't ever come near me again, or I'll walk out of this house for good."

"Look at me," he urged. "I've said I'm sorry. Just look—"

She turned her head. The expression in her eyes, the contorted twisted look of her mouth, shocked him. He sighed, lay back, and rolled over.

Presently, unable to sleep, he got up and went downstairs for a drink. After one whiskey he had another, then a third. Half the bottle was empty before he fell into a heavy doze on the library sofa. He woke as the first sounds of activity echoed from the kitchen; then, only half-recollecting the night's scene, he got to his feet and climbed the stairs heavily to the marital bedroom.

Charlotte was already dressed, looking, he thought, exceedingly plain in brown, with puffed eyes staring condemningly from her plump, pale face. He wondered how he could ever have wanted her.

"Hullo, Charlotte," he said, "you look as though you've had a night on the tiles."

She stared contemptuously, then said, "I'll have black coffee sent up. Obviously you need it."

He flung himself on the bed.

Before she went out she said, "I shall be sleeping in the dressing room from now on, William. It can be made quite attractive, or if you prefer it, you can have it for yourself. . . ."

As the meaning of her words penetrated his brain and aching head he said, sharply, "Don't talk such bloody nonsense. I'm not having the servants gossiping about our conjugal differences—"

"Of course not," she agreed with assumed pleasantry. "There will be no need. You see, I'm going to have a child, William—yours, of course. And ladies in such a condition are automatically afforded privacy and consideration from sexual obligations. Everything will be considered in perfect order."

She swept out, not waiting to see his reaction to her bombshell of a statement.

William at first was quite stupefied; then, as the truth gradually registered, a certain complacency replaced his former anger.

A son, he thought, a legal son, not visualizing for one moment it could be a girl. Nicholas would be pleased. And a respite from nightly lovemaking might even be beneficial in the end. He'd have more energy for the mines and the tricky business of reopening Wheal Flower.

As for Hannah's boy: for the first time the situation held a titillating significance. One son in wedlock, one out of it—and no one knowing except Charlotte, who'd keep her mouth shut for the sake of her own dignity.

Perhaps the future wasn't going to be so bad after all.

So it was that an hour or two later William informed Donna not only of Charlotte's pregnancy but of their mutual wish to adopt Matthew as companion for the coming baby. By then facts were slipping into clearer perspective in his mind. The horror of Hannah's death was beginning to assume its true proportions. He took no blame for it, no moral obligation, because from the start of their association she'd known where she stood. The thought of her suffering and degradation disgusted and affronted him. He hoped that great hulk of a brute Pete was caught one day and made to suffer for it. Meanwhile he'd do the best he could for the

boy; Charlotte would eventually come round and realize she'd married a human being with normal feelings.
Her fit of rage and resentment would pass. Women
were temperamental creatures, cold one moment,
warm the next. One could never rely on their moods.
Only the earth was strong and constant, and the rich
dark feel of it—its hidden wealth and challenge, where
man could pit his strength and wits and physical need
without the fret of feminine whims or interference.

Wheal Flower! Wheal Blair. Once again the latter
rose in imagination to taunt him, and he thought of
Trefyn. He'd get the better of young Connor yet,
somehow, sometime, and without Juliet's help. The
old mine would rise once more from its grave, with
the pumping rod strong and rhythmic against the sky.
There would be steam there, and men singing. Maid-
ens working and rich ore salvaged from hidden levels.

He was sure, at that moment, of his capacity to win.
But he did not know Trefyn.

## 7

The news that Charlotte was already pregnant caused a stir of approval through the house. Nicholas and Donna were particularly gratified, although Donna insisted she didn't intend to be alluded to as "granny" or even "grandmother."

"Having a grandchild is one thing," she said, "being thought old quite another."

"What do you expect the child to call you then?" Nicholas asked.

"*When* it's born, whether a boy or girl, I shall become . . ." she paused a moment, then added, "'Donny,' I think. Yes . . . that will do. Half granny and half me."

Everyone laughed dutifully except Charlotte herself, who was conspicuously quiet over the congratulations and reception of her news.

"Are you sure you're doing the right thing in keeping Hannah Marne's child now?" Donna asked her daughter-in-law later. "I should have thought you had enough to cope with without taking on another unnecessary responsibility."

"Oh yes, I'm quite sure," Charlotte replied. "I've always heard that two children are easier to handle than one, and Matthew's a very good baby. Beth and Elise are wonderful with him, and I suppose we shall have a nanny—"

"Suppose? Of *course* you will," Donna said emphatically. "All the same . . ." she sighed. "It worries me thinking of that . . . that tinker's child being brought up as a Trevarvas. I suppose you think me a snob. Once I wasn't; when I was a girl I believed in democracy and equality with all my heart. Why, at one time I was in love with a miner, Jos Craze his name was. His father managed Wheal Faith, my father's mine. He wanted me to marry him and go to America . . ." Her voice trailed off as a flood of memories swept through her.

"Why didn't you?" Charlotte asked.

"I suppose I didn't love him sufficiently, or perhaps I loved Trencobban, our home, too much. My father died at that time, and I knew in my heart I had to stay. Then I met Nicholas."

"I see."

Donna stared at her reflectively. "No, I don't think you do. You're so much more . . . contained . . . than I was, and possibly not quite so single-hearted." She waited a second or two and, when Charlotte didn't speak, added, "Do you love William?"

Charlotte's face became blank. "I shouldn't have married him if I didn't."

Donna patted her hand. "That's all right then. But you must expect difficulties sometimes. The Trevarvases aren't always easy to get on with. Come to that, neither am I. You'll have your ups and downs, but that's what makes life exciting, isn't it?—not knowing what's coming next."

Her smile was encouraging, sweet, but a little strained. The orange eyes were puzzled. She wished Charlotte was more impulsive and confiding. Her air of self-possession was off-putting and rather irritating, holding, even, a hint of condescension. Clearly, the young woman she'd approved of so warmly at the start as wife for her eldest son had unsuspected hidden depths in her. It was to be hoped she didn't turn out to be an upsetting influence in the house. There'd been too much of that lately, what with the upheaval of Ianthe's sudden return and departure, and Juliet's ridiculous infatuation for Trefyn Connor. Jason too. Her heart stirred and warmed when she thought of him. Although she would miss him when he'd go to Paris, the knowledge that she'd got Nicholas to agree was gratifying, and now that the battle was over she could relax without the fear of having to disappoint her favorite offspring. So she put any niggling worries concerning Charlotte aside and devoted herself instead to helping Jason plan his future.

Juliet was not quite so optimistic. She had the perception and imaginative ability to sense the strain between William and his wife, and she was vaguely troubled.

Unhappiness always depressed her, and there was only one person who could help her at such times: Andrew. So on a warm day in June purposefully she set out to meet him on his return home from visiting a widow, Mary Polgrove, whose husband had recently died. For years Josiah Polgrove, who'd been a miner most of his active life at Penmartin, had suffered from silicosis and had been unable to do anything but putter about his small garden when he wasn't confined to bed. Through sympathy and a sense of duty to a loyal worker, Nicholas had insisted to William that the Polgroves should be allowed to retain their home as long as the man lived. Now it was Andrew's unpleasant duty to remind the poor woman that she would have to leave. The granite cottage was designated as mining property. Workers' cottages were badly needed now that plans for reopening Wheal Flower had been approved. Extra labor was necessary for shaft sinking and additional equipment for fresh workings. New homes would be built eventually, but in the meantime every possible building had to be utilized and, if necessary, restored.

Therefore Mary Polgrove had no choice in the matter. Pity and sympathy could not keep her. She had to go.

Juliet had overheard Andrew protesting to William and Nicholas and watched him, later, take off, with his shoulders at a dejected angle, limping more than usual as was habitual when he was downhearted. The cottage was less than a mile from Polbreath and could be reached by a field path cutting to the left from the back of the house toward the sea. It stood above the road and was apart from the rows of buildings situated nearer the mine.

As he'd anticipated, Andrew had found the meeting a chilling business.

"Go? Where will I go then?" Mary had protested with a faint quivering of her lower jaw, anxiety furrowing the brows above the lined face. She was a tiny woman, with shoulders rounded from age and hard work. Her eldest son, Nathaniel, had died in a mining accident ten years before; her younger, a farm laborer, taken by typhoid. Their photographs hung on either side of her husband's, over the mantel, facing a framed sampler on the opposite wall. It was a very small parlor but neat and clean with stone steps leading up to the one bedroom, which was partitioned into two. The primitive kitchen was at the back.

"You tell me, surr," Andrew had heard her voice persisting, "where will I go? This has bin my home for more'n forty years. My two boys wuz born here. My man wuz laid out up theer above in the same bed where I had Nathaniel an' Jacky. There's memories here, surr. Memories count more'n gold when you've lived long as I have done."

"I know, Mary. And if I had my way, you'd be secure here for life with a good pension—"

"Pension? I doan' want no pension nor charity. Jus' to stay here where I do belong. That's all I ask of the good Lord an you, surr—"

"But you're getting older each year. A time will come when—"

"I'm not able to wash an' clean an' keep mysel' decent," she'd interrupted. "When that day comes, Mr. Andrew, I'll be ready to meet my maker an' they can tek me to the workhouse for the leavin'. But no one can say this cottage edn' tidy an' clean so far. I've a bit saved up, there's potatoes an' greens still growin'. Will Trevarvas's promised me a young pig for rearin'. I won't want for nuthen' to kip a body alive so long as you do let me stay in my home, surr."

"Haven't you any relatives you could join?"

"Why should I plant myself on kin as doan' want me? One sister's all I have, Truro way. An' there's lots of things we doan see eye to eye 'bout. Younger than me she is, set in her ways—"

"But she wouldn't refuse you a roof?"

"She's God-fearin', if that's what you mean. But God-fearin' folk edn' always the kindliest, I've found."

*No*, Andrew thought wryly, *she's certainly touched on a home truth there.*

He'd left saying he'd do what he could, but leaving her with little hope that eviction could be delayed for long. As he made his way across the fields toward Polbreath, he could not dispel the picture from his mind of her small gray figure watching him from the doorway. His leg began to pain him, as it always did under stress. Memories returned. Memories of other gray figures, small Boer farmers without food or shelter—a hundred thousand of them or more—dying in concentration camps organized by Kitchener and Lord Roberts while their farmsteads burned and children perished, denied food or proper medical attention.

If he'd known then a fraction of what he knew now about war, he'd never have joined the Army. Under the façade of toasting, gallantry, and the celebration following the relief of Mafeking, he'd allowed himself for a time to be deceived by a sense of rightness and victory well deserved. But gradually, at odd moments, old nightmares had returned. With his inherent quality of sanguine good-fellowship, he'd succeeded in the past in allaying them. But lately he'd known there had to be a change in his existence. He could not go on as one of the privileged few destined to order and rule the lives of those less fortunate, without the means of alleviating distress when it arose. Mary Polgrove was a case in point. Because of the law, and Nicholas and William's power to enforce it, he had to see tradition ruthlessly observed, regardless of the suffering entailed.

He didn't blame his father, who had generally shown compassion if possible. But when the final showdown came, business and common sense registered first.

The cottage was needed. Wheal Flower came first. Mary therefore was the automatic victim of power and big business.

He saw Juliet coming to meet him where the grassland sloped down to the lush valley of Polbreath. She was wearing yellow, and as she drew nearer he noticed she had a bunch of bluebells in her hand. With the sun spilling an aura of light over her russet hair, she gave an impression of sudden gold against shadow, of rich young summertime against the gloom of wintry memory. He realized he'd not seen much of her lately, and his expression lifted in welcome.

"Hullo, Andrew," she said, "I thought I might meet you. Was it very awful?"

"What?"

"The meeting—with Mary Polgrove. I heard you talking to William about it. I think it's a shame the way he deals so high-handedly with other people."

"It's his job," Andrew said. "As for the meeting, yes it was pretty bad."

"Oh, dear." She sighed.

"What's up?" Andrew queried, forcing a smile, "Trefyn not come up to scratch or something?"

"Don't be stupid, I'm not a child."

"So you keep insisting. But I know you're not." He touched her fingers lightly. "Don't force things though—with the parents I mean. Just hope they'll come round, and keep your fingers crossed."

"Is that what you're going to do, about Mrs. Polgrove? Go on wishing?"

He paused before answering.

"I don't know. My whole future looks rather . . . glum, shall we say? . . . At the moment."

"What do you mean?"

"To tell you the truth, I'm not sure myself, although I've done a good deal of thinking."

"I know. And you haven't said a thing to me. You used to. What's the matter, Andrew? Everyone somehow seems under a cloud since the wedding—everyone except mama and father, that is, and they're . . . well, it rather disgusts me the way they carry on."

"What do you mean?"

She wrinkled her nose. "Such sly glances. And in the conservatory yesterday . . . they were *kissing*. Imagine it, at their age."

"Oh, stop it, Juliet, you're talking like a child. They're normal human beings, and mama's still quite a young woman, so what do you expect?"

"I expect them to practice what they preach and behave with dignity," Juliet answered defiantly. "If I so much as mention Trefyn's name, I'm apparently demeaning myself. . . ."

"Oh, I see. Jealousy."

Her eyes flashed. "Of course. If they can be so sickeningly obsessed with each other, they should surely make an attempt to understand me."

"Logically yes. But logic doesn't always account for human behavior."

"No. And I'm sorry to be bothering you. Especially when you're upset."

"I'm not so upset as completely flattened and disillusioned," Andrew said. "In fact—and this is strictly between you and me remember—" His eyes demanded a promise.

"You can trust me. You know that. Go on."

"I've practically decided to throw it in."

She stopped walking and stood facing him with astonishment on her face. "Throw it in? What?"

"The job. Doing William's dirty work. This bailiff business—it's not my line, Juliet. I don't think I can take it any more—solving problems, soothing folk down who've got a damn good case for grumbling, learning to live with a system and knowing all the time it's rotten to the core—" He broke off, breathing heavily and rapidly in a manner that told Juliet he really meant what he said.

"Oh, but surely you're exaggerating," she protested. "I know it must have been upsetting having to tell Mrs. Polgrove about the cottage. But to *leave!* You! Father would be upset, you know that, and it's not all grind, is it? There are good bits. You've always got on with the tenants so well."

"Admittedly. The jolly good fellow. What?" He mocked in his hale-fellow-well-met Army voice.

Juliet looked away.

"I've caught you in a bad mood," she said, "I'm sorry."

"Oh, it's all right." He paused, then added more reasonably, "I've a hunch you wanted to talk about something. William and Charlotte was it?"

"Yes. I'm sure they're not hitting it off. But that doesn't matter. Not now. It's *you.* What you said about throwing things up. Please don't."

His hand closed on hers, squeezing the palm for a moment before he dropped it and started walking on again slowly. "I may have to."

"But what would you do?"

There was a short silence between them during which she noted quite small things: the glint of a butterfly's blue wings passing by, the sweet throaty trill of a blackbird from a May tree, and from the distance somewhere a cuckoo's call. The air was heady with bluebell scent and the lush smell of young thrusting grass and bracken. Yet Andrew looked so sad. Sad with a composed resignation that made him remote, almost a stranger.

"I'm thinking of joining the Brothers of St. Luke," he said presently, adding, "don't let it shock you Juliet—"

"But . . ." her voice faltered, "that . . . that monastery place do you mean? The one Father Strawn came from?"

"Yes."

"It's *Catholic* though. You can't. They're monks. They don't marry or do anything normal. Oh, Andrew, you *couldn't*."

"Listen, Juliet, don't misunderstand me. I haven't decided yet, and the seminary's not a closed order. I could be sent anywhere at anytime to help those who needed it—the poor and sick. And there's a pretty long probationary period anyway. Time to get accustomed to the way of life. It's not as though I'd be shutting myself away from *people*." His eyes searched hers anxiously for approval. He was disappointed.

"It would be wrong. I'm sure of it," she said bluntly. "Vows of celibacy—no fun, no marriage, no children, no proper life with a family—and you've so much to give, Andrew, in an ordinary way. People like you, and you get on with them. The very thought of you dressing like a black crow in trailing robes and singing and praying all day is horrible."

His mouth tightened. "Actually the praying part would be the least of it, for me."

"There, you see! You've admitted it. You'd be a rotten monk—"

"Brother," he corrected her.

"It doesn't matter what you call it; it's the same thing."

"Oh, dear. I seem to have put my foot in it. I hoped you'd understand."

"How can I? William's marriage is bad enough. I mean, I liked Charlotte, I still do, in a quiet sort of way. But I can't see it lasting. He needs someone to face up to him with more fire and spirit."

"I think she's got it."

"Well, anyway, he's tied himself down, and you can't say the atmosphere's pleasant. But *you!* a priest— it's ridiculous. You've never been particularly religious." She gave him a very straight look before asking with chilling insight, "Is it a compensatory thing, Andrew?"

He flinched. She noticed the small nerve jerking in his cheek.

"What do you mean?"

"Because of your leg? A sort of inverted vanity? To show you've suffered and know a little more about certain things than most people—war, I mean, and men dying? Oh, I don't mean to be unkind. You're the best of all of us at Polbreath. Jason or William can't hold a candle next to you. William's utterly selfish and mine-mad, and Jason's all arty-crafty—especially

crafty. The way he sucked up to Mama was awful.
*Art!* I don't think he's that talented anyway. All he
wants is the high life with some phony French set
where he can throw father's money about and pretend
he's a budding Matisse. I can just imagine him lounging on some vulgar chaise longue with women drooling over him, making him think he's God. He'll grow
his hair of course, and smoke cigars. The rich ones do.
Oh—" she broke off briefly. "I'm being unfair, aren't
I?"

"Yes, you are. Jason has talent."

"It's because of you I'm upset."

"But if it's right for me, you shouldn't be."

"It isn't right though. That's the point. I'm sure it's
not."

"How do you know? I could easily say the same to
you."

"What about?" she said sharply.

"Trefyn Connor. I've never once suggested you'd be
making the mistake of your young life to marry him."

"Why should you? It's natural to love someone. And
I do love Trefyn . . . desperately."

"There are different ways of loving," Andrew
pointed out. "I've lived longer than you."

"Just a few years, that's all."

"And in those few years I've experienced things I
hope to God you never know. . . ."

"You mean the war and killing. I hope so too," she
said soberly. "That's what's so wonderful about Trefyn. *One* of the things, I mean. He wants to protect
and preserve."

"Good for him."

"But in a normal, practical way. He's not cutting
himself off from life, as you would be if you join that

. . . that . . . brotherhood. What about women, Andrew? It's something I've never asked before. But—"

He gave a short laugh. "My dear child—or rather, sister, I can assure you my sex life up to date has been normal and not without certain pleasure and gratification. I had a mistress abroad and later fell in love with a nurse who was massacred by the Boers. Probably for that I should hate the Dutch race, but I don't. I simply deplore the lust and greed that makes war possible and the hypocrisy of those that run them. I enjoyed being a 'hero' for a period and had a damn good time out of it. But it's over now. Forever."

"You can't tell. You may change again."

"True, too true," he said more lightly. "And now, Juliet, shall we stop the conscience-probing? Thank you for meeting me and taking my mind off Mary Polgrove. I'll have another go at William and father tonight, but I doubt if it will have any effect."

"I shall go and see her myself tomorrow," Juliet told him. "I *might* be able to help in some way."

"You might. But an additional word in Nicholas's ear would probably do more. See her first, then tackle him."

"All right."

The next morning Juliet saddled Firebrand and rode to the cottage, taking the longer route by lane and then along the high moor road. Later she intended to call on Trefyn. But now she'd given Andrew her promise she preferred to get the sad business out of the way first.

Mary had been cleaning the small front window when she arrived. In the morning sunlight it winked gold against the gray granite. There was no garden in front, but at the side of the cottage leading to the

back, a scrap of land showed a few greens waving between brown earth scattered with small stones and
grass. An old dog was sniffing at a bone in one corner. He was a mongrel—half sheep dog, half terrier—
with mournful eyes and odd ears, one pricked up and
one down. When he saw Juliet dismount he left the
bone, barked, and waddled forward.

Mary came to the door. "Down, Tim," she said, and
to Juliet, "he won't hurt you, miss. It's Miss Trevarvas,
edn' et?"

Juliet smiled and nodded. "How are you, Mrs. Polgrove? I haven't seen you for a long time."

"No. You was a child last time we met. At school."

"Yes. Well, time passes. I'm . . ." Now that she was
facing the tired bent woman she wondered whatever
there was to say that hadn't been said already. "I'm
sorry your husband died," she added. "I came to tell
you that all of us—well, Andrew and I, anyway, are
going to do all we can to see you stay here. I'm not
supposed to interfere in business matters. But I don't
call this business . . . it's just trying to be fair."

A faint smile touched the thin lips that were networked above with tiny lines drawn inward from the
thin cheeks. The clear light struck cruelly from a sideways angle across the worn features. The flesh was
crumpled and withered from too much work all her
life on too little nourishment. The eyes appeared colorless and sunken, with a watery film over them. She
was not yet seventy, but she looked ninety.

"Well, miss," she said, "you'd better come in. If
there's anythin' to talk about, best say et sittin'. These
legs o' mine edn' so good as they once wus."

Juliet followed her inside and took a proffered chair.
The room was clean but badly in need of repair. A

trickle of water had oozed down the wall from a crack overhead in one corner, and plaster and paper was needed where it had crumbled and fallen away. A small fire burned warmly in the grate. The place felt damp.

"Ought you to be living here alone?" Juliet asked unthinkingly."

"No, my dear, I shouldn'," Mary answered. "I sh'd have my man with me who shouldn' have died from silicoss—or silcis or somethun' they call et these days—from that old mine. An' Nathanial and Jacky too. Good sons they were. Born here. All my life's bound up in this little place. There's things need doin' o' course, but with a little help I could have et real nice agen. It'll come, mind you. When I'm gone et'll be made smart an' fresh for the ones who tek over—furriners probl'y. Germans I shouldn' wonder, 'cause them Germans is skilled, they say. I've heeard Mr. William's bin talkin' about tekkin' a couple on. News travels, Miss Juliet, even to these old ears."

Juliet looked away uncomfortably. "But you don't know, not yet," she said. "I've just told you—Andrew and I are going to do all we can. Try not to worry too much. It won't help you—"

"That's true, my dear; nothin' will. Still, et's good of 'ee tekkin' the trouble to try. Like your mother you are—"

"*No.*" Juliet's voice was vehement. "We're not a bit alike. She—"

"Oh, yes you are," Mary protested. "In the old days before she married your father she wus always tryin' to better things for workin' folk. The Penrozes wus all alike, 'specially her father, your grandpa. Why, 'twas she had that monument put up, to them an' Will

Craze, and the rest of the miners—" she broke off, eyeing Juliet shrewdly. There was a short pause, then she continued, "Mebbe she's changed a bit—or forgotten. The Penrozes had hard luck at one time, and et's when things are difficult folks come together. The Trevarvases are different. They've never had to want for a thing. Riches can blind you, Miss Juliet."

"Not me," Juliet said stubbornly. "And times are changing. Trefyn says—"

"Trefyn?"

"Trefyn Connor."

"Ah. Him."

"Do you know him?" Juliet couldn't help asking, with her cheeks a deeper pink than they'd been a moment before, her breath a little quicker.

"No, my dear. Only tales, an' when you get to my age you tend to disregard much of those."

"Yes."

"Furriners o' course—the Connors. No one knowed where the man came from. Ireland some say—others from the sea."

"The sea? What do you mean?"

The old woman peered at Juliet closely from her small tired eyes. "I doan' rightly know, and that's a fact. I remember 'et though—that day he 'peared as ef from nowhere. One moment he wasn' theer, the next he was. Just like that. But he had the gift o' charmin' all right. Look how he did get that proud Gentry girl, Miss Elinor. Some do say he whistled women just as he did birds an' foxes, an' creepin' adders. An' say what you like, 'twasn' natural. Well, she learned to rue the day he wed her, that's fer sure, poor thing. Not that I had much use for that family—hers I do mean.

The Gentrys for all their wealth was a mean stuck-up lot—"

"And I expect you think we are too?" Juliet said quietly.

The thin hand touched hers. "No, no my dear. Not you. A heart you've got. But Mr. William? Hm! When I do think o' what he's in mind I reckon he's a stone there, an' that's the truth." She sighed, got up, and stirred the fire. "You'd best be goin', Miss Juliet. Thank 'ee for comin', but tedn' no good. Him an the master'll have their way in the end; the rich always do."

Little more was said after that. Juliet left the cottage with a feeling of futility and the frustrated thought that Mary Polgrove was probably right. William, as always, would win, because according to the law, right was on his side, and he hadn't the imagination to see anyone else's point of view but his own.

Instead of going immediately to see Trefyn as she'd planned, she rode back to Polbreath in a spurt of indignation. When she reached the drive, William and Nicholas were walking across the moor from the direction of Penmartin. She drew Firebrand to a halt and waited.

"Well," Nicholas said, "you look very rosy. Had a good canter?"

Juliet dismounted. "No. I've been to see Mrs. Polgrove. I was going on to Trefyn's later—" a note of defiance crept into her voice, "but I changed my mind."

"Good," William remarked calmly. "The less you see of that bastard, the better."

"He's not a bastard and don't you dare talk like

that," Juliet cried. "Mind your own life, William, and leave me to mine."

"Now you two, stop it!" Nicholas said sharply. "And you, Juliet, just calm down and tell me what you were doing at Mary's cottage."

"Listening to her," Juliet replied with her eyes flashing. "Learning and seeing for myself what being a Trevarvas means. You're very proud of the family name, father, and so am I, in a way. But not when I see the kind of thing William's doing."

"What the deuce are you talking about?" William said turning brick red.

"Oh, you know very well, so don't pretend," Juliet replied with active dislike on her face. "I've tried to get Trefyn to sell that land to you, but—"

"I don't bloody well want your help—"

"Don't you? I think you do. You're a greedy snob, William—you'd do anything in the world for power. But without me you won't get it, because I shall tell Trefyn not to sell on any account."

"You little cheat. Blackmail, is that it?"

"Yes, yes it is," she said. "Either you let Mary Polgrove keep her cottage or I'll fight tooth and nail for the Connors. Do you understand?" Her chin was outthrust, her gray eyes icebright with fury.

Nicholas took her arm. "Juliet, control yourself. It's a long time since I put you over my knee, but if you go on in this tone, I'll do just that, understand?"

She flinched, started to speak, but with a great effort of will resisted and was silent.

"And you, William," Nicholas continued, "no more tirades or bullying. I'm master here, and you'll do what I say. If I decide to let Mary stay on at the cottage, she'll do so. If not, she'll go."

Juliet's face brightened. "Do you mean you haven't decided?" she asked quickly.

"No," Nicholas told her. "Mrs. Polgrove is leaving. The property's going to rack and ruin, and if you'd used your eyes sensibly you'd have realized she'd be too old to care for herself much longer. A time comes when sentiment's useless. Action has to be taken for the good of everyone concerned, regardless of personal feelings. So in future please try and keep out of men's affairs, Juliet. Another thing—" He paused, looking at her determinedly, with a dangerous glint in his eyes, "keep away from Trefyn Connor, do you understand? I realize you like riding over Rosebuzzan, but there's no need to touch the farm. Now, remember what I said, both of you, or there'll be trouble."

He strode away, leaving William and Juliet facing each other.

Juliet was the one to speak first. "You're a rotten cad, William," she said, "and I despise you."

"And you're a spoiled brat who needs a good horse-whipping," he said before turning to follow his father.

She laughed sneeringly. "Oh, I *see!* So that's how you treat your women. Poor things. Poor Charlotte. No wonder she wants something to love. What a pity the baby isn't yours, William. Or . . . or . . ." Something in his face took her aback—more than that—acutely shocked her. She couldn't be sure, of course, but truth, like a ruthless hand, seemed to sear and change his features with a mask of guilt and momentary shame.

It couldn't be, she thought. Surely not . . . not William's . . . Hannah Marne's child.

A moment later the aberration—illusion, or whatever it was—had passed, leaving William's face as it had always been: hard and a little contemptuous. But one glimpse had been enough. As William turned on his heel and walked sharply to the house, Juliet knew that doubt now would always be in her mind, and that every expression she saw on the baby's face, every small characteristic of personality and looks, would hold significance and meaning. She'd guessed for some time that William had women; she'd heard vague tales of his meetings with Hannah, which she'd taken with a grain of salt. But *this!*—and if it was true, which she didn't much doubt—oh, what a hypocrite he was, and Charlotte must be a saint.

Polbreath that evening, with its emotional undercurrents and warring ideologies, seemed a suffocating prison of conflict and doubt.

She had not seen Trefyn for some days. Her need for him was suddenly overwhelming.

*I must see him* she thought, *I must, I must.*

When the house was quiet, at about eleven-thirty, she dressed desultorily in a thin frock, slipped a loose cape over it, and in a pair of slippers set out for the moor. The night was warm, almost hot. As she let herself out quietly by the side door a copper moon was already rising in the sky. She didn't risk going to the stables for fear of rousing anyone, but set off on foot for the Connor farm. If the walk took an hour, she didn't mind. Sleep was far from her, her senses were alight with summer magic, the bluish gold-streaked dusk, and earthy scents of grass and sleeping flowering things—most of all her own longing, longing for Trefyn.

She walked quickly and lightly, exulting in the soft feel of the turf beneath her feet, and the brush of bracken and foxgloves against her body. When she reached the valley lane and took the turn round the hill, she saw a light burning near the stables, and knew with a leap of the heart that Trefyn was still up and about somewhere. She quickened her pace and was running when she got there. He was just returning to the house, a tall dark figure silhouetted against the moon—strong, lean, a young god of the night, beautiful and proud in his manhood.

She rushed toward him and flung herself against his chest.

"Oh, Trefyn, Trefyn, I missed you . . . I wanted you so."

Her arms went to his neck; his lips were on hers. There was an earthy smell about him, faintly redolent of animals and the sweet tang of hay.

His mouth traveled to her neck and the silky softness of her shoulder where the cool flesh was damp with thin mist, and the excitement of love.

"I want you too," he murmured.

"You said once there'd be a time . . ." As the words faded on her lips the moonlight caught his eyes, lighting them to darkness and molten flame.

"Not here," he murmured, "Jet's only just gone to bed. I know a place . . ."

"Where?"

He didn't reply, but released her gently, whispering "Sh . . . sh . . ." with a finger against her mouth. Then he slipped back toward the stables, leaving her standing by the darkness of the wall, tense with longing and excitement, conscious of her own heart beating heavily against her eardrums and of mounting heady anticipation. Everything had become a world of mystery, of black shadows and silvered light with elongated shapes cast strangely from the moon's glow.

During those few moments of waiting, the very earth emitted an ancient sense of identity rekindled from far-off times. She glanced up to where the moor's summit rose stark and clear to the sky. The primeval standing stones seemed magnified, imbued with an encroaching elemental life under the golden globe of the moon. Once, history said, those same relics had seen sacrifice and magic rites performed. Juliet shivered, visualizing a prone body helpless on a cold altar with a white-robed figure poised and ready with sword raised to strike. As a child the thought had frightened her. But her nurse had laughed. "You've been dreaming," she'd said. "Those things are only old granite. Do you know what *I* was told when I was a little one?"

"No," Juliet had answered.

"They said they were naughty little girls who'd wandered when they should have been asleep, and been turned into stone. So you just close your eyes now and go to the Land of Nod."

Juliet had not been sure which was the worst—the idea of sacrifice and Druid priests or girls turned into stone. Even the Land of Nod itself had sounded frightening. Only Nicholas, then, had been able to comfort her. "Think of all the small things sleeping there," he'd said, "birds and badgers and baby rabbits. There's nothing can harm you on old Rosebuzzan, love; it's just a place."

A place, yes. And now she was grown up and waiting for her love to take her there. *Oh, Trefyn,* she thought, *come quickly.*

Almost the next moment she heard the steady, subdued sound of hooves and footsteps, and his figure appeared, leading his favorite colt, Bran.

"Here we are," he said in a low voice. "Come along, up with you." He hoisted her onto the animal's back, and they moved at a slow pace to the lane, taking the curve from the gate up the valley between the dark hills. As they rounded the bend, a blurred light cast its beam momentarily across the track.

"Someone's heard us," Juliet said. "Is it—"

"Jet perhaps. Who cares? You?"

Juliet laughed, "I don't care about anything except you. And I never want to go back . . . never . . . never . . ."

His free arm tightened round her waist. "No promises," he said, "no words, no vows, oh, Juliet . . . my love . . ."

A faint tremor of wind carried his words away. She half-turned her head, with his mouth brushing her cheek, before he kicked the colt to a brisker pace. The farm now was completely out of view. All was loneliness and extreme quiet except for their forms silhouetted against the thread of track and the rhythmic hollow echo of a horse's hooves.

Almost at the end of the narrow valley, just before it widened into a desolate stretch of furze and bog that reached eventually to the opposite coast, a narrow path turned sharply to their left, cutting between bracken and boulders up the hill.

Trefyn headed them along it, urging the colt with softening words through the wilderness of encroaching briars and undergrowth. The straggling bushes clawed black now under the stars and climbing moon. Nothing was clearly visible but the receding mine stack of Wheal Blair to their left, outlined starkly for a moment, then swamped into shadow beyond the curve of the hill.

They continued for a time, with no words between them—nothing but the deep inner awareness of unspoken passion intensified by the silence of the lonely night.

Then Trefyn suddenly reined.

"There," he said, "do you see it?"

Staring over her shoulder, Juliet saw the glint of water; a pool of glittering light encircled by a few pale boulders and drooping fern. A dew pond.

He lifted her down and carried her to the water's edge, where he eased her to her feet. Bemused, in a state of wonder, she stood staring, with her hair tumbled about her shoulders, her long thin skirt washed to a pale greenish glow through the shadows. Trefyn withdrew her coat and let his hands rest lingeringly on the sheen of flesh—of neck, arms and rounded shoulders—before easing the bodice and belted waist.

The soft material slipped easily from breasts and thighs, falling like a nymph's shroud over a crouching thorn bush. As she removed her constricting underwear he did the same, and a moment later was kneeling naked with his arms entwined round her white body, traveling downward over the slender swelling curve of thighs to knees and calves of the long slim legs. His mouth touched her feet and moved upward, caressing each quivering muscle with passionate reverence. As his hands reached her waist she was drawn down to him, her ripe young breasts crushed tight against his firm male form. She quivered, with her arms outspread; his manhood swelled, and her spirit and flesh were unified in a desire stronger than reason, life, or death itself, but was complete surrender and extinction—a momentary darkness holding the pulse of all that had ever been and was to come.

As the thrust of love took her to its heights, a little moan left her lips. Following the searing blindness of consummation, she was aware vaguely of Trefyn's lips drawing the sweetness to him, of his dark eyes slowly coming into focus above her. The tumult gradually eased, with the mountainous force receding, leaving them still entwined but quieting into gradual awareness and peace.

He rolled from her and lay watching her lazily, one arm spread over her stomach. She turned to him dreamily. "Oh, Trefyn, I never thought . . . I never dreamed . . ."

"Sh . . . sh," he whispered. "No words, darling. No talk. Such a waste . . ."

He kissed her again; her hair, temples and smooth cheek. Her head lay on his shoulders. A film of thin passing cloud momentarily dimmed the moon, leaving only velvet darkness above. Then it had gone, and the silvered light was everywhere. Moths fluttered by bushes and ferns. The earth hummed with the muted chirrup of grasshoppers and small buzzing insects. Summer, though hushed, was thrillingly alive. Juliet suddenly sprang up, her body a white column of fire against the dark hill. "I'm going to bathe," she said, and ran from him, lithe as a young fawn, into the pool, splashing its clear cool water over her, kicking her feet with the air.

Trefyn went after her and they sported and played together, laughing, splashing, caressing each other, letting shivering streams of coolness ripple their limbs. She had never thought such joy was possible. And when, gasping, the game was over, he lifted her up, with his hands gentle on her smooth wet skin. Proud as a young god, black curls glistering in a shivering beam of light, he held her tight against him for a moment, standing as lovers of ancient times must have stood in days forgotten by man. Then he laid her down and loved her again, a king of the old world, and she his queen.

At last, as the first faint ray of early dawn dimly lit the eastern horizon, they dressed and wandered hand in hand to where the colt was already standing, sniffing the tang of thin rising mist. Before they mounted, Trefyn took her two hands and pressed his lips to her forehead.

She spoke then, knowing everything must be all right. Nothing ever, now, could destroy or mar one moment of their passionate coming together.

"When can it be?" she said. "How long?"

"What?"

"You know . . . our . . . our . . . you're going to marry me, aren't you Trefyn?"

"I don't think you need ask that," he said. "As soon as you like—anytime. Tomorrow or the next day, or the one after that. There are rules aren't there? Red tape and registrars, licenses. And your parents—"

"They don't matter. There'll be no trouble. They'll come round." Her voice was confident, though a niggle of doubt persisted. "They've *got* to," she continued. "Anyway, it'll be easy if you sell that land to William, and you will now, won't you, Trefyn? It'll make all the difference. And to us, too. We'll be able to have a lounge built on, and . . ." her voice ran on heedlessly, so filled with plans and visions of the future that she was unaware of his form stiffening or of the sudden hardening of his lips and dying fire of his dark eyes that left them narrowed and cold, swept of all lingering desire.

"What do you mean?" he said, so coldly she was abruptly startled. When she saw his face it was as though she was looking at a stranger's for the first time.

"I . . . what I said . . . about the land. If you let William have it—"

"I see. So *that* was it. At the back of your mind you were scheming all the time how to get your hand on my property for your precious brother. William would be satisfied, you thought, and your father would be indulgent—perhaps. Into the bargain you'd change things here and have a fancy parlor and a maid so you could entertain your rich friends. 'Trefyn will do anything for me now,' you thought, 'because I've bought him with my body—'"

She was shocked. "You don't believe that. You can't."

"Why shouldn't I? It's true, isn't it? If you loved me so much you wouldn't have brought up that matter of the land now. You wouldn't even have thought of it. Oh, Juliet—" the rage died into hopeless negation. "You haven't the first idea of values. You're so—ruthless. Such a snob. I told you didn't I?—" His voice rose again fiercely. "I told you at the very beginning the way my wife would have to be. And I haven't changed. Neither have you. That's the hell of it. We're rivals, Juliet, enemies fighting for different things—"

"But we love each other—"

"Love?" he laughed. "If you said 'all right Trefyn, William or Nicholas don't matter a damn, I'll come to you as I am, on my knees, willing to scrub floors and cook and clean—' then I might believe you. But—"

"Why should I?" she cried with her temper rising. "Why should I go down on my knees to you, or scrub floors and do all your other beastly chores, if it's not necessary? You call me a snob, but it's you—*you*. Boss-man, that's what Judy called you, *and* Jet—"

"Yes, exactly. Boss," he said, looking down on her coldly. "And you have me that way or not at all. I can't help being myself any more than you can help being the spoiled daughter of Nicholas Trevarvas. I want you still; I guess I always will. But not on your terms, Juliet. It wouldn't work. Now, hadn't we better get started? I'll take you as far as the lane—" his hand went out to her, the other held the bridle.

She struck his arm aside. "Let me alone. I don't want your help—" She dove away from him down the narrow track through the bushes. He followed and caught her after the first few yards, swinging her round sharply. His jaws were set, his eyes flaming.

"Behave yourself, will you? I'm getting you back home. Now shut up, Juliet, before I lose my temper properly—"

Knowing there was nothing else she could do, she obeyed him mutely, too angry to cry but with such desolation in her she wished, briefly, she could die.

The summer dawn had come quickly. By the time Trefyn lifted her from the colt's back at the turn of the drive leading to Polbreath, the sky was already half-light, lifting to a greenish pink glow over the distant sea and cliffs. She turned to face him once, before rushing swiftly away along the tree-lined avenue.

"You've spoiled everything," she said bitterly. "*Everything*. All you think of is yourself. It's a good thing I've found out in time. They were right after all—all of them—" Through the uncertain light he could not see the glimmer of tears behind the thick lashes, was aware only of the desperate anger of her voice, the frustration and cutting temper.

"Think well, Juliet," he warned. "I take only so much—"

"I don't need to think. You've shown what you are." She was away before he could reply, a pale shadow receding and finally caught up into all the other transient shadows of early dawn.

For a minute he stood watching her, erect and motionless, with the young horse quivering restlessly. His eyes were hard and unswerving, his mouth set. Then, with a sharp movement he had swung himself to the saddle and was cantering away, increasing speed to a gallop round the turn of the lane.

As she reached the drive of the house Juliet walked more slowly, keeping carefully in the shadows of the wall. A glimmer of light shone from the kitchens, but the window adjoining the side door was dark. It seemed unlikely anyone would be about there at such an early hour. The door was still unlocked as she'd left it, and it was easy to slip in, closing it quietly behind her. By then, tiredness was claiming her. All she wanted was to reach her room before discovery and the inevitable tirade of questioning that would follow.

She ran on light feet to the main hall and up the stairs, thinking how much easier it would have been if William and Charlotte hadn't confiscated the east wing. In the house all was still dark, except the faint fitful glow from stained glass and occasional dormer windows. The portraits of proud, long-dead ancestors seemed to peer from their frames as she passed, their faces ghost-pale and condemning. She shivered, partly from weariness, mostly from reaction and a sense of utter negation and loss. At the top of the stairs, taking

a corner leading to her own room, she knocked into a
pedestal that held a bowl of some foreign blossoming
plant. It crashed and fell to the floor with a shattering
thud. She stood for a moment, horrified, looking down
at the mess, still trembling from shock and fatigue.
The door of a room behind her opened, and a woman's figure emerged in a white nightdress with thick
dark hair tumbled over her shoulders.

Donna.

Juliet straightened up, fighting for composure. "I'm
sorry," she said. "I didn't mean to wake you—" her
voice was soft and shaken.

"Where have you been?" her mother demanded.
"What are you doing at this time of the morning,
dressed like that?" A hand went out, gripping the
dewy shoulder sharply. "You're wet," the cold voice
continued. "You've been . . . you've been . . . no,
you needn't say. I can guess." Her grip hardened.
"You've been with that . . . that man—Trefyn Connor, haven't you? And don't lie to me, it's written all
over you. You should be *ashamed*, creeping out like
any slut in the night—"

· Juliet pulled herself free. "How *dare* you." Indignation rose shrilly from her throat. "Don't touch me. And
don't call me a slut. If my father heard you he'd—"

"He'd agree with me and be extremely angry."
Donna interrupted. "You're not too old to be pun-
ished."

"Don't be ridiculous. Go away." Juliet said contemptuously. "Leave me alone. I dislike you utterly,
just as you dislike me; you always have. You've never
loved me or tried to. You've never understood—"

"That's a *terrible* thing to say—"

"Yes, it is, but true." She turned with a rush, but

Donna grabbed her arm again, and at that very moment Nicholas came from the bedroom.

"What's all this?" he enquired, looking from one to the other. "Do you want to raise the whole house? What's the meaning of this screaming like fishwives at each other—"

White-lipped, Juliet faced her father, "She called me a slut, just because I . . . because I . . . went for a walk . . ."

"Is this true, Donna?" Nicholas's voice was hard, formidably cold.

"Quite true. And you should know why. Ask her. Ask our precious daughter why, and where. If I lose my temper, you'll agree, I think, I had good cause."

Nicholas put his hand beneath Juliet's chin, forcing her to look up at him.

"Well, Juliet?" he said.

She hesitated, wanting to lie, trying to find the courage and failing miserably.

"I went to see Trefyn," she said. "It was such a lovely night. I couldn't sleep. There were things I wanted to talk about . . ."

"And was that all you did? Talk?"

"No. We—we bathed, in a pool. The dew pond."

There was a long pause, then Nicholas said heavily, "I see. You bathed, in a dew pond."

"Yes."

"And what else?"

Her lower lip quivered. "What do you mean, what else? We love each other; at least we *did*, until . . . until . . ."

"Until what?"

"He wanted me to . . . to . . ."

"You see," Donna interrupted. "She's quite shameless. She admits it. You've always spoiled her."

"Hold your tongue," Nicholas snapped. Donna flinched. "Now, Juliet, continue," he said sternly. "What exactly did Connor want you to do?"

"He wanted me to stop William from trying to get that land—the Wheal Blair bit . . ." she prevaricated with a half-triumphant glance at Donna. "And I made it clear I wouldn't. I told him he should sell."

Nicholas sighed. "Well, if that's all it was . . ."

"How can you be so gullible, Nicholas?" Donna couldn't help saying.

"And how can you be so crude, madam?" Nicholas retorted. "Enough's been said already in full hearing of anyone awake. Go to your rooms, both of you. We'll talk about this later."

"And remember, Juliet," Donna added as a parting shot, "we're going to the Courts for dinner tonight, so perhaps you'd better get yourself under proper control, have a good wash and sleep, and pray hard that Desmond makes you a firm proposal of marriage before any whisper of this disgraceful episode comes to his ears."

"Pray for him?" Juliet flashed contemptuously. "For Desmond? To marry me? I wouldn't have him at any price. And I'm not going to the Courts tonight. You can tell them I've a headache or any lie you like. I shan't be there."

She rushed away, and a minute later the door of her room slammed loudly, leaving Nicholas and Donna staring after her helplessly.

Nicholas glanced coldly at his wife. "You haven't learned much tact in all these years," he said. "And slut's hardly the term I'd have expected you to use. Juliet's simply headstrong and impulsive—like you when you were young."

"I didn't go bathing naked with young men in dew ponds through the night!" Donna replied sharply.

"No. Coves were more to your choice, if I remember rightly," Nicholas reminded her shrewdly, "and you were considerably older. So don't for heaven's sake play the perfect prig. It doesn't suit you."

A warm flush stained her cheeks. "You don't seem to realize the implications of this—this whole thing," she said when they were back in their room. "Juliet's compromised herself. Can't you understand? And with Trefyn of all people—an Irish tinker's son!"

"And Elinor Gentry's also."

"What has that to do with it?"

"Oh, quite a bit, I should have thought," Nicholas said calmly. "Genes. A mixed bag can be healthy I've been told. And you don't even know Connor's stock. You're only guessing."

Donna gave an ironical laugh. "*That* doesn't take much intelligence."

"Well, what about it? She might easily do worse."

Donna gasped.

"Nicholas! You sound as if you *approved*."

"I can assure you, I don't, but I'm certainly not going to throw my own daughter out or have her treated as a pariah simply because she had a little fun on a summer night with an attractive young horse-breeder who knows his job and has the guts to stick to it."

"You mean you're going to let things slide? Not even—"

"Use my horsewhip? Certainly not. I'm as concerned as you are about her. But what's happened is over, and there's nothing, simply *nothing* we can do about it. So do you mind trying to be rational and a little generous to your daughter for once? And another thing—" he cast an overt glance at her back and proud set of the head turned against him. "Are you listening?"

"I could hardly not be."

"Stop the matchmaking. I just won't have it, Donna. Young Court's all right in his way—likable, but brainless. My daughter deserves something more stimulating. I can understand her kicking."

"I wasn't matchmaking."

"No. But you were having a damn good try."

Donna sighed, shook her heavy hair back over her shoulders, pulled on a lacy wrap and went to the dressing table.

"I'm not going to argue. It's always the same when Juliet's name crops up. If I try to discipline her or even make a suggestion, you're up in arms. It's not right or fair. I love her, too, you know."

Nicholas, softening, crossed to the chair, bent, and let his lips rest lightly on her cool shoulder. "Of course. I know that. But you're a little jealous perhaps?"

She jumped up and swung round, orange eyes bright under the tumbled fringe of dark hair. "*Me?* Of my own daughter?"

He shrugged.

"That's what I said. It does happen you know—a pining for youth again and the wild lost years."

She shivered. "Oh, Nicholas. You make me sound so—so *obvious.*"

He drew her to him. "Forget it now. We'll tackle Juliet later. Together, and quietly."

She shook her head. "No. I wouldn't trust myself. You must do what you think fit. I only hope she's sensible about tonight. This dinner party's been arranged for some time. And I don't want the Courts disappointed."

"Desmond, you mean?"

"Naturally. If Juliet's going to let him down, she can at least be tactful and discreet about it."

Nicholas said nothing more, but he thought privately that Donna was being unduly optimistic. Juliet by nature was neither tactful *nor* discreet, and he doubted that she'd accompany them to the social get-together that evening.

His judgment proved to be correct.

All day Juliet remained in her room behind her locked door, refusing to eat when first Elise, then Beth, each with a tray followed by Donna, insisted she show herself.

"I don't want anything," she called, "I've a headache. Please go away and leave me to rest."

Nicholas also was rebuffed.

"Open the door, Juliet," he said loudly and clearly. "You're being very unreasonable. Your mother's upset."

"Let her be." Juliet shouted. "I hope she is. And you can tell her I'm *not* going to the Courts tonight, and I don't care what anyone thinks. I'm not sorry either. So please—*please* go away."

As Nicholas went morosely downstairs it was with a grudging feeling that Donna might have been right after all. For once his hand itched to treat his unruly, beloved daughter like the child she obviously still was, and spank her soundly.

He didn't realize that Juliet's suffering was far from

that of a child's, having little to do with the unhappy
interlude on the landing. Through the long hours of
the morning and afternoon only one thought had properly registered in her mind: her bitter parting with
Trefyn, which had proved he didn't love her.

Her eyelids were swollen and red from intermittent
crying. Hopelessness filled her with a dull persistent
ache that was pain through her whole body. Everything he'd wanted from her she'd given, and she'd believed he felt the same. But in the end he'd thrown
things back in her face—love, respect, trust. She felt
shamed and lost, hurt almost beyond endurance.

But, of course, one did endure, one had to.

At times she got up from the bed and nibbled a
biscuit or two. Occasionally she wandered to the window and stared out across the summer landscape of
rising moors beyond the lush valley. The clear
weather had clouded, and already thin rain was film-
ing the grass and trees in a shroud of gray. She felt
entombed and lost without sympathy or friends. If
only Andrew had tapped at her door she'd have let
him in, but none of her brothers had made any attempt to contact her. Andrew was probably discussing
spiritual matters with Father Strawn, she thought despondently, and Jason didn't care. As for William, he
only made trouble for her. If it hadn't been for him
and that wretched old Wheal Blair, the scene with
Trefyn would never have happened.

Or would it?

Perhaps so. Perhaps he'd never really cared for her
deeply at all. When she looked back she remembered
that as a child she'd always been the one to follow
him round, and pester him with questions and confidence. He'd seemed so wonderful—his way with horses

and wild things, and of luring baby foxes from their holes; his art of taming and calling birds, which he'd learned from his father, so that they flew at his whistle to perch on his hand. She couldn't remember a time when he'd not fascinated her. Maybe, though, she'd just been a nuisance and he'd not wanted to hurt her feelings.

But now she was grown up—surely that was different.

*He had cared for her last night. He had,* she persisted to herself. They'd discussed marriage. He'd suggested a license as soon as she liked. And then—what had happened? Just a few stupid words from her about that patch of land and he'd gone into a fury, saying cold hard things nasty enough to put any girl into a temper.

Especially after what had happened.

Especially that, she remembered in a confusion of love, longing, and shame because she could still want him so desperately—the burning touch of his hands and lips on her mouth, breasts, and thighs; the sweetness and excitement of their coming together. The first pain, followed by the glory. Yes, to her their mating had held both anguish and undescribable joy. But Trefyn? She could no longer clearly guess what he felt. Donna's words still rankled darkly at the back of her mind: "like any slut in the night . . ."

Her mother. Her own mother, to talk like that. She couldn't bear it. She knew in a sudden flash of decision that she had to get away, leave Polbreath until everything fell into better perspective and she could find proper values for herself. Once she'd made up her mind the prospect didn't appear too difficult. When Donna and Nicholas had left for the Courts that

evening she'd drive herself to Penzance, leave the
horse and gig with the groom at The Admiral, and
catch the night train up country. She'd leave the train
at Bristol and go straight to Clifton where a school
friend of hers, Leonora Marsh, lived with her family.
She'd put up there for the night and write a letter to
her parents confirming her whereabouts. Then after
posting it the next morning, she'd travel to London
and contact Ianthe. Ianthe had told her she'd be welcome at any time, and luckily Juliet had kept the Belgravia address safe. Of course she'd write a prelimi-
nary note to Nicholas—a sane, apparently well-
balanced explanation, informing him of her decision
to stay with Leonora for a time until her mother had
recovered her equilibrium, telling him also of the gig
and horse waiting for collection. The letter would be
left on the hall table.

If by any chance Nicholas and Donna used the gig
themselves for their visit to the Courts, there was always the governess's cart. But she thought that hardly
likely. Donna would wish to arrive by chaise, in style.
Why, Juliet had heard her only recently suggesting to
Nicholas that they should purchase one of the new
motorcars fashionable people were all having these
days. Nicholas had so far objected, saying he'd no liking for being stuck on hills in the wilds of Cornwall,
but knowing Donna, Juliet was sure that in the end
he'd give in.

However, whether they had a motorcar or not in
the future was really of no importance at that moment. What mattered was that Juliet's own plan was
workable, and when she reviewed it critically it did
seem remarkably simple with no complicating factor

likely to go wrong. Involvement with practical matters made her feel better. As she sorted out a few clothes to pack into a small valise, a dim hope flickered at the back of her mind that when he'd discovered she'd left, Trefyn might even miss her. She couldn't quite believe it, but it was the one straw she clung to, the one ray of light in her deep unhappiness, giving her the courage to go ahead.

At five o'clock there was a tap on the door, followed by Donna's cold voice saying sharply, "We're off in half an hour Juliet; the Courts want us there by six for drinks. I hope you're dressed and going to be sensible . . ."

There was a pause before Juliet answered with equal clarity, "I've told you already—lots of times. I'm not coming."

"You're a willful, stupid girl. If I had my way you'd be—"

"Well spanked and put to bed," Juliet interrupted, "Poor mama, what frustration for you. I'm not a child, remember. And please don't shout. *Please*—go away."

There was a drawn-out pause, followed by a click of heels and the sound of Donna's light feet receding down the corridor.

Nicholas tried a few minutes later. "Juliet—for my sake, be reasonable. If you don't come, your mother won't easily forgive you."

Juliet went close to the door. "I'm sorry. I meant what I said, father. You can easily tell them I've a headache. It's quite true. And I'm sure if you explain to Desmond, he'll understand. There'll probably be flowers in the morning."

He made no more attempt to persuade her, and

after half an hour Juliet heard the sound of wheels and the clippitty-clop of horses' hooves receding down the drive into the distance.

A little later, wearing a pale gray coat with a shoulder cape over a rose-colored summer dress, and a small flowery hat perched on her rust-colored, piled-up curls, Juliet went downstairs quietly, carrying her valise in one hand, her reticule and the note in the other. The note was simple. It read:

> Dear father,
>
> I am leaving on the night train for Bristol, where I shall be staying for a time with Leonora Marsh, my school friend who you have met several times. When I get there I shall write to you telling you of my safe arrival.
>
> At the moment I can't bear things at Polbreath. Mama is just too much for me—and her opinions are completely wrong. You can tell her that, and I only hope she believes you. If she doesn't, I can't help it.
>
> Don't worry, I shall be quite all right. The Marshes are dears. I will let you know when I'm returning.
>
> With love to you always,
> Juliet.
>
> P.S. The gig and mare are at The Admiral. Sorry to give you the trouble to collect.
> J.

Beth came out of the parlor carrying a glass bowl of flowers when Juliet reached the foot of the stairs. She paused, astonished to see the valise, and the girl she'd

known from babyhood obviously distressed and attired for a journey. As Juliet put the note on the hall
table, she said, with a touch of disapproval, "Miss Juliet, you're not going away surely? At this hour?"

"Oh, yes," Juliet replied calmly. "Perhaps you'd see
that Peters is informed, will you? I'd like the gig
brought round to the front."

Beth said nothing for a moment, then she asked,
"Does your mother know?"

Juliet's faint smile was icy. "I shouldn't think so, for
a moment; I've only just made up my mind. I've had
an invitation to visit a friend in Bristol, and I'm taking
the chance before there's any argument about it."

Beth's homely face was worried. "My dear . . .
something's upset you, I can see that. But leave things
till the morning—please *do*. It isn't right for a young
lady of your position to set off without a chaperone or
friend at this hour."

"I'm quite capable, thank you," Juliet retorted. "And
you needn't worry about the parents. I've left a note
on the table explaining everything. They'll quite understand."

Jason unexpectedly appeared from the library, looking casual and artistic in a brown velvet jacket, narrow striped trousers, with an overlarge, cream silk
bowtie at the neck. He had an amused smile on his
lips.

"Hullo, little sister," he said in his cultured drawl.
"What's this, a night flight? Fleeing the parental nest?
Good for you."

"It's no laughing matter, Mr. Jason," Beth said
coldly. "Miss Juliet's taken it into her head all of a
sudden to go to Bristol, and I'm trying to make her see
reason and wait till the morning."

"Bristol? Ah!" Jason stroked the tip of his fair beard that had started to grow again. "Now why Bristol? Let me think."

"I'm going to stay with Leonora," Juliet told him shortly.

"The Marsh girl?"

"Of course."

"Hm. I met her once, didn't I? She came here for the weekend. Rather an attractive little bit. Dark eyes and a bosom. Lautrecish! Think I'll come with you . . ."

"Oh, Jason, don't be ridiculous. And get out of my way if you don't mind; as Beth won't order the gig for me, I'll have to do it for myself."

She swept past them both, and rushed down the hall, followed a moment later by the housekeeper and the sound of her brother's laughter.

Five minutes later she was rattling down the drive in the gig toward the lane. When she'd turned the corner leading cross-country through the hills to Penzance, she flicked the horse to a smart canter, only slackening speed at the steep, upward climb overlooking St. Figgans. The rain has stopped, but the countryside was gray in the fading evening light. The hill overlooking Trefyn's farm was barely visible in the distance, and she kept her eyes resolutely from the blurred outline, telling herself she must not think back or picture their happiest moments together. The quarrel had been Trefyn's fault. She was not his servant to be ordered about and made to fit in with his unbearable bossy moods. His behavior following their love-making had been not only hurtful but an insult. If ever they came together again—and surely they must some time—it was he who'd have to do the pleading.

The new wave of anger and indignation invigorated

her, and when she reached Penzance one part of her was almost enjoying the prospect of the adventure ahead.

She stabled the horse and gig at The Admiral, and wanting to stretch her legs after the day's confinement in her room, insisted on walking to the station, allowing the hostler's boy to carry her valise.

When she'd paid him, and arranged with a porter to secure a first-class carriage for her, she seated herself on the platform to wait, hoping the train would not be late. During the ten minutes she had to spare, she sat very erectly, keeping her eyes stoically and unswervingly ahead. In spite of this, she was aware of male eyes turned intermittently upon her, of interested glances, and whispered comments between two matrons who were obviously puzzled and a little shocked to see a young lady of Juliet's type traveling at night alone.

She could imagine their veiled remarks: "An elopement, do you think?" Or possibly, "My dear, she looks familiar. Isn't it Mr. Trevarvas's daughter? *Squire* Trevarvas of Polbreath?" Oh yes, she could easily be recognized; Juliet was well aware that many people unknown to her knew her by sight, and would relish any piece of news worth gossiping about. What did it matter? It didn't affect her in the slightest and would only annoy Donna, who was so set on delivering up a chaste and highly desirable bride to Desmond Court like a lamb to the slaughter.

Poor Desmond.

For a moment Juliet was almost sorry for him until she thought upon how easy it would be for him to find a wife elsewhere. She had no illusions about his lighthearted character. He had good looks and impeccable manners when it suited him. But one pretty filly with breeding would probably suit him as much as any other, and a spell in London or Ireland would be sure to provide a wife equally, perhaps more suitable, to Court requirements than herself.

The train pulled along the platform at last. The porter appeared magically, as if from nowhere with her valise and bag, and a minute later Juliet was ensconced comfortably in her luxurious compartment, with no one to invade her privacy and the prospect ahead of being able to relax for a few hours and recover her composure properly before arriving at Bristol. As the train started off it occurred to her for the first time that Leonora—or the whole Marsh family— might be away on holiday somewhere. In that case what would she do? Write a note from there to her parents, post it, and then continue as soon as possible to London? Or book in at a hotel somewhere?

In the end she decided to put the problem aside until she knew whether or not there was one.

It was quite late and completely dark when the train drew in at Bristol, and Juliet momentarily doubted whether she should inflict herself on her friend at such a late hour. But she needn't have worried. When she reached the Clifton house by cab, most of the lights were on, and she found to her relief that the family was engrossed with friends in a late session of bridge.

Leonora, who found the game extremely boring, was delighted to see her, and for the chance to escape the weekly ritual. She was a bouncy girl of plump proportion with thick yellow hair, a fresh complexion, and sparkling eyes.

"But you must stay longer than one night," she exclaimed, "That's stupid; I've such a lot to tell you. And on Sunday Wilfred's coming. You haven't met Wilfred have you? He's a pet—you'll like him. We're secretly engaged, but of course the parents don't know because he's not quite . . . well, you know . . . 'top drawer.'" She laughed. "As if that mattered; crazy, isn't it? In the twentieth century. And anyway, he's got brains—he invents things, gadgets for motorcars. Imagine it!" she broke off suddenly exclaiming, "But you're tired. Have you had anything to eat?"

"Not for ages," Juliet told her.

"Why?"

Juliet explained about the quarrel with Nicholas and Donna, giving no details.

"Good heavens! You mean you're running away?"

"Only for a bit. I've left a note saying I was coming to you. I hope that's all right?"

"Of *course* it is. If you like, I'll drop them a line telling them you're staying for a month."

"Just one night," Juliet said firmly. "I've made plans, you see. I can't break them."

"Why?"

Deciding it was best not to mention Ianthe just in case Nicholas or Donna came rushing up to Clifton, Juliet replied, "Oh . . . friends. You don't know them. I shall write to father tomorrow myself, of course, and post it from here, so please, Leonora, keep out of things."

"Very well, just as you say." Leonora sighed, adding, "Is there a man concerned? Oh, you needn't answer. It's quite obvious. What's he like? Tall, dark and handsome or fair and forty? Young or old? Rich or poor . . . ?"

She paused, noting a fleeting look of pain and long-ing cross Juliet's face.

"I'm sorry, Juliet, I don't want to pry. And you're hungry; you must be, after only biscuits all day. Come up to your room; Dolly must have got it ready by now, and I'll order a tray for you. Then we can have a real powwow in the morning."

The powwow, however, was short. After a long night's sleep and a good breakfast, Juliet discovered a train for London was due to leave Bristol in an hour's time, during which there was the note to write and post to Nicholas, and the Marsh carriage and horses to be harnessed for her journey to the main station. Leo-nora insisted on accompanying her friend, and when all the good-byes and thank-yous to John Marsh and his wife Mary were politely concluded, there was no time left for private conversation between the two friends.

They'd been on the platform for only five minutes when the train puffed into view, causing a hum of activity: bustling figures and porters carrying bags, whistling and shouting and last minute dives for pa-pers from the nearby stall. When Juliet was safely seated in the corner of a first-class carriage, with her valise on the rack above her, doors were already being slammed, and the guard walking sharply up and down the platform with his red flag and whistle ready. The window was blurred with steam and early fog, and Leonora's face had become a mere pale disc as the engine, with a rumble of wheels, of puffing and chug-ging, to the accompaniment of shrill whistling and hu-man voices, started off, gathering speed until the sta-tion was left behind, and Leonora's figure with its waving arm and white handkerchief was taken into the gray distance and finally lost.

Juliet sat back, trying to focus her attention on the pages of *The Lady Magazine* that Leonora had thrust into her hand through the carriage window. But she found concentration difficult. She could not help being aware of a male passenger's eyes frequently turned in her direction from the opposite corner. He'd got into the train at the last minute and was obviously interested in her, glancing discomfortingly over his newspaper every time she moved or looked up. He was middle-aged, large, wearing formal morning dress under a dark cloth overcoat, and had a broad pale face with small eyes under bushy brows, and an extremely thick moustache waxed to upturned points. Seeing her, he had taken off his top hat and laid it on the seat beside him. Diamonds glittered from his cuffs and tie pin. His whole appearance was ostentatious and a little vulgar, Juliet thought, and in a vague way faintly familiar. She searched back through her mind, trying to place him, but it was no use. Probably she'd seen someone like him in a photograph and was merely being overimaginative, she decided at last. The strangeness and excitement of the journey on top of her flight from Polbreath were enough to give any girl queer ideas. She couldn't possibly ever have met this man.

But she was wrong.

After about an hour he spoke.

"Tell me," he said, "and please excuse, *pardonnez-moi,* mademoiselle if I intrude. Have we not met? Yes?"

Ah. So he was French. That explained it—the lascivious eye, the polite but contrived approach, the air of subtle discriminating desire.

"I don't think so," she answered coldly. "You must be mistaken."

"Perhaps, yes," he agreed. "I thought at first—again my apologies—I thought, surely this young lady, this veree attractive young lady, if I may say so, is the daughter of my veree good friend Nicholas."

Nicholas? Juliet started visibly.

"I surprise you? It was, of course, some time ago. A year? maybe a little less, when I was entertained by a most charming host and hostess, Madame and Monsieur Trevarvas, at their country Cornish home, Polbreath. Their daughter, so like yourself, was at home from college, or as you put it—finishing school?"

Juliet flushed.

How stupid of her not to have remembered.

"I . . . I . . ." she fumbled for words for a moment, then said in a rush. "I'm sorry. I had forgotten."

"Ah, well, no matter. Why should you remember? A formal introduction to a dry-as-dust—is that not how you English put it?—business acquaintance? A meeting that is gone like a puff of wind and forgotten—or shall we say—just ships that pass in the night?"

Juliet forced a smile. She turned her head watching mechanically the passing vista of countryside—trees, fields, distant hills, and hamlets under the lifting veil of morning mist.

"Perhaps we shall meet again one day at Polbreath," she remarked politely.

"I hope so. Indeed I do, mademoiselle," the suave voice replied. And then came the inevitable question, "May I ask if you are traveling far today?"

Realizing her unwelcome companion was probably

going to London himself and would find out in any case, she answered shortly, "I'm visiting friends in town. I've been staying in Bristol for a short time at Clifton. I have a school friend there."

"Clifton! Ah! I know that too," the Frenchman said.

He would, Juliet thought.

There was a short silence, then he said, "You may think me overcurious, but I have a penchant for—or rather a sense of adventure in me that tells me this journey is veree important to you. Yes? A little romance perhaps?" The immense waxed bristles turned upward, revealing a shining row of very white teeth.

Juliet turned again to face him sharply. "Certainly not. I shall spend a few days with my . . . my friends, shopping and seeing the sights, then I shall return. But I don't really understand why you're so interested Mr. . . . Monsieur . . . ?" Her voice died into a question.

He took a card from his pocket and handed it to her with an extravagant bow of his head. "Martellon," he murmured, "Louis Martellon."

She thought back again but couldn't recall the name.

"Thank you," she said. "I shall be able to tell my father when I get home about meeting you. He'll be interested, I know."

"He is a veree *good* friend of mine, as I said, Miss Trevarvas, we have many interests in common. Shipping in particular. So you can hardly blame me for enjoying so much making the acquaintance of his so veree lovely daughter."

Juliet felt herself growing rosy from annoyance and embarrassment. She found the conversation not only boring but exhausting. All she wanted just then was to

relax and prepare herself for the meeting ahead with
Ianthe. It was a strain having to sit so erectly, answering ambiguously and with such care in case she gave
anything away. For all she knew the odious Louis
Martellon might have an appointment planned with
Nicholas in the near future, in which case her name
would obviously be brought up, and her father would
know her visit to Leonora had been mostly bluff.

There'd be a scene, naturally, if he located her at
Ianthe's. But then there'd be a scene in any case. Until
this unfortunate, unexpected interlude with Louis
Martellon she hadn't viewed the future at all clearly.
Her one objective had been to escape from endless
emotional arguments and complications, and especially from Trefyn.

Trefyn.

Her heart ached with sudden, almost unbearable,
distress when she thought of him.

"Excuse me," she said, going toward the corridor,
"it's very stuffy in here. I must have some air."

The Frenchman got up with surprising speed for a
man of his portly proportions. "Allow me, mademoiselle," he said, opening the door. "Can I assist you in
any way? You are not ill I hope?"

His voice oozed sweetness and sympathy, but his
small, lecherous eyes were appraisingly upon her
rounded breasts and slender thighs under the gray
cape. Just as though he was imagining her without her
clothes, she thought with a stab of annoyance.

"I'm quite all right," she answered, passing by him
with her head lifted an inch or two higher and one
hand drawing the cape more closely about her.

She walked sharply down the corridor to the Ladies' Toilette, locked the door firmly, took off her hat,

smoothed her hair; then she had a wash and took a
clean towel which she dampened and held to her tired
eyes with refreshing coolness. In the reticule she
found a bottle of eau de cologne and sprinkled a liberal portion on her handkerchief, applying a few
drops behind her ears. Her reflection from the mirror was comforting, giving her assurance and a sense
of sophistication. She lingered as long as was discreetly tactful in the closeted interior, which had a
luxurious air about it with its basins glittering and
spotlessly clean, and shining taps. The color scheme,
like the carriages, was of gilt and crimson, evocative
of the late-Victorian period which had given birth to
the great steam age of the railways. When she returned to the compartment she stood for a few minutes in the corridor, staring out of the window, then
resigned herself to a further inevitable session in the
company of Louis Martellon. Luckily the train became quite crowded at Exeter, and a third passenger
was ushered in, a fussy, stout, elderly woman with numerous small cases and bags handed in by a porter
and a chauffeur. She was dressed in lavender and
gray, carried a jeweled, silver-chain handbag, and
wore a large wide-brimmed gauzy hat crowned with
flowers and feathers. She appeared petulant, overbearing, and very, very rich. As soon as she was
seated in the corner, facing the Frenchman, she made
it obvious she wanted his place, complaining that she
could not be comfortable with her back to the engine.

She was about to command the chauffeur to find
her another compartment when Monsieur Martellon
got up with a stream of assurances and overpolite gestures, offering his own corner seat.

The lady, who was already pink with rouge, grew

pinker and succumbed readily to his flattery. As she rustled her skirts, the air became heady with perfume. Juliet, who ordinarily would have found her presence distasteful, was relieved. Obviously her father's ebullient business acquaintance would be occupied from that point in furthering his chance encounter with the stranger, especially following her man servant's retreat with a very respectful touch of his cap and the magical appendage of "Milady" before he closed the door.

The train started up again; presently the outskirts of the town were left behind, and Juliet was freed for the time being from male attention. Louis Martellon was so concerned with playing the gallant to her ladyship it seemed very unlikely he'd have time for pressing conversation upon the chilly and unreciprocative daughter of Nicholas Trevarvas.

Her estimation was correct; and when the train at last drew in at London it was comparatively easy for Juliet to step out unobtrusively, find a porter to collect her valise, and hire a cab, leaving Monsieur Martellon fully engaged with their domineering fellow passenger.

It was already late afternoon, quickly fading to a misty summer dusk, as the cab made its way through a threadwork of streets and main thoroughways toward Belgravia. Buildings, rooftops, towers, and chimney pots became blurred into uniformity, clarified only at intervals, when the fog thinned into vague shapes of quivering gray. When at length the driver located the Wycksley mansion, odd lights were already twinkling through the thickening foggy air.

"It'll be a pea-souper in the city later," the man said as he assisted Juliet from the vehicle. "These warm summer nights can be difficult for traffic after the damp we've had here lately." He paused, then enquired, "Well, ma'am, this is where you want, is it, Number 10?"

Juliet looked round at the large building confronting her. It was impossible in the poor light to define its period, but there were steps in front leading between railings to a wide, porched front door, probably early Georgian. The exterior was square and wide-fronted, giving the impression of balconies above. Light streamed fitfully from squares of windows, and the dark shadowed trunks of trees reached and disappeared into the damp evening sky. As the man escorted her to the door, Juliet had a sudden inexplicable fit of nerves. Supposing Ianthe didn't want her? Supposing this was the wrong house and she hadn't read the address properly?

"Just wait a moment," she said, fumbling in her reticule for the card and money to pay him. "Yes . . . I think so . . ." She moved into a beam of uncertain light and studied the number, peering closely. "It's all right," she told the cabby. "Thank you. Just put the bag down. How much do I owe you?"

He told her; she counted the fare and, after pulling the bell, handed it to him. He touched his cap and was moving away when the door opened, revealing a man servant impeccably attired in a butler's formal dress.

"Yes, madam? Miss?" He inquired unblinkingly.

"Is this Mrs. Wycksley's house?" Juliet asked as aloofly as possible, thinking his face looked rather like a flat slab of cheese, "I'm—"

"It is Mr. *Robertson* Wycksley's residence, madam," the man interrupted before she could finish. "Are you expected, may I inquire?"

"No, but I'd be obliged if you'd inform your mistress, Mrs. Wycksley, that her sister, Miss Trevarvas, Miss Juliet Trevarvas, has arrived," Juliet told him coldly.

"Oh." The man appeared momentarily taken aback, then said, still in the flat formal voice and with the deadpan expression on his face, "Please come in, madam. I'll inform Mrs. Wycksley." He picked up her valise and stood waiting for her to pass.

She entered. He indicated a rather ornate chair of no particular style or period and walked majestically down the wide hall, disappearing round a corner.

Juliet sat down and glanced round. The floor was ornately tiled and partially covered with luxurious Persian rugs. Pieces of marble sculpture were displayed at intervals. There was a good deal of lacquer and brass about, intricately carved pieces of furniture evocative of the East, and crystal lighting giving an air of conscious splendor to the interior. Great wealth was obvious. The Chinese influence of the past decade was apparent, combined with a striving also for the Gothic. The windows at the side were Gothic, and arches of the same style had been artificially contrived at the end of the main hall to give a hint of opulent mystery beyond. Although nothing was in harmony or complete good taste, the general effect was certainly theatrical, and Juliet could easily imagine Ianthe sauntering picturesquely from room to room, a cigarette poised from her painted lips, draperies trailing.

A moment after the butler had disappeared—or rather, faded away discreetly to the back quarters—Ianthe herself came through a door halfway down the passage. She was wearing an extremely low-cut,

tightly busted dress in green silk, slit up one side, revealing an orange underskirt. Her dark hair was swept
upward from the back in a roll to the front of her
forehead, where it was caught by a velvet bow and
jeweled pin. A diamond brooch glittered near her left
shoulder; a gigantic flimsy tulle flower was caught at
her waist. She wore makeup, but not so heavy as to
mar her natural beauty, and two rolls of shining pearls
fell from the bare neck and shoulders to her knees. In
one hand was a fan.

Seeing her sister, she looked at first too astonished
to speak. Then she exclaimed, "Juliet! What on earth
does this mean? When Barnes gave your name I
thought someone was playing a joke. My dear girl,
you look—" she broke off helplessly.

"I expect I look a mess," Juliet interrupted, "I feel a
bit of one. I'm tired. But you did tell me to call if ever
I felt like it. And—"

"Of course." Ianthe looked round perplexed and a
little discomforted. "I didn't quite expect you to appear like a bolt from the blue," she added in explanation. "Naturally I'm glad to see you. It just happens
there was no rehearsal this afternoon and I'm having a
little soirée. One or two friends of mine . . ." she concluded vaguely.

Juliet's heart sank. She felt suddenly unwanted. "I'm
sorry. I shouldn't have come—"

"Oh, nonsense." Ianthe pulled herself together. "You
can stay as long as you like. We have plenty of rooms
ready for unexpected visitors, and I know Robertson
will be delighted." The acid sarcasm in her voice was
unmistakable. "All the same, sister dear, I *would* like
to know a little of what this is all about before I go
back to my friends. And I shan't have any time with

you tonight, you know—I've a performance at eight-thirty—"

"It doesn't matter," Juliet said, wanting nothing so much then as to be able to slump on a bed and relax. "I've quarreled with . . . with mama, that's all."

"Ah! I can well understand that. I think most people with any spirit would quarrel with your precious mama eventually. What was it? . . . a love affair?"

Juliet's face betrayed her without the necessity for speech.

"Good for you," Ianthe continued. "I'm surprised you've stuck it for so long. It must be hell for papa."

Juliet's sense of loyalty impelled her to say, "He loves her. They're happy. But they don't seem to understand that anyone else could feel the same way."

"Well . . ." Ianthe touched her shoulder lightly. "We'll talk about things in the morning. In the meantime, darling, Clariss, my maid, will see you comfortably to your room. It's a nice one, overlooking the square, and someone will bring a tray up to you. All right?"

Juliet nodded and replied in a small voice, "Thank you."

Five minutes later Clariss, a pert yet polite maid in black silk and white frilled apron and cap, was unpacking Juliet's few clothes and laying them very carefully in drawers of the elegant rosewood dressing table or on hangers in the wardrobe. In spite of her tiredness, Juliet was aware of the richness of the interior: the pink satin brocade curtains, genuine Venetian lace bedspread over pink silk, and the luxurious thick carpet. Light quivered from crystal chandeliers round the room. The wallpaper was pink striped, Regency style. There was a dressing room and an attached bathroom. Nothing could have been more alluring to tired nerves. Polbreath was ordinary in comparison.

When the maid had gone, Juliet spent some time undressing, washing, and getting ready for bed. From the hall below, muted conversation and laughter occasionally drifted up to the bedroom. She wondered vaguely about Ianthe's soirée and what type of guests she was entertaining. The voices sounded male, but of course from such a distance it was hard to judge.

A little later a tasteful meal was sent up to the bedroom on a tray. Juliet, who'd thought she could not eat, found suddenly she was ravenously hungry. When little was left of the food and the tray had been taken away, she lay for a short time with the bedside light on, reveling luxuriously in the comfort, quite content to forget for the time being the problems and unhappiness of the previous day. Then, forgetting to put the lights off, she gradually slipped into a doze.

She was roused to sudden consciousness by a sharp tap on the door.

She sat up startled.

A wide, bland, male face poked itself round the door—elderly and lascivious, with sideburns; shrewd, slightly bulging pale eyes; and a tight, button mouth above the double chin and heavy jowls. A podgy hand was visible round the door, displaying a number of rings. Juliet clutched her nightdress tightly across her breasts, but the unwelcome stranger did not attempt to enter.

"You're my wife's sister, I presume," he said in even tones. "Welcome, my dear. I hope you sleep well. I'm very pleased indeed to know we shall have your company for a time, and only sorry we have not met before. My name, of course, is Robertson. Robertson Wycksley."

The manner was polite, the voice smooth, but Juliet was discomforted by the personal appraising glint in his eyes. "I . . . I'm pleased to meet you too," she said, not strictly truthfully. "Ianthe's told me about you, of course."

"Ah, well, I hope she spoke well of me," he said with a hint of tartness. "But I won't worry you any further. Tomorrow we must have a nice chat. If you're interested in the theater, by any chance . . ." he paused questioningly "we shall have much in common. I'll say good night now."

"Good night," Juliet replied automatically. The next moment the door had closed softly, followed by the receding tread of footsteps down the landing.

She waited a few minutes, then got up and turned the key in the lock.

So it was that her first introduction to the Wycksley household began.

Juliet had already had breakfast in her room, dressed, and gone downstairs before Ianthe appeared the following morning.

"Oh, there you are!" she said petulantly after a series of yawns. "What on earth are you doing in the conservatory?"

Juliet turned. The conservatory led from the vast drawing room where she'd been idling time away for the past half hour. It had an outer door leading into a terraced garden, and Juliet had been on the point of strolling into the fresh air as her sister came in.

"I was wondering where to go and what to do," she said frankly.

Ianthe rubbed her eyes. Juliet noticed they had dark rings underneath and that with her hair falling untidily about her face she looked considerably older and not half so beautiful. "I'm afraid you'll have to amuse yourself a good deal while you're here," she told Juliet, "unless of course Robertson takes a fancy to you, which he probably will. He likes women young and fresh, although heaven knows he hasn't a thing to give but his filthy lucre. Perhaps that's the challenge—for him, I mean." She eyed her sister with sinister speculation. "But you're not like that, are you, darling? Not yet ripe prey for a worn-out rake?"

Juliet stared distastefully at Ianthe whose figure, in the light of day, appeared less slender and elegant under the diaphanous wrap than in the sophisticated clothes she'd worn at Polbreath. She had a sudden restless urge to be away from the overheated rich interior and to go into the cool morning where she could explore the vicinity on her own, take a stroll round the elegant square glimpsed from her bedroom, and somehow get her thoughts into order so she could decide what to do. Coming to Ianthe had seemed such a bright idea following her quarrel with Trefyn and her parents, and now that she was here it would be undignified to rush immediately back to Cornwall. But she knew she couldn't face a prolonged period at No. 10. She didn't trust Wycksley, and Ianthe had already implied she was in the way.

She waited irresolutely as Ianthe went to a cupboard, took out a decanter and glass, and poured herself a drink.

"Want one?" Ianthe asked before lifting it to her lips.

"No thanks. Isn't it rather early?"

"Damned early," Ianthe said, holding the glass before her for a second, "but who cares? To you, darling, and remember" she paused.

"Yes?"

"I'm not half so bad as I seem. The play's ending this week, you know, and the mere thought of a last night gives me the jitters. Do you know why? Because I wonder each time if there'll ever be another beginning. And that's why I envy you. You're so young. Still, let's not compare. Comparisons can be so odious. And anyway, why are we standing here? Come into the breakfast room and watch me peck at food. Whoever sent you to the drawing room?"

"No one. I was just wandering round."

"Very dangerous when Robertson's on the prowl."

"Oh, Ianthe, don't be silly."

"My dear child, I'm not. He's a real old wolf, in his own particular way. Oh dear!" she made a moue, "you *do* disapprove, don't you?"

Juliet didn't reply.

Fortified by the drink, Ianthe took Juliet's arm and steered her to the door. "Try and cheer up, pet," she said. "In about an hour I'll be in fine form. Acting's an exhausting business anyway, you know, especially when you've to fight so hard to keep your place. If it wasn't for my husband, I'd have been out on my ear long ago. Did you know that?"

Juliet shook her head. "Of course not. How should I?"

"Exactly. You see, I'm not sure you know the first thing about what you've run into," Ianthe said more gently, ushering her sister down the hall into a cosier, smaller interior. "It's just one long strain when you've nothing but your looks to rely on. You see, I've no particular talent, no strong dramatic sense . . . I'm just a kind of puppet, willing to be used in any way Robertson thinks fit. . . ." She paused, going to a sideboard where breakfast dishes were still warm. "Sit down, Juliet, and listen to me." She buttered a piece of toast, poured a strong cup of coffee, and drew a chair up to an inlaid fireside table. "Here—" she insisted, indicating a low-backed chair opposite. Juliet obeyed automatically.

"I can quite understand why you ran away from home," Ianthe continued, "and I'm not trying to get rid of you. But life here's no good for a young girl, and I mean it. Oh, it's all right for me, I'm not young anymore—and I chose it. But I wouldn't again, not if I was your age. I'd—"

"Yes?"

"I'd damn well stay at Polbreath, or go back as soon as decently possible and fight your overbearing mama, Donna Penroze. She *caught* our father, you know, or didn't you? She set out deliberately to get him and was so clever and sly about it she succeeded in the end. I loved him so much, Juliet, I think he's been the only person I really ever *have* loved, properly. But after *she* came everything was different. I was just a very poor second. You may think I sound possessive and mean, but that's how it was, and how I'm made."

"What about your . . . about Robertson?" Juliet asked awkwardly. "Didn't you mind about him at all?"

"Not a fig," Ianthe answered ruthlessly. "He was just a means to an end, a kind of revenge, if you like. So you can't exactly expect us to be good mates, can you? Oh, I've not been without a little lovenest occasionally, as I'm sure you must have heard. But a lover or two—when you've had one you've had the rest, although each time you go on again, hoping it'll be different from then on. It never is though. Now after this little homily, it's your turn. Tell me about the rest."

"What rest?"

"Oh, darling, it wasn't only Donna who drove you to your wicked sister's arms. The man? the wonderful gallant who so ungallantly let you down. Who is he?"

Juliet flushed. "He did not let me down, and he isn't ungallant. His name's Trefyn. Trefyn Connor. And it's all . . . well, a kind of misunderstanding."

Ianthe stared, and after an astonished pause said, "Do you mean that Gypsy family? The Connors near Polbreath—the Gentry woman's son?"

"Yes. He's not a Gypsy though," Juliet asserted. "He's . . . he's quite unusual."

"Then why on earth are you here?"

"It doesn't matter." Juliet answered. "I don't want to talk about it, and I'm not going back. So please stop asking questions, Ianthe. Do you mind?"

"Yes. I mind very much. I feel like a bit of gossip. However, we'll leave it for the moment." She poured herself a second cup of coffee. "Want one?"

"No, thank you."

Just then Wycksley came into the room.

In the morning light he did not look so raffish or dissolute as on the previous evening. He was wearing a black velvet smoking jacket with a cream silk shirt and black bow tie. His trousers were narrow-cut pin-stripe, and in his coat lapel was a white carnation. The expanse of jowls and double chin were offset by his general air of urbanity and elderly savoir-faire.

"Good morning, my dears," he said with a chilly glance towards Ianthe. "How pleasant to find two young women conversing pleasantly in the early hours." He took a hunter watch from his breast pocket. "But it isn't so early after all, is it? I'm sure your charming sister would appreciate it if you dressed properly and took her round the garden of our limited domain, Ianthe."

"Oh, no, Mr. Wycksley," Juliet said quickly. "I'm quite able to look after myself—" she broke off, realizing how formal she sounded.

"*Mister?* Now, now, what a way to talk. I'm your brother-in-law, remember, and who knows, I may have a little plan for you up my sleeve?"

"Plan?" Juliet stared at him puzzled as Ianthe looked contemptuously away.

"Certainly. I can pull strings, young lady. I'm a man of many parts, you know, and may be prepared—just *may* be, remember—to give you a very promising debut into a stage career. . . ." His voice faded suggestively. Juliet's cheeks glowed.

"Don't be ridiculous, Robertson," Ianthe exclaimed rashly, "Juliet's not interested in acting. It's unfair to—"

"Oh, but I am," Juliet contradicted quickly. "I always have been—"

"Ha! So you see, madam," Wycksley said with his pale eyes protruding more than usual, "it would be better if you held your tongue and allowed Juliet to speak for herself. It just happens that I'm toying with the idea of financing a new play—dramatic romance, laced with titivating comedy, that would possibly provide quite a choice little part for your sister. Not a leading role, of course," he added, smiling genially at Juliet, "but a very helpful stepping-off part, something most young women would give their eyes for. So think about it in the meantime. I shall do the same, and when I've reached a firm conclusion we'll go into things properly."

"Thank you," Juliet murmured.

"Robertson," he reminded her.

"Robertson," Juliet echoed.

"I may not see either of you until this evening," he said, before leaving the room. "I shall be at the theater tonight Ianthe, so have your wits about you, and don't make farce of that little scene with Vincent in the third act, or you'll have no chance of acting opposite him again—or anyone else—with my approval in any of my productions."

The door clicked sharply. Ianthe turned in a whirl of fury to face Juliet. "You little idiot," she said, "now see what you've done. Making me quarrel with Wycksley at this moment of all times when I was doing my best to get back into favor. That ridiculous blurb about 'stage debut'—and you falling for it. Don't you realize he tries it on with every attractive woman he meets, if she's young and naïve enough? I'd already warned you beforehand. Well, hadn't I? *Hadn't* I?" Her voice was shrill, two bright spots of color burned on her cheeks.

"I don't think you'd mentioned anything about me acting," Juliet said. "And anyway, I can't see what's so wrong. You don't know me so very well, do you? You've no idea what I'm really like, what I'm good at, or what I want to do with my life—except marry Trefyn, of course. I did tell you about him. But it may never happen. And if Robertson gives me the chance of—of going on the stage—well, why not?" She lifted her chin defiantly. Her clear eyes were so full of life and light and fire Ianthe was momentarily silenced. Her young sister was certainly a beauty, she thought grudgingly, and was depressingly aware at the same moment of her own gradually fading looks.

"Oh, well," she said relapsing into sullen quietness, "if you're determined to walk straight into the lion's jaws, that's your own affair I suppose—" She took a cigarette, placed it in her longer holder, and puffed ostentatiously before adding, "I'm not at all sure I oughtn't to write to papa and tell him what's going on."

"Don't you dare, Ianthe," Juliet exclaimed. "If you do, I shall simply run off somewhere else and leave you to deal with things—mama as well."

"You're a sly puss, aren't you, darling?" Ianthe said calmly. "Threatening me with Donna Penroze. I'd as soon invite a snake into my house, which you very well know."

"You exaggerate," Juliet said. "She's not as bad as that. She *is* my mother after all. I don't think you ought to say such things."

"Oh, dear. I'm so sorry. Now—" Ianthe's voice changed from mockery to quick impatience. "For heaven's sake, stop arguing, Juliet. You bore me. I have to be placid and get my face and nerves into order for tonight, on top of which there's a short rehearsal this afternoon. Wycksley's on the warpath, and you're in my hair! So do you mind leaving me now. Go! Quick—vamoose."

Juliet opened her mouth to speak, then changed her mind and shut it again.

She spent the morning idling about the immediate locality, finding a certain glamour in that area of imposing residences and garden squares so graciously laid out for those of quality to enjoy. The early mist remained all day, giving the strange impression of

moving in another world, another sphere of existence.
Everything seemed slightly insubstantial—even the
horse's hooves and passing vehicles had a muted
sound, and though London's busy thoroughfares were
only a short distance away, the quietness round No. 10
was strange, as though silence had been specially contrived for those rich enough to pay for peace.

At moments Juliet's thoughts turned to Cornwall,
and she wondered with a sudden short shock what she
was doing in London by herself when her family and
Trefyn were so far away. Ianthe, though her sister,
was a stranger; and although she might be trying in
her own way to make Juliet feel at home, it was obvious she didn't really want her. Robertson had been
more genuinely welcoming than his wife, but of
course he liked young girls—or so Ianthe had told her.
But then, Ianthe might just be being nasty. Perhaps
she was jealous.

Once the idea took hold of her, Juliet could not
shake it off. She didn't want unpleasantness with her
sister, but the thrill of ambition, of feeling she might
be considered Ianthe's rival, stimulated her. It would
be so wonderful to make a triumphant bow over the
footlights—to have an audience acclaiming and applauding her, to be toasted as famous actresses had
been in the past, and perhaps even have King Edward
himself admiring her from his box. A stage career was
not considered disgraceful anymore. Many actresses
had married into the peerage and become titled ladies
and the wives and mothers of dukes. It must be wildly
exciting, she thought, to have noblemen drinking
champagne out of one's slipper and being met at the
stage door every night by a number of would-be lov-

ers carrying huge bouquets of flowers. The idea, of course, was unlikely in her case, but just possible. Robertson had obviously sensed she might have talent, and if it turned out to be true . . . Her heart quickened at the thought.

It would mean so much to her—not just the fame and the fact of being able to prove to Donna and Nicholas, especially her mother, that she had a mind and personality of her own, but because of Trefyn. Once he knew she could make her own way and become famous in her own right, he'd surely try and make up to her for that awful quarrel and the unhappiness he'd caused her. He wouldn't want her to scrub floors and churn butter and be just a "yes, Trefyn, no, Trefyn" kind of woman. When he recognized she was unique, he'd be willing to make friends with her family, sell that stuffy bit of land to William, and they'd have a nice home with all the things she'd been brought up to expect.

This was all she wanted really—just to marry Trefyn. Maybe, she thought with an unexpected hint of mischief, she'd do a spot of flirting first—lure on a gallant or two a little, allowing them to kiss a hand or her earlobe. Without meaning to, a giggle escaped her. The idea of kissing an earlobe was so ridiculous.

Then, just as quickly, all humor suddenly vanished. Probably the whole thing was just wishful thinking anyway, and even if it wasn't, nothing would really matter without Trefyn. He might not approve of actresses. He might not miss her sufficiently even to know she'd left Polbreath. Any sneaking idea she had that he'd come rushing to London to find her was probably just a stupid dream.

The thought was so depressing she pushed all memories of Cornwall to the back of her mind and made her way back to No. 10.

Ianthe was out when she went into the house, but Wycksley wasn't.

"My dear young lady," he exclaimed as she entered the hall, "I've been waiting for you—"

"But I thought you said—" Juliet interrupted.

"—you wouldn't see me till evening; so I did, so I did, my dear," the suave voice continued. "But things have changed since breakfast time, and I have a very interesting proposition to put to you." His small mouth was stretched into an ingratiating smile, his pale eyes bulged with anticipatory appreciation. Juliet felt the back of her neck grow damp. "So come into the library, dear," he said, reminding Juliet of the nursery rhyme, "Won't you walk into my parlor, said the spider to the fly." "We can chat better there."

For a moment she hesitated as he continued, "You're not nervous are you? I can assure you you've no need to be. I'm only thinking of your own prospects—and the chance of a lifetime that would make most young ladies jump for joy."

With a quickening heart, Juliet forced a mechanical smile to her lips; then with Robertson Wycksley's hand on her arm, she allowed herself to be ushered to the room.

## 8

When Nicholas and Donna returned from the Courts and found Juliet's note, Nicholas's first instinct was to rush to Bristol and fetch her back. "The little madam," he said explosively, "putting on a headache when all the time she had a carefully worked-out little plot in her head to do a night-flit. I could—"

"I know you could, so could I." Donna agreed grimly. "But leave her a bit. She just wants to cause a scene and have you run after her making a fuss. Anyway, if she's gone to the Marshes she'll be all right. They're a nice family. And to tell you the truth, to have her off my hands for a bit will be a rest. She is *tiring* Nicholas."

Nicholas regarded his wife broodingly for a few moments.

"Very well," he agreed reluctantly. "But if I don't hear from her in a few days I shall make it my business to take a trip up."

Two days later the letter arrived, in which Juliet

apologized briefly for having left so suddenly. The Marshes were all well she wrote, and Leonora was delighted to see her. She'd let them know when she was returning, and would they please tell Andrew to think well about what they had been talking about and not do anything *she* wouldn't.

"Now what does she mean by that?" Donna asked suspiciously.

Nicholas shook his head. "I haven't an inkling. But Andrew's been in a peculiar mood lately. Doesn't talk much. No contact between us. The Mary Polgrove business has worried him. But it's more than that."

"Yes, I know." A worried frown creased Donna's brow.

"Do you think it's anything to do with that Trefyn Connor? Juliet and Andrew were always close. He may be on her side."

"Oh, I don't think Trefyn has anything to do with it," Nicholas answered, "not where Andrew's concerned. But I'd like to know something of what's been happening with Juliet and him."

"You don't think there's anything *really* wrong. That we should know about?"

"If there was she'd hardly say." Nicholas said wryly. "Juliet's as reckless as her mother in some ways, and quite capable of going her own wild way. All the same I think I'll take a walk down to the Connors this morning. It's time young Trefyn and I had a talk. I'm not going to have him upsetting my daughter to this extent for nothing. He'll either give me a satisfactory explanation or I'll know the reason why."

"Be careful, Nicholas," Donna told him, with the color bright in her cheeks. "He's clever, you know, and cunning like his father. He won't admit anything, and it would be undignified to lose your temper. Why don't you just ignore his existence like I do?"

"Because he's been ignored too long already." Nicholas said shortly. "Whatever else he may be, it seems to me young Trefyn's a force to be reckoned with—even if it has to be with a horsewhip in the end."

His mouth was grim. Seeing the dangerous light in his eyes, Donna clutched his arm. "No, Nicholas. Whatever happens, not that. You'd only play into his hands. Juliet would be sorry for him and blame you. I know I'm not generally very clever about handling my own daughter, but to harm Trefyn—obviously—would only drive her straight into his arms. You must know that. And we've got enough worries and complications on our hands already, what with Andrew's moods and Charlotte and William as they are. Besides . . ." she gave him a long considering look "you're not twenty years old anymore, and Trefyn's quite a hefty young man . . ."

"Are you suggesting—"

"No, no, I'm not suggesting you couldn't put up a good fight darling. But why should you have to? I love you, don't you see? I don't want my husband with any precious spare bits missing?"

His eyes glowed as he looked at her, then he swept her up into his arms, with his lips warm on her mouth. "Witch!" he said, putting her down again. "Very well, I'll be quite civilized and treat him strictly as gentleman to gentleman."

"Gentleman to peasant," Donna corrected him.

"Oh, come now. We needn't be so precise. He's Elinor's son, remember?"

"I always thought Elinor was a bit of a throwback," Donna said tartly.

"Now, now, no cat's eyes. For that matter, most of us are in one way or another."

"I do hope you're not going to turn into one of those dreadful labor people who think all men equal," Donna said quickly, "the Tim Hardie, John Macdonald kind."

An amused smile touched Nicholas's lips.

"Donna, my love, you've become a snob with the years," he said bluntly. "There was a time I remember when you wanted to be matey with everyone—especially the miners and their families."

"That was different."

"How?"

"Helping people isn't being *of* them."

"Quite. Lady Bountiful—a very charming role, I'm sure. But when you were younger . . ."

"You're thinking of Jos of course," she interrupted quickly. "Well, yes—I was at the romantic age. Idealistic, I suppose, in a way. But then, my father was alive. He was . . . unusual, you know. I really do think he put his workers first. That doesn't mean to say he forgot his responsibilities and place in society as a Penroze."

"Exactly. And he didn't play the heavy father either," Nicholas said. "That's what you're trying to din into my thick head, isn't it? Treat young Trefyn with gentlemanly contempt, yet leave him in no doubt where he stands with Juliet. Is that how your father managed you and Jos?"

"No. My father died, and I met you. So the problem was settled."

"Eventually," Nicholas agreed dryly. "But it took some doing on my part. I should remember that if I were you. Try and see things a little from your daughter's point of view. In the meantime I'll get off to the farm and find out exactly how the land lies at that end. I'm afraid William's started a feud over the Wheal Blair business. I can see his point: with a good bit of outlay and development the mine might be productive again. But I wish to heaven he'd forget about it."

"He won't," Donna said decisively. "I know William. He's set his heart on it, and when William does that, nothing will put him off."

"I'd call it sheer bloody obstinacy," Nicholas said. "Why in heaven's name can't he be satisfied with Penmartin and Wheal Flower? He's got a wife too, something he seems to be forgetting these days, and too soon. Why did he marry at all if he didn't mean to pay the girl a bit of attention? You mark my words, Donna, Charlotte won't put up with things as they are forever."

Something doomlike and prophetic in his voice startled her to attention. "What do you mean . . . as they are?"

Nicholas flung her a dark look. "Never mind. But William should watch his step. I didn't mean to say this, Donna, but perhaps I should. Why do you think our lusty eldest son has been prevailed upon to take Hannah Marne's boy into the house?"

Donna stared. As full implication of the words sank in, a little of the color drained from her face.

"You don't mean . . . you can't think . . ."

"What I think isn't the point; it's Charlotte's business and William's. But it's just as well you have an open mind on some matters. And clearly Charlotte isn't quite the trusting, innocent bride of some months ago."

"I can't believe it," Donna gasped after a pause. "William and that . . . that . . . no I won't, I *can't*."

Nicholas shrugged. "Such things have happened before. The point is, be as nice as you can to her, Donna. She may be on the dull side, but it was you who wanted the match, and say what you like, the girl has courage and a conscience."

"Why didn't you mention this before?" Even in her own ears her voice sounded hard, wooden.

"My dear Donna, you're usually very quick on the uptake. And I didn't see the point of upsetting you unnecessarily."

"You've upset me now," Donna told him sharply.

"You'll get over it," Nicholas said, more lightly than he felt. "The little fellow seems a healthy enough child anyway—full of fight and shout."

"How *can* you!"

"Oh, Donna pull yourself together. If it's any consolation, we've no proof. And as the baby's being adopted, there'll be no problems."

"You don't know. I wish—"

"Well?"

"I wish Charlotte hadn't been so pigheaded in taking him. It's not going to help the marriage."

"No one can help that but William himself, and there are times when I think I neglected my duty by that young man when he was a youngster. He should have had more of the stick than he got, thanks to his doting mama. You were always far too lenient with the boys, Donna, and hard on your daughter."

Donna did not reply. She knew it was true, and sensed it was partly because Juliet was in many ways so like she had been at her age. If she'd been a gentler, less willful character, relationships, between them would have been so much easier. She'd looked forward to having a daughter; both she and Nicholas had longed for one as the youngest of their family. But her imagination had pictured a sweet, amenable little girl with the pretty manners and fair looks of her own mother. Instead had arrived the determined russet-haired, bawling young Juliet, who had caused tumult and argument from her earliest years. Jason from the very beginning had come nearest to Donna's ideal, and there were times she almost wished he was the only one, though Nicholas, of course, would have been affronted to know it, Juliet being the apple of his eye.

She was still churning a little resentfully over her husband's preoccupation with his daughter, when Nicholas set off five minutes later for the farm.

The air was fresh, with a wind blowing from the sea. As he crossed the valley road, shadows scudded from the flying branches of the trees, clawing across the lane with the greedy semblance of giant fingers. Rosebuzzan loomed brilliantly clear against the sky. A few clouds already feathered the distance. By evening, he thought, there would be rain.

Before he reached the building round the bend of the track, he met Jet cutting down from a lush field carrying a basket of mushrooms. She was wearing a dark dress with a red and white checkered apron, and a red handkerchief tied over her black curls. Her eyes, dark as sloes, confronted him watchfully, enigmatically, making him feel like an intruder. This irritated him. Her alien blood was all too apparent in the brown skin, graceful lithe movement of her young body, and defiant pout of her perfectly formed mouth. She was all Connor, and though no man worth his salt wouldn't feel a quiver of desire, he resented her more, and addressed her sharply.

"Is your brother about?"

"I suppose so."

"Can you tell me where I'm likely to find him?"

She shrugged. "With Matt, I expect."

"Who's Matt?"

"Our new man. A groom."

"Thank you. I take it he'll be at the stables then."

"I should think so." Her mood suddenly changed. "I'll walk back with you if you like. He *could* be in the loft. He's got a den there now where he does the accounts. I can give him a call and see."

"I only want a short talk with him," Nicholas said as they went on.

There was a brief silence, then she said, "about Juliet, is it?"

Nicholas glanced down at her quickly. "You want to know too much, young lady. My business is with your brother."

"He tells me most things," she said calmly. "He's expected you before this."

"Has he indeed!"

"Oh, yes. Well, it's natural isn't it? They're very thick you know, Juliet and him—and Trefyn knows how you feel about us. A Trevarvas and a Connor. Oh, dear!"

Nicholas did not speak.

"And yet on your own I don't think you'd be so bad really," she continued in her soft intimidating way, "in fact, I think I could quite like you."

He stared straight ahead, willfully ignoring the implication of her remark, and almost at the same moment a briar caught his face. He put up a hand, and the gesture jerked the girl's arm. Her basket fell, scattering the mushrooms over the ground.

He bent down to pick them up. Her slim, warm, brown fingers touched his. He glanced up confused, with a sudden distracting warmth flooding his body. She was smiling at him, her pearly teeth caught on her full lower lip. The sweat was damp on his neck. His pulses leaped. God! he thought, could a man never be free of his nature? He pushed her hand away, as anger replaced the aberration of brief desire. "Behave yourself," he said. "Remember who you are, and who I am."

She laughed. "You're not so different from anyone else after all, are you, Mr. Trevarvas? My mother always said you were a rutting hypocrite."

The short silence that followed was electric. Then Nicholas said, "Your mother was a mentally sick woman, which is why I shall ignore that remark."

"I'm sorry," she said in a low voice. "I shouldn't have said it."

"No."

"I'll leave you then," she said abruptly. "I'm going to the lower field. You'll find Trefyn at the stables."

She cut away from him down a narrow path to the right. He walked on moodily, feeling in some odd way he'd not only let the girl down but himself. He should have talked to her, tried to stimulate her throughts in some other direction. She was no older than Juliet. What a life it must-have been for her as a child with that crazy Gentry woman and her tinker husband for parents. The idea of Juliet becoming involved with the family shocked him. Donna was right, he told himself as he reached the farm path, marriage be-

tween young Connor and his daughter was unthinkable.

Unthinkable, yes. But possible?

He was not reassured when he saw Trefyn and a
man—presumably Matt—walking from the farm toward the stables. The young fellow had a sturdy look
about him, and walked well, with an air of pride. He
was almost a head taller than the other man, loose
limbed and broad, wearing knickers and leather gai-
ters. His hair, black as his sister's, shone bright in the
sun; but his skin was fairer—honey gold against the
blue shirt. Even from the distance Nicholas was impressed. A handsome young buck likely to turn any
girl's head; and Juliet had fancied him since childhood. Hardly the type to write off, as Donna had suggested, as a mere peasant. This young man was a
force to be reckoned with. More Gentry than Connor,
but with all the wily charm, probably, of the latter.
He quickened his pace, and seeing he meant business,
Trefyn left his companion and went to meet Trevarvas.

"Good morning," he said, "can I help you?"

"You may be able to," Nicholas answered bluntly. "I
hope so."

"Well?" The dark eyes stared very directly at the
older man—farseeing strange eyes, burning with vitality between the narrowed lids. At one moment they
appeared almost black; the next, when a beam of light
caught them, held a curious intermingling of gold,
brown, and deepest blue. Unfathomable, but above all
knowledgeable and keen. The features, too, were pur-
poseful and resolute, set in a noble mold. Nicholas
was taken aback. He'd been prepared for a challenge,
but not of such a genre. It was as though all the

inherent, most devastating, qualities of the Connors and aristocratic Gentrys had been assembled by cunning nature to produce this one outstanding male offspring. For the first time Nicholas understood Juliet's infatuation, and was sorry for her.

"We have to have a talk," Nicholas said, deciding it was better to come straight to the point, "about my daughter."

"Very well, I'm ready. Let's go this way, to the lane. I guess it's private—for you and me alone."

"You're quite right."

They walked down the path and at the bottom turned to their left, taking the curve below Wheal Blair. Trefyn glanced up toward the ruined mine stack with the hint of a smile on his lips. "That's not the bone of contention this time, I take it?"

"Not directly. I simply want to know what's going on between you two."

"Do you now! Does Juliet know you've come?"

"No. Juliet's gone away, to Bristol," Nicholas said, watching Trefyn closely. He noted a slight jerk of surprise cross the young man's face, but only fleetingly. The next moment the handsome features had settled into uncompromising calm.

"Has she? Well, I hope she enjoys herself. A holiday, is it?"

"Don't play with me," Nicholas said shortly. "You know very well what I'm talking about. She was out with you the other night until morning, and consequently upset her mother so much there was a very unpleasant scene. I'm not going into details of that, it's none of your affair. But I think I've a right to be put in the picture. My daughter did not run away for nothing. Will you kindly explain?"

Trefyn shrugged. "My dear Mr. Trevarvas, lovers do have quarrels, you know. Don't worry. She'll come back."

*My God!* Nicholas thought, *the impudence of it.* "And what's that supposed to mean?" he said, restraining with difficulty any obvious show of temper.

"Quite simple," Trefyn answered with a hard, icy edge to his voice. "When her temper's worn off she'll be back like a bird to her cage . . . or home. Perhaps I know Juliet better than you do. She's willful and unpredictable, but—"

"You—"

"Let me finish. She goes where her heart is. And the truth is, we love each other. I've not treated her in any way cheaply or as she didn't want. I'm ready to marry her any moment she wishes. But on my terms. She'd done her best to get me to please you by letting you have those acres above. She's devoted to you, that's another thing, and you don't help her by interfering. You only tear her to pieces—"

"You have the effrontery to tell me how to treat my own daughter?"

"I'm trying to point out that you could make things a whole lot pleasanter all round by leaving us to settle our own future. Juliet's young, yes, but she's mature. And another thing, she's quite capable of leading a woman's life instead of a dressed-up doll's. When she faces that one home truth everything will be fine for us—with or *without* your consent, sir. Naturally we'd prefer friendliness to quarreling, but take it from me— if Juliet has to make a choice between us, she'll choose me in the end."

"And you'd be happy—quite content to have my daughter cut off from her own family and all the things she's been used to, just to bed down with you in that . . . that shack of a place, after Polbreath?" Nicholas said incredulously.

For the first time a shadow of discomfiture crossed Trefyn's face. "It won't always be a shack of a place," he said stubbornly. "I'm working hard. Extending. The few crops we have are thriving. And my shire stud's going to be one of the best in the country—eventually. Capital's been limited from the beginning, but we're managing to save a little."

"By 'we' are you alluding to your sister?" Nicholas said coldly.

Trefyn looked startled. "Of course. We share."

"And you'd wish Juliet to live as she does—half-wild, a drudge to a small farm with no cultural interests whatever?"

When Trefyn didn't answer Nicholas continued. "Well? Your sister. Are you proud of her?"

A flash of temper destroyed briefly Trefyn's composure. "What the devil do you mean?"

"You know very well. Jet's in danger. She needs companionship and education. Don't tell me you're unaware of that."

There was a short uncomfortable silence before Trefyn said more quietly, "That's what I'm working for, partly, so I can send her to some college or finishing school—I don't quite know what yet. But that's one of the things Juliet's got to understand. Jet matters too."

"And yet you won't consider selling the Wheal Blair site to my son? No, no, don't interrupt. I don't want it; to my mind it would be a bad deal. There are possibilities that's all, and you'd get a damn lot more than it's worth. Yet—"

Trefyn caught his arm. "Look there. You see that?" He was pointing to the stretch of flat land bordering two or three lush fields below the hill. "The fields are good soil now," he said, "providing most of our produce. That strip of land above is needed for grazing purposes and exercising the horses. I'm not just being bloody-minded, Mr. Trevarvas, I *need* those acres. They're my future. Or don't you believe I have one?"

Something in his direct gaze nonplused Nicholas. He felt intimidated, up against a brick wall, and aware there was little he could do to extricate himself. Young Connor was not only clever, he had a conscience and the stubbornness of a mule.

"Very well," he said, "I can see there's not much point in discussing things. But I warn you, young man, I'll do all that's humanly possible to prevent my daughter having anything more to do with you."

"Fair enough." Trefyn answered. "If you want to take that line, go ahead. I'll do the same. Juliet will marry me whatever you say. Not because I'll have to persuade her, but because she'll want to. And you needn't remind me about consent and the law. There'll be some way round. If not, we'll wait. So let's call it quits, shall we?"

Nicholas gave him one hard, furious stare, then turned and walked sharply away down the lane, striking the hedge viciously with his cane, and inwardly cursing the day Elinor Gentry had thought fit to deliver Connor's son into the world.

## 9

Three days after Juliet's departure Charlotte suddenly announced over dinner that if Nicholas and Donna were willing, she would like to move to the lodge that stood back from the road, at the end of Polbreath drive. It had been empty for a year following the death of the old gardener who'd lived there on his own since his wife Betsy succumbed to influenza.

Donna was aghast. "Why should you go there," she said, "especially in your condition when you need a little extra looking after. With the—the baby too—Matthew. The idea's impractical, Charlotte. Having housework to contend with on top of everything else, and William's meals—he has a good appetite, you know. Of course, you could eat with us, but what a traipse in bad weather—"

She broke off, dismayed by the obtuse, stubborn look on Charlotte's face.

"I'm quite strong," Charlotte said, "and I think it

would be better for both of us, William *and* me, to have more to do."

"Here, steady on," William said with a hint of belligerence. "Why should we move from a perfectly satisfactory, comfortable home just to have more to do?"

"A woman needs responsibility," Charlotte said with maddening calmness. "Things have been made very easy for us here, and I'm grateful. But a family should be a self-contained unit, and I'm thinking of the future. Children can be so easily spoiled with a lot of grownups fussing round. Either that or . . ." she hesitated before adding "pushed out. With Matthew being adopted it would be so easy for him to sense any resentment—"

"Matthew!" William exclaimed. "You speak as if our whole existence is going to center round him."

"A certain amount of it will," Charlotte pointed out.

"Please stop arguing, you two," Donna interrupted. "I said from the beginning you shouldn't have taken Hannah's boy in, especially when you were expecting one of your own. But I don't think you need fear Nicholas or I or any of us would dream of allowing a child to feel inferior—"

"All the same," Charlotte persisted, "the lodge would make a pleasant home if it was painted and brightened up. I—"

"I'm afraid not, Charlotte," Andrew said quietly. "I had the surveyor round recently. It's in a deplorable state—riddled with dry rot and woodworm. Old Treviss had just let it slip into decay. I'd tried to get something done about it before, but he was a stubborn old chap and refused to let a workman into the place. Only the walls are really sound. And the drainage was never good. You couldn't possibly live there. No one could without health hazards. I'd wondered whether it could be made fit for Mrs. Polgrove, actually. She's without any home to go to when William takes over her cottage. But the place is only fit for demolition. I'm sorry."

William glanced at his wife ironically, with a hint of triumph. "So now perhaps you'll try and settle down," he said curtly.

There was an embarrassed silence broken by Donna saying, "More gravy, Jason?"

Jason grinned impishly, throwing a wicked glance from Charlotte to William. "Count your blessings, children," he said. "Cook's gravy is very good."

The meal continued after that in comparative silence. When it was over William followed his wife upstairs to their own quarters. Some knitting in white fluffy wool for the coming baby lay over an armchair in the sitting room. Elise came out of the small bedroom as they entered and said, "Little Matthew's had his bottle and is asleep, Mrs. William. Will you need me any more now?"

Charlotte shook her head. "No thank you. You'd better get back to the kitchen. Mrs. Paynter may need you."

After Elise had gone, Charlotte, ignoring William, picked up the knitting, rolled it up carefully and put it into a bag. The domestic gesture irritated him more than any heated argument would have done. He returned to the door, locked it, and faced her.

"Well?" he said, "Haven't you anything to say for yourself? Wasn't that a damned fool thing to do, stirring up resentment, making my mother think you were ungrateful with that stupid talk about moving to the lodge?"

Charlotte stared at him with stubborn coldness. "It seemed to me a perfectly reasonable request. And why should I be grateful? Your mother's only anxious to keep us under her roof because she can't bear any of her sons to show independence."

"You have a vicious streak in you, Charlotte," he said. "When I married you I—"

"You didn't expect it, no. You just thought if you *had* to marry—which was expedient under the circumstances wasn't it?—it might as well be dear old plain Charlotte who'd give everything and expect nothing but to be a convenient doormat and alibi for your secret little sex orgies elsewhere. Well, you made a mistake. I don't like being used, William, and I don't intend to be. You've married me, and I expect you to provide for me as other men do for their wives. I want a home of our own, so we can—"

"Quarrel in privacy and spit and fight to our hearts' content with no one knowing? Is that your secret dream, Charlotte? A nice little lust nest—"

Charlotte's face flamed. She brought her hand smartly up across his cheek. He stared at her, then laughed. "So I was right. Beneath your homely front lurks quite a greedy libido." The smile died from his mouth. The eyes darkened. One hand closed harshly on her plump forearm.

"Come here, Mrs. Trevarvas. It's never too late to learn. I've been very tolerant with you mostly . . . very gentle, I think. Maybe it's been a mistake."

He lifted her up, held her for a moment, then laid her flat on the floor. She gasped as he pinioned her, and struggled for a moment, turning her face to one side. His weight was heavy on her. One hand forced her head round again. She could feel the other fumbling with her clothes and his. The male force of him was strong in her body; there was no tenderness there, no love. But in spite of her disgust and anger something in her responded—a deep primitive need that was both triumph and defeat.

When it was over she didn't immediately get up, but lay there staring at the ceiling, hating herself and him. Once she glanced at his face. There was no shame there as there had been the last time, only a mild, bitter cynicism that seemed to drain any last vestige of pride from her.

He grasped her hand and pulled her to her feet. "That's what you wanted, wasn't it?" he said. "No different from the rest, after all."

"Don't you—"

"And don't tell me not to dare," he said crudely, "I shall dare as often and whenever I like. You see . . ." he paused then said slowly and contemptuously, "I know now what your game was in taking Hannah's child. It was to make me pay, wasn't it? Your weapon for revenge, for having me toe the line whenever you felt like it—"

"Oh no, William, no, *no*—"

"But it won't be that way," he said, jerking his tie into place. "I'll call the tune, Charlotte, and you'll do the running from now on. Now, for heaven's sake, tidy yourself."

As she moved dejectedly to the mirror a child's wail came from the adjoining small room.

"My son wants your attention," William said brutally. "You'd better be quick about it. Now we've got him there's going to be no neglect."

Charlotte flung him a look of hate before leaving the sitting room.

William smoothed his hair, slipped on a jacket, and five minutes later was cutting along the seaside of the moors toward Wheal Jakke. Below the Marne cottage he turned down to the place where he'd so often lain with Hannah. Reaction had already set in following his interlude with Charlotte. He felt ill at ease and dejected, conscious that in some way he'd demeaned himself—not by what he'd done, but through omission and cowardice in the first place. For the first time he realized with acute shock that in rejecting Hannah he'd lost the one thing that could have enriched his life. Her presence seemed everywhere—in the wind's sighing through the faintly browning bracken and heather, the quiver of silvered light through the clouds over the gray stones, and in the salty drift of brine from the sea. As his palm touched the smooth surface of the stone, he seemed to sense her skin beneath his hand, recalled the countless times they'd lain together in passion, safely hidden from prying eyes. Oh, the warmth of her, the sweetness, the hurt in her eyes when he walked away that last time, and his final cold denial.

His head dropped suddenly into his hands. He sat crouched and still as the standing stones of the moor above. He could not visualize life ahead with Charlotte. He should have married Hannah and been damned to the family.

Now it was too late.

Hannah was dead.

Only her son remained. But, by God, he told himself suddenly with a savage stab of resolution, young Matthew should have the best he could give. Everything he worked for—all that physical strength and brain could achieve for the mines, should have dual purpose and survive as a living testament to this fruit of his loins born of Hannah's flesh.

Presently he got to his feet and strode on toward Wheal Jakke.

Of Charlotte he didn't think at all.

Perhaps she sensed it. Bitterness flooded her as she lulled the child to sleep and laid it back in its cot at Polbreath. She knew William would never love her, and she realized in that moment of awareness she'd done a dangerous thing in accepting Matthew. But the choice had been hers; she'd insisted, and there was no way of putting the clock back.

From that moment any compassion she'd felt for the baby—and at first there'd been a great deal—died. Henceforward her attitude was to be one of duty only. Perhaps one day, if she tried hard enough, some shred of respect and affection might be salvaged for her marriage. At least, she thought, she bore William's name, which was something he could not take away. And time was a healer. This was her one hope: time.

To alleviate frustration caused through his domestic problems, William rode to Hayle next day for consultation at Harveys concerning expenditure over the possible Wheal Flower project. The rough figure given was considerable, but not as large as he'd feared. The tricky and unknown factor of the whole operation was, of course, the building of the dam, which was a matter for the engineers. With his appetite whetted William set off for Redruth forthwith and was lucky enough to find Robert Carnforth, one of the most skilled mining engineers in the country, in his office.

Carnforth, at first dubious, became more interested when William explained that veins running in Wheal

Flower's direction from Jakke had given proof of low-lying tin lodes. "The three mines run in cooperation could give the richest ore yield in Cornwall," he said. "If the water could be safely stemmed, the cost would be well worth it. And I don't see why there should be any problem there."

Carnforth gave William a shrewd glance. "Water's always a problem," he said. "And you should know, Mr. Trevarvas, that safety's an ambiguous word in mining. There's never any guarantee—absolutely."

"You don't have to tell me that," William said with an edge to his voice. "Isn't that what makes any new venture worth its salt?"

"No. Not when men's lives are in the balance. The opening of an old mine can be about the most hazardous undertaking we engineers have to face. Before starting on a project of the kind you're talking about, we'd have to be ninety-nine and a half percent sure. And labor costs would be considerable. But, of course, you realize that."

"Yes."

"Very well," Carnforth said after further discussion, "I'll come over next week—Monday morning, if that suits you, and bring a colleague with me. But we shall need a second opinion later. Harold Thomson of Derby's likely to be in Cornwall in a fortnight's time. It might be a good idea for him to look over the site."

"Certainly," William agreed. "Nothing better. I'll leave things in your hands then."

They parted five minutes later, and when William got back to Polbreath he informed Nicholas of the meeting.

Nicholas frowned. "Don't you think you should have consulted me?"

"It didn't occur to me," William said. "Your interest in the mines recently has seemed only secondary to the estate. I wanted to get on with things."

"With my money," Nicholas pointed out abruptly.

William flushed. "I didn't anticipate you'd cut up rough. Unless . . . there is any financial difficulty?"

"No," Nicholas told him. "And I don't want any. The thing that puzzles me is why you're so dead set on expanding all the time, William? Haven't you got enough on your hands without going like a bull at a gate into other problems?"

"Not practically," William said. "There's enough to do, yes, superintending—settling disputes—business commitments, markets, all the rest. But the whole set-up's ready-made. I've a right to do my own thing, haven't I? Or don't you agree?"

Nicholas didn't answer at first, then he said, "What's needling you, William?"

"I don't know what you mean."

"Oh, come on now. This spurt of enthusiasm isn't only for work's sake. Anything wrong on the domestic front?"

"What makes you ask that?"

Nicholas shrugged. "I'm not blind. Charlotte isn't exactly radiant. And you've only been married a matter of months."

"That's the trouble I expect," William said shortly.

"What do you mean?"

William faced his father squarely. "Possibly I shouldn't have married at all."

Nicholas went to his desk, opened it, and took two cigars from a box. "Here you are—" William took one automatically. "And now a drink." When the two men were settled more comfortably, each with a whiskey,

Nicholas began again, "You've married Charlotte whether you like it or not."

"Yes, thanks to my doting mother."

"You're a man, aren't you? So don't put the blame on her. Charlotte's a good girl. You could have done far worse, and she's having your child, William—my grandson. Or daughter. Perhaps you did marry too quickly on the rebound; now, keep your temper and just listen to me. I know very well about you and Hannah. But you should put all that behind you now and think of the future. Anyway . . ." his eyes narrowed and darkened. "You've got the boy, haven't you?"

William looked away, saying nothing.

"I shall do right by him," Nicholas said with no trace of emotion in his voice, "and I hope you do right by Charlotte. Try and make her feel wanted. And if it makes you feel any better, I'll go halfway to meet you over the Wheal Flower business."

William's heart lifted. "You will?"

"I'm not going to pay your bills or be responsible for any debts incurred, which I hope won't happen. What I propose to do is settle a certain sum on you, making you sufficiently independent to run your own project. I shall, of course, have certain shares; in a proper deed drawn up I shall be indemnified against damage to either of the other mines, and insured on behalf of the men's safety. The sum I've in mind at the moment is fifteen thousand pounds."

William's stomach churned with excitement.

"In repayment I want you to show responsibility and restraint in your own personal life. And if I hear of any disreputable behavior toward Charlotte, you'll be out on your ear with my boot in your backside. That's plain speaking, William, and I mean it."

William's jaw was outthrust when he said, "You don't mince matters. But I'm grateful. All I want is a chance."

When Nicholas told Donna later what he proposed to do, she was at first amazed, then doubtful. "But is that wise? Such a large sum. And what will the others think? Andrew and Jason?"

"Andrew's beyond me at the moment," Nicholas said bluntly, "God alone knows what he does think about these days. As for Jason, he can't complain, neither can you. He's having a more than generous allowance for Paris, which he'll doubtless fritter away on studio parties and women when he gets there in the autumn. No, none of them can complain. My real worry is Juliet."

"It always has been," Donna said pointedly. "Why I don't know. She's had the best education any girl could have, pretty clothes—above all, nice friends."

"Friends supplied for her by you."

"Oh, don't be stupid, Nicholas. All parents want the best company and security for their children— especially daughters."

"And look what it's done for ours—sending her off in bad blood on a wild-goose chase to Bristol."

"Bad blood? *Goose chase?*" Donna laughed but without humor. "The Marshes are most respectable, and Leonora's the nicest friend she has. I'm thankful she did go, and only hope when she returns she'll be in a better mood."

"*When,*" Nicholas said moodily.

Donna sighed. "Do stop fretting about her. Things

could be far worse. In Bristol she's not able to lurk round the Connors every spare moment, for which we should be grateful. She may even meet someone else to take her mind off that . . . that Gypsy."

"I doubt it," Nicholas remarked dryly. "And he's not a gypsy, Donna, as I've pointed out time after time. He's a shrewd, strong-minded young chap with more looks and charm than are good for him. Not the kind a girl easily forgets."

"Well," Donna said after an uneasy silence, "if there's no change when she comes back, we shall have to do something."

"Such as . . . ?"

"Send her abroad perhaps. Why not? She isn't terribly accomplished, Nicholas. It might even be an idea for her to have painting lessons. I've heard there's a very good academy for young ladies in Paris. Jason could keep an eye on her—"

Nicholas laughed. "My dear love! What an optimist you are. Jason? I don't think you've the first idea of your son's propensities and limitations. The last thing he'd want would be to saddle himself with a sister. And I can't see Juliet in the role either."

"No," Donna agreed. "She'd probably give him the slip and end up in some disgraceful stage turn with the Folies Bergéres."

"Probably," Nicholas agreed.

Actually, at the very moment this conversation was taking place Juliet herself was having Wycksley's proposition put to her.

"The play I'm thinking of financing, my dear," he was saying with his shrewd eyes assessing her possibilities, "is experimental—dealing with the emotional reactions of two women to a certain situation." He paused. Juliet was seated on a decorative garden bench in the conservatory of the Belgravia home, looking unusually vibrant and lovely in an orange dress generously supplied from Ianthe's wardrobe, which fitted and suited her to perfection. "The drama is an original work written by a protegé of mine," Robertson continued in the same silky, even tones. "I consider it has potentials—considerable potentials, given the right cast." Juliet waited.

"It's just possible," her elderly brother-in-law continued, "you might fit one of the feminine roles—not the lead, you understand, which would go to Frances Bellingham, but as her opposite, her foil. Youthful exuberance and naïveté as opposed to cool sophistication and chic."

"Frances Bellingham?" Juliet queried. She'd vaguely heard the name but couldn't remember in what play.

"She was very well known before her rather disastrous marriage, the suave voice continued, "and now wishes to make a comeback. I believe I can use her talent to the advantage of all concerned. And as you, my dear, have already told me of your stage ambitions . . . well, I think with certain instruction you would fit the roll of Susie admirably."

"Oh, but . . ." Juliet shook her head as the wild rich color flooded her cheeks. "I'm not sure. I've only acted in school plays. I'm not a professional actress, I've had no experience—"

"Ah," a fat forefinger was waved in her direction, "that is just the point, my dear. Your entire lack of sophistication. Your naïveté and natural charm. I believe audiences would take you to their hearts, which would make the dramatic finale the more poignant . . ."

"You mean *theater* audiences?"

"Of *course*, my dear. What else? But it is a small theater—the Beehive—very intimate and friendly. You could call it almost 'my baby.'" He smiled, with one thumb and forefinger enfolding the top layer of his two chins. A ridiculous feeling of nerves churned Juliet's stomach, setting her heart racing uncomfortably.

"I'm not sure . . ." she said. "I might—I might not be any good. I mean—"

"Now, now, what nonsense. You'd only have to be your own beautiful self . . ." His pale eyes narrowed slightly. She was too elated to notice the tip of his tongue circling the dry lips, or the tremor of his hand. Only one thought registered: the fact that Ianthe's elderly husband was offering her the chance she'd so often dreamed about—an opportunity on the road to fame; something, if she achieved it, that must surely bring Trefyn to her side again, admiring, loving her.

She felt suddenly overcome by the heat, the steamy geranium scent, and the excitement. "Do you mind if I—if we have the door open?" she said. "It's a bit hot in here. I feel—"

"My dear child, of *course*." He went to the outer door, opened it a little, letting in a gust of fresh air. Then he came back, snipped a white carnation from a pot and brought it to her with a feathery stem of maidenhair fern.

He bent down and placed it in her hair. "There! How charming you look. Such an ideal Susie."

Juliet composed herself. "Could you explain the plot? Tell me what Susie has to do?"

He spread both hands out, with a nonchalent shrug of the shoulders. "My dear, it is simple. As I said, an experimental piece—*Drawing Room at Night*. Except for the very minor role of the butler, there are just three characters—Eloise, the beautiful, sophisticated stepmother of the young girl, Susie. Eloise is what you would call the *femme fatale* of the piece—a woman with the art of captivating any male who sets eyes on her. Susie is eighteen years old, returning from boarding school in Switzerland with a young man, Anton Clare, presumably her fiancé whom she hopes to marry shortly." He paused, taking a deep breath. "They reach the home of the widowed Eloise late one evening—Susie all excitement, full of enthusiasm, bubbling good spirits and passionate love for Anton. At first it appears he feels the same for her. Then gradually, disenchantment, or rather enchantment for Eloise sets in. And here you have the drama: Susie's desperate bid to keep her lover's attention, and her stepmother's fatal charm gradually taking precedence, until disillusionment for Susie is complete.

"Eloise of course has the most difficult part to play. *You* have explosive emotions to suggest—Eloise remains for the most part static, apparently cool, conveying though, by the flicker of an eyelid or merest gesture of a finger, a world of power and meaning— the power of Eve over Adam through the ages. It is you see, a play not of action, but one more of suggestion." He waited, then continued: "The theater—the fashion of drama is changing, Juliet. In twenty, thirty years time, the old and current style of declaiming will be over. We shall see a revolution of the art—a far subtler representation of human emotion and conflict. I believe this play to be a forerunner of the style to come. And just think, in the final scene—what a powerful dénouement. You—the innocent young girl, disillusioned, broken." He sighed, took a deep breath, and continued, "And, Eloise—enigmatic, watching Anton's final capitulation to her sexual allure with a cynical, aloof, travesty of a smile about her lips—" He broke off, entranced by his own rhetoric. Juliet tried to imagine the scene, and in her bewilderment couldn't.

"I'm sure I'm not the person you want," she said. "I don't think I'm capable."

"But you *are*, my dear. You have only to be *yourself*."

"What about Ianthe?"

His face changed and became hard. "Ianthe? She's hardly young enough to make a convincing Susie."

"But—"

"Forget her," Wycksley said petulantly, his lower lip quivering irritably. "Ianthe should conserve her energies with more dignity. She's wasted herself, I'm afraid, and I do not allow anything of a second-rate nature in my cast."

A stab of indignation made Juliet say rashly, "Ianthe's my sister. I don't think she'd like it."

"While she's under my roof she'll accept my decision," Wycksley retorted with an unbecoming heightening of color.

"All the same, to call her second-rate isn't kind," Juliet persisted stubbornly. "No, I'm sorry. I couldn't possibly hurt her like that."

Robertson was spared having to reply by Ianthe's unexpected entrance from the drawing room.

"Don't be so ridiculously honorable, darling," she said. "Do what my husband says. He's quite right, you know, I should make a disastrous Susie, whereas you'd be enchanting." There was no rancor in her voice, only a mild cynicism. "Unless," she continued, "you're thinking of going home." The smile fell from her face suddenly, leaving it bleak and strained. "I would if I were you."

"Do you mind holding your tongue, madam?" Robertson said, his pale eyes popping with anger. "This matter is an affair between Juliet and myself. Another thing, I will *not* have you listening at doors. Do you understand?"

Ianthe laughed. "You were declaiming so loudly I didn't have to."

"Oh, please," Juliet said, "please don't quarrel. I—"

"Quarreling? This is a habitual occurrence where Robertson and I are concerned. I'm used to receiving the brush-off. But don't let it bother you. Just go ahead and take what's offered—if you want it enough. My husband may be a brute, but his judgment's shrewd where protégés are concerned." She paused before adding significantly, "Generally."

Juliet got up, taking the flower absently from her hair and laying it on the seat behind her. Wycksley picked it up. "Your carnation, my dear. And don't let this little scene disturb you. Think about it well, and let me know as soon as possible. Plays don't wait, you know, and you've your future to think about, haven't you?"

The bland smile had returned to his lips. Something covetous about his expression mildly put Juliet's nerves on edge. She left him standing there almost motionless, aware that Ianthe's eyes also were following her. Her first impulse was to tell Wycksley as politely as possible at the first opportunity that she'd considered things and decided after all that she couldn't accept the part. Her plans, however, changed overnight.

Lying wakeful for some time between silk sheets,

watching the networked shadows flung by moonlight against the curtains, memories of the scene with Tre-fyn and her mother's anger returned in a torment of unhappiness. If she returned immediately to Pol-breath, there would be further scolding and recrimi-nations—more blatant attempts to have her married off quickly to the boring Desmond Court. All of them—Trefyn included—would be expecting her to re-turn shortly, subdued and asking to be forgiven. Well, once more the tantalizing thought returned: this was the chance to prove that she was something more than a Victorian Miss fit only for sewing samplers and sheets and running a house. She was a personality as well, though not one of Judy's "new women" exactly—because she thought suffragettes were unfeminine and generally plain to look at—but capable of causing a stir and making a reputation that might even go down in history books. *Could* she? Had she really the inherent qualities suggested by Robertson?

On impulse she jumped out of bed, switched on the bedside lights, and ran lightly to the mirror. Her cheeks were flushed in the subdued, becoming glow, her eyes limpidly bright and glowing.

She lifted a hand to the neck of her frilly nightdress and let it fall to her feet. Her body was reflected al-luringly from the glass, shadowed subtly in warm pinks deepening to softest mauve, round curves of stomach and upthrust young breasts. She lifted a hand, touching a rosy nipple gently, recalling the warm hunger of Trefyn's lips—his hands on thighs and the wild thrill of their bodies mating. *Oh, Trefyn, Tre-fyn*, her heart cried, *if only you were here*.

But he wasn't. Neither was she where she should have been—in his arms—because of Donna's narrow-minded class consciousness, and because of Trefyn himself, who'd refused to make that concession on her behalf over the land for William.

Let them worry and wait, she thought; she'd show them. One day Donna, who'd always seemed to resent her, would be proud of her, and Trefyn would be once more worshipful and adoring as he'd been at the dew pond, without reservations or conditions.

Unconsciously a small secret smile touched her lips. Her hair was a dusky molten cloud over her shoulders. She was fully conscious for the first time of her own beauty. And it was just at that moment that a floorboard creaked outside the room. Instinctively she turned abruptly, gathering the long hair protectively over her breasts. Her heart almost stopped beating as the doorknob appeared to turn slowly, and a faint crack appeared between wall and wood. She stood frozen, wondering if an eye really watched through the narrow aperture, or if it was only her imagination. She rubbed her eyes, and when she looked again all was closed and still. There was no sound from outside. But she discovered her heart was beating almost uncontrollably. She waited a moment, then ran to the door and turned the key hurriedly in the lock.

Who had it been? Some prying manservant? The young footman perhaps who had eyed her so admiringly that same morning? Or . . . Wycksley? Surely not. He wouldn't be so stupid. Perhaps after all she *had* been just seeing things that weren't there. However, she determined in future to keep her room securely locked when she was inside.

It was some time before she slept that night, but when she did she had no dreams, and awoke feeling refreshed.

When Robertson saw her later she told him she'd agree to take the part of Susie, and the following day Wycksley drove her to the Beehive, a small theater tucked away in the vicinity of Piccadilly, where he introduced her to the producer of *Drawing Room at Night*.

## 10

Juliet had been at her sister's for less than a week when rehearsals for *Drawing Room at Night* started at the Beehive. The theater was small, tucked away from any main thoroughfare, not yet lit by electricity, and with exceedingly cramped dressing rooms and wings. The hall also was small, but high with two circles. The stage, though, was large in comparison and had been scheduled for further improvements and modernization at a future date. The whole atmosphere was "arty" and experimental. Wycksley himself had invested most of the capital for purchase of the property, and the plays put on were modern for the period, acted mostly by repertory companies and progressive actors and actresses of promising talent.

"Don't let the rather humble premises put you off, my dear," Robertson said as he showed Juliet round. "From here more than one famous name has already emerged. It is a testing place—a trial forum, you could

say—and I have every confidence in your ability to
make the grade."

He spoke with confidence and slight pomposity, his
round eyes under heavy lids turned sideways upon the
alluring curves of her youthful bosom. Trying to ignore the glance, Juliet said, "I shall do my best, Mr.
Wycksley."

"Robertson."

"Robertson," she echoed mechanically, feeling the
back of her neck and hands grow damp with nerves
and embarrassment.

"And now, my dear, I want you to meet Claude
Ferrier, your producer, and, of course, Frances. Frances, darling . . ."

He raised his voice slightly and the actress appeared from the wings as though she'd been waiting
for a cue, followed by a pale-faced middle-aged man
with ginger sideburns, wearing a monocle and a
floppy, spotted silk tie to complete a sand-colored velvet suit. His hair was longish, his manner slightly
vague and condescending, but the light eyes were
shrewd, belying the artiness.

Frances was blond and willowly, extremely beautiful, appearing from a distance considerably younger
than her years.

Both professed great pleasure at meeting Juliet, but
Frances's slanting green eyes had an appraising suspi-
cious glint in them, and although her tones were
creamy soft when she said, "Darling, *how* lovely to
have someone so fresh and young in the cast," those
cold eyes of hers were not. Yet Juliet could complain
of nothing in her manner. She was extremely helpful
during the two hours they spent there, explaining
more of the rudimentary rules of stagecraft than

Claude Ferrier, who was mostly busy conversing with Wycksley.

"Tomorrow," Wycksley said, when they left that afternoon, "we shall have a brief read-through of the script, and next week, probably, you will meet the author. I like to have the scene properly set—or rather, Ferrier does—before any conflicting opinions are aired. Authors—especially playwrights you know—are inclined to be interfering given a chance. And we can't have that. Claude and I see absolutely eye to eye over these things. That's one thing you have to concentrate on in the theater, my dear—know what you're doing." His podgy hand tapped Juliet's playfully, lingering slightly longer than was necessary. She drew her fingers away gently. He sat back in the carriage, staring straight ahead. Her own gaze was fixed deliberately on the maze of passing streets which eventually turned into the main thoroughfare.

Juliet wondered vaguely what Ianthe was doing, and how she'd receive her when they got back to No. 10. Her thoughts were disturbed by Robertson saying suddenly, "About money, my dear . . ."

Juliet, startled, jerked herself to attention. "Oh, I—I'm all right, thank you. I brought some with me, and I can always—"

"No, no. I shall insist on paying you a proper salary. That is only fair." His voice was smug, determined, almost as though he'd bought her, she thought. Her mouth closed.

"I haven't even started on the play," she said firmly. "I'd rather not take anything yet, if you don't mind, not until I know if I'm going to be any good."

"Nonsense. I insist. You see, Juliet . . ." His voice was cajoling, holding at the same time the condescending quality of an adult's argument with a child, "there are matters involved you probably have not considered." He paused as she looked at him in surprise.

"What?"

"Well, clothes for instance."

"I'm not without. And I can always—"

"Send home?"

She flushed.

"Ianthe—"

His face took on the mottled, angry look she so disliked and was beginning to dread. "I certainly don't intend to allow you to depend on any borrowed wardrobe of Ianthe's," he said more coldy than she'd heard him speak so far. "To begin with, Ianthe's taste is flamboyant and not entirely seemly. I've seen her on occasions lately looking quite ridiculous."

"I don't think you should—"

"Talk of your stepsister—forgive me, your halfsister—in such a way? No, no. You're quite right. I must guard my tongue. However now that you know my feelings I'm sure you'll agree to my suggestion. You must have clothes befitting your status and own style, and for that you'll need money, a proper salary. So no more quibbling, my dear. Tomorrow morning Frances will accompany you to her own modistes and help you decide what is necessary for a most beautiful young actress's wardrobe. I shall see your salary is paid in advance, monthly. So that will ease a number of small problems, won't it."

Juliet was not all convinced, but realizing Wycksley meant to have his way, she was silent, and presently, to her great relief, the carriage drew up at the doors of No. 10, leaving the topic temporarily closed.

Wycksley inserted his own key into the front door. Juliet passed by in front of him, and just as she entered the hall a door, some distance down on the right, opened, revealing a female figure with a number of grimacing faces grouped behind her. Her dark hair was loose round her shoulders, and she was wearing a bearskin pinned from one shoulder and at the waist. One breast was bare. Obviously she had little, if anything on beneath. The effect was ludicrous, and to Juliet quite shocking, because the macabre vision was none other than Ianthe, and she was obviously drunk.

Seeing them, she tottered forward on bare feet, waving a wineglass aloft.

"Your h—h—health, dear s—sister—" she mocked, "and long may y—you reign, tra la—!"

"Long may you reign—" came in an echo behind her.

Wycksley stiffened. With a feeling of sickness Juliet saw Robertson's hand tighten on his silver-knobbed walking stick, heard him say in a thunderous voice, "My God, madam, if it wasn't for your sister, I'd—" He struggled for words, almost choking.

Juliet caught his arm. "Please," she begged. "Oh, please, it's my fault. She's been upset, I don't want the part. I—"

"Nonsense, nonsense. You've got it." Robertson forced himself to restraint. "Go to your room, madam," he said to Ianthe, "and if you care for your own skin don't ever expose it in this way again. As for you, *all* of you—" with his head thrust forward he lunged ahead, waving the stick this way and that, "Out—*out*—"

There was a squealing and shouting, the crash of a chair tumbling over, as a number of disarrayed figures went plunging down the hall with coats and wraps flung haphazardly round their heads and shoulders.

A footman emerged as though from nowhere, like some giant major-domo come to restore order. Ianthe's disorganized little retinue disappeared through the open door, which was closed with tremendous aplomb and dignity on their undignified retreat. Wycksley seated himself, gasping, on a hall chair and sat there for some minutes mopping his face, which had quickly turned from mottled red to a sickly gray pallor.

"Are you all right?" Juliet asked, realizing for the first time that after all he was little more than a greedy, ambitious old man who could quite easily expire from a heart attack at any moment.

From almost halfway up the stairs, Ianthe turned, clinging to the wrought-iron banisters. She laughed. "Of course he's all r—right, he's always all—all right. Don't w—w—worry d—darling. He'll sur—survive."

She slumped suddenly on the stairs, her head on her knees.

Juliet made a gesture to go to her, but the butler interposed. "Just leave her to me, madam," he said, "I know how to handle her."

He marched up the stairs purposefully, and lifted Ianthe up in his arms.

Juliet watched helplessly, feeling for a few moments she was going to faint.

Then, ponderously, Wycksley got to his feet and offered his arm. "Allow me, my dear," he managed to say in a thin voice. "I think we both need a little pick-me-up."

Unresistingly, Juliet let him escort her to the library.

The rest of that evening was a subdued affair. Robertson was unsmiling and morose at dinner. Ianthe did not appear at all until later when she made a belated appearance in the drawing room for coffee. By then it was almost nine o'clock, and she'd managed to assume an air of pathetic dignity. She was wearing a gown of gauzy black. Her face was free of makeup except for a dusting of powder, and the dark rings under her eyes gave her the washed-out, fragile quality of some pining Dame aux Camelias. A single diamond ornament glittered in her hair. Her slender fingers were ringless, her manner composed, yet the hand enclosing her fan was restless. Every minute or two she outspread the fragile object, wafting a wave of perfume through the air. Juliet was intensely sorry for her, because she sensed that beneath the elegant exterior fear lurked; fear of Wycksley because of her outrageous behavior.

"Are you sick, madam?" he questioned once, sharply. "If you can't keep still, perhaps you should retire again so your sister and I can have a little peace."

"Oh, *no*, please," Juliet said quickly and, before Robertson could intercede, continued breathlessly, "Would you like to go out, Ianthe? Just for a walk? It would—"

"Certainly not." Wycksley's voice had the impact of a pistol shot. "Young ladies do not go walking in London at night unescorted by gentlemen. We've had enough scandal here for one day."

Ianthe shrugged and smiled wryly. "My husband's quite right, darling," she said with a sideways glance at Wycksley. "This isn't Cornwall, you know. There are rules to be observed." She sighed and added, "I'm sorry for breaking them and landing you in such an embarrassing scene."

"Just see it doesn't happen once more—" Wycksley said before Juliet could reply. "And take care in future that none of those—mountebanks—enter my house again."

Ianthe's mouth tightened, her eyes blazed, but she managed to keep silent. "In fact," the rasping voice continued, "it might be quite an idea for you to have a change, madam."

"A change?" Ianthe's voice shook slightly.

"A trip abroad, perhaps, or a cruise to refresh your mind and take stock of your position."

"Oh, no." Juliet's clear young voice was firm and filled with indignation. "If Ianthe goes, I shall—I mean it. After all . . ." she swallowed nervously, "she was only having a party. Lots of people dress up at parties—"

Wycksley gave her a shrewd glance over his glasses. "*Indeed!* Do they, miss? And like that? Some deranged whore masquerading as a tiger? Oh, I think not, I think not, my dear. Still—" he forced a humorless smile to his primped-up mouth, "just for your sake I'll endeavor to forget the sorry business this time. And you in your turn must never mention going away again. Do you understand?"

"If you say so, Robertson," Juliet answered guardedly.

"And now, what about a hand of cards? Do you play, my dear?"

"Whist and snap," she answered, hoping neither game would appeal to him. She was disappointed.

"Excellent. Excellent. Ianthe?" His pop eyes turned coldly on his wife. "Is your head sufficiently clear for snap?"

Ignoring the insult, Ianthe replied, "I think I can meet the challenge. Even whist if you prefer it."

"Very well, whist," he agreed. "Get the cards, Ianthe."

The next hour dragged. At last, shortly after ten o'clock, Wycksley himself suggested retiring, and thankfully Ianthe and Juliet, remembering not to appear too keen, both complied and said good night.

Before undressing for bed Juliet stood at the window, looking out over the moon-washed London square. The impersonal strangeness of the city enveloped her. The grayness of pale pavements streaked with elongated black shadows from the trees oppressed her with the haunted quality of being lost in some cold nightmare that had no relationship to her real self. She had an overwhelming longing for Polbreath, picturing the lonely moorland hills rising dark over the sea and valley road. She opened the bedroom window a little, closed her eyes, and drew the cool summer air into her lungs, picturing the gray farm by Rosebuzzan and Trefyn's figure outlined by the stables. She thought of her father; her brother William who'd wanted Hannah and married Charlotte; Jason; and her favorite, Andrew, too, who meant to be a monk. Then her mother, Donna. Why had her mother not been able to need her in the way she wanted? She'd tried so hard to make her love her when she was a little girl, and even at boarding school had secretly envied girls of her own age whose parents had spoiled them completely. Donna had never spoiled *her*—her upbringing had been strict where her mother was concerned, the parental hand frequently sharp, though she'd never told her father. If she had, there'd only have been further trouble that would have reacted unhappily on Nicholas—and not for the world would she have worried him unnecessarily.

The fact that he must be troubled now upset her. But perhaps he wasn't. Knowing she'd gone to Leonora's would surely satisfy him for a time. But later? She tried not to visualize his concern when she wasn't soon back—tried to believe he'd really be proud of her when he learned of *Drawing Room at Night.* Deep down, though, she knew he wouldn't be. Oh, poor father! If only Trefyn would miss her and come hunting wildly for her through London. If only he'd walk through the door of No. 10 one day, looking just as he always had: proud, free, with his dark head held high, lips and eyes expectant with longing, chin stubbornly set, one strong arm thrust out to pull her to him and take her away from this place—this unhappy rich home where her own sister lived so shamefully at the mercy of the callous old man she'd married. No play would matter then; no fashionable audiences or applauding crowds. She'd follow Trefyn eagerly, so willingly, and it would be heaven once more to feel the Cornish winds and fine rain on her face, to hear the mournful, high screaming of the gulls flying, and the plunging boom of waves on the rocks.

But Trefyn wouldn't come—not yet, not until something jerked him to his senses. She had to be herself, and *prove* she was worth more to him than just a domestic chattel to fuss over one moment and disregard the next.

A slight cough tickled her throat. The London air was so thick and damp; there was no scent in it of heather or fresh spring water. No drift of salty wind from the sea. Only cloying vapor faintly pungent with smoke from the distant, crowded areas.

She closed the window, turned, and went to the bed. The maid had already turned the sheets down; her slippers had been put by ready, and her thin wrap laid over the lace spread. Somehow her few simple possessions looked inadequate for the sumptuous bedroom, reminding her that the following morning she was to go shopping with Frances Bellingham.

She did not sleep well that night and when morning came was glad to get up and go downstairs. Breakfast was already laid in a small parlor used specifically for the purpose. She had coffee and a roll, and was frowned upon by Wycksley who came in just as she was finishing the meal. "No sausage? No bacon or egg?" he said. "But you should eat, my dear, with rehearsals starting so soon. Good nerves help good acting. And a little more weight would do you no harm, no harm at all—" He walked over prancingly to the sideboard, lifting the silver covers of the dishes one by one. Juliet noticed what small feet he had, and what a portly stomach.

"I wasn't thinking of my figure," she said. "I'm not very hungry."

He helped himself to a liberal portion of liver and bacon. "I hope you weren't too upset by the regrettable scene yesterday," he said, returning with a heaped plate to the table. "You should know by now that your sister has an extremely odd sense of humor and a very uncertain temper."

"I haven't known her very well since I grew up," Juliet said, not wishing to discuss her sister.

"No, of course not. You're so young." He gave her his characteristic bland smile. "And what are you doing this morning? Ah yes, I remember. The shopping expedition." He took his watch out and glanced at it. "Nine-thirty. Don't mind me, my dear. If you want to get ready, run away now and titivate yourself. It's very unlikely you'll see Ianthe before you go."

With great relief Juliet excused herself and went upstairs. She idled away time glancing at a fashion magazine taken upstairs the evening before, wondering what styles and color schemes to choose. By the time Frances arrived she'd decided that yellows, browns and rust shades were the best for her hair. But when they reached the modiste's, a select shop off Regent Street, she was persuaded that blues and grays were more favorable to the limpid gray of her eyes and delicately tinted complexion. As the expense of the chosen wardrobe was to go down on Robertson's account, there was no problem of money, but Juliet was reluctant to spend excessively. Wycksley might insist the outlay was necessary, and that she was entitled to have the very best in the cause of her new career, but she resented being obligated to him, and several times was on the verge of argument with the two women. On one occasion when Frances was insisting on her having a flame-shaded, high-waisted dress with an immense wide-brimmed hat to match, trimmed with large curling ostrich feathers, she refused obstinately saying, "You said blues and grays were my colors, and if they are, I don't see myself in all this bright red. I'm sorry, I couldn't possibly wear it."

"But madam—"

"Juliet, dear—" from Frances, "it's so *effective*. You should have at least one or two outfits to make an impression—"

"I don't want to make an impression. I want to be myself," Juliet insisted stubbornly.

"Oh, very well," Frances was clearly annoyed, but tried to keep her temper. "We shall have to decide on the emerald green instead then."

Juliet, who would have found the shopping interlude stimulating on her own, was disgruntled and finally bored by the chattering interference of the modiste and the actress.

"Well," Frances said as they drove away after an excessively tiring morning, "I hope Robertson approves of our choice."

"I expect he will, as you made it," Juliet said rather pointedly.

Frances was silent for a moment or two, then she said, struggling for patience, "I do hope you're not going to be difficult, dear. I don't *want* to inflict my opinions upon you, but if we're going to work together—which Robertson is determined upon—there are certain matters where you'll have to be advised. You know nothing of the theater, do you? and have not long left school. So shall we try and cooperate?"

"Of course," Juliet said stiffly. "But clothes are very personal, aren't they?"

"So is the theater, my dear. The most intimate yet exacting criteria in the world. Without being ostentatious one has to be always just a little larger than life, if you know what I mean."

Juliet answered in the affirmative, but her thoughts were wandering. Coming from the opposite direction, almost in the middle of the street, were three women wearing drab dark clothes with large boards slung from their necks. MRS PANKHURST LEADER OF ENGLISH SUFFRAGETTES was printed in bold black type on one; on another, larger still, VOTES FOR WOMEN.

Some commotion was being caused. A policeman was already hurrying to the scene to clear space for traffic. Juliet was suddenly interested, recalling the odd-looking girl, Judy, who'd been staying with Jet and Trefyn and her breezy references to the "new women."

"Will they be arrested?" she asked.

"I certainly hope so. Such monstrosities are an insult to our sex. A woman's business is to be beautiful, men's to run the country. The sooner this ridiculous movement is squashed, the better. If women want to dabble in men's affairs they should be prepared to go to war with their husbands and risk dying."

"Some do, don't they?" Juliet said sweetly. "Florence Nightingale did in the Crimean War. There was a whole book about her in our school library. And then—"

"She didn't fight or shout or stride about looking ugly, wanting to attack politicians and lay down the law in Parliament. She was a nurse. That's different."

Realizing that Frances had the uncomfortable knack of always turning an argument to her own accounts, Juliet was silent. But a renewed sense of loneliness had descended upon her. As the cab rattled to the door of No. 10 she wished with acute longing for a moment that she could shut her eyes, then open them and find before her the steps and wide porch of Polbreath, with her family waiting to forgive and receive her.

But, of course, there was nothing to forgive—nothing,

she told herself fiercely. Donna's anger and Trefyn's cruel unfairness, combined, of course, with her own wild temper, had driven her away. She had been insulted by her mother and despised by Trefyn. Until they missed her sufficiently to come and find her, she wanted nothing more to do with them.

*Nothing.*

Ah, but she did, she thought a little later when the clothes, carefully unpacked from their layers of tissue paper, had been shaken out by the maid and hung in the wardrobe. Most of all she wanted Trefyn. What did fine clothes matter when her body so ached for his arms round her, and her spirit yearned for the feel of the fine moorland turf beneath her, for the humming of bees in her ears where the yellow gorse was thick and the heather blew, and for the mournful sighing of the wind round the ancient standing stones of Rosebuzzan.

What was Trefyn doing at that moment, she wondered? and Jet? Lucky Jet who had no troublesome family trying to force her into a stupid marriage.

Her dark mood deepened and was only checked when Wycksley sent a message up to say he'd like a few words with her before lunch, as that same afternoon they were going to the Beehive for a brief read-through of the script.

The next few days rushed by in a whirl of activity— of comings and goings from No. 10 to the theater, of criticism and encouragement, of reading one passage over countless times before going on to another, and of a growing feeling in Juliet's mind that she would never make a satisfactory Susie.

Such moods, though, were generally when she was tired, and Wycksley was quick to buoy her up again with flattering remarks. "Ah, that touch of anger suits you," he said once. "Be yourself, as your producer says. Let your own exuberant spirit be free—within bounds."

It was the bounds that worried Juliet. There were so many of them to think about—pauses, voice inflection, and, when they got to gestures, movements, and entrances, knowing exactly when to enter and how many paces to move across the stage. There were also a number of "nots." Not to have one's back to the audience, not to shield any other of the cast yet to appear perfectly natural, and never under any circumstances to "declaim," yet clear production of the voice was essential.

It was all extremely confusing. This process had been going on for a week when Ianthe said one afternoon, "You're looking washed-out. Are you really enjoying being Robertson's performing protégée?"

"No," Juliet answered honestly.

"Then why go on?"

Juliet's mouth became stubborn. "Because I have to."

"Why on earth?"

"I'm not going to be a failure," Juliet told her. "I mustn't be. You wouldn't understand."

"Why wouldn't I? How do you know?"

Juliet flung her a speculative frowning glance. "Because I don't think you've ever loved anyone. Except father perhaps. . . ."

"There's no perhaps about it. I loved him, yes. I still do. I always will. As a matter of fact I was thinking of him. He'll be worrying, you know."

"He thinks I'm with Leonora. He trusts her."

"But how long will that go on?"

"Oh, Ianthe do stop questioning me," Juliet said irritably. "I don't probe into your life."

"My life is a scandalous open book, darling, there's nothing to probe into. But you're different. Anyway, think over what I've said. I don't like the idea of you being in the clutches of that big bad wolf I've married." She walked out of the lounge in her usual languid way, leaving Juliet to her own reflections.

Ianthe's references to her father troubled her, and if she'd known how upset he was becoming over her absence, she'd have worried more.

At Polbreath, Donna was becoming actively concerned about Nicholas. "You're looking so *weary*," she said one evening. "And it's Juliet, isn't it? You're fretting."

"Juliet *and* William," he said. "And then Andrew. What's the matter with him, I'd like to know? None of our children seem particularly satisfactory at the moment."

"You're forgetting Jason," Donna said tartly. "You can't complain about him. He's being most helpful in every way. And William? What's wrong there?"

"His marriage," Nicholas said shortly. "He and Charlotte aren't sleeping together, and they both seem truculent."

"Expectant mothers often are," Donna pointed out. "You weren't. You were just—"

"Yes?" Her orange eyes were alight.

"A damned nuisance," he said, and kissed her.

"Oh, Nicholas," she said in a changed, strangely gentle voice, "how I love you. Remember that, won't you, however domineering and difficult I may seem sometimes, whatever happens in the future—I love you so much that without you I think I'd die."

"My dear love," he said with his lips against a temple where a dusky curl nestled. "Why this nonsense about being without me and dying?"

She sighed, then smiled. "I don't know. Things, especially lately, have seemed oppressive sometimes; not physically, but as though something sad was in the air. It's hard to explain. I've been remembering too. Thinking back to the past when I went up to the stones that night in the fog, and the time I set fire to the headland because I thought you were in danger. Oh, my love—you won't leave me, will you? Not ever?"

He drew her closer, "Not while I live, Donna."

She shivered. "And that's a sad thing to say too—while you live . . . What about after?"

"Who's to say? But I can promise you that while a fragment of me—spirit or flesh—endures anywhere, you'll be with me, love, and I with you. Now," his tone changed, "cheer up, and no more gloomy talk. Tomorrow perhaps—"

"Yes?"

"We shall hear from Juliet."

But the next day the letter that arrived was not in her handwriting but in Louis Martellon's.

"My dear friend Nicholas,

This is just to tell you that I am leaving town shortly for Wales and, if convenient, would enjoy so very much a brief break at Polbreath. I have a little tip for you—is that not how you put it?—concerning shares in a new company to do with the production of cotton goods produced abroad that I think would interest you. At a very *minimum* price. But enough of business. I can be your way on the 3rd or 2nd of next month, and will contact you later to see if my visit is in order.

My regards to yourself, your beautiful wife and family—

Sincerely
Louis Martellon.

P.S. By the way, I had the great pleasure of traveling up to London with your charming daughter Juliet about a fortnight ago. She informed me she was going to town on a visit to friends after staying the night in Bristol. I very much enjoyed the encounter. But no doubt she has informed you already of our meeting.

L.M."

After reading the note, Nicholas stood for a few moments motionless, the piece of paper held tightly in one hand. His face had gone ashy gray. Donna noticed the giveaway muscle jerking near one temple, the outthrust set of his jaw, and as the seconds ticked by, the two vivid patches of color staining the strained skin of his high cheekbones.

"Nicholas—" She took a step toward him. The letter dropped to the table.

"She's not in Bristol," he said, wheeling round and facing his wife suddenly. "The little madam to have—" he broke off, gripping the polished surface of the wood to steady himself. The expression in his eyes frightened Donna. Her hand touched his arm tentatively.

"Who? Calm yourself. What are you talking about?" Her eyes glanced down at the paper. "Juliet, I suppose. Is that it?"

He thrust the note at her. She glanced at it automatically, then said, "Well? Why are you so shocked? Isn't it quite in keeping with her character? What you'd expect?"

"*No,*" he answered explosively. "By God, no. I thought I knew her. I never dreamed she'd have lied to me. Pretending she was at the Marshes—"

"But Nicholas, she probably was," Donna pointed out reasonably. "You can easily get in touch with them and find out." She paused, then continued, "It's quite clear to me. She got off there en route and stayed a night perhaps, as a blind, and wrote that letter to keep us satisfied. Then—off again, the little cheat, probably to Ianthe's."

"Yes . . ." Nicholas's breathing eased; a little natural color returned to his face. "You're right. Ianthe . . . !"

"I never agreed with your having Ianthe back for so long," Donna could not help saying. "She was a bad influence from the beginning. Still . . ." Her voice softened, "I suppose in a way it's understandable. But from the moment she entered the house Juliet became more defiant. And now—"

"Oh, stop it, Donna," Nicholas interrupted sharply. "It's not Ianthe I'm worried about—where Juliet's concerned. It's that—that plausible old rake she married. The whole decadent setup. Look what he's done to Ianthe—and *she's* my daughter too, Donna. She had values until I let her down . . ." He drew a hand over his forehead wearily.

"But you didn't, Nicholas, you didn't."

"When I married you I did—not through the act. I'd

have married you anyway, I loved you. But through *neglect*. The little things . . . oh, my God—"

"Nicholas, Nicholas . . ." Donna shook his arm fiercely, "you're not to say these things. They're not true. You didn't neglect Ianthe, you spoiled her, just as you've always spoiled Juliet, or she wouldn't have behaved like this—"

"Well . . . ," he wrenched himself free, "there's going to be no more of it. If Juliet's with Ianthe, I'll find her and bring her back and keep her here if necessary under lock and key. I'm not seeing another girl of mine ruined and corrupted by the debauchery of that filthy crowd. You haven't the first inkling of the insidious power of a certain section of town life, Donna. Twenty or thirty years ago it was different. Vice was hidden and to a certain extent controlled. Now it's become a rampaging disease. Drugs, sex orgies, free speech, degrading habits, and all under the cover of feminine rights; white slavery—and money, money, *money* to promote it—"

Donna gasped. "Nicholas, I didn't know—I've never—"

"You know *nothing*, Donna, about certain things; and I never meant you to. But it's right you should now, just so you understand."

He took his watch from his pocket and glanced at it. "If I hurry I've just about time."

"For what?"

"To catch the London train. I'll take a small case and go the short cut to Penzance—"

"But the gig won't—"

"On Pluto," he said. "Pluto will make the pace."

Donna resisted at first, ran to the door and stood there with her arms outstretched.

"No, Nicholas, *no*. That stallion's wild. You've always said so—untamable was your word. *Don't, please* don't."

He put both hands on her arms and forced them firmly but gently down, holding her hands in his.

"My love, I have to. What are you worried about? If Juliet's at Ianthe's, we shall return tomorrow. If not, I'll locate her, never fear. Now—" He bent his head, kissed first her cheek then her lips. "Please love, don't fret." The next moment he was striding down the hall to the stables.

Donna, realizing nothing she could do or say now could stop him, packed a bare minimum of necessities in a small light case, and five minutes later, with the cold fear still gnawing her, she watched him ride away up the drive, a dark figure on a dark horse against the gray sky—proud and reckless as the Dark Horseman of her youth who'd wooed and won her so relentlessly and wildly those many years ago. The sense of loss in her was inexplicable and frightening. When his flying form had disappeared round the bend into the lane, she still stood for some minutes, watching with numbed nerves, eyes glazed and only half-seeing.

Presently she forced herself to move and tidy her hair, then went downstairs.

Beth was coming from the parlor as she turned the curve of the stairs. Donna's expression disturbed her. "Is anything wrong?" she queried, "You look—worried, my dear," the last two words, a remnant of the old years, slipped out unconsciously.

Donna smiled. "Only myself. My wretched nerves. I don't like my husband riding that vicious creature, Pluto. He's uncertain."

"Mr. Trevarvas is an excellent horseman," Beth reminded her. "I don't think you need worry."

Normally Beth's words would have proved prophetic, but on that certain day a mist clung to the hills, and the light was uncertain along the narrow track that wound past the slope below the higher hump of Rosebuzzan. Nicholas, determined to catch the train, gave the stallion its full head, kicking the animal to a dangerous speed through the clutching wilderness of furze, thorn, and clumped heather. The distorting air billowed in damp, ghostly shapes as the animal, mane and tail flying, plunged ahead recklessly, snorting with joy at the unexpected freedom.

Sensing too late the horse's mood, Nicholas attempted to rein a little, but Pluto was beyond control. Bushes and gray writhing branches became gyrating, threatening claws of destruction. Leaves were caught and whipped against the eyes of man and beast; damp earth and stones showered into the mist. A gull screamed as it rose with a tremendous flap of wings before the black hooves. There was a bellow and snort—a tremendous rearing into the air, and Nicholas was thrown off sideways—thrown and dragged, his feet caught in the stirrups, leaving his head thudding against every rock and stone, for every yard of that last desperate journey.

His body was found two hours later by a shepherd from a farm Gulvarrick way. With the help of a laborer he was carried to a nearby pub and a doctor called. Life, it was learned, was quite extinct, and he had probably died in the first impact of the fall.

* * *

When Donna heard she did not speak at first. Her
face went gray, the lips tightened into a bloodless ef-
figy of a mouth. The orange eyes froze to the semblance of bleak glass. Beth went forward to comfort her,
but she drew rigidly apart. Even Jason was of no use.

Then at last she said, "Fetch him home. I want him

William took charge from then on, leaving Charlotte

"*Please—*" Charlotte begged, "please don't look like
that—cry, do anything. And remember, remember you

Donna's glance was withering, almost inhuman.
"What use are you? Any of you?" she said with cold
contempt. "He was my life, and now it's gone."

Charlotte's homely face winced. She made one more
attempt to comfort and thought Donna was going to
strike her. Then the upraised arm fell. The stiff back
turned, and the erect figure walked rigidly like that of
an automaton to the window.

"I'm sure you mean well," she said jerkily. "But
please leave me, and see no one comes near me until
they bring Nicholas back."

No one moved for a moment. Andrew who'd come
to the door hesitated before he said quietly, "We must
let the girls know."

Donna turned. "What girls?" she said with a remote
iciness that was worse than any anger, any hate.

"Your daughter Juliet, and Ianthe."

"I have no daughter," she told him. "Juliet killed
him. I never want to see her again."

"If she comes near this house," Donna continued re-

After the funeral you can contact her if you wish, but never, *never* let me set eyes on her again."

Her manner was so inflexible, her expression so strained Andrew realized she was beyond reasoning with.

"What are we going to do?" he said to William. "They have a right to be told. And yet—"

"Leave it," William said shortly. "If mama feels that way, her wishes should be respected. There'll have to be an inquest, I suppose, and then the funeral to be got through. What good could Juliet do, anyway—nothing except harm, especially with Ianthe trailing along with her."

"*If* she's at Ianthe's."

"That's the point," William said, "we don't know, do we? And if there's any criticism, we've got a perfectly valid excuse."

"And Jonathan?"

"Oh, my God! I forgot about him."

"The eldest son?" Andrew pointed out wryly.

"He's probably abroad somewhere."

"I'll contact that aunt—Joanna something or other—what's her name?"

"Vencarne?"

"No. That's the title. Funny isn't it, to think our aristocratic half-brother will be a lord one day?"

William shrugged. "It's stamped all over him, always was. I never felt the slightest tie. But you'd better get on with it Andrew. Her name should be in the address book."

With so many practical issues to be dealt with, the full tragedy and reality of Nicholas's death did not properly register until after the inquest, when the sad trappings of the funeral arrangements were in process.

Jonathan was eventually found to be in India and therefore could not possibly be back in time for the service. The rest of the family, in deference to Donna's wishes but against Andrew's principles, did not contact Ianthe until it was too late for her and Juliet to reach Cornwall for the burial. William, as head of the house in Jonathan's absence, sent a wire to Ianthe saying, "Father died in accident. Funeral today. If Juliet with you keep her there. Mama no wish to see her. Writing. William."

Later that day when the traumatic business was over, a return telegram was delivered to Polbreath, simply addressed to Trevarvas family. It read, "Juliet here. Both very distressed. Will never forgive you for not contacting earlier. Ianthe and Juliet."

When Donna saw the fragile slip of paper she tore it into bits and said, "*Forgiveness.* There can be none anymore between us." Her mouth was hard, her eyes frozen. Only Andrew, who'd learned through experience to recognize grief almost beyond bearing, understood; he knew too that no words could give comfort, and that although in time something of the old Donna might revive and live again, she would never be the same. And religion would not help. Her only religion had been Nicholas. Memories would endure, but memories, to a personality of her vitality and physical awareness, would prove sterile: the soft summer wind on her face, the lifting of a hand to the empty air where he'd once walked; the imagined presence in the lonely bed; the listening ear ever on the alert for the sound of his voice, for the galloping thunder of his horse's hooves over the moor and down the drive—these would provide no peace or warmth for her; in the end she'd have to accept that there was nothing left of him she knew. God was a mere illusion to her—a dream created by weaker personalities for their own comfort.

Donna was too proud to delude herself.

If only, Andrew thought frequently in those early days, she could find for herself even a frail glimmer in her own being that was sufficiently selfless to glimpse the wider reality. But he doubted she ever would.

He felt for her acutely; she was his mother, a human being. But the gulf in character between them was widening. William, sturdy and gusty with life, was likely to be of far more help to her than he could ever be. And of course there was always Jason, her favorite.

On the day following the funeral Andrew said casually, "I suppose this won't change your plans, will it? About Paris, I mean."

Jason gave him a shrewd look. "Are you expecting it to?"

"No, it was just a thought."

"Yes. Well—I don't know."

"Look, I wasn't suggesting—"

"You don't have to. Damn it, Andrew, I've got a heart. I mean, she does rather have this thing about me, and with the old man going so suddenly . . . it's bloody rotten for her—"

Andrew stared at him, temporarily taken back.

"Do you mean you're actually considering throwing the whole thing up? What you've been fighting for these past few years?"

Jason shrugged. "Well, you can paint anywhere, I suppose, and there'll be more work needing to be done here. You too—"

"What about me?"

"Come off it. It doesn't take half an eye to know you've been itching to test the water for some time."

Andrew paused before commenting; "You're cleverer than I thought."

"That's part of my art, brother mine. Deception."

Andrew thought for a moment then he said, "All right, and if I have, what about it? The same thing applies to both of us."

"Not quite," Jason said, "I've heard from several quarters you've an eye on holy pastures new, and though I don't approve, I wouldn't try to stop you."

"How the devil did you find out?"

Jason laughed. "Ah, that would be telling. The point is, if you feel strong enough about it, why don't you go ahead? I can take on from here. I might even cut quite a figure as 'the young squire'—master, bailiff or estate agent—whatever you like to call it. I think I could do it, I know the ropes, and old William would always be in the background as major-domo. Anyway, as long as tin and copper endure William will be content. I sometimes think . . ." he added wryly, "he should have commissioned me to sculpt a woman in copper and taken her to bed with him. And that's sacrilege at the moment, I suppose."

"No," Andrew answered. "Protective armor. Quite permissible. I know what you're feeling." He gripped Jason's shoulder for a second, because he'd caught the glint of tears in his eyes. "Buck up, old son, you'll get through. We all will."

"Yes, I guess so."

"And I'll think over what you said—if you meant it."

"Take it as settled," Jason said. "I've a hunch it'll work out."

"All right," Andrew said abruptly.

And from that moment he had no hesitation in making firm plans.

The following week he put them to Father Strawn.

## 11

Juliet sat slumped on the couch, staring yet seeing nothing. Her mind was a blank of despair through which only one thing registered.

Nicholas.

"He's dead," she said. "My father's dead, and she never told me."

"She told neither of us," Ianthe said bitterly, putting her arm round her sister's shoulders. "You have a particularly nasty bitch of a mother, haven't you? Of all the low things to do, that's about the rottenest I've ever heard of. And my precious half-brothers too. They must have known where you were. And anyway, what about me?"

Juliet glanced up. Ianthe's face looked old. Even under the makeup her complexion had paled. A blur of tears flooded her eyes. Juliet looked down again, pressing her face against the full breasts which felt icy through the thin wrap.

"I can't believe it. I *can't*. I just won't," she said with a sudden tumult of emotion.

"You've got to," Ianthe told her, and her voice was harder, more composed. "Nothing we say or do can alter things. Anyway . . ." the bitterness returned, "perhaps he's better off."

Juliet jumped up. "Don't say such things. It's not true. He loved life." There was a drawn-out pause, in which memories stirred with agonizing pain. "It's not fair."

"Of course not. Very few things are in this old life."

"Ianthe—"

"Yes?"

"I think I must go back."

"Why, for heaven's sake?"

"Just to be there. To be near. I feel kind of . . . faithless here."

"Oh, don't be ridiculous. Do you think they want you? You know *she* doesn't. And the rest are all afraid of her, poor things. Still . . ." her eyes narrowed, "if you want to throw yourself on their pity—demean yourself before that Gypsy lover of yours, give up the play, everything—do. Go ahead. I don't mind, although Wycksley will. Not that Robertson bothers me. We know exactly where we stand now."

"What do you mean?"

"He can't divorce me, darling. I've got him by the ear. He took his erring spouse back after she'd been . . . ever so naughty. If he tries anything in future, the boot will be on the other foot. And won't he look ridiculous, the stupid old so-and-so." She lit a cigarette and walked casually to the window. Her figure in swathed black appeared provocative, almost snakelike above the frothing hem, though her hips were seductively full.

Juliet was shocked by her ability to readjust—to return so quickly to habitual cynicism after the news of their father's sudden death. But when Ianthe turned it was obvious the mood was merely a pose. The mouth, though set, had a tremor to it. The eyes were too bright and brilliant. Whatever veneer she put on, Ianthe was suffering.

Pity for the worldly woman whom she hardly knew, but was so close to in blood, stirred Juliet to brief self-forgetfulness.

"I won't go," she said. "I'll stay. You're right. No one seems to bother about . . . about us. And there *is* the play. I *have* promised."

"Oh, that . . ." Ianthe took the holder from her lips and blew a coil of smoke into the air, "don't worry about it. I don't doubt for a moment my cunning husband has other luscious little cards up his sleeve." Her expression changed. "And what about your Trefyn? Won't he be missing you?"

"I don't know."

"Well, it's up to you. It's your life. If he wants you enough I expect he'll come and get you. As a matter of fact, Juliet, I don't want to be responsible for you. You're welcome to stay here as long as you like. You titillate Robertson and make things easier in that direction. But I don't want you on my conscience— what's left of it."

"I shan't be, I can make up my own mind," Juliet said stubbornly. "I want to do *Drawing Room at Night*." And it was true. Action of some kind seemed the only means of alleviating unhappiness and despair. The wound of her father's death went deep, but Trefyn's apparent neglect added cruelly to it, kindling as well a bitter defiance in her which whispered every time she thought of him: *Let him find me, let him suffer and want me. If he doesn't, I don't want him.*

And so rehearsals, after a tiring but promising start, went on. Wycksley was enthusiastic and made a great effort at diverting Juliet's thoughts from straying too frequently to Polbreath.

"You must always think of *my* home as yours," he said more than once, his pale eyes popping with genial affection. "You are on the crest of a new life, my dear . . ." and Juliet, with an unexpected quirk of humor, saw herself, in imagination, being launched from the top of an immense wave into a mighty sea of splashing success.

The opening night had been scheduled for the end of August for, hopefully, a successful autumn run.

William arrived unexpectedly at No. 10 in July, wanting to take Juliet back with him.

"You've been here too long," he said sternly, after explaining full details of events leading to the accident. "It's time you observed the decencies and took your proper place with the family."

Juliet stared at him. He was looking somber but handsome in his dark clothes, with the black band symbolic of loss and respect round his arm.

"My proper place?" she said wonderingly, "What's that? With mama hating me and threatening to bar doors. Don't be ridiculous, William. There's no place for me at Polbreath anymore. And if there was, I wouldn't want it, without . . . father." Her voice trembled on the word.

William tried a softer approach. "When people are

shocked and under great stress they say things sometimes they don't mean," he said calmly. "You can't altogether blame her, under the circumstances."

"What circumstances, William?" Juliet demanded,
with rising color. "You mean *you* blame me too, don't
you? You think *I* was responsible for the accident, just
because I wouldn't put up with mama's bullying and
tempers, her bourgeois determination to get me married to that dull creature, Desmond Court—?" she
broke off breathless.

"Desmond's all right," William said lamely, "better
than that tinker's son by far."

"Leave Trefyn's name out of it, if you don't mind."
Juliet said hotly, "and don't try and force anything.
I'm not coming back."

"You could be made to," William replied with his
temper rising. "You're under age."

Juliet laughed, "Try it, you just try it," she said,
with her eyes blazing. "You're only my brother; do
you think any judge would listen to you, after the way
you've managed *your* life? And do you think after
how mama's behaved she'd get any sympathy? I'm living with my sister, anyway, and I've got a career
ahead. Wycksley's got me a part—a very good one in a
new play. I'm going to make a name." She turned
away, realizing her words had a childish ring and not
wishing William to see the confused distress on her
face.

Just then Ianthe came into the room, followed by
Robertson.

"Throwing your weight about, William?" she demanded. "I wouldn't if I were you. It's not done in
sophisticated society. Get back to your mama and loving wife. I rather believe Juliet's had enough of you."

Juliet didn't speak.

Wycksley coughed and went to the sideboard. "Have a drink," he suggested, bringing out a decanter and glasses.

William eyed him morosely. "No, thanks," he said abruptly, "this is hardly a social occasion. I've no time to waste. My sister apparently prefers the ways of your establishment to her home, and as I don't wish to be embroiled in an argument, I'd obviously better go."

"As you wish, sir," Wycksley agreed with portly dignity. "But should any of you feel inclined to attend the occasion of her stage debut, I shall be delighted to send complimentary tickets, should you let me know."

"Well done, Robertson," Ianthe said with a hint of grudging admiration when the door had closed. "Your aplomb was marvelous."

"I hope I have not yet forgotten how to conduct myself in front of ladies," Wycksley said pompously.

During the days and weeks that followed, Juliet became outwardly obsessed with her dedication to the part of Susie, resolutely turning her thoughts from Polbreath, determined almost fanatically to have a personal triumph in the play. The producer, impressed with her zeal, was not completely happy with her performance."

"She is vigorous," he told Wycksley, "superficially lighthearted, but I can't get her to relax. I have doubts she'll get the character over to the audience."

Robertson sighed. "Please see she does," he said coldly. "It's your business to, and important to me."

"Very well, I'll do my best."

But dealing with Juliet at that time was like coaxing human emotion from steel, artistically impossible.

She received a letter from Andrew one day saying
he missed her, but could understand her prolonged
stay in London. "I expect mama will recover in time,"
he wrote,

> but things are difficult at present. She is deter-
> mined to run the whole lot of us—Charlotte and
> William included—and though we realize it's be-
> cause of losing father, this doesn't make things
> easier, practically. I have decided to join the Or-
> der as a lay Brother, which of course means noth-
> ing final—probably I shall spend part of the pro-
> bationary period training abroad at some mission
> hospital. If so, I shall make a point of seeing you
> first. Jason's taking over from me. Strange, isn't it,
> after his fight to get the Paris business settled?
> But he seems quite determined, almost enthusias-
> tic.
>
> I had a word with Trefyn recently. He's an odd
> chap. When I mentioned you he went very silent
> and withdrawn, but I could see your flight has
> hit him hard. The foal bred from Red King is
> doing well, and I've a hunch he's going to suc-
> ceed with that small stud. If you still feel as you
> did about him, don't leave him in his misery in-
> definitely. He might kick! I'm not trying to
> frighten you, but he's not the sort to put up with
> too much for too long.
>
> Well, I don't think I've any more to tell you at
> the moment. All success with the theater if it's
> still on, and greetings to Ianthe.
>
> > My love, Juliet,
> > Andrew

The letter, rather than cheering Juliet up, depressed her. She couldn't visualize Andrew as a celibate aesthete in monk's robes, and his references to Trefyn were too slight and noncommittal to be helpful. What, for instance, did he mean by "not the sort to put up with too much for too long?" And why hadn't Trefyn at least sent a word to her? By now he surely realized the quarrel had been at least half his fault, and if a man loved a girl it was his business to make the first move.

Or wasn't it?

She was brooding with the letter in her hand when Ianthe came into the parlor. "What's that?" she said, "News from home?"

Juliet handed her the letter. Ianthe read it desultorily and handed it back. "You've made your stand," she said, "stick to it. I told you at the beginning you should go back, but you chose to be here. Don't shilly-shally, darling, it does no good. If your black-eyed swain wants you enough, he'll come and get you. Oh, Juliet . . ." for a second or two real feeling showed in her face, her voice was warm, "you're such a child. In outlook . . . experience. I just don't know how to advise . . . what to say. If you were a hardened creature like me, you'd damn well enjoy yourself while you could, and that's what I'd tell you to do. 'Gather ye rosebuds while ye may'—a lover or two on the way—what's it matter if it gives a bit of sweetness? But you're not like that are you? You're the same as Andrew, a bit of a puritan at heart, and heaven knows where you got it from. Certainly not . . . father."

"Please don't talk about him, Ianthe. I can't bear it."

"Very well. Yes, I agree. But remember, real life

isn't what it seems to be in Cornwall. War's probably brewing, and—"

"War?"

"Don't you read? The Triple Entente business with France and the East has upset Germany. A year . . . two years, three, four . . . and we may all be dead. Who knows?"

"You sound so cynical."

"I am. But don't take it too seriously. I have a wonderful capacity for being wrong, as my marriage to Wycksley proves. By the way—"

"Yes?"

"What about dear brother William and his wife? Is it working?"

"What do you mean 'working,' Ianthe? I told you about the child, and the little boy, Matthew, they've adopted."

"Yes, so you did. I wonder why."

"What?"

"Why they so willingly accepted a perfect stranger's offspring, and a peasant's at that. Of course with my perfectly foul mind it's not hard to guess. That burly brother of yours had obviously been a bit of a ram in his spare time."

Juliet glanced down.

"Well?" Ianthe persisted, when she didn't speak. "*Is* the baby William's?"

"I think so," Juliet answered. "I'm not sure."

Ianthe laughed.

"Poor Charlotte. I thought her extremely dull at the party and can't understand what William saw in her. But then I don't suppose *he* did. It was what they call expedient. And the woman was murdered, wasn't she?

Oh no, I forgot. An open verdict." When Juliet didn't reply Ianthe shrugged and went out.

A few days later Juliet found another letter addressed to her lying on the hall table. One glance at the handwriting told her who'd written it. She picked it up with trembling fingers and tore the envelope open. Her heart quickened, setting her whole body shaking for a moment.

> Juliet—
>
> Are you coming back? or have I got to come and drag you by the hair of your head? You're behaving abominably, know that? And I haven't really time to waste chasing after a spoiled young woman who doesn't care a damn about anyone but herself. If I *have* to make the journey, you'll be sorry.
>
> Incidentally, I got your address from Andrew,
>
> Trefyn.

Juliet felt a tide of warmth flood her. A secret thrill of excitement and triumph because Trefyn was angry and obviously worried. That was a good thing, she thought; it showed he cared. But she wasn't going to give in, not yet—and never completely. He needn't think he could love her one moment and scold the next—tell her just what to do and when to do it. She wasn't a bird to go flying to him at a whistle, or one of his strange little wild animals who'd go running at a call or crook of his finger.

And yet—a faint smile touched her lips—in a way she was; wild and passionate and longing for him to sweep her up into his arms. She closed her eyes briefly, imagining the closeness and warmth of him;

the sensuous possessive grasp of hands round buttocks and thighs and breasts, the hardening force of male need against her; the exquisite hungry pulse of her own desire. She wanted him; oh, how she wanted him. Through her deep longing even her father and the sadness of his death were forgotten, and all her world was once more Trefyn—the overpowering, flowering awareness of his maleness and thrilling ability to subjugate and take her to the darkest recess of human passion.

Very slowly the moment died. She opened her eyes and found herself once more with reality: the elegant, sophisticated surroundings of Wycksley's town house, with Cornwall taken into the mists of another life—a world almost of legend, she thought, glancing through the window across the square, a yesterday of wild unspoiled moors and primitive menhirs where fable was still so strangely intermingled with fact, and the rich earth belched steam kindled by man's greed. A great homesickness filled her. Her instinct was a sudden wild desire to be racing through the winds round Rosebuzzan, with Trefyn after her. Or perhaps completely on her own, so she could find some secret place where she could be her real self, knowing that never again need she be parted from the place she so loved.

That night she slept badly, torn between a desire to return to Polbreath and her ambition, which seemed to her then almost a duty, to make a success of Susie in *Drawing Room at Night*. At one point, about two o'clock, when her vitality was at its lowest, she almost decided on the former course.

Then, the following afternoon, matters were taken out of her hand.

She was in the conservatory when a maid appeared to tell her she had a visitor. "A visitor? Who?" Juliet demanded with an irrational hope quickening her pulses.

"A Mrs. Trevarvas, Miss Juliet," the maid said. "She seemed very . . . anxious to speak to you immediately, miss. Shall I show her into the drawing room?"

Juliet was about to answer in the affirmative when a voice she recognized only too well said from behind them, at the door, "There's no need at all. What has to be said will take only a few minutes."

Juliet turned and gasped.

Donna stood there, with the greenish yellow-gold light from the glass full on her face, which was pale and strained, tight-lipped with unforgiving condemnation. She was dressed all in black, with a long black veil pushed back over her plumed hat.

Juliet's face had gone white. "You can go," she said to the maid.

The girl hesitated for a moment, then muttering something under her breath, she went out, closing the conservatory door behind her. The two women stood facing each other, until Juliet said, "Won't you sit down . . . mother?"

"No, thank you. I won't remain a second longer in your company than is necessary. I've made this journey specially to see you and make things perfectly clear." She paused, while Juliet touched her dry lips with her tongue. Then Donna continued, "In case the telegram was not sufficient, I want you to know from my own lips that I consider my husband's death your entire responsibility and that I no longer regard you as any daughter of mine. If it wasn't for you, he'd be alive today. You murdered him. I hope you remember it for the *rest* of your life. Never dare to show your face at Polbreath again. What you do with that lusting tinker's son is your own affair, just so long as I never have to set eyes on you while I live—"

"But mother—" the hatred on Donna's face silenced her. Without another word the rigid figure turned stiffly and walked out, not looking back once.

Juliet stood dazed and shocked, listening mechanically to the light tap of receding footsteps followed by the sharp click of a door closing. Then, suddenly crumpling up, she half fell onto a seat, as the air curdled and revolved into sickening darkness.

She must have fainted. She came round to find Robertson bending over her, with a glass in his hand.

"Drink this, my dear," he said. "And don't let that— that creature distress you." His breath was warm against her cheek. Like a child she responded to comfort—any comfort, even his—unaware of its source or motive. Sobs came presently. He patted her hand, treating her superficially as a child in need of reassurance.

"Don't you worry, my dear, you're safe here. You must think of this always as your home, which it is, isn't it? Your mother—forgive me saying so—is unbalanced, a little mad, I'm afraid. Forget her and what she said—"

"But about my father. She—she—"

"I know, I know. I heard enough. Don't think of it. People like her should be locked up. They don't know what they're doing. There is only one course for you to take, Juliet, and that is to pull yourself together and concentrate on your career."

Presently, recognizing the sense of his words, she controlled herself and went up to her room.

Ianthe was waiting for her. "That woman's a witch," she said. "However did a nice girl like you get herself such a frightful mother?"

Juliet swallowed before replying. "She couldn't have meant it. It's what Robertson says—she's demented, because of what's happened. I don't hate her; but I could—so easily at the moment."

"*I* do," Ianthe said, "I detest her; I always have. And this proves it; no one with any decency in them could act like she has. I said it before, and I was right. By the way . . ."

"Yes?"

"Wycksley's already discovered, through his usual devious means, that father's not forgotten you in his will. We'll be hearing any day I expect."

"As if that mattered," Juliet said.

"Oh, but it does, darling. Money is very important. Especially in your case, isn't it?"

Juliet was not unaware of the significance of the words. They alluded to her future with Trefyn, of course. But at the moment even this seemed unimportant, something dimmed to insignificance by the hatred seen in Donna's eyes.

Because of rushed days filled with regular rehearsing, constant journeying between the theater and No. 10, social occasions which even Juliet could find no excuse to miss, and the trivial babble of Ianthe's friends—disturbing any hope of peace at the most unexpected hours—summer passed toward autumn hardly noticed by Juliet. Occasionally she was shocked to realize how quickly the first night of her stage debut was approaching. The changing season would be obvious in Cornwall, with moors turning from green and yellow to brown, and the valley deepening to rich russet aflame with gold and crimson before the leaves fell.

In London nature was less obvious, except for an increasing nip in the air and the networked tracery of trees becoming more clear daily against the graying skies. Sometimes there was fog, when the shadowy shapes of passing vehicles and the swathed, unreal forms of people emerged like looming ghosts through the thickened air, making Juliet herself feel unreal, as though she were a character in a dream.

Ianthe had a friend, Paul Tenière, a Frenchman who was a keen photographer and also an enthusiast of the new and developing cinematograph industry. He had equipment and a projector, called a "Kinetoscope," designed on Edison lines, which he had brought to the house and used to show story films depicting original fictional adventures as fantastic as Méliès's *Le Voyage dans la Lune*.

This new art irritated Wycksley, but he generally put in an appearance when his wife's little clique was watching, because he was shrewd enough to recognize that it could be big business in the future. The fact that Tenière was also Ianthe's newest lover did not worry him so long as she was careful not to air the relationship too tastelessly in public. His interests, both of an earthy and financial nature, were by now concentrated almost solely in Juliet, although he frequently had doubts about her acting ability. The promise he'd sensed at the outset of the rehearsals was not maturing according to plan. Too often she seemed rigid and mechanical, speaking her lines with vigor, but as though her mind was elsewhere. At periods when they were driving back from the theater, he tried stimulating her with tactful criticism, always putting the onus on the producer.

"Our good friend thinks perhaps you should not *try* quite so hard," he said once. "Just relax, my dear. We want the audience to love and suffer with you. So you must be *natural* above everything else. But of course," patting her hand, "you will be, I am sure, when it comes to the test. That's what I told him. 'The dear girl won't let me down, or you,' I said. 'Have faith.'"

"I'll do my best," Juliet said.

And with an appraising glance at the perfect profile by his side—the burnished, silky glint of copper curls brushing the ivory pale cheek, and shadowed sweep of dark lashes on the high cheekbone—Robertson thought, *You will, my dear, you certainly will, in one way—or another.* And the idea of the "other" was so stimulating the suggestion of failure was not at that moment so very distressing. If Juliet failed in the part of Susie, she had an adequate understudy thirsting for the part, which would leave his wife's young sister conveniently available for the more personal role.

Ianthe tried to put Juliet on her guard. "Just watch the big bad wolf," she said more than once. "You may be innocent darling, but don't carry it too far, Robertson's got his eye on you, and believe me, being bedfellow to the old reprobate's no fun. He's like a latterday Henry the Eighth—the appetite's still there, but not the punch, if you see what I mean."

Juliet saw, although she didn't want to.

"I don't need your warning, Ianthe," she said coldly. "There's nothing between Robertson and me, and there certainly won't be. So you needn't worry on my account."

"I don't darling. I just gape. You've got me

stunned—to have such a sublime faith in human nature. Wycksley—though you may think so at the moment—is no pool for charity. Why should he be after all? He owes you nothing for being my sister—in fact, he probably considers that a liability. However," she gave an expressive shrug of her elegant shoulders, "you'll make your own bed, as they say; just see you don't blame me if it turns out to be a decidedly distasteful one."

Juliet didn't reply but after Ianthe had gone she was so consumed with homesickness she decided, on the spur of the moment, to write to Charlotte for news of Polbreath, knowing if she got a reply it would be factual and nonbiased. The answer came quickly, almost by return post. After a few brief allusions to the domestic side of the household and the problem of catering to the numerous officials and engineers come to inspect and advise on the Wheal Flower project, Charlotte turned to the difficulty of dealing with Donna's moods. " . . . she has gone very cold and withdrawn," the letter ran,

shutting herself in her room, often for a complete day at a time, yet when I attempt to organize or take charge she resents it and makes a scene. I'm trying to be philosophical, but it's not easy. As you know, Andrew will be leaving this winter. I shall miss him. As for William and me—well, what can I say, except that we jog along without too much argument. Rather a sad commentary on married life, isn't it, after only a few months, but sometimes I'm quite grateful that William seems more married to his tin than to me. I'm rather tired. I think the baby will be large. My body feels like a ton sometimes. The doctor says I should take more exercise, but walking wearies me. Little Matthew thrives. I know everyone thinks I shouldn't have taken him, but he's a loving child, and I believe even William's a bit intrigued.

There's really very little more to say, Juliet. I expect you can read between the lines. I haven't seen or heard anything of Trefyn or his sister. Do keep in touch with me, I feel rather cut off.

Yours,<br>Charlotte

Juliet put the letter down with a queer feeling of frustration. The note was colorless, ambiguous, and boringly reminiscent of Charlotte's homely personality.

It *was*, however, a truthful commentary.

William was becoming increasingly irritated by his wife's cumbersome presence about their limited quarters. Charlotte had not blossomed as many women did with pregnancy. Her face had grown haggard and heavy-eyed; her complexion—never particularly clear—had taken on a drab, yellowish tinge. When he was forced to notice her he could not help comparing her with Hannah, and cursed himself for being too shortsighted in his choice of a partner. He spent more and more time in the vicinity of Penmartin and Wheal Flower, and when his frustrated sexual instincts demanded appeasement he took off to Penzance where the obliging widow of a sea captain always had a warm welcome. She owned a tavern, the Goat and Bell, inherited from her father who'd been half Breton. She was good-humored, lusty, and completely uninhibited with a rich laugh and a more than satisfactory bank balance. There were no illusions between them. She and William enjoyed what they had together as they'd have enjoyed a good meal with relish and no talk.

"My word, Jan," he'd say afterward, or words to that effect, "you're putting it on in front *and* behind," and she'd laugh heartily as her backside resounded with a smart slap. "Go on, you," she'd say, "you're no shadow yourself, you great bull, you," and he'd more likely than not fling himself upon her again, pulling her nipples and thrusting into her with the hearty lust of any primitive male animal.

Spiritually, romantically, or ideologically, they had nothing in common, and on his return to Polbreath he was quite aware he'd settled for second best. This didn't bother him. Hannah had gone, and Charlotte could no longer stimulate in him anything but a boring sense of mild guilt. It was difficult to imagine he'd ever found her in the least desirable; the memory of their marriage night was now embarrassing. He felt in some way betrayed—that by devious means and enticement of her body she'd bound him, through conception during that short period, to a lifetime's bondage.

Any earlier thought he'd had for the coming child was quickly fading. Ironically—since Charlotte herself had insisted on Matthew being brought to Polbreath—it was only the young boy who held any interest for him.

Charlotte must have realized his feelings—or lack of them. Her eyes which he'd once thought fine, were now generally hard and accusing—though, at moments, reminding him of those of a cow who'd lost her

calf. He wished with irrational impatience for the
birth to be over, knowing she was suffering and not
well, and angry with himself that he could do nothing
for her, feel nothing—not even genuine sympathy. On
the rare occasions the Major called at Polbreath, William made an attempt to appear polite and "matey"
with his father-in-law.

"My girl's done you proud, my boy," he said once.
"Five months married and an heir due before the
year's out. Jolly good, eh?"

"Oh, father," Charlotte protested miserably, "please
don't."

The Major looked briefly downcast. "Said something wrong, have I? You're all right, aren't you, girl?
Nothing wrong?"

"Charlotte's perfectly fit, Major," William answered
for her. "She has everything she needs, and all the
medical attention necessary."

"Oh, well, in that case—good, good," was the unsatisfactory reply, and William knew his own words had
not provided suitable conviction.

Even through her own unhappiness Donna was
aware of the marital difficulties, and although she
tried her best to blame Charlotte, she was under no
illusions concerning her eldest son's shortcomings.
Though in looks he sometimes reminded her so
acutely and painfully of Nicholas, in character he
measured up in no way to the man she'd so loved.
Only Jason provided any comfort—his buoyant happy
nature was infectious and as the days passed he succeeded even in making her smile sometimes. The fact
that he'd sacrificed his hard-won battle to go to
Paris—and with no apparent bitterness—for her sake,
touched her.

"I shall have a studio built in the garden somewhere, or maybe in a field," he told her. "The country here's as good as any foreign landscape. Better probably. Poplar avenues and vineyards have been overdone by the Impressionists. Don't worry, mama. Painting can be done anywhere, on a mountain or in a back street. And anyway, I always rather fancied myself as a squire figure. I shall take to leggings and lemon waistcoat and have a hell of a time with tenants' daughters, doncherknow?"

His smile was warm, whimsical. His blue eyes bright with sympathy.

"Oh, Jason," she said, running to him and drawing his head onto her shoulder. "What should I do without you?"

"You'd get by, you'd survive," he said stoically, "and one day . . ." He drew apart, regarding her very seriously.

"Yes?"

"You'll make friends with Juliet again, mama."

"*No*." She stiffened and turned away.

He followed her and planted a kiss against her neck. "Yes, you will, for your own good. It's not good to quarrel or hate. A damned waste of life and time. Know that?"

"You sound like Andrew," she said, diverting the subject.

"That suits me. I rather admire him."

"Why?" Her voice was sharp, holding a hint of derision.

"Because he knows what he wants to do and means to do it."

She laughed mirthlessly. "You mean to cut himself

off and spend his time praying. What use is that to anyone, Jason?"

"I've no idea. But then, I've not fought in a war or seen men die. I've not made my way from cottage to cottage on a gammy leg trying to do a bit of human good only to be thwarted every time by William and his bloody mines."

"Jason!"

"It's true. William may be a handsome bastard, he *may* have a heart somewhere in that great body of his, but I'm deuced if I've ever seen a sign of it."

Donna felt forced to say, "He hasn't the gift for showing his feelings."

"Hm! I wonder. It depends what kind of feelings, and where," Jason replied pointedly. "It's a pity he doesn't show a few for Charlotte."

After such short discussions Donna usually felt a little better, simply because her thoughts had been diverted from herself; but inevitably sadness and loneliness returned, increased by her own bitterness toward her daughter. As the days shortened to misty evenings over the moors, she felt strangely without purpose, and quite disinterested in the approaching birth of her grandchild.

Meanwhile, in London, the first night of *Drawing Room at Night* drew near. Juliet steeled herself to a show of enthusiasm and exuberant portrayal of the part, though inwardly she lacked confidence.

Ianthe, at her request, went to the dress rehearsal which took place on the afternoon before the appointed day. Wycksley sat next to his wife, watching, and from the irritated tapping on the chair arm, Ianthe knew he wasn't pleased.

"She's nervous," she said briefly during the interval. "Dress rehearsals are always hell. Anyway, you know very well you were taking a chance. Juliet's had no experience of the stage. At heart she's an unsophisticated character—a country girl. I hope you remember that, Robertson."

He glanced at her, scowling. It was very seldom these days Ianthe was unwise enough to cross him.

"Kindly leave me to manage my own affairs," he said shortly. "And attend to your own."

"Oh, I do, I do," she said, lifting her cigarette holder from her lips and puffing a series of smoke rings ostentatiously into the air. "But I *must* remind you, husband mine, that Juliet is my sister, and that I happen to have a shred of feeling for her. Also . . ." she paused before adding with a hint of malice, "she has a very handsome young Romeo tucked away in the wilds of Cornwall, to whom she's quite madly devoted. Her code of values is completely different from mine or yours. For the sake of your own dignity, I think you should remember it."

"You're insulting," he muttered under his breath, "and you look quite ridiculous in that—that silver turban thing. Or is it a bathing cap?"

Ianthe smiled wickedly. "Designed for a sultan's harem," she said. "Only I got it from a sheik—a friend of mine. Apparently they're going to become all the rage in select society."

Wycksley did not deign to reply, but the mottled deepening red of his complexion clearly signified what he felt. There were times when he decided even a contested divorce action would be preferable to continuously having to accept Ianthe's outrageous behavior and jibes. But then he'd probably have to pay out more than was acceptable to his shrewd business mind, so he let the matter drift each time, and ignored as much as possible his unsatisfactory domestic situation.

The first night arrived, jolting Juliet with a sudden sickening feeling that she couldn't possibly face the audience; she would faint or collapse; turn and rush from the wings at the last minute and run—run—run—away from that stuffy, crowded theater and the cynical, watchful face of the producer—from Wycksley's bulging appraising eyes and Ianthe's half-amused concern—rush to the station where she could hide and wait until a train came that could carry her back to Cornwall and Trefyn. Why had she ever thought she could be an actress? Already her throat was constricted and she had to keep saying her first lines mechanically over and over through her mind in case she forgot them. Her hands were damp and icy cold. Waiting in the wings to make her stage entrance, followed quickly by Linton Wells her stage lover, she was only dimly aware of him whispering, "You look ravishing. Bear up, darling once you're on, you'll be all right."

They had all told her that—Ianthe, the cast, the producer, stage manager, Frances, and Robertson. But she couldn't believe them anymore. She couldn't act like Susie, because she didn't feel like her; she knew the ridiculous scarlet costume and flappy red tam-o'-shanter didn't suit her and were wrong for her hair. She had to fling her beret off, of course, as soon as she appeared on the elegantly devised drawing-room set, shake the ribbon from her russet curls, and rush into Frances's arms. Frances, as Eloise, would remain cool,

poised, condescendingly tolerant, then graciously offer her hand to the handsome, shy young man approaching with such diffidence. Then the emotional
conflict would gradually begin. Susie's slow disillusionment would be only faintly obvious at first, becoming a mere background for Linton's increasing involvement and capitulation to the ravishing older
woman. The finale would explode in a hysterical
scene in the third act. But to Juliet, the whole play
now seemed artificial and contrived—a party piece
merely devised to display and publicize the ravishing
personality and brilliant talent of Frances Bellingham.
In real life Juliet knew she'd have dressed seductively
in subtle shades and refused to be downcast by her
rival's wiles. She'd have used every means in her
power, every ounce of skill and feminine subterfuge
to keep her lover by her side. Then if it came to a
fight, eventually she'd behave like a tigress rather
than lose Trefyn.

Trefyn!

But of course the play had nothing to do with him.
Trefyn was far away in Cornwall. If he'd been within
miles of this beastly theater, he'd have come and
swept her away. He would surely. Or didn't he care
enough? Didn't it matter to him at all that she was
marooned here with no one to support her but Ianthe
and her pop-eyed elderly husband? In a flash, a burst
of spirit returned to her. She'd show him—oh, yes she
would. Here was the chance to get notices in the papers, her name in lights, and her photograph in all the
fashionable picture papers and magazines. Her limbs
trembled; gradually a glow crept to her cheeks under
the makeup, and her eyes sparkled, She wouldn't fail;
she couldn't—she *mustn't*.

She felt a gentle dig in her back. "Your cue in a minute," Linton whispered. "Keep your nerve—you'll be fine."

A moment later she saw Frances get up from the chaise longue and move to a window, heard the sharp snap meant to indicate the opening of a door that was her entrance cue, and, hardly realizing it, found herself obeying instructions and rushing on to the stage.

Linton followed, and hesitated behind her. Frances turned. "Susie, darling," she said in her marvelously husky voice as Juliet flung herself like a bomb at the perfumed, bejeweled breast, almost knocking her over. "My dear child—what excitement." She paused, still smiling, though her eyes were narrowed in an expression the audience did not see. "And *such* a surprise," the calm tones continued. Then, looking toward Linton, "Who—who is this? A friend, obviously."

"He's—it's Linton, my—fiancé," Juliet said with a genuine gulp.

"Oh—" there was a pause that shouldn't have been there at all—a ghastly moment in which Juliet searched for words. Then she suddenly remembered. "This is my—my stepmother, Eloise—Linton—"

Linton moved forward and took the gracefully extended hand. From the audience somewhere there was a faint but obvious titter. Perspiration gathered uncomfortably under Juliet's makeup. She knew she was making a muddle of the part—she'd been gauche in her meeting with Francis, or rather Eloise, and she realized suddenly she'd forgotten to throw off her abominable beret.

She instantly remedied the mistake, but the gesture was ill-timed, and the woolly object went whirling like a pancake into Linton's face.

The audience roared with laughter.

He was furious, but kept his head sufficiently to say on his own initiative, "What a madcap you are, Susie."

Frances, expert at improvising, inserted a few more lines unwritten in the script, and brought the interlude to its proper cue again, from where Linton continued.

The rest of the act was a nightmare to Juliet.

"I can't go on," she said in the interval, "I can't, I can't."

"No. I quite agree," the producer told her. "You were quite unbelievably *terrible*."

Juliet made a dash for the dressing-room door. He caught her and pulled her back. "Now listen to me, young lady," he said sternly, "if the matter had been left to me I'd have fired you after the first reading, but as Mr. Wycksley's sister-in-law you had to be allowed a chance. This play, though, is not a farce, which you seem to think it is. I feel insulted and ashamed for the cast and the author that you have made it one. Luckily we have a proficient understudy—"

"You mean—"

"I mean you'll go on to that stage for the second act," he told her ruthlessly, "you'll say a few lines—I don't care a damn what—then you'll fling yourself on the ground in hysterics or a faint, I don't mind which—the curtain will come down, and I shall appear quickly with my apologies to the audience for your sudden collapse and illness, telling them the play will continue with your understudy, the accomplished Gillian Vance, as Susie."

He paused. His usually pale face was beetroot red. "You understand?"

Juliet nodded humbly.

"*Good.* And no comic interlude, or I'll bloody well wring your pretty neck."

"I didn't mean—" Juliet protested feebly—"I didn't mean to be funny. I—oh well, the whole thing was wrong for me anyway." Her voice rose, "I didn't want to wear this horrid stupid red or make cow's eyes at Linton. And no girl in love would ever—*ever* act the way you tried to make me."

"Indeed. Well, this doesn't happen to be your play or your production, and I'm not at all interested in your opinions on love. Just do what I say—collapse on the stage, drop down or fall dead. It doesn't matter a damn to me so long as you remove yourself from this theater."

Insulted and shocked by his words and manner, Juliet was flooded by a seething tide of angry emotion. Very well, she thought, if the odious man wanted outrageous behavior, he should have it.

She no longer cared what the crowd or Wycksley or Ianthe or anyone thought, and when the curtain went up again she proved it by such a display of hysterical abandon her performance apparently carried conviction.

"But you were *superb* as a mad woman, darling," Ianthe said later as they drove back side by side from the theater. "Even my dear husband must have thought so, didn't you, Robertson?"

He didn't reply. There was no indication on his bland face what his thoughts were.

Ianthe, though, was highly amused.

"You're the best actress I've seen for years," she said.

Juliet kept up a stoical appearance as long as possible, but once the reaction set in, when she was alone at last in her bedroom, her nerves completely gave. Her stage debut!—and such a fiasco. Tears unwillingly flooded her eyes and broke in a stream down her cheeks. She put both hands to her face and let the sobs come, her body wracked with distress and disappointment. To think she'd made such a charade of herself!—appeared so ridiculous and gauche in front of all those people, making them laugh when they should have been twisting their handkerchiefs and weeping for her.

What would Trefyn think if he ever heard? It wasn't likely, of course, but these things got about. Newspapers were always ready for a tasty bit of gossip, and if anyone at Polbreath got an inkling of what had happened, it would penetrate somehow to the farm. The servants talked and giggled. Old Abel Price, who'd once worked in the garden when Nicholas was a young man and now had a cottage on the estate, was always perusing papers. Polly Trewhella, the postmistress at St. Figgans, sent him a copy of the *Cornish Weekly* every Monday, and Abel would be certain to spot any item mentioning the Trevarvas name. He was an old gossip, devoted to the family, but just couldn't be trusted to keep his mouth shut.

It would be terrible if Trefyn got to know of her disgrace. Not only that—he'd be so sure of himself, so confident of his power over her, and able to say . . . what would he say? She shivered at the thought, and cringed. She loved him and wanted him passionately—

but not to have him crowing over her and thinking of her as just a woman to be used and put in her place when he felt like it. She wanted him always to worship her as he had that night at the dew pond before they started to quarrel over the wretched Wheal Blair business.

The memory of that heady, wonderful night filled her with a renewed agony of longing—longing so overwhelming she could hardly bear it. She jumped off the bed suddenly and started to undress, wild thoughts churning through her mind of where to go and what to do in the future. She *couldn't* return to Polbreath—not yet, anyway. That was impossible. Her mother hated her and had said she must never show her face there again. Trefyn would despise her for being a failure, and throw her childishness in her face. Andrew might already be closeted in some dreary monastic cell near Devon, and William had never really liked her as much as her other brothers. Jason was tied to mama. No, there was simply no one in Cornwall to whom she could turn. Her father, the one person who'd have protected and taken her in his arms, was dead. Because of *her*, Donna had said, and that was a cruel thing to say. Cruel and untrue—it must be. If Nicholas had really died through her fault, then she wished she could die too. But it wouldn't have happened if he'd not ridden that wild stallion. He could have chosen the gray or the mare, Tamsy. Pluto had always been uncertain—her father had said so time after time—not at all like his sire, the first Pluto. He'd known the danger and needn't have taken it. And surely Donna must realize it. In the end perhaps she'd see the truth and take her dreadful words back. But in the meantime Juliet had to face the prob-

lem of where to live. In her miasma of dark depression
she didn't care much where it was, just so long as she
could get away from Belgravia and Ianthe and Wycksley as soon as possible. Obviously she couldn't stay
at No. 10 after tomorrow. She'd let Robertson down,
and though her half sister didn't appear to mind—
rather the reverse, in fact—Ianthe's amused irony was
suddenly distasteful and intolerable to put up with.
The Marshes would take her in at Clifton, but the gesture would mean a sort of charity, and Juliet loathed
the thought of that. So what was the answer?

She leaned forward over the dressing table with her
head in her hands, trying to think. The rich glossy
cloud of her burnished hair tumbled over her shoulders, half-covering the creamy breasts.

She'd already removed her underbodice and loosened her stays which were crumpled toward her hips.
Her white petticoat lay half on the floor.

So might Degas have painted a study of a ballet girl
relaxing.

And so she appeared to Robertson, as he turned the
knob of the door softly and stood for a moment entranced—only looking much more vulnerable and desirable, a nymph, half-woman, half-virgin, bathed in
an aura of subtle, sensuous light.

Before she heard, or was aware in her distress of
anyone's presence, he crept in with pursed-up anticipation on his round moist lips, eyes wide and desirous
above the pendulous cheeks, breathing heavily as he
approached her, amazingly lightfooted for so heavy a
man.

It was his breathing she heard first. Startled, she
looked round and jumped up when she saw his large
figure looming so close in its crimson satin dressing

gown. He stood for a second, smiling fatuously. Instinctively she reached for clothes to cover her naked-
ness, and discovered to her dismay that everything
was crumpled round her waist. She bent down to retrieve her bodice, fumbling with wildly beating heart
and shaking fingers to shield herself. But a podgy
hand stopped her. "My dear—" an insinuating, sly
voice said softly, almost in a whisper, "don't be
afraid . . . you're surely not afraid, of _me_—
Robertson? I only want to help you my dear . . . to
be your guardian and friend. . . ."

Her breathing quickened, she tried to draw away as
fingers tightened on her skirtband, giving a sudden
jerk that released it completely, sending its froth of
frills to the ground. Before she quite realized what
was happening, the stays too were quietly and insidiously claimed, leaving her completely exposed except
for the calf-length embroidered drawers. She stiffened and opened her mouth to protest. Wycksley's
hand came up over her lips, while the other located
the remaining buttons of her underwear. The drawers
fell, leaving the podgy fingers free on her buttocks,
tightening and squeezing as his revolting bulging
form, with the dressing gown already fallen open,
closed upon her. She started to struggle wildly, but he
did not desist. "Sh—" he muttered, his breath hot and
rasping on her face. "Don't worry—no risk, my dear—
we won't—there are other ways—" she realized, with a
wave of disgust stronger than her first sense of rage,
that his flesh was limp and flaccid against her own.
He was playing with her body in a revolting, unspeakable way.

She made a violent lurch from him, suddenly managed to bring a hand against his damp face, clawing

at it so wildly he gave a short sharp shriek of pain, and released her. She kicked him savagely and started screaming. She screamed and screamed, and rushed to the far side of the bed; with his pendulous face thrust forward he followed her. "You little bitch," he said, his eyes maddened, mouth drooling. "I'll have you—you little madam—I'll teach you what pain is—" he already had a hairbrush in his hand. She looked round wildly for a weapon with which to defend herself. There was nothing. So she screamed again, so shrilly and loudly he stopped for a second or two, staring at her, momentarily shocked yet still savoring the minute ahead when he'd have her at his mercy, the sweet tender flesh his possession to torture and defile.

And it was during the brief respite that Ianthe appeared. "Well, well," she said, smiling in the doorway, "up to your old sport again, Robertson?"

He spun round, drawing the dressing gown close about him.

"You filthy creature," Ianthe continued contemptuously, "you sadistic old man. Get out, do you hear, or I'll get the police. I won't spare you this time, Mr. Robertson Wycksley. You and your talk of *divorce!* My God! *You.* You're about the sickest thing ever born. Go on—go, and leave my sister alone or I'll see the whole of the London press knows of this in the morning."

Wycksley's mouth thinned, then opened, gasping for a second like a great fish gasping for life. He was breathing heavily as he drew himself up and attempted to speak, but the words ended in a mere splutter of sound. He went through the door without another glance at Juliet or his wife, closing it with a snap behind him. Ianthe seated herself on the bed.

"I'm sorry," she said coolly, "but I did warn you."

Juliet didn't answer. She was already dressing fren-ziedly, snapping her corsets, pulling up her drawers and adjusting her petticoat and skirt with fingers that had gone icy cold. Her mind would register nothing but the urgency to get away from that suffocating, luxurious house which to her had become a place of evil. Ianthe watched, waiting for a reply as Juliet pulled a bag from under the bed, opened the elegant wardrobe, and one by one wrenched the few clothes she'd brought from Cornwall off hooks and hangers.

"Juliet—" Ianthe began again, "don't be stupid. Where do you think you're going at this time of night?"

"I don't know, and I don't care—anywhere," Juliet said recklessly. "I can—"

"Walk the streets?" Ianthe asked bluntly.

"I can go to a hotel somewhere."

"Have you any money?"

"Yes, enough."

"Hotels are expensive. And if you're going back to Polbreath, you'll need the—"

Juliet swirled round. "I'm *not* going to Polbreath. And don't try and make me. Don't dare tell William—"

Ianthe got up suddenly and took her sister by the shoulders. "Darling, as if I would. I may be all sorts of a . . . bitch, but not that kind. All the same . . ." she paused while Juliet's stiff body relaxed a little "I've got to know *something*. London's not Polbreath you know . . . there are all kinds of nasty people about. Pretty foul things can happen to an innocent like you wandering about alone—"

"What does it matter?"

"Of *course* it matters." Ianthe's voice changed into sharpness. "Now, before you go you're damn well going to tell me where, or at least give a clue, or I won't allow it. I simply won't."

Juliet stared at her blankly, trying to get her thoughts into order. Then she remembered. Judy. Of course—she'd go to the strange place Judy had told her about—the queer lodging house near Camden Town. Judy would let her join her, she was sure of it, at least for the time being, and she had her address somewhere in her purse. She rushed for her coat and found the piece of paper in the pocket. "Here, that's where I'm going," she said, handing it to her sister. "She's nice. She stayed at Trefyn's in the summer—to paint."

Ianthe studied the address and looked doubtful. "Good heavens! But that's a—a funny sort of neighborhood, isn't it? I mean, hardly *our* style."

"Who wants to be *our* style?" Juliet said bitterly. "Anyway, I'm going. Tonight, or tomorrow early, and no one's going to stop me, either you or anyone else."

Ianthe's mood abruptly changed. She shrugged. "I'm not your jailer. And God knows, I've no right to play the moralist. It's just—maybe I was thinking of that young man, partly. If you love him, Juliet, don't spoil things, or yourself. It's so easy. One wrong step can ruin a life. And I should know."

Juliet softened. "Oh, Ianthe, I'm not stupid. And I'm not ungrateful either. But Wycksley!—" she shuddered, "I've got to leave. I must. Don't you see?"

Ianthe nodded. "All right. We'll get you a cab. If I bother about the chaise this time of night, it will be sure to cause a complete furor with the servants.

Heaven knows, they must have heard enough already. Still . . ." her voice became dry, contemptuous. "no doubt that wily husband of mine will be clever enough to have thought of an adequate excuse by morning—'my poor young sister-in-law,' you know—an attack of hysteria—unfortunate, most unfortunate. My wife had not informed me of her complaint—an inherited disease—"

Juliet looked aghast. "Ianthe! He *wouldn't*."

"Oh yes, my dear, he would. Anything to save his own flabby skin."

The younger girl flinched. "I must hurry, mustn't I? About the cab . . . I could—"

"If you insist on going now, I'll get the boy to call one. He's trustworthy and won't talk. Anyway, what does he know to talk about? You'd better finish dressing now, quickly, before Robertson gets the idea of having all doors barred. Oh, don't worry, I think it highly unlikely; probably he'll be as glad to see the last of you safely off the premises as you are to go. Now I'll nip downstairs while you collect your things. Write that address out for me clearly, in case Andrew or your loved one contact me. I won't be more than five minutes."

She hurried out quickly, leaving Juliet to push her remaining odds and ends into her case, pack the rose-colored dress, and put on instead a gray blouse and skirt under the gray cape. She tied a scarf over her small hat, and when Ianthe returned she was ready.

"The cab should be here any moment now," her sister said, "and here's something to tide you over a bleak spot—" she pushed a handful of notes into Juliet's hand.

"Oh no, Ianthe, I can't."

"You can and you will. It'll ease my mind. My goodness! It's not my idea of life to have to fret over the fate of a silly bit of a girl with no more sense in her pretty head than I have in my own. Now, what about that address. Got it?"

Juliet handed it to her.

"Don't expect to see me though," Ianthe remarked caustically. "I'm not one for visiting the poor and deprived. Poverty sickens me. But if saintly brother Andrew turns up, I'll be able to hand on information."

"Not William though."

"No, certainly not William."

Juliet made an effort to smile.

"Thank you for—for helping me, Ianthe."

"Help?" Ianthe laughed. "No sob stuff darling, and no lies. I'm about the rottenest influence any innocent could fall under. But in a queer way—although you're Donna's daughter—I rather like you. So cheer up, keep your chin high. What about a pick-me-up?"

"Oh, no, I—"

"Oh, yes." Ianthe disappeared briefly and returned almost immediately with two glasses in her hand.

"Quaff it up, quick. The real stuff darling—whiskey." She forced one glass into Juliet's hand and held the other in front of her. "To us, darling, or rather, you. And may the rest go to hell."

Five minutes later the cab was rattling away from Belgravia, with Juliet sitting inside, dizzy from emotion and the drink, not knowing how exhausted she was or what lay in front of her.

## 12

It was quite dark when the cab drew up outside the looming shadow of the house. No lights penetrated the rising mist except those of the few vehicles passing and the dim glow from odd squares of windows that gave Juliet the strange impression of hostile eyes watching. She felt unreal, detached from herself, and a little frightened. As the cabby poked his head round and said, "This is it. This is the place," two women with an unfamiliar accent jostled each other, laughing. The shadow of a man followed. Somewhere from down the road a girl shouted. Because of the general muffled silence, every noise there was seemed intensified. Juliet clutched her cape at the neck and stepped down onto the damp pavement, paid her fare, and a moment later the vehicle was moving off again, leaving her standing hesitantly by the iron gate. She could see, vaguely, a few steps leading to the door. There was a railing bordering a narrow strip of ground—it could hardly be called a garden—and steps from there also going down on her left to a basement. The whole atmosphere in the darkness was chilly and depressing. It was hard to imagine the rollicking Judy she'd met in Cornwall living in such a place. Supposing she didn't? Supposing she'd left and gone somewhere else, or supposing the driver had been wrong about the address?

Realizing nothing could be gained by hesitating, she forced herself to the door and pressed the bell. Following its dull buzz there was silence for a moment, then the hollow tread of footsteps from inside. The door opened, sending a wan beam of light across the flagstones.

A thin pale face framed by red hair drawn back into a knot stared out inquisitively.

"Yes?" The tones were abrupt, almost intimidating.

"I—I'm looking for—" Juliet's voice faltered. She realized, with a shock, that she'd never known or asked for Judy's surname. "Her name's Judy—" she continued in a rush. "I never—I mean I've forgotten what else. We didn't know each other well, but she told me to come here if I needed her. And—" she broke off helplessly.

The pale countenance came nearer. Juliet noticed how very bright the eyes were, screwed up and penetrating under thick brows. "Come in," the clipped voice said abruptly. "You look rather . . . well, not exactly one of us. But I expect you mean Judy Welsh. Wait here, I'll go and see. Most of my tenants are in their rooms by now, you know. It's late."

So she was the landlady, Juliet thought as the woman turned, walked down the flagged hall, and up the staircase. Juliet glanced round at her surroundings which were lit by only a small-powered bulb hanging without a shade from the ceiling. The interior appeared shabby and as uninviting as the outside. Brown oilcloth, rather worn, covered the stairs. There was a cheap-looking table by the side of wall pegs where coats were hanging, but, incongruously, the chair next to it was obviously a genuine antique that had seen better days. Near the foot of the stairs, stuck on to a yellowish bulletin board, were several notices and placards—one an especially large reproduction of the head of Karl Marx and, facing it on the other side, a large poster boldly printed with VOTES FOR WOMEN above a photograph of Emmeline Pankhurst. There was another, smaller hand-inscribed placard which said something about equality and welcome to all.

Juliet tried to feel composed and relaxed, but it was difficult.

She had to wait only a few minutes before two figures emerged at the top of the stairs, and as the wan light caught their faces she saw with relief that one was Judy's. She was looking rather incongruous in an old tweed coat over a flannel nightdress, and her eyes and mouth were opened wide in her round face.

"Juliet Trevarvas," she cried, rushing down the last few stairs, "Golly! what a surprise. What's this all about? My word, you look half-dead. Gosh! What's happened?"

"I've left home," Juliet told her, "and I remembered what you said about calling if I needed help. I'm sorry to be a nuisance, but—"

"Don't be silly," Judy said quickly. Then, turning to the other woman, "This is a friend of mine, Agatha. Juliet, meet our friend and landlady, Agatha, Miss Grant. This is Miss Grant's house, Juliet, and we rely on her—absolutely." There was a pause before she continued once more to the ginger-haired lady, "She *can* stay here, can't she, Agatha? She's quite forward-thinking really, and she *does* have the stuffiest home life—"

Miss Grant surveyed Juliet doubtfully. "All my proper rooms are filled," she said. "I should have to clear a storage room, and I'm not sure it would be suitable for your friend."

"Oh, but it would—it could be, I'm sure it could," Judy protested enthusiastically. "And she could share my bed until then. Honest injun! Agatha, it would work. Juliet's just what we want—you know someone who's sick of the old rich life and wanting the new . . ."

Even then Agatha Green did not entirely agree. But when she'd considered the proposition for a few moments longer, she said, "Very well. For tonight, anyway. I'll think things over, and in the morning we'll have a talk. But of course you can't possibly share that narrow bed of yours. I've a spare mattress upstairs. If you'll help me carry it down, Judy, we can rig things up on the floor. It is aired, of course. I always keep things ready in case there's an emergency."

An hour later, when the two girls were ensconced in a small room hardly more than eight feet square furnished only by the bed, mattress, narrow washstand, one inexpensive chair, and a few of Judy's personal possessions, Judy, staring down from her pillow on Juliet's recumbent form, tried to explain.

"We all have just one room of our own," she said. "There are about eight of us—Katinka, she's half-Russian but her parents are separated, and she does typing somewhere, in the daytime. Then there's Mr. Singh—he's an Indian but not rich like some of them—he studies law in the British Museum mostly. There's

Carl Berloiz—he's a German, he does journalism; and Maidie—she works as a waitress half-time at a café—quite near here. Her husband beat her up *terribly*—so of course she's *absolutely* antiman, if you know what I mean, and goes on all the marches with Agatha—"

"Marches?" Juliet queried sleepily.

"Of course. Suffragettes. Agatha's one of the leaders. She's stupendous, absolutely inspiring when she gets going." There was a brief silence while Judy got her breath. Juliet waited, trying to keep awake.

"Peter Richard's a poet. He's sort of vague and dreamy, but he writes the most thrilling stuff; once you get the hang of it you're drawn into another world—absolutely. Mind you, it's not easy to understand at first. But Stephanie, who's the daughter of a duke or somebody who had a baby and ran away—she thinks he's a positive genius. She doesn't have to go out to work, but she does the cooking for us, breakfast and a meal at night. She's got a bit of money, you see, and puts it all to our cause. Freedom. You'll like her, I think . . ."

Judy was still recounting the ideals and the personalities of the establishment when Juliet completely lost the drift of her words and fell asleep.

The morning came misty and gray, with a thin rain blowing down the London streets.

Juliet woke wondering at first where she was.

She'd been dreaming, all through the short restless night, of the granite standing stones of the moorland heights of Rosebuzzan and of a dark figure on a dark horse emerging from the clouds and waiting there for her to join him. She could not see his face. At first, it seemed to be her father trying to tell her something, and through the sighing wind he was calling and calling, and she knew he didn't blame her for running away; she was forgiven. She tried to reach him, struggling against the angry elements that swept the hillside—pulling herself up by the blown heather and clumps of furze—her arms and hair scratched and torn, while the clouds and mist thickened and blinded her. When the air cleared, a shaft of light penetrated the blackened sky, and for a moment the figure towered stark on the skyline. She hurried on, gasping for breath, knowing that in a moment he could be gone and lost to her forever.

Then, when she drew close it was not Nicholas's face confronting her but Trefyn's. His black curls were blown from his forehead. His eyes were wild and bright as stars in the darkest night. One arm was outstretched, with a spear held high before him.

She was filled with fear, because he was no longer the Trefyn she knew, but a hunter ready to strike—a proud young god reborn from some legendary sphere come to conquer and claim what he most desired. And she knew she was lost. She turned to run, but her feet wouldn't move. Through the rushing wind she felt herself caught in a grip of steel, and as the great hooves pounded she was swung in front of him and carried away into a swirling abyss of deepest, wildest pain and joy.

When she woke to reality her heart was pounding, and her whole body was drenched in sweat. She opened her eyes fearfully and saw Judy bending over her. The small room looked gray and filled with shadows in the early morning light. Her own case lay open on the floor beside her mattress, and Judy's clothes and knickknacks were scattered about everywhere.

The window was shut but the air felt chilly and damp. The sound of voices from below somewhere echoed up the stairs, and in the street there was the rattle of milk cans, a car, and horses' hooves passing.

In a rush the events of the previous day and evening swept through Juliet's mind.

"How are you?" she heard her companion ask, "Sleep well?"

"Well, I *did* sleep," Juliet replied grudgingly. "But it's cold here, isn't it?"

Judy jumped out of bed and started flapping her arms over her chest and out again, followed by a number of athletic exercises. "You'll get used to it," she said cheerfully. "And once you get warm this way it's the real thing."

"Haven't you—couldn't we have a stove or something?"

"Oh, we've got one," Judy told her, pointing to a small gas fire plugged into one corner. "But there's a meter. You have to pay. And it jolly well gobbles up the pennies. Anyway, it's not winter yet."

"I've got money," Juliet told her, ignoring the last remark.

Judy stared at her before remarking solemnly, "I wouldn't go saying too much about that if I were you."

"Why?"

"Well, I mean . . . you're not supposed to have much money here. Everyone's equal. Don't you see, it's the principle?"

Juliet didn't, but she merely said, "I expect I'm tired and that's why I'm cold. If I give you what's needed, will you put it in?"

Judy shrugged. "Just as you like. But it seems a

waste. The kitchen's always warm, and Agatha or Stephanie see we have a good breakfast—porridge and a boiled egg generally, and lots of toast if you want to make your own."

Juliet didn't feel she could eat a thing. She had a mild headache and was still suffering from the shock of her disastrous stage debut and from Wycksley's monstrous behavior.

"Of course . . ." Judy continued, "we pay for meals when we have them. Sometimes some of us can't afford it. But if you'd like to sign something and be a full-timer—you know, bed, breakfast and evening meal, you can. That means you pay the full board every week in advance. But most of us prefer to be free. Well? Come on, cheer up, you *do* look glum."

Juliet made an effort to oblige. She got up, found what change was needed for the meter, handed it to her friend and started to dress.

Pulling the old coat over her nightdress, Judy went out on to the landing. There was a rattling near the door, the sound of coins dropping, and the quaint figure returned again.

"Our meter's on its own on the left," she said. "But if Agatha finds you a room for yourself, you'll have another. And I say—"

"Yes?"

"You will tell me, won't you, about what happened? I don't want to be nosey, but I'm sure something exciting's gone on—something about Trefyn, is it?"

"Partly," Juliet answered. "Not only that though. My . . . my father died."

Judy stood silent for a moment, gaping. Then she said uncomfortably, "Oh . . . I'm—I'm frightfully sorry. I didn't know. I shouldn't have bothered you of course. I talk too much. But that's *me*. Please forgive me."

She looked so contrite and so comical standing there only in a bodice and long calico drawers, her hair falling over her shoulders in two pigtails. Juliet relaxed and managed to dispel a threatened rush of tears.

"It's all right," she said, "you weren't to know. The awful thing is it was my fault."

"What on earth do you mean? What bosh! it couldn't be. You wouldn't hurt a fly, especially your father. You're just all mixed up. That happens sometimes when things are too bad to bear. You look round for someone to blame and pick on yourself. But—"

"*No.*" Juliet's voice became harsh, strained. Her throat so constricted she could hardly breathe. "It wasn't like that at all. If I hadn't run away it wouldn't have happened. He had a fall you see, from his horse. He'd found out I was in London and was coming after me. It was a wild stallion—Pluto. And—and—"

"Well then, he was silly to ride such a creature, wasn't he?" Judy said with forthright honesty. "That was *his* choice, not yours, and he shouldn't have gone chasing after you like a madman, should he? Parents don't *own* children, and you're grown up—"

"*He* didn't think so." Juliet replied sadly. "He loved me so much."

"Love isn't possession though," Judy protested. "And it never works in the end. Trefyn's the same sort you know—like your father in a way. I've told you that before, and I know I'm right."

When Juliet didn't answer she continued, slightly uncomfortably, "Well, when you want to tell me the whole thing you will, I guess. But for goodness sake, don't get all heated up and miserable thinking it's *your* fault. That's sheer masochism, and a sort of indulgence if you can put it in its proper perspective. Now come on, Juliet, finish dressing and we'll go down to breakfast. Tonight I'll introduce you to Mr. Singh. He's got the most *marvelous* detached sort of philosophy. You never see him ruffled or in a state—"

"Yes, yes." Juliet interposed quickly, "but where do we wash? Is there a bathroom or anything?"

"One," Judy told her, "and it'll be taken now. Everyone makes a rush in the mornings. But there's a tap along the landing. You can take the jug and get some water."

"Hot?"

Judy burst into laughter. "You really are funny, Juliet. If you want a bath—and that's the only hot water you'll get, unless you go downstairs when the stove's free and boil some—you have to tell Agatha twenty-four hours in advance. Something about boosting the boiler you see—and expensive."

Realizing there was nothing else she could do about it, Juliet took the jug and went despondently for the water.

"I always wash at the tap," Judy said as she came back. "It's easier, because you've got to bother going to empty the bowl if you don't. I suppose—I suppose it'll be a bit difficult for you at first—adjusting, I mean. But you'll learn an awful lot, you know, about other people. And that's important if you're going to do anything worthwhile. There aren't really many geniuses—writers or painters or—or anyone who hasn't had to just fight their own way up—"

"I'm not a genius," Juliet said bluntly, "and I don't want to be."

"But you must have an *aim*," her friend exclaimed. "I don't believe you could possibly be one of those awful drifters who roll along, on inherited wealth, or live off other people—men or rich old women."

"There are people who just live, I suppose," Juliet said, after scrubbing her face vigorously. Judy's soap was a crude, plain yellow kind and stung her cheeks.

"Oh, well, we'll talk later. Come on, hurry up, I want to take you down myself."

Presently the two of them were hurrying down the two narrow flights of stairs, and a third which led to the basement. The kitchen was a long room with a tiled, uncarpeted floor and a large stove at one end with gas rings and an oven and a fireplace. There was a narrow table pushed against a wall where Agatha stood, officiating and pouring tea from an immense brown china pot. Two or three tenants, guests, or whatever she liked to call them, were ladling porridge into bowls or dropping eggs into a pan. Smaller tables covered by oilcloth were placed under the tall window facing Agatha. Juliet glimpsed the branches of a wan-looking tree tapping at the glass. Her spirits sank. If this was Judy's "new world," she found it, so far, very depressing.

Mr. Singh was just leaving when they arrived. He wore a turban, a dark gray suit, and was a sad-looking man with mournful eyes that peered enigmatically from his brown face. Judy introduced him to Juliet; he was extremely polite, greeting her with a series of bows every time he spoke. Their conversation was about the weather and the state of the world, which Mr. Singh considered one must be sufficiently composed to view in proper perspective.

He's a Sikh," Judy said, when, following further

bows, he left. "You'll be impressed when you know him. That's why having a bath's so important, you see."

"Having a *bath*? What's that got to do with Mr. Singh?"

"Oh, of course, you didn't know. He bathes every day—it's the only time he takes his turban off. So of course no one else gets much chance to use the bathroom except at certain times. Now . . ." her manner changed abruptly, "what're you having, an egg? Come on, it'll only cost a penny. There's porridge first, of course. I always have it before I set off for the den—"

"What's the den?"

"I work there when I'm not in my room or at the zoo, sketching. It belongs to Peter. He's a photographer, and he lets me borrow his cubbyhole when I want it. Here he is—Peter . . ."

Juliet began to feel dizzy in the whirl of introductions while boiling eggs, collecting tea and toast, and trying to absorb the trend and information of Judy's conversation.

When they were both seated at a table, Peter came over to join them. He was a fair, pale young man with a golden moustache and light blue eyes. He wore a floppy, spotted tie with a black velvet jacket that had seen better days, and drainpipe trousers.

Juliet thought he looked tired and extremely delicate. What he thought of Juliet was obvious. He made no secret of his admiration. "Cornwall!" he exclaimed when Judy had given a brief introduction and background of her friend. "Fancy that, but I should have known."

"Why?" Juliet asked curiously.

"Your hair. You seem to carry the sun in it."

THE PROUD HUNTER 341

"Oh, but—that's—that's not true," Juliet said, laughing uncomfortably. "I'm not even fair."

"Ah. But I wasn't talking of color."

"Peter sees differently from most of us," Judy said, attacking her egg with relish. "Essentials . . . quality. That's true, isn't it, Peter?"

He nodded. "Exactly. Light and shade of personality show if you train yourself to see it. That's what I try to do. Of course I'd have liked to paint, but I haven't the cash. The outlay's too heavy. One day though I bet we'll have proper color photography. That'll be the time. Only I'll be kicking up the daisies by then."

"Now Peter," Judy said severely, "don't go all morbid. Who wants to think about dying anyway?"

The meal passed in a daze for Juliet. When it was over Judy went off with Peter to his den, leaving Juliet to have her talk with Agatha.

In her small private sitting room, which was furnished with a few good pieces (but sparsely, to avoid any pretenses to class distinction), Agatha told Juliet a small bedroom was available for her if she wished to take it. The sum mentioned for rental seemed extremely small, but with her piercing eyes bright on Juliet's face Agatha added, "Everyone under my roof is supposed to have a purpose. I take it, being a friend of Judy's, you must have one, so we won't argue about that. But it's quite clear to me you come from a very different background from most of us. What your finances are I don't know. If you feel you can comfortably contribute a little more to joint expenditure, you are allowed to do so, but that is entirely up to you. One thing I must stress strongly: we are all equal here. That is our guiding aim; equality of sex, race, and class. We also have a weekly meeting when any problems are discussed. This is held in what was once my family dining room, before my parents died. It has been converted into a common room. Most of the women here are suffragettes, which Judy has doubtless told you. But our interests are also wider, comprising welfare work whenever possible. Of course . . ." she looked away momentarily.

"Yes?" Juliet queried.

"Any resident such as Mr. Singh is allowed absolute privacy. We force none of our ideas on those of a set religion. But I hope, Juliet, that you will join our special group aimed to further the rights of women."

When Juliet did not answer she sighed and said, "Well, we shall have to see, shan't we. Now perhaps you would like to see the room I have."

Juliet agreed automatically, knowing that whatever her feelings she would accept for the time being.

The room was a little larger than Judy's, but furnished in the same cheap rather dreary way, although a pair of cheerful blue curtains hung at the sides of the window shade. Agatha took the cord and it jumped up with a rattle. "Quite a nice view, really," Juliet heard the clipped voice saying, "overlooking the garden. Most of our tenants have to face the road."

Juliet looked out. The garden consisted of a large, worn lawn of faded yellow grass with an ancient, tired-looking sycamore in the middle. There was no other bush or tree in sight—only red brick walls showing the remains of leafless creepers straggling over them. Three large dustbins stood near the shed at the right of the house.

"Yes . . . yes, I see," Juliet murmured vaguely.

"Well?" The voice had become sharp. "What about it? Do you want it?"

Juliet swallowed. "Of course. Thank you very much."

"Hm, you'd better bring your case and clothes up then, and we'll discuss the terms, whether you want to pay in advance each week, or by day."

"Oh, weekly would be best, I think," Juliet said.

And so the matter was concluded.

Juliet was accepted as a tenant of Agatha's community, and for the first few days she wondered how she was ever going to bear it. From the very beginning, despite Judy's friendship, she felt isolated and apart. Much to Agatha's disapproval, she would not go on the first march, which took place the following Saturday. Instead she went shopping and bought herself a new dress, which appeared to cause suspicion. Only Peter seemed to show any real understanding and sympathy, and when a fortnight had passed he made a surprising suggestion that was to alter the whole course of her future.

## 13

One bright autumn day when Judy had gone out sketching somewhere along the embankment, Peter suggested Juliet should take a look at his studio. "It's not elegant," he told her, "but big. Plenty of room to work. I thought you might like to help me."

"Help?" Juliet echoed, astonished. "How could I? I don't know the first thing about photography."

"Ah, but that's the point. You wouldn't have to."

"What do you mean?"

"Come and see," he insisted. "Sooner or later I reckon you'll be wanting a job, and a girl like you couldn't be expected to go for just anything—not like cleaning or the usual thing . . . you know, catching some fancy bloke's eye—"

Juliet studied his face closely, wondering whether he meant to be insulting, or was merely trying to make advances. From his expression she saw it was neither. He was completely serious, and though she knew he admired her very much she felt nothing par-

ticularly personal in his attitude. Although she hadn't
had much experience of sex—her one affair had been
with Trefyn, Trefyn had always been the only one—
youths like Desmond Court had generally tried on
first acquaintance to touch her hand or make sentimental, sly suggestions. Peter never did. He seemed
content just to look at her and admire as one admired
an attractive painting.

"He's fallen for you," Judy had predicted. But Juliet
felt he hadn't, not in a conventional way. So feeling
suddenly curious, she agreed, and that afternoon they
set off for Peter's studio. The air was chilly and the
sky was gray, but with a clear grayness that threw the
lean, dark branches of the few trees into networked
relief by the roofs and chimneys of huddled houses. It
was a curious neighborhood of rather desolate small
buildings crowded into dingy streets occasionally interspersed by large dwellings evocative of an earlier,
wealthier area. These were being gradually converted
to lodging houses, and the adjoining squares of gardens
had an uncared-for appearance. Fallen leaves lay tumbled on the worn grass and paths—a few still clung to
the spreading arms of chestnut and sycamore, hanging
above the railings like yellowed dead hands, Juliet
thought with a hint of morbidity. Small shops
crouched in unexpected places, and narrow alleyways
stretched haphazardly from the wider thoroughfares.

"Best not go anywhere like that on your own," Peter
told her.

"Why?"

He gave a laugh that sounded more like a cough.
"You're an innocent," he told her. "Easy to see you
don't know London. Ever heard of white slave trade?
Thieves? Thugs?"

"Thieves, of course," Juliet answered.

"They're not the worst," Peter answered grimly. "You just watch out, Juliet. Keep to the main roads round here unless you're with someone like me."

They went on, took a turning to the left, and soon reached a tall narrow building wedged between two shorter ones. There was a greengrocer on the ground floor, with steps leading through a door at the back that cut upward abruptly from a dark entry. "Follow me," Peter said, "my room's at the top—an attic you could call it, I suppose, but it has lots of possibilities. If I ever had proper cash to convert, I might even move in, with Oswald."

"Who's Oswald?" Juliet said, following him up the rickety stairs.

"He's my partner," Peter answered after a pause. "You may meet him."

"Oh. I didn't know you had anyone doing things with you."

"I don't, he does the selling side," Peter said ambiguously, "and a bit of designing."

Juliet was out of breath when at last, after a number of turns and mounting three flights, they reached the top. Peter led her along a narrow landing that smelled of dust mingled with a curious odor of some kind of chemical that she couldn't place. He put a key in a door, pushed it, went through ahead of her, turned, gave a comical, decorous little bow, and said "*Entrez!* Here lieth my dream. Here I am king of all I do survey."

Juliet paused a moment, then passed before him into the room. It was very long and must have covered the whole of the premises below. There was a dark curtain at the far end, cutting off probably a third of

the interior. The furniture was sparse, consisting of a
stained wooden table, two inexpensive chairs and a
shabby, leather-covered sofa with stuffing poking
through a hole. A tripod with a large square object on
it, presumably a camera, stood by the table. Peter
waved an arm toward it, saying something about
adaptor and emulsifier—mysteries that were mumbo
jumbo to Juliet. "And that's my developing room," he
added, pointing to the curtain. "The darkroom they
call it nowadays. But I don't suppose you're interested
in technicalities?"

"No," Juliet admitted truthfully. "Not really, and I
don't see—"

"You don't see what you could possibly do here," he
interrupted. "No. Well, I'll explain. Only I've got
something to show you first. Sit down, do. I'll heave
the things out."

Juliet seated herself on the softest-looking portion
of the sofa, which creaked ominously under her
weight. Peter went to a roughly made cupboard and
dragged out a large box. He pulled it to the couch and
opened the lid, then lifted from it a parcel wrapped in
brown paper. "Here you are," he said untying the
string. "What do you think of them?"

He was holding a bundle of cards and prints, most
of them of females—portrait photographs and daguerre-
otypes of heads and shoulders—all of them beautiful,
with hair elegantly arranged and eyes looking outward with a soulful, holier-than-thou expression.
Above bosoms discreetly covered and swathed in frothing tulle and chiffon, swanlike necks rose delicately,
turned at alluring angles to show gently tilted chins at
their most complimentary angles. Nearly all these

were printed on cards for posting, with fancy borders of flowers and birds, and sometimes with an inscription beneath that said "Sweet memories never die," "Dreaming of you forever," "Until we meet again"—or something similar.

Juliet looked at them one by one, screwing her brows up, but with a faint, growing idea of what he might be going to suggest. "Very nice," she said when she'd examined the collection. "Who does the borders? They're very . . . dainty, aren't they?"

"I suppose you'd call them sentimental," Peter said grudgingly.

"Well, yes."

"Still, they sell. And that's what you have to think of when you're in business. Oswald's the artist, of course. I just do the photographs, then they're printed. But you wouldn't be interested in the process."

"No."

"That doesn't matter. It's a model I want."

Juliet gasped. "A *model*?"

"Yes. *You*."

She laughed. "But how *ridiculous*. I couldn't, of *course*, I couldn't."

"Why not?"

"Well, I mean . . . I'm not . . . I don't do that sort of thing—"

"What sort of thing?"

"Pose. It's like—like selling yourself." Her cheeks were red at the very idea. "Oh no, Peter. I really couldn't consider it."

"But you've got things all wrong," he said. "I suppose that's because of living in Cornwall all your life. If you'd stop to think—"

"I *have*," she told him with a flash of temper. "And don't talk of Cornwall like that. As if it was some sort of—of simple backwater—"

"Isn't it?"

She lifted her chin up and said coldly, "I think I want to go now, if you don't mind."

He touched her shoulder lightly. "Just listen to me," he said placatingly, "I didn't mean to be critical or offensive. I think you've been damn lucky being able to grow up by the sea. But in London standards and the way of life are quite different. There's nothing wrong in just having your face photographed—is there, for heaven's sake? It simply means other people will be able to admire your looks. If I wanted you in the nude, that'd be . . . well, I could understand it. But in a way I'm offering you fame. Girls would envy you for looking so beautiful and young men would stick your likeness on mantel shelves and in their studies and wish they could give you flowers and kneel at your feet—"

He broke off as Juliet suddenly started to laugh.

"What's the matter now?" he asked. "What's so funny?"

"*You.* I was really cross a moment ago, but the way you put it—the idea of young men kneeling at my feet! I could just imagine them kissing my toes!"

"That's not so odd as you seem to think," Peter said with all seriousness. "Still, if you mean to take me as a joke—"

"Oh, I don't. And it's kind of you to offer me a job. But—"

"I'd pay you a proper wage," he said, "not large because I can't afford it—yet. But some day, if I'm lucky, society women will be mad to have my name beneath their photographs. Actresses too, like Lily Elsie, Mrs. Seymour Hicks, Sally Cooper, and—oh, the whole lot of them."

He waited, watching her expression change as a range of possibilities raced through her mind. After a pause she asked, "Do you mean these cards will really go through the post?"

"Naturally."

Perhaps Trefyn would get one, she thought, with excitement stirring her. She could even send one herself if she agreed to Peter's wild suggestion—no name signing it of course, and no handwriting, just his address on the other side in capital letters.

She picked up one of the cards and examined it. At the tip in small type was printed "Famous Beauties," and below the photograph the name of the lady.

"I shouldn't like that," she said, "not my name."

"In your case it wouldn't be needed," Peter told her. "You're not known yet to the public. But eventually, believe me, you would be—as the "Golden Girl." There could be a Golden Girl series—

"But I'm not golden. I'm red—well, auburn," Juliet protested.

"It doesn't matter. It wouldn't show. Oswald would probably manage a yellow tinge, a sort of aura in the background."

Juliet found herself weakening. Peter made the project sound exciting and important, and since her family had abandoned her, would it matter what they felt? Even if they ever saw her likeness, which seemed unlikely.

Trefyn, of course, was quite a different matter. She would want him to know what was going on, want him to be angry and jealous—so jealous that he'd come raging to London in the end, demand her return, perhaps even try to carry her back by force. But he wouldn't be able to because Peter and Oswald would be there, and she'd smile tauntingly in Trefyn's face and tell him condescendingly that at the moment she had obligations to face which didn't permit her immediate return to Cornwall. The thought of his reaction stimulated her. Once he saw her after their long parting she was sure everything would work out. A glimpse, a touch of hands, a flare of temper between them even would mean contact and eventual coming together. Nothing mattered really except loving each other. She wanted him—oh, how she wanted him— boss man or not. Just so long as he didn't demand the impossible: to have her at his feet like any Indian squaw. Her mind was so lost in anticipation and exciting visions of the future she had to be jerked to attention by Peter saying, "Well? What about it?"

"All right then," Juliet said with a defiant toss of her head. "I'll have a try and see what it's like. But I warn you, I'm not very good at sitting still."

Peter smiled. "You won't regret it," he said. "And I know Oswald will be over the moon about it."

Oswald appeared ten minutes later. He was carrying a case and had an odor about him of paint and turpentine. In appearance he was completely unlike Peter: broad, dark, with a square jaw, untidy hair, and wearing a shabby overcoat that flapped open, revealing paint-stained overalls. His trousers were noticeably frayed at the edges, and Juliet was surprised that such a neglected-looking character could do such fine work.

Peter introduced them and explained that his proposition had been accepted.

Oswald grinned, holding out to Juliet a hand which, though inky-looking, was delicately formed for his large frame.

"Sorry I look such a mess," he said. "Been working. I can't be clean and turn out good designs at the same time. But old Peter will verify I'm not always like this."

Peter nodded. "When Oswald's dressed to kill he's the most devastating, heart-stealing cad with women in town," he said. "So beware."

Juliet was quite aware that Oswald approved of the arrangement and that he was impressed by her looks, but in spite of his obvious admiration, she felt he was quite uninterested in her as a woman. There was no warmth for her, no subtle undercurrent of desire that was usual from the young men she met. His attitude was impersonal. Yet his eyes, when he glanced at Peter, glowed and were bright with friendly affection. Affection was certainly the word, she thought, as his arm slipped round Peter's neck; and sensing the mysterious relationship between them, she was discomforted, though she couldn't quite understand the reason.

The routine of her sessions posing for the photographs started the following week, commencing at ten in the morning and ending each afternoon at three with an hour's break at one o'clock. Generally Juliet ate at a small café nearby, occasionally joining Peter in the studio where they made sandwiches and coffee. Sometimes Oswald turned up, and at those times, feeling unwanted, she had a snack on her own in her room at Agatha's.

Once she got into the routine she found the work simple, but tiring. The constant effort of keeping her head up, or gracefully turned like a delicate slender flower on a stem, made her muscles stiff. But the wage Peter paid her was quite good, and meant she did not have to dig into what remained of her own money.

Judy highly approved of the venture. "Everyone here will respect you more," she said. "It makes you properly one of us."

The statement, though well-intended, inwardly irritated Juliet. She didn't particularly want to be labeled "one of them"; she certainly had no wish to go marching through the London streets like a sandwich man with a placard on her back; and the idea of being treated on equal terms as a male didn't attract her in the least. "And of course," she heard Judy continuing, "you'll have no trouble with Peter or Ozzy."

"What do you mean?"

"No secret kissing or cuddling business," Judy replied. "They're buddies."

"Buddies?"

Judy gave her a poke, "Oh, go on. You can't be *that* innocent."

"I don't know what you're talking about," Juliet said shortly, walking away. But from that moment she began to notice things—small personal details of attitude and responses between the two young men that disturbed and puzzled her, but she told herself that their friendship was none of her business and that the important thing was their civility and thoughtfulness where she was concerned.

Gradually though, as the autumn days lengthened and drew towards winter, she began to long for a change. The fogs and gray buildings, the dreary gardens and leafless trees, the constant grinding of

traffic, the shadowed figures passing huddled into
their coats depressed her. She wanted the sweet, wild
tang of Cornish air from the moors, a glimpse of gigantic waves flinging their fury against the gaunt
cliffs above the cove, and most of all for a sight of the
Connor farm round the curving lane below Rosebuzzan. Sometimes she stood at the open window of her
small London room with eyes closed, trying to pretend the damp wind carried a hint of heather in it.
But there was nothing save thick cloying mist, pungent with city smoke, and there were no wild birds
near, except sparrows cheeping and the occasional
crying of a lone gull flown inland from the Thames.
*Why don't you come, Trefyn?* she thought frequently
with actual physical and emotional pain. *Why don't
you appear suddenly and take me home?*

She would walk about the district, occasionally
searching in a frenzy of loneliness for his face, yearning for him to appear unexpectedly from a group of
pedestrians or round a corner—even for a look of him
somewhere on another's face. But it never happened.

Her sense of isolation deepened. However cheerful
she might appear on the surface, she was lonely. She
longed even to see her mother so the terrible rift between them could be healed. She wrote once, but the
letter remained unacknowledged. And she knew she
was still blamed—however unfairly—for her father's
death. She toyed with the idea of visiting Ianthe, but
the memory of Wycksley was so repulsive she rejected
it immediately.

One foggy afternoon Peter said, "What's the matter
with you, Juliet? You don't seem to have any life in
you. You're strained. We've had a dozen tries at that
last position, and none of them really worked—"

"I've got a headache," Juliet said. "And I don't think it's any use going on today. Do you mind if I go? I'll make it up some other time."

"All right, yes, maybe it would be better," he agreed.

Five minutes later Juliet was making her way down the threadwork of streets toward the main road. The fog had deepened during the last half hour, and was a furry thickness in her throat; all she passed—vehicles crawling ponderously with lights emerging only as blurred eyes through the grayness, buildings that seemed to be lurching over the pavements, human beings feeling more than seeing their ways—appeared contorted and unreal; ghost shapes against a phantom background. At a corner, under the wavering, curdled beam of a street lamp, she paused to get her bearings.

The stooping shape of an old woman, bent over in a black coat, stumbled against her. Juliet winced. A haggard face, briefly caught in the wan foggy glow, glanced up. It was a lined, hooknosed, almost mannish countenance, but the cracked voice was frail and full of pleading as a bony hand gripped Juliet's wrist.

"Help me, dearie," she begged. "Help me to the road. My old eyes are that dim, and this light—" she broke off, coughing.

Stifling her repulsion, Juliet allowed the contact and was about to move ahead with the old creature when she felt, with a shock, the hard fingers enclose on her wrist in a viselike grip. She tried to shout, but a strong hand was on her mouth, another pulling her to the wall, where no light could penetrate. There was a brief struggle, then further darkness as the figure straightened, becoming a column of shadow in the billowing mist.

Juliet kicked and instinctively thrust up her knee. At that moment the glimmer of a torch pierced the fog, and she saw with terror a hand—a hand with something poised to stab. A needle? The sudden memory of Judy's and Peter's warnings registered, and with it came strength. She gave a violent movement, freed her face, and screamed. The figure released her abruptly, and lurched away, running, into the enveloping darkness. Juliet stood panting, leaning against the wall, while her heart and breathing eased.

"Are you all right?" A friendly female voice asked. "What happened? Was you attacked?"

Above the light of the torch Juliet saw a kindly middle-aged feminine countenance staring at her with concern.

"Yes," she answered. "I was helping an old woman, and—and—"

"There now," her companion said. "You needn't say. They turn up round here on days like this, the devils. You shouldn't be out alone, my dear; not with the trade that goes on in these parts. Your old woman was probably a dressed-up hulk of a man. White slavers they are—always on the lookout for pretty girls like you to ship aboard to foreign brothels and harems. P'raps you didn't know about such things. Hm. Lucky I happened to come along. Another minute, and—oh dear, don't faint on me. Come on now, there's a pub round the corner. It's something strong you want and no mistake."

Too shocked and exhausted to resist, Juliet allowed herself to be led to a small place with a sign creaking above it, where she was given a stimulant and then coffee.

Later when she recounted the incident to her

friend, Judy, at first sympathetic, became shrewdly critical. "As things turned out you were all right," she said. "But you were taking a risk going along with anyone. After all, that 'friendly woman,' as you called her could easily have been one of a gang. It isn't always the nice-looking ones that are good. They could be the most dangerous of all. You just remember that in the future."

Juliet thought a moment, then said with a touch of mischief, "But you're always saying women should be equal with men. They're not, you know—they never will be, in some things. There are times when they need protection. Anyway, Judy, I'm not a pioneer or politician, and I know I'm a disappointment to you. I'm sorry about that; you've been good to me. But after this afternoon, I really don't think I can stay much longer at Agatha's. It's—it's somehow morbid—to me."

"Where will you go?"

Juliet shrugged. "I don't know, the Marshes perhaps."

"And be a sort of social parasite."

"Oh, don't be silly."

"There's Peter, too. Are you going to let him down? Just when he's getting his series going?"

Juliet didn't answer for a moment, then she said shortly, "He'd soon find someone else."

"I don't think so. Girls who look like you are generally on the lookout for something else too. And with Peter—well, you know how he is."

Yes, Juliet thought, she was beginning to realize his potentialities or lack of them, and she was discovering also that the setup, combined with his involvement with Oswald, was beginning to mildly sicken her. She longed for something to happen—something exciting and pleasantly romantic to break the tediousness of those long gray days before Christmas.

At the end of November she had a letter from Andrew with a note enclosed from Trefyn. With hands that trembled she opened the note first.

"Where are you, my love?" it read,

> and who and what do you think you are? One day I'll find you—my God, I will, and then you'll be sorry. Sorry for the wasted hours we could have had—the passion and the loving. Time doesn't wait, Juliet, and remember—there's no blackmail in love. You either want me or not. You either return when I call, or—what shall I do with you? What—what—*what*? One moment I could beat you, you stubborn willful brat, the next I'm so sick with passion I curse myself for a fool. But have you I will. Andrew wouldn't give me your address, but he's sending this on to you. He's a good chap, but damned if I understand him.
>
> Juliet—remember the dew pond. Don't you dare ever forget.
>
> Trefyn

Delicous thrills of excitement trembled down her spine. She read the note twice more before opening Andrew's.

"Juliet," it said,

> I've had a duel of words with Trefyn, who almost came to blows with me when I wouldn't tell him where you were. He was furious, but restrained himself remarkably well. A forceful, un-

usual character, that lover of yours. I'm not interfering or wanting you to come back to Polbreath
yet, because it seems to me you should work out
your own future. Anyway, my main news is that
Charlotte's had her baby—a girl. She had a rough
time but is recovering quickly. William unfortu-
nately appears cold and bored by the whole business. He's polite but offhand and distant to poor
C, and takes no notice of the child at all—possibly
because she looks so far as though she's going to
be Charlotte all over again. But of course babies
change quickly, I believe. I hope this one will, for
everyone's sake. They already have a Nanny, a
girl engaged through a Plymouth agency. She's
extremely pretty, and William's eyes are often on
her. Charlotte watches him like a hawk. Mama is
still frozen and cold to everyone. I haven't seen
her cry once since father's death. It's not natural.
Jason's the only one she really talks to. I wish I
could do something, but there seems nothing.

As you know, I had intended to be at the Seminary by now. But owing to the tragedy I thought
it better to stay at home a little longer. Now my
plans are changed. I'm going to Africa with two
of the Brothers as part of my probationary period. The work will be as medical missionary as-
sistant in remote jungle areas. I've been studying
hard in my spare time, and I know I'm doing the
right thing. So you see, you needn't picture me
enclosed in black robes, praying and meditating
all day. I shall be working like hell to save life
instead of destroying it. If that's being a crank in
your eyes, I can't help it. But please try and understand.

By the way, on the 12th of this month I'm taking a trip to London for two days. I shall probably stay with a friend of Father Strawn's, but would like to take you out for dinner on the 13th. Don't worry, no talk of religion—we could eat at a cosy little place I know in Soho, L'Oiseau Rouge—an intimate, attractive restaurant run by a Frenchman and his Spanish wife. The food and wines are excellent, and we could make it a happy occasion. If I don't hear to the contrary before then—and time's getting short—I'll call for you at your friend Agatha's about seven. So get out your best bib and tucker and be your own beautiful self. All the news when I see you.

Love,
Andrew

There was a lump in Juliet's throat, her heart had quickened with emotion as she slipped her brother's letter into her pocket. Trefyn's she read once more before placing it safely into the bag she always carried. No one must see it—no one. It was not a very polite letter, but it told her all she wanted to know—Trefyn was still thinking of her and wanting her.

The days dragged for her until the evening of her meeting with Andrew. She did not go to the studio that afternoon but spent it in her room, relaxing, after having a bath arranged for the previous day. This was rather disapproved by Agatha, who considered bathing at such an hour an unnecessary luxury not entirely according to the rules of the household. It might interfere with the boosting required for Mr. Singh's early morning ritual, she said tartly. But if Juliet was willing to pay something extra to go to the "common fund," she'd make it an exception just this once.

Juliet had been more than willing. With what she'd earned from the Golden Girl modeling and the generous sum already contributed by Ianthe, the problem of finance did not arise at the moment. She was slightly discomforted by Judy's attitude, which was critical at first of Juliet's capitalist circumstances. But her friend had eventually relented, and said good-naturedly, "It's your life anyway. That's what we stand for. I've a feeling though you won't be with us long."

So had Juliet.

The new dress she'd bought recently had certainly been a brain wave, she thought later, when she studied as much of herself as was possible through the narrow mirror. It was of green velvet, cut smartly with a lace front inserted into the tightly fitting bodice. The neck reached fashionably high to the chin, and was also of lace, edged with delicate ruching. The gracefully falling skirt touched the tips of her best shoes, but she knew Andrew would hire a cab that would deposit them comfortably at the door of the restaurant. She had a chiffon scarf for draping over her auburn curls. These she carefully arranged in a roll high above bangs from a center part, in accordance with the current style.

Her reflection told her she looked lovely, and she wished desperately that Trefyn could see her. Still, there'd be other men, she thought defiantly. She was used to being stared at by the opposite sex, and if she gave Andrew a hint he might make a point of seeing Trefyn again when he returned to Polbreath and letting him know how admired she was in the restaurant. She knew she was being childish. But after the terrible tragedy of her father's death and the effort recently of trying to settle into a dreary existence that didn't really suit her, it was a relief to be vain and feminine again and able to dress up in attractive clothes without being frowned upon.

Andrew arrived promptly. Juliet was waiting expectantly in her room with her ears on the alert for any buzz of the bell and sound of voices below, her cape lying on the bed, ready to be flung round her shoulders at the first sign of his presence. When she heard it she rushed downstairs, and saw for a second Agatha's stern face glancing upward under the light, before Andrew strode forward, looking impeccable in his evening clothes. Agatha turned and discreetly disappeared down the hall. A moment later Juliet was in Andrew's arms.

"Oh, Andrew, it's so *lovely* to see you. Oh, I—" she broke off, laughing.

"Come along now," Andrew said, "slip your coat on, the air's damp. I've a cab outside. We can chatter all evening if we want."

Forgetting to put the flimsy scarf over her curls, Juliet passed before him through the door, half running down the few steps and iron gate to the pavement. A typical London mist was rising, and the cabby's face was a mere blurred disk in the night air. Andrew helped her into the cab, and the next moment the road was echoing with the hollow sound of horses' hooves and wheels as they drove at an easy pace through the darkness. Questions fell in a rapid pace from Juliet's lips—questions concerning Polbreath,

Charlotte and William, Jason, and Donna. When brief answers had been given she said with an excited undercurrent in her voice, "And Trefyn?"

Andrew took her hand, squeezed it, and said, "He's crazy about this new foal of his. Says it's going to be a winner."

"Oh."

"But I should add not half as crazy as he is about a certain young woman called Juliet who at the moment is putting him through hell."

Juliet smiled secretly, but aloud she said, "He's asked for it, you know. He can be quite insufferable."

"So can you," Andrew told her.

"Why?"

Andrew stole a look at her. Her profile was proud and mysteriously lovely against the dusky evening which was pinpointed now with the glimmer of intermittent lights from shop windows and increasing traffic.

Andrew waited for a grinding motor vehicle to disappear before he said, "You'll have to come home some time, you know. You can't go on living this life forever. Mama will need you when she's got over the shock."

Juliet felt herself stiffen. "Don't talk about it. She never will. She's never really wanted me very much. And now—" a shiver ran through her. "She hates me—because of father."

"You mustn't think that. When people are so distressed they say things they don't mean."

Juliet turned her head to look at him, and just for a few moments he saw not a girl but a woman seared by a terrible inward agony. "I don't want to be re-

minded about father," he heard her saying. *"Please,*
Andrew, I can't bear it."

"I'm sorry. I shouldn't have allowed the subject to
come up."

There was a long pause. When at last she spoke
again they were nearing Piccadilly Circus, where the
world of dimmed shadow became the misted quivering realm of Theaterland with colored signs and lights
shattering the fog to silvered particles of brightness.

The Soho restaurant was small, as Andrew had told
her, tucked away between two larger ones. It was
tastefully decorated in blue, cream, and gold, with
mural wall panels of pastoral scenes. Small tables
were placed in alcoves discreetly lit by cunningly devised lighting. Wines glittered from a bar at the far
end of the room, and waiters were hovering quietly
and yet alert to give any service necessary.

A table had been reserved in Andrew's name, and
the food was excellent. Warmed by the very good
Madeira, conversation between them flowed and
lightened. Juliet became aware at intervals of envious
glances from women and desirous ones of the men.

Andrew was careful to keep topics on the future
rather than on the past, and Juliet learned that he was
returning to Polbreath for only a few days before sail-
ing from Falmouth for Africa.

"But are you *sure,* Andrew?" she asked. "It seems so
queer—you of all people going off with priests to live
with savages. And when you get back what will you
do? Go to that place and shut yourself away? I can't
see—"

"Don't try to. Not that far," he interrupted. "It's the
present I'm interested in—getting away from our hide-
bound little Society to something a bit more active

and helpful maybe, though I certainly don't profess to be a saint, and for heaven's sake, don't try to think of me as one. When I return—or perhaps I should say if— I may find I was mistaken and can't stand the life at all. Nothing's settled, Juliet, it's just a tryout. And now, what else do you want to know?"

Deciding not to broach the subject of Trefyn again, she answered, "The new baby. You said she was like Charlotte. Is she still?"

"As far as I can judge, poor little thing."

"You mean William's still cold?"

Andrew laughed shortly but without humor.

"Between you and me, love, big brother William's behaving like a first-rate cad—where Charlotte's concerned. Of course she is a bore, poor girl, and he should never have married her, but there you are. She'll either have to lump it or take off."

"As bad as that? He doesn't . . . I mean, he doesn't ill-treat her, does he?"

Andrew's voice was ambiguous when he said, "That depends what you mean by ill-treatment. He's got a woman in Penzance—strictly between you and me, this is—and he returns late, sometimes oozing sex and drink. But as they don't sleep together—he and Charlotte I mean—it may not worry her."

"How perfectly horrid."

"No, just the nature of the beast. He should have had more guts and married Hannah, then everything would have been all right in the family nest."

Juliet thought for a moment, "How's Matthew?" she asked.

"Oh, he's thriving. And strangely enough—though perhaps not so strange after all—about the only human being at Polbreath just now who my handsome elder brother seems to have any affection for. Ironic, isn't it?"

"Yes."

No more was said concerning Charlotte and William, but later, when the evening was over and Juliet had said a tearful good-bye to Andrew at the door of Agatha's, her mind wandered back to the short period immediately following the wedding when everything appeared to be going so well between them. Pity for Charlotte filled her—it must be dreadful, she thought, to be plain and unwanted and so despised by her husband that he took a mistress before they'd had a year together. She couldn't help feeling, as well, a touch of contempt for her sister-in-law. Why hadn't she fought him and taken some action? Men like William needed someone to stand up to them, to gain respect. But then Charlotte had always been quiet and placid, calm when she should have shown temper and rarely able to fight back except with reproach from her brown eyes. They were nice eyes, fringed with stubby black lashes, quite her best feature, but too placid somehow, like a gentle cow's, which William would find exceedingly irritating when he was longing for a touch of physical combat.

Actually, at the very moment Juliet was envisaging the unsatisfactory relationship between her brother and his wife, matters were quite different from how she pictured them.

There was a scene going on at Polbreath. At that late hour William had mistakenly invaded Charlotte's room following a visit to Penzance. His state of dress, general air of bemusement, and other factors—including the betraying odors of alcohol and strong perfume—told their own story only too clearly.

Charlotte, who was on the verge of sleep, was jerked suddenly fully awake and jumped out of bed. The small oil lamp she always kept burning on a table in case either of the babies in the night nursery cried or the nanny wanted her, threw a fitful glow round his large figure. He closed the door and stood staring at her, faintly bewildered at first, until her plump form in its cotton nightdress properly registered. Her brown hair was pulled from her broad face into a pigtail. Her appearance at first faintly amused him; she looked so like an old-fashioned wooden doll in the absurd garment, which was gathered tightly in frills at each wrist and buttoned close under her chin.

"Hullo, Charlotte," he said clearly but with that certain thickness in his voice she'd learned to dread, "you look ravishing, quite, *quite* ravishing."

And then he started to laugh.

Perhaps if she'd held her tongue and disregarded the sarcasm, he might have left her alone and retreated to his own quarters.

But she didn't.

An irrational, quite uncharacteristic, rage seized her.

"Get out," she said, "leave my room instantly do you hear—you—you great filthy boor. I know where you've been—what you've been up to—with some woman, haven't you? Well, I've had enough, *enough* I tell you—"

"Have you, now! have you," he said swaying slightly, "so have I, madam, so have I. That doesn't mean I'm not capable of more—if my lady wife wishes."

He ambled toward her slowly. She backed away. "Don't touch me, William," she said. "If you do I'll scream—" Instinctively her hand reached for a small paper knife lying on the bedside table near a book. He moved abruptly and snatched it from her, then he clutched the neck of her nightdress, and jerked her forward so her face was brought close up to his.

"Stab me, would you? Trying to goad me? Yes—that's what you want, isn't it? Under your prudish airs you're sick for sex—"

She broke free and ran to the other side of the bed, white-faced and breathing heavily.

"Don't you *dare!*" she said, in more of a gasp than a cry. "I *hate* you, William, do you understand? You're loathsome to me. Beastly. And tomorrow I'm leaving. Tomorrow—" her voice became very clear and hard "—tomorrow I'm packing my things and taking the babies and nanny to my father's. Since Nicholas died you've become insufferable. I can't live with this sort of thing, or with you anymore. I *won't.*"

She was trembling but tried not to show it. He walked purposefully to where she stood, appearing in no way desirable but a challenge now to his male pride and authority.

"Won't you, indeed?" he said, pushing her down on to the bed. "I'm not sure I relish our marital relationship either. But by God, Charlotte, there'll be no walking out on me, and no stealing of my children, d'you hear? And if I catch you leaving Polbreath, I'll bring you back and beat the devil out of you—and I mean that—"

She cringed but managed to say, "You're nothing but a low-down laborer—" before he bore down on her, ripped the nightdress down the front, exposing her large plump form which was heavy and uncomely from months of inactivity. The breasts, ripe and heavy still from suckling the baby, sagged sideways. All pretensions to a waist had gone.

His first impulse to take her in contempt faded, like a pricked balloon, into sudden revulsion. The fear in her eyes and the quivering of the large thighs—partly through hate, partly desire—sickened all feeling in him to derisive dislike. Any lingering sexual emotion in him went flaccid and cold. He brought the garment over her again and jumped up, hastily rearranging his clothes as he went to the mirror. Then he turned and said, "Perhaps after all you were right. Marriage between us is a pretty humiliating business. I don't like you and you've certainly no cause to put up with me. Go to your father if you want, and take the baby. I'm sure the Major will be pleased to have you, considering the hefty allowance I'll make. But the boy will remain here."

She didn't answer and was lying on the bed as he'd left her, with her head turned away, when he reached the door.

Having recovered himself, he paused there briefly and said with a faint touch of shame, "I'm sorry it should have come to this. Why the devil you married me beats me. You must have known the kind of man I was. And about Hannah. You were a fool, Charlotte— what did you think you'd gain by thrusting her boy under my nose? Shame me? Have me under your thumb so you could flaunt your damned virtue in my face very time I had a bit of a fling? Did you think for one moment you could wipe a single memory of her from my heart?"

She still refused to answer.

"I said my heart—" he persisted. "Did you hear that, madam? Or have I got to come and shout in your ear?

I loved her. And thank God I can admit it at last. *Love*—not the sort you understand, all smug and respectable with a ring and vows to cage it—but fire and warmth and sweetness—"

Her voice came cold from the pillows then. She turned and looked at him. Her eyes were wounded in the lamplight, but her mouth was hard, her voice contemptuous when she said, "You're mad. And if you don't go, the servants will hear."

He turned on his heel abruptly and without another word went out, shutting the door behind him with a snap.

He went downstairs quickly and out the back door. The night was clear, with a golden moon hanging in the velvet dark sky. There was no wind, but small sounds stirred the grass and undergrowth. The hump of Rosebuzzan was streaked with shadows clawing to the valley road.

William was no longer tired. The unsavory episode with Charlotte had purged him of physical need. Even the thought of Hannah had diminished into reasonable perspective. Women, after all—*any* woman—filled only a part of life. Roots—real roots—though bred of sex, stretched far deeper and farther, extending and spreading through the very bowels of the earth itself, giving richness and wealth from its soil, a reason for living and toiling and savoring its potentials.

Copper. Tin.

Instinctively and without thought, he walked down the drive and took the lane and track toward the Connor farm. On the way he passed the old man, Abel, who'd once worked for Nicholas.

"Evenin' surr," he said as William approached. "Nice night edn' et?"

William paused. "What are *you* doing out at this hour?" he asked.

"When you get to my years, surr, you doan' sleep so much," the old fellow replied. "You get to dreamin' of old times and wonderin' what et be all about—livin' an' dyin', an frettin' y'r guts out for sumpthen' as goes like a puff o' wind in th' end. That old mine now round the bend, 'twere workin' in my great-grandfather's day, he wus a cap'n then, I've heerd. Now—nuthen. Nuthen but a great black skellington an' an empty shaft hole. They ole' stones though up theer on moor—stood theer before the good Lord was born. D'ye know, surr, I've heerd Joseph of—what's the name—Arimathea or some such like—comed theer with the young Jesus preachin' or on some mission. Whether et be true or not I doan' rightly know. But on a night like this with they shadows streakin' the hill, a voice seems to whisper to me: 'could be', 'could be.' All manner o' ghosties seems a whisprin' sometimes—"

William waited until the oration was over, then he said, "Isn't it time you were getting back to your cottage, Abel? The air's sharp."

"Yes, surr. When I can pull myself proper to my feet. These old bones edn' so jaunty as they once wus."

William took the old man's arm and helped him up. "I'll see you safely home," he said. "I was about to turn back myself."

The journey to the cottage, though short, took quite a time because of Abel's arthritis, and when they'd said good night William, still restless, continued down the lane in the opposite direction for a short distance.

Then he cut round the base of the moor which brought him eventually to the high coast road overlooking the site where Trencobban had once stood, marked by the monument erected by Donna.

He crossed the lane and went down the narrow track toward the derelict patch of ground not far from the ravine leading down to the cove below. Though there was no wind, the boom of the waves echoed with hollow persistence as they broke against the savage cliffs. Only a few tumbled stones indicated any building might once had stood there, and no one who'd not known the sturdy mansion as it had been in Donna's youth could have envisaged its stately stern frontage with stables and courtyard at the side. William had seen two faded photographs. But they had been inadequate and quite incapable of reproducing the simple grandeur of structure. And the surroundings were missing. There was no color—no light and shade, no crashing of waves or wild crying of sea birds, no sound of the eternal ocean breaking on the shore. Such things could be only ghost figments conjured up by the mind.

William, having walked farther than he realized, suddenly felt physically tired. He moved to the simple granite slab, his grandfather's memorial, and put his hand on it. As he stood there he was seized by a strange emotional stirring that gave him an overwhelming sense of "belonging," of being a part of something—a heritage—completely beyond his comprehension yet something that at all costs he must not betray.

Beneath his palm it seemed to him unknown vibrations quivered and made contact—and a greater understanding than his own mind recognized flooded his whole being. Did a ghost hand touch his shoulder? Was the voice of the sea the voice of something or someone else speaking? Or was it merely his own manhood coming to terms with life?

Whatever the answer, he knew, as he made his way back through winter's tangle of brown heather and furze, that in the future he'd make an effort to keep his mind more firmly on values. He was no saint and never would be. His mold was of the earthy kind. But before Charlotte left he'd do what he could to restore a little dignity between them. No man worth his salt should shame a woman utterly. Take her back he could not and would not. But, though distasteful to him, he could at least apologize—for marrying her in the first place and then rejecting her.

Perhaps even in the end they might be friends, though he doubted very much Charlotte would agree.

## 14

The old man Abel was seated on his usual boulder huddled into his coat, eyes on the moorland slopes, when the fire started. It was a cold afternoon in mid-December with a wind blowing and the light was quickly fading. He was about to heave himself up and make his way back to his home, realizing the walk in his condition had been a mistake, when he saw the red glow deepening the sky by the Connor farm. At first he took it for a sudden flash of dying sun; then he realized it was in the wrong direction and that there had been no sun that day. He started to tremble. His arm was shaking violently as his hand closed on his stick. A queer kind of panic rose in him. He remembered the day a quarter of a century ago when fire had taken Trencobban—how Donna, the young mistress of Polbreath who'd once lived there, had ridden Saladin, her colt, in an attempt to salvage what she could, and how she owed her life to Jed Andrewartha, the ruthless one-armed character who'd rushed to the

inferno and saved her. A bitter, terrible night it had
been, with the old house creaking and groaning before it died. Oh, houses had hearts—there was no
doubt of that in Abel's mind as he watched now a
yellowing tongue of flame shoot and curdle above the
hill, followed by smoke and angry, hungry crimson.
The high wind blew against him, holding an acrid,
bitter smell—the smell of burning wood and timber.
He started to cough, while his whole frame shivered.
He shouldn't be cold—not with that great bonfire in
the distance, he told himself—but shock on top of the
biting wind, had chilled him, and his old heart was
bounding against his ribs like the thudding of a weary
old horse wanting to be free. The horses!—what would
he do, that poor young fellow, if his animals were
taken? In imagination he already saw them racing and
plunging through the smoke and flames—magnificent,
powerful creatures they were, too proud and fine by
far for such an end. Some folk liked hunters and the
racing kind, but he'd always been one for the mighty
giants—the thunderous shires and cart-horses of noble
ancestry who'd once pulled chariots and shown brav-
ery greater than humankind.

*Must get help,* he thought, forcing one stiff leg before the other, *must get there somehow—to the big
house.*

But it was hard to make any progress at all, and as
he started to cough the stick fell to the ground. He
made an effort to reach it, failed and fell. There was a
searing pain in one hip, an agonizing tearing across
his chest as the coughing intensified and became one
long hacking sound through which all energy that was
left formed into a knot of breathless gasping for air.

No one saw or found him until much later, and by

then it was too late. He could have been a tumbled lump of rock lying by other boulders in the tangle of dried undergrowth.

And round the bend of the hill, Trefyn fought like a madman to save his stud, helped by firefighters from various farms, by hoses fed from the stream and pool above, by beating and every means possible to combat the blazing fury. Jet, half choking, with clothes and hair singed, face blackened and streaming, plunged after her brother time after time, laden with buckets of water that proved of little use.

"Come back!" she screamed as Trefyn appeared, a figure of fury and lightning speed, leading the mighty stallion through the billowing hungry smoke and flame to the verge of the inferno. The horse reared, snorted, and bellowed. One of the men wildly attempted to lasso him, but Red King plunged away down the slope to the stream, flinging himself into the water where he lay for minutes, reveling in the coolness. Then he stood up, head magnificently posed against the reddened gray sky, nostrils flared, before taking off toward Polbreath.

By the time the fire engine reached the farm, the worst was over. The stables and the back part of the house had gone. The stud and livestock, including the two prize mares, had been saved; all but one—the precious colt that, next to Juliet, was the most treasured thing in Trefyn's life. For a long time, when all was quiet except for a few tired crackles of furze and timber, he knelt by the charred body, staring into the shocked glazed eyes. Though the glossy fur was burned from one side, showing blackened bone, the head was merely singed, as beautiful in death as it had been in life. Trefyn bent his face, letting his mouth rest briefly on the still warm nuzzle. Tears coursed slowly from his eyes. He said nothing and hardly moved until Jet's hand closed on his shoulder.

"Come along, Trefyn," he heard her say, "you can't do any good, and your hand's burned."

After a moment he got to his feet and let her lead him back to the house. "It's all right at the front," she said mechanically, "the sitting room and the bed-rooms—we can manage."

Trefyn slumped onto a chair with his head on his hands.

"I'll make coffee," she said mechanically. "The gas ring in my room's all right." She moved to the door, turned and continued, trying to comfort him, "Red King was all right, wasn't he? You can breed—"

He jumped to his feet quickly.

"Red King! I forgot. My God—where's he gone? I must get him—" he rushed away, pushing Jet aside while she called, "Don't, Trefyn—please wait a bit—"

If he heard her, he took no heed; he just raced out through the front door, down the path and gate, calling the horse in his own particular way. His hands were to his mouth, hair blown back from his white face in the wind, eyes screwed up, still smarting from smoke and grief, scanning the landscape. The stream was a mere empty thread of silver under the evening sky, the moor quickly fading to night's uniformity. He changed course and took the lane leading to the valley road. It was then he saw the unmistakable, proud shape of the stallion, bridled, being led by the broad figure of a man.

William.

In the cold gray light they came face to face. And it seemed for that long moment before either spoke that the opposing forces of primitive chieftains from earlier times were brought together in confrontation.

Then William said, "He came our way. I was able to take him. He's a fine beast."

"So was the foal." Trefyn said, taking the bridle.

William gave him a hard look. "I'm sorry about it," he remarked. "If there's anything—"

"You can do?" Trefyn interrupted bitterly. "Haven't you done enough?"

"What the hell do you mean?"

"Do you imagine I don't realize you've been waiting for something like this for years?" Trefyn said, hardly aware of his own words. "I wouldn't put it past you even to have connived at it—"

"Why, you foul-minded young upstart—" William shouted, lifting a fist, "if it wasn't for the fire and what you've gone through, I'd knock you to hell for that—"

"*Would* you?" Trefyn said, thrusting his lean-jawed, blazing face close against William's. "You just try it, man, and you'll wish you'd never heard the name of Connor."

William let his arm drop and forced himself to say placatingly, "Forget it. When you see straight maybe you'll find a shred of gratitude for getting your bloody stallion back in one piece. My groom had a kick, and one of my arms is practically broken. Keep him under control in the future, and see your stables are properly built when they go up again. Hay's dangerous kept in lofts above live creatures."

He turned sharply, striding at a quick pace down the track, his whole mind and body seething with indignation. As he reached the corner he saw a girl's form racing down a narrow sheep track leading from the farm between clumps of gorse bushes and boulders. He paused. She was out of breath, and her face was streaming with perspiration that had worked most of the grime and smoke away. Her hands were scratched and scorched, her dress torn. But even in such a sorry state she had a wild Gypsy beauty of her own.

Jet.

"What do you want?" he said.

She eyed him fiercely. "Don't harm Trefyn. And keep away. He loved that foal. It was his life—almost. Or can't you understand that?"

Her dark eyes, almost black flecked with curious green sparks, challenged him. He wanted to touch the thin, quivering limbs, and smooth the unruly, tumbled hair from her forehead to make sure she was real and not some fiery sprite kindled from the elements and his own imagination. Pity, too, was in him, a rare emotion in his experience. But he kept his hands to himself.

"I understand," he said. "And I've no wish to hurt your brother now. Only, look after him. Keep him away from Polbreath."

"Do you think *I* can keep him away?" she demanded, "do you? Or anyone? No one can make Trefyn do what he doesn't want."

She shook her hair from her face, and added, "He's all I've got, I'd *die* for him," before turning quickly and plunging away again up the path with the speed of some untamed wild thing into the darkened shadows of bushes and rocks.

William walked on, head thrust forward broodingly, trying to erase her image from his mind. It was difficult. There was nothing about her like Hannah except a certain quality of untamed passion. But it was enough to remind him of all he lacked. Of depths in his nature that were unfulfilled. He grabbed a thorn stick from a nearby bush and swung it aimlessly from side to side, beating undergrowth, prodding furze and bushes, occasionally kicking a stone or two with his boot.

In doing so he detected, with a quick shock, something odd crumpled beyond the side of the lane— something that could have been a boulder lying near a greater one, but wasn't. He took two strides into the withered bracken and gave the thing a prod. It was soft but didn't move.

He bent down, and kneeling, peered through the gray light at the still form. A smell of tobacco emanated from the worn tweed coat. As William's hands traced the rough surface he saw a cap lying nearby. Automatically he picked it up, gave it one glance, then turned the white face toward him. It was quite cold now, and no breath came from the bearded lips. The eyes were wide open and staring, as though molded in glass.

"Poor old fellow," William whispered to himself automatically, "Poor old Abel."

He lifted him up as though he'd been a child, and carried him back to Polbreath.

"What have you got there?" Donna demanded shortly as he went in through the side door.

"The old man," William told her. "Abel. Connor's foal was not the only casualty tonight. We shall have to have the doctor, of course. Someone had better fetch him."

Donna did not move.

"Well, mama," William said, "will you allow me to pass?"

"Have we got to have him here? Can't he go to his own cottage?"

William stared at her coldly before passing by. When he reached the parlor he laid the old man on the chaise longue.

"How dare you?" he heard a woman's voice whisper bitterly from the doorway. He looked back sharply. Donna was standing there, white-faced, her eyes pinpoints of orange under lowered brows. "Nicholas lay there last," she said, "after your sister killed him. It's *his* place—sacred. The cushion bore the mark of his shoulders—it's not been touched since he died." She walked slowly into the room. "Take him away, William. I won't have that draggled old creature on my husband's place."

William, ignoring her command, strode toward her and took her by the shoulders.

"Go to your room, mama. I'm doing what my father would have done, and when you come to your senses you'll know it. And don't tell me what to do any more. I'm master now until things are settled with Jonathan. You no longer hold the whip. And another thing . . ." he paused significantly, "if Juliet returns here—*when*—she'll take her proper place in the family because I say so. And there'll be no more tirading on false accusations. My father died because he did what he chose to do on his own responsibility. Do you think you're the only one to miss him? Do you?"

She flinched as he shook her slightly.

"We all do," he continued, "but we have to accept the fact. He's dead. *Dead*, mama, and it's time you acknowledged it. Now just quiet down. Take that look off your face, and go and have a rest upstairs on your bed. I'll see about old Abel."

He released her. Without another look at him, Donna turned and obeyed him mutely, knowing for the first time there was a force in the house she could no longer combat—William—her eldest son, who for those few agonizing moments had reminded her so poignantly of Nicholas.

She went upstairs and flung herself on her bed, but not to rest as he'd suggested. Instead, a tumult of anguished sobs broke from her—not of anger or resentment but in an overwhelming tide of grief and release from the long killing strain of stoical pride. Until then she'd deluded herself with the belief that hardness could dim loss. Now, suddenly, she knew there was no opiate for pain like hers. Only time could help. Time and somehow coming to terms with widowhood.

*But oh, Nicholas,* her heart cried, *how am I going to live without you?*

Presently, worn out by physical and emotional exhaustion, the tumult died within her, and she slept.

But there was no sleep for Trefyn. Only the slow formation of a plan taking shape like granite in his mind; a plan that first must have a sound basis and prove to him a rightful cause beyond any human doubt.

When he heard of Abel's death, he knew. The old man, one-time servant to the Trevarvas family, had been prowling about the moor on the night of the fire. Tobacco and matches had been found in his pocket. That he'd died from a heart attack didn't register at all.

"He did it," he said to Jet with deadly ruthless precision in his voice. "I'll make them pay—sometime, somehow—for Velvet's death."

"But Trefyn, you don't *know*," Jet protested, "the doctor said—"

"Doctors? Doctors can be bribed by wealth," Trefyn asserted, "*his* sort, anyway—William's."

"What can you do though? It isn't as if you can do anything. Besides, I don't believe it. And think of Juliet . . . " her voice faded, became tentative and placating.

"I am," Trefyn answered.

"Then if you love her . . ."

Trefyn's eyes narrowed when he looked at her. "If? Don't be a fool, Jet. Except for you, she's about the only thing I *do* care about. But she's a Trevarvas. And for that she'll have to make amends."

Jet shivered. Her brother at that moment did not appear quite human, and all she could do was to leave the subject, hoping in time he'd put the fire behind him. There'd be a great deal to do in the immediate months ahead; rebuilding and replenishing stock and, with luck, breeding successfully again from one of the mares, so that another foal sired by Red King could take its proud place in the new stables.

One day he'd forget the bitterness. He'd have to. Like a shadow, memories from the past shivered bleakly through her, and it was not Trefyn's face she recalled anymore but that of her mother, Elinor Gentry, whose own bitterness had so soured her life that it had eventually killed her. *Please don't let it happen to Trefyn,* she whispered aloud, unknowingly. *Let him love again.*

She didn't realize, how could she? The passionate desire and longing in her brother for Juliet was already taking its own ruthless course toward fulfillment and expiation of the past.

\* \* \*

Before Juliet was hardly aware of it, Christmas came
and went. She joined halfheartedly in what festivities
there were at Agatha's establishment. There was a
party on Christmas Eve in the common room, followed by a march on Christmas Day when Agatha, in
defiance of religious custom or belief, led a gathering—mostly women—advertising feminine rights and
equality through the locality, including Regents Park.
Juliet, Mr. Singh, and a few of the other tenants remained behind, although there was a full get-together
at night when a number of less privileged and unem-
ployed were entertained by the household. Judy gave
impressions of music-hall characters; and a skit on
current social conditions, devised by Agatha herself,
was produced on a temporary platform erected with
planks.

The next evening Juliet attended a party at Peter's
studio. There were less than a dozen present, including Oswald and four of his friends—extravagantly
dressed young men who discussed art and the "new
thought": Freud, Jung, and the philosophies of Hegel,
Kant, and Karl Marx, while seated on the floor, drinking cheap brandy followed by strong coffee. Only
three women were present—Juliet herself; a tow-
haired, masculine-looking female with a thin colorless girl companion; and Judy. The fair woman, whose
hair was cropped like a man's, had a hearty manner of
slapping anyone available on the back and smoked cigars with the bravado of an established moral revolutionary. Judy appeared to enjoy herself immensely.
But for most of the time Juliet was intensely homesick
for Polbreath.

She'd heard from no one in Cornwall except Jason,

who sent her a letter that included a silk scarf and best wishes from them all. Andrew, he said, had already sailed for Africa, and mama was a little better, gradually recovering from Nicholas's death. The letter had been forwarded from Ianthe's.

There was no word from Donna herself, and Juliet had not expected it.

Nor had Trefyn written.

She felt isolated and deflated in spirits, and when two o'clock passed she got up abruptly and said she was leaving.

Judy made a face. "Oh, *must* you? *Why?* We're only just starting, aren't we, Ozzy?"

Oswald gave an ambiguous fuddled smile. "Quite. Only just."

"Oh, come on, be a devil," Bobby the tow-haired woman said, putting her arm round Juliet's shoulders. "I've got a script to read first, just a snippet—start of a new novel, matter of fact—"

Juliet pulled herself free. "I'm sorry. I must go. I'm really tired."

Judy was huffed, but insisted on accompanying her. "Why do you have to be such a spoilsport?" she demanded querulously, walking back through the cold streets. "Heaven knows, we don't get all that much fun round here. I think you might have stuck it a bit longer. Bob's a genius, you know. Peter says she'll be a second George Sand when she gets properly started."

"Oh, I *see*," Juliet said shortly. "*That's* who she's aping. I might have known."

"What's the matter with you? George Sand was a remarkable woman," Judy replied tartly. "Everyone of any importance admired her—men *and* women. She was the mistress of lots of famous men, you know—Alfred de Musset and Chopin, and she was all for equality, even at that time. If you read about the golden age—"

"Oh, stop it," Juliet said. "I'm sick of equality and intellect and the new age. Go back if you want. We're near the main road now. No harm can possibly come to me."

But Judy grudgingly insisted on going with Juliet all the way back to Agatha's. And when they reached the house she said, "I suppose you're right. *I'm* tired too. I've just realized it. Sorry I was a bear."

"It's all right. Only I'm certain of one thing—no more of Peter's parties for me."

Judy flung her a whimsical smile. "The trouble with you is," she said, "you're lovesick."

"Don't be silly," Juliet told her. But she knew it was true. .

On the following evening Ianthe caused a furor by arriving unexpectedly at Agatha's to collect her half-sister for an evening out. She was wearing a luxurious purple silk gown with enormous bell sleeves edged with ermine under an ermine shoulder cape. She had an extravagantly wide-brimmed hat trimmed high with flowers and feathers, and the skirt of the gown, though frothily full at the hem, was slit at one side to reveal a titillating glimpse of shapely leg when she moved in a certain way.

Mr. Singh and Peter, from the back of the hall, gasped when they saw her. Agatha, who'd opened the door, drew back in dismay.

Juliet was just coming downstairs. "Ianthe!" she exclaimed, hurrying forward. "What are you—?" she paused, saying to Agatha, "This is my sister, Mrs. Wycksley, Mrs. Robertson Wycksley. Agatha—"

The introduction was never properly concluded. Agatha drew herself up rigidly and said, "I quite understand; I'll leave you then. You've got things to talk about, I suppose." She turned and retreated.

Ianthe laughed. "Of course she's heard of me. My dreadful reputation. Oh dear. Never mind, darling, if they throw you out, you can always return to No. 10. Robertson wouldn't notice you. He's found another protegée now. The point is, I've come to abduct you for an evening—"

"Oh Ianthe, what do you mean? Don't be so silly."

Ianthe's eyes, looking larger and darker than ever with the liberal use of kohl, widened.

"Dear little sister, I'm not being at all silly. Heavens! what a hole this is. How can you ever stick it? Now you're just going to have a taste of fun and the bright lights for a change. We're having dinner at the Café Royal with two very dear friends of mine—Julius Saroyan, my latest lover, a patron of the arts, and *very* rich, my dear; and Claude Bellon, the *honorable* Claude, who's dying to meet you. No—don't interrupt. It's all arranged. I've got a dress for you to change into at Marietta Anson's—I've known her for years—she's an actress, twice divorced, with two lots of alimony to keep her very comfortably in her gorgeous West End home. Then we'll take off, and if you like, you needn't come back here at all—" she broke off, smiling radiantly.

"Ianthe, I *couldn't*," Juliet said, "I'm not that sort of person. I mean—"

"I know, darling. You're young and innocent and in

love with a Gypsy. But don't you see, that's so romantic? Claude will be fascinated. He won't *try* anything, darling, he's in love with an Italian count anyway. And do you imagine I'd let you come to harm?"

"No. But—"

"No more buts. Get your best shoes and cape—the rest are all waiting for you. Hurry now. I've a cab outside. I didn't bring the carriage in case Wycksley got curious. He knows about Julius, of course. But if he knew I was after you, he might object." In the end, dazed and overwhelmed by Ianthe's exuberance, Juliet gave in and five minutes later was being driven with her sister to Marietta's luxurious home.

The room she changed in was a dream of exotic beauty, furnished all in cream and gold and palest rose. Marietta, an aging blonde but still ravishing to look at from a few yards away, was gushing and faintly amused as Juliet stared speechless with wonder at the gauzy blue dress provided. It was cut low at the bosom but not tastelessly so, and was sewn with glittering sequins. A maid appeared to dress the luxurious curls with a silver ribbon and one white artificial rose. There was perfume, powder, and makeup of every shade in small gold-knobbed bottles. But these Marietta discarded as unnecessary.

"*Non!*" she exclaimed. "Not for you, *cherie!* You are the natural type—yes. A true English rose."

Ianthe was giggling when she and Juliet left for the Café Royale where they were to meet their escorts. "You'd think Marietta was French, wouldn't you? That's what she wants. But my dear! If you heard her holding forth in her natural lingo, you'd have the shock of your life. Talk about true Cockney! But she's fun—a real trouper."

"We had a dressmaker at Polbreath like that," Juliet said reminiscently. "Her name was Miss West. She was very plain, and stuck pins into you."

"On *purpose?*"

"Yes, I think so," Juliet answered. "She was probably jealous."

Ianthe patted the slim, gloved hand. "You're learning, darling," she said. "Have no illusions about people—especially women—and you'll find life a whole lot less heartbreaking. That's why I don't believe in all this equality business. If women had the chance, they'd be tyrants, simply because the plain ones are so much in the majority."

"You're a cynic, Ianthe," Juliet said. "And anyway, you exaggerate."

Ianthe shrugged. "Of course. Don't believe all I say. Most of it's façade. But—"

"Yes?"

"Be nice to Claude. He has influence with Julius—socially—and Julius is very important to me."

Juliet found that being nice to Claude was not difficult. He was engagingly polite, courteous, blond, and elegantly dressed, listening attentively to her every remark yet making no indication of any personal demands or expectations of her. Julius was very different—dark, heavy-browed, with a sensual quality about him intensified by his full, firm lower lip and chin, the brooding glance of his black eyes every time he glanced at Ianthe. Juliet could not help envisaging their lovemaking, thrilling at the thought—which inevitably took her mind back to Trefyn.

The meal was an exotic interim enlivened by a very old and rare blend of champagne chosen by Julius, who was an authority on wines.

When they left the Café Royale they went on to a nightclub where the new dance, the tango, launched by Mistinguett, was exhibited by those daring enough to expose a leg. Ianthe, who'd changed her hat at Marietta's for a gold turban trimmed with osprey, took the floor with Julius, pelvis and stomach thrust forward, shapely leg outrageously on view as she gazed languorously up into her lover's face.

The whole episode passed like a dream to Juliet. An unreal, stimulating dream that left her, however, feeling completely exhausted. Although Marietta had invited her to stay the night, she chose to return to Agatha's. It was past one o'clock when she inserted her key into the lock. There was no light at all except from a small oil lamp left burning on a chest on the top of the first flight of stairs and a thin glimmer streaming from beneath Agatha's bedroom door at the end of the hall.

The whole house felt unwelcoming, desolate. She realized with a sudden stab of cold truth that she hadn't really enjoyed a single moment of her time there. She was no pioneer or fighter of causes. Her only rare moments of interest in London had been at Ianthe's, when she'd so stupidly believed she could be a fine actress.

Of course she couldn't. She wasn't an actress at all. She didn't belong to the artificial world of theaterdom or sophisticated society. She couldn't pretend to be anything but what she was—herself!—Juliet Trevarvas whose roots and heart were in faraway Cornwall where the wild moors stretched to the relentless sea and the winds blew free from the stone-capped heights to the valleys below. In a surge of loneliness and passionate longing she decided she couldn't stay another day in London. She'd pack her bag and leave, get on the first train in Penzance and find somewhere to stay until she got the courage to face her mother. William would stand by her—he'd have to. He was her brother. Oh, what an idiot she'd been to stick at her stupid job with Peter for so long.

Golden Girl picture cards! how ridiculous they were, and how soppy she looked with all that fussy stuff round her neck, suggesting she'd nothing on below or beneath. And with her eyes so soulful and sad-looking.

"You look angelic," Peter had said. And what a lie. How could she?—when she didn't feel angelic at all? When her whole heart and mind and body were longing to fling defiance and anger in Trefyn's face—to wave one of the stupid things in his face and say, "There! Look what you made me do! That's *me* in the photograph; do you recognize me? People buy me and put me on their mantelpieces. I go through the post and silly young men drool over me. Even dukes, Peter said. Because I'm beautiful. And Oswald's colored some of them . . . made my cheeks all pink and put a yellow light round my hair—"

What would Trefyn say to that? Why, he might even have had one of them already. As she undressed for bed she realized, sobering down, it was hardly likely he would. The first batch of postcards were now only just circulating, and very few of the colored ones had been done. Besides, who'd send him one? Certainly not Judy who was too immersed in her painting and in her own affairs to bother about Trefyn.

But—Juliet's heart almost stopped beating when a wild idea suggested itself—what about herself? She could print his name and address, just TREFYN CONNOR, MOORVALE FARM, NR ST. FIGGANS, PENZANCE, CORN-WALL, and post it anonymously. He'd not know who it came from, but he'd recognize her and surely be jeal-ous—so angry that he'd come looking for her at last and carry her back in a frenzy of love and desire.

Despite her tiredness a secret little smile of triumph and longing touched her lips. It must work out that way, she insisted to herself. It *must*. She'd have to stay on for just a few days longer, of course, to see what happened. And if he didn't appear—if she had no word from him—well, she'd think out a further plan. It had been stupid and weak of her to be depressed and ever imagine for one moment they would not come together in the end. She'd known from childhood that they belonged to each other. And hadn't she proved it, at the dew pond? No marriage vows could be more enduring or sacred than those wonderful moments when he'd claimed her with such pride and absolute commitment.

He'd recognized it, too. Hadn't he chided her in his letter for wasting one moment of passion by leaving and running away?

With her underclothes fallen from her tilted, rose-tipped breasts, she went to the small chest of drawers, took out his two cherished notes, and read them over and over again. When she crossed to the mirror and saw herself with them clasped against her, thick hair tumbled in a dark cloud round her burning cheeks, eyes brilliant, even in the wan light, she hardly recog-nized her own reflection. So vivid she looked—so filled with explosive life and yearning, though a few moments before she'd been tired and drained of en-ergy.

She slept fitfully until morning, and went to the studio later for her usual session of posing. When time came for leaving she asked for a sample of the most recent Golden Girl photograph.

Peter was surprised. "I didn't think you were keen on them," he said.

"I'm not. All the same I'd like one. I think I have the right."

"Of course."

"And a colored one, please."

"But we haven't many yet. What's the idea."

"Never mind," she said rather shortly. "It will be an advertisement for you though."

In the end he agreed. Juliet got her sample card; she addressed and posted it that same evening, in time to catch the late mail.

The next few days dragged by for Juliet with fevered interims of waiting and longing and imagining Trefyn's reaction when he received the card. She said nothing to Agatha or Judy of her intentions to leave, although Judy sensed something.

"What are you up to?" She asked once curiously. "Something's happened, hasn't it?"

Juliet shook her head. "No, nothing. But it will," she prophesied, "you just wait."

Judy sighed. "I hope it won't be too long, that's all, whatever it is. Peter says you're not concentrating."

Juliet just smiled maddeningly and turned away.

Two days later her prediction concerning the waiting proved correct.

When she reached Agatha's one evening after a late sitting, her landlady was waiting for her on the stairs, looking distinctly put-out, with tight-lipped condemnation on her face.

"There's someone waiting to see you—in my sitting room," she said coldly, "—a—a young man. I had to ask him in as he'd come a long way, he said. But you should understand it's against the rules of the house for female tenants to have gentlemen calling at such an hour. If I could have got rid of him I would. But he just sat down in the hall, saying your sister had directed him and he intended to stay until you came back." She paused before adding "I must warn you, Juliet, he's a domineering hot-tempered character. Not at all the type of male I encourage on my premises."

With a wild leaping of her heart Juliet said, "In your sitting room, did you say? Oh Agatha, thank you— *thank* you. I can take him upstairs—"

"You'll do nothing of the sort. You'll get your conversation over as quickly as possible, then show him the door. Forward-looking we may be in my establishment, but respectable. Please remember that in the future."

*Future?* Juliet thought in a daze of exhilaration, *if it was Trefyn the future was going to be all changed. And it must be Trefyn. It must be.*

It was.

When Juliet entered he was waiting by the small window that looked out onto the dusty garden. He turned as the door opened, and her first emotion following the excitement and relief was of shock. He looked so smart in a long, double-breasted black coat and shoes shining with polish below striped trousers. Though clean-shaven, he still had thick, dark side whiskers and was holding a pair of butter-colored gloves. The details, of course, didn't register at first. All that mattered was that Trefyn stood there: a tall, broad handsome figure, with no smile on his lips, only a brief narrowing of his eyes as they fell on her. Then, after a perceptible pause, he said, "Well, Juliet? Here I am."

She rushed toward him, hoping and longing for him to take her in his arms, but he didn't.

"You'd better get your things packed, hadn't you?" he said in calm, controlled tones that somehow puzzled and chilled her.

"Why? What do you mean?"

"Just that," he said. "Surely you don't imagine I've traveled hundreds of miles tracking you down just to go back again empty-handed?"

Her heart started hammering. "What do you mean?" she said with a stubborn thrust of her chin.

"What I said. Pack your clothes, Juliet. We're leaving. I'm booking you in at a respectable hotel for a night or two while I do what is to be done. Then . . . we'll go back together to Cornwall."

She was dazed and bewildered. This wasn't at all the reception she'd expected when she and Trefyn met again after their long parting. She'd visualized recriminations and forgiveness, following a few hot words perhaps, then kisses and the feel of his arms around her. But there was none of this—only a stern, apparently cool Trefyn Connor with a ruthless determination about him she could not understand. She felt her temper rising.

"You say what we're going to do. *You* say," she retorted hotly. "You've a nerve, haven't you? What makes you so sure I've any intention of returning to Cornwall?"

"I haven't, but you will all the same," he told her. "And if you make a scene, Juliet, I'll make a far worse one, I assure you. I'll put you over my knee here and now like the naughty girl you are and give you such a sound spanking the whole household will come racing down to witness the amusing scene. Do you understand?"

She shivered, inwardly seething with chagrin and anger, but realizing he meant it.

"Very well, if you have to be such a bully. But I'd like to know, if you don't mind, just what your reason is—your plan, if you have any."

He smiled, though the smile had little humor in it. "I'm never without a plan. You surely know me well enough to remember that." He waited, noting with a stirring of desire the perplexed frown between her lovely eyes, the quickened breathing and beating of a pulse in her neck above the rounded bosom. Then he continued, "I have applied for a special license, Juliet. We will be married at a Registrar's within a few days, and after that—"

"Yes?" the question left her lips as a sigh.

"There'll be a fine new house for us at the farm," he said, still not touching her. "Just a few little things to be done when we get there, of course. But in the end you're sure to like it."

"Oh, Trefyn—"

"You won't recognize it," he continued, still in that even, calm voice that troubled her. "Everything's quite, quite different now."

On impulse she rushed back to him and lifted her face to his.

"Kiss me, Trefyn, please kiss me," she begged. He put both hands on her shoulders, bent his head and let his mouth briefly touch hers—more, it seemed to her, as a duty than in desire. She withdrew and went to the door. Then she turned and said, "I don't understand you."

"You will," he told her, keeping his tones level, though every nerve and sense in his body was clamoring for her. "Once you're my wife everything will be clear. Don't worry, Juliet. Be quick now, hurry up and get ready so we can be away. There's sure to be a cab somewhere near."

Without waiting to argue, she obeyed him mutely.

Five minutes later they were driving down the main thoroughfare away from Agatha's toward a new destination.

She did not look back once. The whole episode of her stay there seemed to her now like a dream.

Stealing a look at Trefyn's hard profile outlined against the window, it was difficult even to believe everything she'd longed for was at last happening— Trefyn Connor was going to marry her.

She longed for a clasp of his hand, a touch on her breast or a single warm glance from his eyes.

But there was nothing. No sign at all that he loved her.

Tomorrow, though, it would be different, she told herself stoically. He was tired now, and trying to punish her for running away. Tomorrow things between them would be warm and passionate and filled with happiness. Tomorrow Trefyn would be the one she'd always known and fallen in love with. She didn't realize the bitter tricks that time could play or what lay ahead for her when they returned to Cornwall.

## 15

The hotel was really more of a boarding house, for "ladies only," in the vicinity of Kensington. It was quiet, very select, furnished quietly but artistically, and run by two sisters, the Misses Vance. Miss Flora was tall, thin, and rather elderly, with pale blue piercing eyes behind her pince-nez. Miss Ruth, shorter and rounder, had a kindly, fussy manner, but Juliet guessed she usually did what her sister suggested. Both wore high-necked long dresses with hand-embroidered bodices in delicate pastel shades. There was one maid servant called Fanny, a daily helper to do the rough work named Miss Porter, and a cook. Miss Flora allotted the rooms to her guests, which were never more than six in number. She was also responsible for the flower arrangements. Her sister dealt with the menus which were discussed between herself and the cook each evening for the following morning. If visitors required a light evening meal, they ordered one in advance. But most preferred to dine out. If anyone wished to be out after ten-thirty P.M., they had to ask for a key, which was only granted when Miss Flora was satisfied all laws of respectability would be strictly observed.

Juliet's bedroom was a delight after the cubbyhole of the place at Agatha's. There was a rose-colored carpet on the floor; flowered pink and white curtains hung at the windows, and a white silk spread covered the bed, beneath a pink eiderdown. An electric lamp with a pink shade stood on a small bedside table. Everything was scrupulously clean and tidy, with a faint smell of lavender permeating the air.

When Miss Flora had gone, Juliet sat on the bed with a sigh of comfort. The mattress was springy and soft, and she knew in spite of her excitement she'd sleep like a log that night. The primness, after the revolutionary atmosphere of Agatha's and the sophisticated wealth of Ianthe's, didn't worry her at all. But she was intrigued and mildly amused that Trefyn should have chosen such a place for her—Trefyn with his love of lonely places and wild animals, who could tame any creature that came his way and whistle birds to fly to his hand. He was staying in lodgings near Tottenham Court Road, he told her—kept by an Irish woman, the widow of a friend of his father's who'd once bred horses. There were little matters of business to be discussed, so he was taking the opportunity to get certain things settled while he was in town. Juliet had asked why she couldn't stay there too.

"Not suitable," Trefyn had said rather shortly. "We shall be together in the daytime, and as we'll be married in a couple of days, I want you to be somewhere safe and cozy until then."

Remembering what had happened at the dew pond, Juliet had been bewildered by his peculiarly conventional attitude, but she'd not argued, simply said, trying to tease him, "Suppose I run away, Trefyn?"

He'd looked at her then with the old hot flame in his eyes and said, "But you *won't*, my love, will you?"

And she'd answered, "Of *course* not, Trefyn. You know that." She'd wished, though—oh, how she'd wished—he'd take her in his arms and say he loved her.

But he didn't.

During the whole two days they were in London seeing the sights and visiting all the notable places possible like Hampton Court, Kew, the Tower, all the parks, and eating at restaurants and select places she'd never have thought Trefyn could afford, he never once made reference to his feelings for her unless she pressed him. The past was never mentioned between them.

Once she said, "Are you *sure* you want to marry me, Trefyn?"

And he replied, "Do you imagine I'd have gone to all this trouble and expense if I didn't?"

"Say yes," she insisted, "*say* it."

But he'd merely said rather coldly, "Don't try and bully me with words, darling. It won't work. Soon you'll know."

His evasion bothered her. Sometimes when she appeared not to be noticing she could feel his glance upon her, was aware with a rush of longing of the old bond warm and desirous between them. At other times, though polite, he seemed withdrawn, almost a stranger. But then, she told herself optimistically, this was probably because he didn't like London and was as dazed as she felt at the thought of marriage. Even about their future he was ambiguous. After his first reference to the fine new home they were to have, he carefully steered away from the subject whenever she tried to bring it up.

It was difficult for her not to explode with irritation. But she managed to control herself, wanting nothing in the world to provoke a quarrel or jeopardize their wedding.

So she was married to Trefyn, still in a state of unreality, by special license at a Registry Office near his lodgings only three days after his appearance at Agatha's. Her age, on the license, was given as twenty-one.

She wore the gray coat over her rose-colored dress, and carried a simple bunch of white lilies of the valley. The Irish woman, Trefyn's landlady, and a man friend were witnesses and the ceremony seemed so short Juliet wondered, at first, if it had really happened.

There was no proper reception or wedding breakfast, just sandwiches and champagne in the rather dreary parlor. Juliet was not surprised at that. She guessed Trefyn had already spent more money than he could really afford. And in any case, what did any such superficialities matter when she was at last actually his wife?

She had believed, though, they'd spend the first night of their marriage in some small, not too expensive hotel, and when he told her calmly they were traveling overnight to Cornwall she felt a stab of disappointment. She *wanted* to get home, of course she did. She'd been tired of London for weeks—months— and the thought of Trefyn's promised new house excited and exhilarated her. But the journey was so terribly long. It would take nearly twelve hours, perhaps more; hours when she could have been lying close in his arms, with his hands and lips caressing every inch and curve of her warm, naked young body—precious moments of beauty to be remembered and treasured all their lives.

Instead they were to sit stiff-backed in some stuffy, smoky railway carriage, conventionally dressed, with other dull, weary-eyed people probably facing them, rustling newspapers and occasionally nodding off into a doze. When she'd run away from home those months before, it had been quite different. She'd traveled first-class, and in spite of the obnoxious, fussy little Frenchman, the carriage had been wide and comfortable. But Trefyn had told her such expense was unnecessary.

"You're my wife now, darling," he'd reminded her as they set off for the station, "and will have to do a little conforming, I'm afraid."

Forgetting her resolve not to lose her temper, Juliet said sharply, "You mean we're going to travel like servants? *Third*? Lucy, a maid we had at Polbreath, said the carriages were terribly stuffy, and—"

Something in Trefyn's face stopped her. His lips were set, his eyes hard when he said, "Just like servants then, if that's their style. You're no longer Miss Trevarvas of Polbreath, remember? You're Mrs. Trefyn Connor." He paused, then added, "And see you don't forget it."

As if she could, she thought. As if she'd ever want to. All the same, if it hadn't been for the cabby, the fact that they were nearing the station, and that she didn't want to start the journey with a quarrel, she'd have flared up at him with a tart answer, showing him, however bossy he was, that she didn't intend to be a mere "yes" wife—the kind Judy so despised.

However, she kept silent, and soon they were making their way through the station barrier to the platform.

Although the train journey passed like a tired dream in a haze of unreality, it seemed endless. At moments she allowed her back to sag, pushing her chin forward onto her chest. She slept on and off in this manner for periods at a time, and did not know then that Trefyn's hand pressed on hers briefly, or that his eyes softened at the sight of her youthful vulnerability. Conscience smote him once or twice when he thought of the shock ahead of her. Had he been unfair? Was it, after all, unwise of him to imagine he could tame her wild spirit in the way he intended? She looked so innocent, so lovely, and in every way desirable with the long lashes shadowing her cheeks, her lips softly parted as a child's could be, hands limply folded on her knees. But she deserved it, didn't she? She'd given herself to him, then flung it in his face—publicized herself like any cheap prostitute with her face on picture postcards for any man to buy. She was also a Trevarvas. Sister of the man he hated, the man who'd destroyed—murdered—the lovely creature that was the fruit of years of breeding and caring for and endless hope.

Memory of the fire still seared his mind whenever he allowed a picture of the joyous, proud young animal to return. Mostly he pushed it away. But he knew that even when the first acute anguish was finally eased he'd feel at intervals the soft thrust of the muz-

zle in his hand and hear to the end of his life the ago-
nized whining of its death pangs.

Someone should pay. It was only fair. Juliet could
help. He loved her, but she had things to learn—not to
make a show of herself, or think any family owned
others with the right to steal and kill the birthright of
those less endowed. So when he felt himself weakening he forced his eyes away, took his hand from hers,
and stifled the passionate longing in him to hard resolve.

It was already light when the train drew in at Penzance station; gray but fine, with winter sunlight
streaking silver over the harbor and sea. She felt a
rush of warmth as the well-known view came into
sight, showing St. Michael's Mount rising like a fairy-
tale castle from the water, and the sails of fishing
boats bobbing gently Newlyn way.

"I'm so glad to be back," she couldn't help saying as
Trefyn took their bags from the rack. He said nothing
but bustled her onto the platform, urging her quickly
to the barrier. Most of the passengers had left the
train earlier, and the few who got out there Juliet did
not know. She was surprised that Trefyn had not arranged for his man or Jet to meet them with the carriage. After all his recent expense it seemed odd to
hire a cab. Still, perhaps he just wanted to please her,
she thought optimistically. His quietness could mean
he was just as excited as she was, deep down, and was
trying to appear aloof and dignified. And yet, somehow, that was not like Trefyn. He'd always acted just
as he felt; he'd been spontaneous and full of changing
moods that followed quickly one upon the other, like
the transient sunlight chasing shadows over the wind-

swept hills. This quality had always been one of his greatest charms. Oh, *Trefyn*, she thought, trying desperately to penetrate his reserve, *do look at me. Smile . . .* be *nice.*

But he hardly glanced her way once during the winding journey through the hills to the farm, and as the curling road narrowed to the track that eventually led by the base of Rosebuzzan to the opposite coast, tenseness seemed to deepen between them.

"Look, Trefyn," she said as they passed the old mine stack, "look, you can see it. The dew pond."

His eyes slid momentarily to a flash of silver where the pool lay above in its own bright circle, but she did not see, and he said nothing.

Just before the farm he told the driver to stop. "We'll walk from here," he said.

If the cabby was surprised he did not show it. "Very well, surr," he said, drawing the horse to a halt. Juliet obediently got up and followed Trefyn out. The fare was paid; the man nodded, gave a flick of his whip and a click of his tongue. The next moment the vehicle was rattling away, and Trefyn and Juliet were making their way toward the farm. Juliet wanted to carry her own case, but he refused.

"It's not far, my darling," he said, "You'll have plenty to do later. Don't grudge me showing a little chivalry to my new wife." His lips were smiling when he looked at her, but his eyes weren't. She couldn't understand him. Just for a moment she was acutely apprehensive and on edge. Her pace must have slowed. He touched her arm, then withdrew his hand quickly and said sharply, "Come along, Juliet. Surely you're not tired already."

The short walk round the curve of the hill wasn't

more than a hundred yards, and as they took the
bend, the front of the house emerged as it had always
been—cream-washed, with its top windows and roof
faintly tipped with early sunlight. She frowned in per-
plexity.

"But Trefyn . . . I thought you said . . . I
thought—"

"Well? What did you think?"

"You said a fine new house," she reminded him.
"Don't you remember—?"

"Of course."

"Then what . . . where is it?"

He grabbed her hand. "I'll show you."

He pulled her along, carrying the two bags in one
hand, while she half tripped against loose stones at
the edge of the track.

"Come along." He forced her into a run by the side
of the building, and when at last he suddenly stopped,
pointing, she gaped in astonishment and horrified
amazement, her skirts still held above her ankles, revealing white embroidered petticoats grimed with
dust and soil.

She swallowed nervously, viewing the scene with
shock: the charred remains of the dairy and burnt-out
kitchen quarters, the blackened patches of earth lying
round, and desolate space where the stables had been.
Her heart began to pump painfully. Her skin became
cold and clammy. What was the matter? What did it
mean?

She turned her face questioningly to Trefyn's. He
was staring down at her with an expression on his
face, cold and enigmatic, which, faintly amusing to
him, she did not recognize, could not even begin to
fathom.

"I don't understand," she said feebly.

"But you will, my love. You will."

"What?"

"It will take time," he said, "but in the end you'll have it all—a fine building with a new parlor and everything your greedy little heart demands."

"But—"

"*Everything,*" he said with a different, stronger note in his voice . . . "when we've once built it."

"*We?*"

"You and I, Juliet," he said. "We'll start together from scratch and watch it grow, brick by brick, plank by plank, solid walls and a firm roof: the Connor farm, or house, if you like. And you will run it as a wife should, when it's finished. *My* wife. I'll carry you over the threshold, and then our life will properly begin. Until then you'll work like a boy and do as I say."

"And if I won't?" she asked with fury mounting in her, "if I run away—" she broke off, outraged by his duplicity.

"Then I'll catch you and bring you back," he told her. "Wherever you run to I'll hunt and find you, and there'll be no peace or forgiveness or pretty words. I'll tame you as men tamed their women in primitive times: with a decidedly hard hand, my love."

Her chin came out obstinately. "You're a brute, Trefyn Connor. I hate you."

"Hate on," he said coldly, though his eyes flamed. "I've hate in me, too—for that brother of yours who destroyed my farm and killed my foal, for the whole Trevarvas breed that gave you such airs and graces, and your own damned insolence in flaunting yourself for lusting males to drool over. You sent me that card, Juliet—Did you really imagine I wouldn't guess? What else did you do, I wonder? Who was he . . . the man who pictured you in that sickening flimsy finery? Or wasn't it there at all really? Was it something just laid on afterward for respectability's sake?—" He broke off, not really believing it, but trying to.

Her face had gone very white. "What I did in London's got nothing to do with you, Trefyn," she said in icy dead tones. "You weren't my keeper, and you're not now. No one will be . . . not ever . . . ever—" she turned and tried to rush away, but he stopped her and pulled her back, leading her to the front door where he pushed her through.

"The bedroom's ready," he said, "and Jet should be waiting with tea and something to eat. You'd better tidy yourself and take off those ridiculous clothes. There are overalls and breeches on the bed that should fit. Try them, Juliet. You'll find them better for work than frilly skirts."

Before going out he paused at the door and added, "I shall be sleeping in the barn by the new stables until the house is ready, so you can feel quite free to relax and titivate yourself in your spare moments. I shan't intrude."

For some moments after the door had closed, Juliet stood motionless, as though turned to stone. She only moved when Jet appeared with a cup of tea in her hand.

"Drink this," she said, "it will make you feel better. I'm sorry about Trefyn, but . . . it'll pass, you know. He hasn't got over the shock yet, about the fire. And when you sent that photograph . . ." her words died feebly. She shrugged.

Juliet took the cup from her and said with stony

deliberation, "I shan't stay, you know. I shall go home to Polbreath."

But she didn't.

When morning came she was still there, and after a tempting breakfast which she ate mechanically in one of Jet's dressing gowns, she got up, washed, and struggled into the breeches, shirt, and woollen jersey that fitted perfectly.

The previous day had been spent mostly in wandering round the farm and wrecked premises, inspecting the new stables which had already been built, and helping Jet in the improvised kitchens and what remained intact of the house. Trefyn had returned to Penzance later in the morning on some business matter to do with new stock, which had left the two girls free to sort out domestic arrangements and somehow get the future into perspective. Jet had explained about the fire, which had shocked Juliet profoundly.

"No one told me," she'd said, "but then no one wrote to me at all in London, except Andrew, and he's gone now, abroad somewhere."

"Yes, I'd heard."

"Anyway . . . you say Trefyn blames William. That's *awful*. William wouldn't do a thing like that . . . he's not the kind of person. And to believe old Abel was in it. It's—it's ridiculous."

"I know," Jet had agreed. "But I can't get Trefyn to see it. He won't even see the doctor—you know, the one who examined the poor old thing."

"What good would that do?"

"It might prove to Trefyn that Abel was ill anyway and couldn't have climbed up to the stables. Oh, I don't know, Juliet . . . he's just dead set on believing the worst. But of course *you* didn't help."

"What do you mean?"

"That photograph. It was a stupid thing to do. He's the jealous kind, especially of you. And you won't ever change him."

"I don't want to," Juliet admitted, "except . . . it's rotten to blame William. William has lots of faults, of course. He's not my favorite brother, and marrying Charlotte like that was mean—just to please mama and get out of the scandal with Hannah—"

"So you knew about that?"

"I think most people did. Still, he wouldn't play such a trick on Trefyn. He's not a criminal."

"I know," Jet agreed in a surprisingly dreamy way. "I think he's marvelous, all things considered. I mean, having such a bossy mama, and goody-goody brother like Andrew. Then being caught by that dull woman, Charlotte—"

"Andrew wasn't goody-goody," Juliet interrupted quickly. "You don't understand. You never knew him properly."

"No, William's the only one I've properly talked to, and he's quite, *quite* different, isn't he?—strong and exciting. A real man. That's the kind I like!"

Juliet glanced at her curiously. "How well do you know William?"

Jet shrugged. "Well enough. We meet sometimes, just by chance . . . on the moor or in the lane."·

But Juliet didn't believe her. Any meetings she'd had with her brother, she sensed, hadn't been by chance at all. And she wondered what would happen if Donna heard. There'd be a row obviously. But without Nicholas to back her, mama wouldn't be able to do a thing about it.

Jet probably sensed Juliet's disbelief. She'd lifted her

chin for a moment, shook her black hair from her
shoulders, and said defiantly, "Oh, all right, we like
each other. Why shouldn't we? We're the same sort—
not clever or cultured or highfalutin like the rest of
your family; We know what we want, and if we can
we get it. William will probably get free in the end,
Charlotte will divorce him. And then—"

"How do you know she will?"

"Because she's easy and good, and William will pay
her well. Her father hasn't a bean you know, and he'll
be all for it."

"Well . . . I wish you luck."

For a brief time Juliet's mind had been diverted
from her own unsatisfactory position to wondering
about Jet and William. But later she relapsed into
moody rebellion. Jet had noticed and said, "I
shouldn't be too angry if I were you. Just play Trefyn
up. Go his way and make him think he's married a
soppy 'yes' girl. Carry a few bricks and swoon over a
bucket." Her eyes had brightened with mischief, "Or
at least try. In his own way he's soft about you . . .
he'd never see you hurt or sick, although I wouldn't put
an old-fashioned walloping beyond him. But then, you
wouldn't mind that, would you?"

Juliet's cheeks had flamed. "Don't be silly. I'd bite
his hand."

"Good for you. I hope I'm in at the fun and games."

Lighthearted as Jet's words had been, Juliet had
ruminated over them, and the following morning
when she went out to the tumbled back of the farm,
looking like a boy in the breeches and jersey provided
by Jet, her lovely hair pushed under an old cap, she
surprised Trefyn by her meek answers when he said,

"Good, I hope you're prepared for a morning's hard work."

"Of course, Trefyn," she said unsmilingly, with her eyes raised solemnly and unblinking to his face. "I'll do my very best. Not that I'm terribly good at lifting, I broke my arm when I was young. But the other's really strong. Don't worry. I expect there's a knack in building houses. And I had such a good sleep last night. It was wonderful. Sleep makes such a difference, doesn't it? I hope you were comfortable. It seems such a shame you hadn't a proper bed."

Trefyn stared at her speculatively for a moment before saying, "Don't try any tricks, darling. This isn't an act. You're going to damn well pull your weight, or else!" and he frowned, adding, "And don't think you can fool me, either. You're as strong as a young mule, and just about as stubborn."

Juliet felt the warm color flooding her cheeks. But she controlled her temper, and when the short confrontation was over she was curiously deflated, thinking how stupid it was to be sparring and arguing when they should have been acting in the manner usual to a newly married couple passionately in love. But *did* Trefyn really love her in the way she wanted? During the weeks that followed there were tired times when she doubted he loved her at all. Except for Sundays, each morning was one long chore of hard work: carrying and lifting and mortaring, mixing and stirring the sticky stuff in buckets, getting stiff muscles into activity and sweating under workmen's clothes despite the hard cold weather. When either of the two men was free he gave a hand, and Jet occasionally took time off from the kitchen to assist in the manual la-

bor. Trefyn was withdrawn and silent most of the
time, sometimes stealing an enigmatic look at her
from withdrawn, narrowed eyes, but he seldom spoke
except at mealtimes or when work was finished for
the day, and then only on general subjects. Each evening after supper he went to his quarters in the barn
adjoining the stables where he stayed until the following morning.

Every night when Juliet had flung herself into bed,
she thought of him and wondered if he had pangs of
loneliness for her. But she was too tired to keep
awake, and sleep, when it came, was heavy and
dreamless.

Gradually the burned-out part of the house took
shape again, with larger kitchens, dairy and back parlor. As the weeks passed Juliet found she didn't tire so
easily. Her skin was browned from the fresh air, sun,
and cool winds from the sea. The color in her cheeks
turned from delicate pink to deep rosy gold. The
spring came early that year, starring the ditches with
celandines and early primroses, and bringing a drift of
pink thrift to the cliffs and headland.

When it was time for the roof, Trefyn and one of the
men tackled it.

"You've plenty to do on the ground," he told Juliet.
"It's no woman's job to lay slates and climb ladders.
What use would you be with a broken ankle?"

How *dare* he, Juliet thought, clenching both fists
fiercely. One day she'd show him; one day when the
wretched farm was completed, with everything
freshly painted, spic and span and as charming as she
could make it, she'd pack her clothes, face him, and
say: "There, Trefyn Connor. I've worked like a laborer, seen everything's right inside—even made the

curtains myself. You've a lovely home now, a house any woman would be proud of. But you've no wife. Good-bye, Trefyn. Our marriage can be annulled, I'm sure. I hope you soon find someone more to your taste than me."

She rehearsed similar speeches a hundred times or more, visualizing his reaction and shock with bitter triumph. He'd make a scene probably, but it would make no difference. He couldn't keep her by force forever, and she'd not even give him the satisfaction of looking back; just walk down the path and through the front gate with her head high, swinging her hips and shoulders in contempt. Further than that last defiant gesture she never thought, simply because the idea of a future without Trefyn was hard to contemplate. She wasn't sure, even, that she'd act that way when the moment came.

One afternoon when she went to pick wild daffodils from a small patch of woodland near the stream, she saw William with Jet half-hidden in a dip at the side of the lane. They were standing very close. William's arm was round the slim young figure, and his head was bent, with his lips resting on her black hair. Her face was lying against his shoulder. But when she looked up, Juliet could imagine the look in her eyes.

Feeling suddenly despondent and no longer interested in the daffodils, Juliet turned away, envying their obvious passion for each other, and saddened by her own inner torment. She was hurrying back along the lane when they suddenly saw her.

"Juliet!" she heard William call. "Wait."

She took no notice, just quickened her pace, hoping they'd be too engrossed in each other to bother about her.

But William quickly caught up with her and pulled her round to face him. "For heaven's sake, Juliet! What's the idea? Afraid to talk to me? Has he threatened you or something?"

When she didn't speak, he shook her sharply. "Well? Answer me; you know who I'm talking about. That young scoundrel, the man you married, what's he up to? Sending you out looking like a ragamuffin boy."

"He didn't send me. I came for daffodils, and I like my clothes. I feel free."

"*Free?* Cooped up in a burned-out hole of a building, working yourself to the bone like any gypsy? Now look here, Juliet, I've got the setup. Jet's put me in the picture, and I'd 've been along to knock the fellow to kingdom come, if she hadn't stopped me. And know why? Because she says you'd make a devil of a fuss and tell me to go to hell." He paused. "Is that true?"

Juliet thought for a moment, then said, "Yes, William, I think it is. Besides, you know mama wouldn't have me at Polbreath."

"Not by choice. But I'm master now. I know it's not easy thinking of father's death. But facts are facts. Another thing . . ."

"Yes?"

"I'd like you home, and I know Jason would. How do you imagine we feel about your mad-headed marriage? I could have told you the way it would be. Vengeance, that's all he thinks of, vengeance against the Trevarvases—any single one of us—because of the bloody fire and his precious foal. He blames *me!*" William thumped his chest, "Can you imagine me going in for arson, however much I hate the fellow's guts and everything else about him?"

Juliet shook her head. "No," she admitted.

"As for Abel, that poor old bloke. Why, it's farcical."

"Yes. And Trefyn will see it in time," Juliet managed to say with more conviction than she felt. "Please don't do anything rash, William. If he doesn't—if things go on as they are, I'll let you know. Truly."

"Hm!" William regarded her doubtfully, then he said, "In the meantime why don't you tell that young buccaneer of yours to get his head examined. It might be a good idea for him to have a word with the doctor about Abel, too. He'd only a matter of weeks to live anyway, and would have dropped dead before he'd gone a few yards up the slope."

Just at that moment Jet came cautiously toward them. "Have you told her, William?" she asked.

"What?"

"About us?"

William looked briefly discomforted. "This isn't the time and place. Better leave things for a bit."

"Why?" Jet's voice was defiant.

Juliet laughed. "Oh, you needn't bother. Everything's quite obvious, William. I've guessed for some time. Anyway, while you're married to Charlotte you can't do much about it, can you? And what about mama? You're a fine one to tell me how to manage my life, you know."

William turned abruptly. "Run away, both of you. I should be back at Polbreath by now."

They stood watching him as he strode down the lane to a tree where his gelding was tethered. He swung himself into the saddle, glanced back once and then was away, galloping toward the main valley road, a dark figure on a dark horse, reminding Juliet poignantly for a second or two of Nicholas, her father.

* * *

Young summer came, and by the end of May the farm
was rebuilt and enlarged, with the painting and deco-
rating completed and only a few minor adjustments to
be made. All that day, except for the groom, everyone
on the farm had worked feverishly until a late hour,
and as dusk came a curious air of peace and fulfillment encompassed not only the building but the
whole landscape, shrouding the moors and distant line
of land and sea into muted, misted uniformity.

Trefyn was completely silent over the late meal,
and Juliet, though inwardly excited, was shy and
withdrawn. Jet prattled artificially about things that
didn't really matter—how warm the mellow walls of
the new sitting room were, bringing out the golden
tones of their best carpet, what fun it would be to
have a really large kitchen to work in; and that they
should have Mrs. Beaton's cookery book to try out
new recipes on the fresh stove. The stables too!—they
looked splendid painted in that fresh bright green,
and it would be nice for Trefyn to sleep in the house
again. Well! wouldn't it?

At that point she'd broken off uncomfortably,
seeing Trefyn's eyes slide meaningfully toward Juliet
who was looking straight ahead with a rather haughty
look on her face.

Oh dear, Jet thought, she did hope her sister-in-law
wasn't going to be difficult now, just when Trefyn
was unbending. She looked so beautiful, too, in a
green dress William had sent from Polbreath—tight-
waisted and cut low on the shoulders—and wearing
her auburn hair pinned in a roll on top, leaving a
fringe curling above her clear gray eyes.

If Jet could only have seen into Juliet's mind she'd

have known Trefyn's young wife had no intention of being difficult in a hot-tempered way, just unapproachable. He had said more than once that if she dared go away he'd hunt for her and find her, and bring her back from wherever she was. Well, this time she didn't mean to go far—just someplace where she could be at peace for a time, sort herself out, and wait.

Wait for Trefyn. She'd know how to behave when they faced each other. For months he'd treated her no better than a hired laborer. It was her time now to tease and taunt a little.

As she slipped out of the door when Trefyn had gone to the stables and Jet was occupied in the dairy, she knew exactly her destination. She was wearing a cape and had changed her slippers for a pair of strong shoes. Soon, she guessed, the moon would creep from its veil of mist and the moors would be silver-bright below the stars, rising gradually until the whole landscape was a world of mystery and slipping shadows— of light and dark, peopled by the fantastic beings of her childhood's imagination. So she walked quickly, almost running through the violet dusk down the slope toward the narrow track that led upward to the summit of Rosebuzzan. It was strange, after her years at boarding school and the months in London, how well she remembered almost each boulder and bush, each twist and turn of the way. When she was a small girl of seven she'd escaped from the house one afternoon and gone there with the dog Jody, a black retriever. At the top of the hill they'd sat by the old standing stones and watched the sun sink in a ball of fiery red beyond the opposite hills and sea. It had seemed then that witches and dragons haunted the landscape, and if it hadn't been for Jody, she might have stayed until the mist came up and really frightened her. But the dog had been restless and led her down again. At the bottom she'd glanced back, and the stones were very clear and dark against the evening sky. Awe had filled her, because she'd sensed in a moment of unchildlike awareness an ancient wisdom reborn from earliest times—a secret knowledge formed through countless centuries that was inbred in the very granite itself. She couldn't explain it. But since then the old stone circle had held special meaning for her and had been always her retreat in times of doubt or stress.

And so it was once more.

The moon, as she'd predicted, had risen when she got there, and the valley below was a billowing, milky-white sea of mist. Around her the grouped stones stood strong and tall as ancient gods guarding their territory. She touched one, and then, pulling her cloak closely round her, sat down with her knees up, hands clasped round them.

How quiet it was. Except for a faint stirring where a mouse or rabbit scurried, there was no sound at all, no quiver of wind even, just the calm summer air fragrant with heather, thyme, and the salty, faint tang of brine from the sea. As the mist rolled in vaporous waves below, she caught at intervals a glimpse of Polbreath's roofs and towers, and her mind turned to Donna, her mother, who'd always seemed to resent her and now hated her. She recalled the time so long ago, before going to boarding school, when she'd prayed hard for love between them. But love hadn't come. And now, probably, it was far too late. Anyway, Trefyn came first. *Oh, Trefyn,* she thought, *please come. Please find me here.*

She hadn't really expected it to happen, but it did. One moment she was a solitary, crouched figure with long hair broken from its ribbon, free about her shoulders—a shadowed sprite-shape of the night among the greater shadows of the stones; the next there was movement and the approaching sound and shape of a horseman riding toward her. He came from the seaward side of the hill and was dark against the night sky. The horse was dark, too. For a bewildered moment it seemed her father rode there, or her father's ghost.

And then with a rush of excitement she realized it was no ghost or figment of her imagination, but Trefyn.

As he dismounted and took the great animal by its bridle, a silver glitter of light caught his face, accentuating the high cheekbones, dark eyes, and proud chin into vivid clarity. His mouth was unsmiling but softened with desire. The black curls, blown by the ride, were lit to pale fire by the moon. His tall, erect body held the arrogance of some legendary young monarch as he tethered the horse to a tree and came purposefully toward her.

She got to her feet, breathing quickly, with such a tumult of feeling in her she swayed for a second, struggling with an overwhelming longing intermingled suddenly with resentment and gathering defiance.

For so long he'd tyrannized over her, treating her like any hired workman—watching her daily fetch and carry for him, heave bricks, plaster and paint, tramp about in male breeches, hiding her femininity under

ugly jerseys and overalls—as he ignored her rights as a
wife and left her frigidly alone at nights when he took
off to his precious stables. She'd put up with it all
because she'd loved him and had hoped each day that
tomorrow would be different. But it hadn't been.
He'd gone on and on, thinking he'd only to lift a finger and she'd come running when he called. Well . . .
Mrs. Connor she might be in name, but theirs so far
had been an empty marriage, and bitterness flooded
her to see him so certain of himself, so damned cock-
sure now that all he'd aimed for had been achieved.

She steadied her nerves, straightened into a rigid
pose, and with only a yard between them said with
her clear eyes blazing, "What are you doing here, Trefyn?"

He was too astonished at first to answer. Then, with
one hand outstretched he said, "No more games, Juliet. You know very well."

"Don't touch me," she said in an icy whisper. "I'm
not your slave anymore. The time for scraping mud
from your boots is over, Trefyn. It's finished."

"What's finished?"

"Everything, I think—with you and me."

He reached for her arm and pulled her to him. "Finished? It's not properly begun yet. For weeks, months,
I've loved, lusted and longed for you. Do you think it's
been easy—"

She pulled herself free, took a step back, disturbing
a bird that rose squawking into the air. "Yes, for you,
because you're that kind—proud, arrogant, domineering. Oh, if you realized the contempt I feel for your
insufferable moods and gypsy ways—"

"Gypsy is it? Tinker? Is that how you think of me?

When I believed—" he broke off, his face very white in the fitful light.

"Yes, yes it is—" she cried as her heart pounded wildly against her ribs. "And you're on Trevarvas land, did you know? This bit of the hill belongs to Polbreath—so don't touch me Trefyn—leave me alone. Go back to your fine house and your precious stud. I've done what you wanted and it's odd, isn't it—I don't want you anymore. Once I'd have died for you. Now, I just don't care."

She turned and rushed quickly down the slope overlooking the coast. On the edge of the cliff to the west a beam of moonlight shone pale across the moors and glassy sea, momentarily throwing the solitary granite memorial to her grandfather into stark silhouette. Farther on, the black shapes of distant mine stacks, including Penmartin, and Wheal Flower soon to be opened again, rose, symbolic of man's power, against the sky.

She stood for a moment or two, as a rising wind from the sea brushed fresh against her face, blowing the molten cloud of hair in a flying stream behind her. Her throat was thick with emotion, every limb in her body felt suddenly tired. But at last, she told herself, at last she was free. Free, as Judy and Agatha would have wished, of male dominance and power. Free to be self-sufficient and alone.

Herself.

Just Juliet Trevarvas, with not a thing or person to care about or worry over in the world. She could live her own life now and be content.

Suddenly, without any warning, knowledge hit her, and she knew it was a lie. Without Trefyn nothing mattered.

MARIANNE HARVEY

Nothing at all.

She turned to go back, and he was there, standing by a bush, watching. "Oh, Trefyn," she said, "I thought . . ."

He strode forward and took her in his arms. "What you thought is of no account," he said with his lips warm against her ear. "Tinker I may be; but you're a witch, know that? A hot-tempered wild one if ever there was."

She lifted her face with the blood pulsing rich and warm in her cheeks. He kissed her, lifted her up, then carried her like a child to the ancient stones—her sanctuary.

Through the warm, steamy summer dusk the scent of bracken, heather, and sleeping bluebells drifted nostalgically in the soft air. He laid her down gently, unfastened the cape, and eased the green silk dress from her shoulders. Then, while she waited, he freed himself from jacket and breeches, and she saw him as he'd been that far-off day at the dew pond, only magnified, stronger, and swelling in his manhood—lithe and golden-skinned, wild as a Gypsy, proud as a king. He lay upon her, resting on his elbows for a moment, before the force that was in him found the deepest recess of her longing and need.

"Let this be our marriage bed," he said before taking her. "No stupid building or walls or roof, just you and I—my only love."

His lips were on her hair, her mouth, her breasts, and navel, till the leap of passion pulsed and claimed her, taking her to the deepest, wildest pitch of human experience. Stars glowed in the sky above, but she did not see; she knew only that by union all she'd been born for was realized—that miracle created of God but bequeathed to man through both the spirit and the flesh.

When the fever of giving and taking had died at last into calm, they lay for some time still entwined. A mouse scurried by their feet; a night bird suddenly sang.

Soon they got up, dressed, and hand in hand wandered to where the horse was tethered. Trefyn unloosed the animal, took the bridle, and slowly the three of them moved down the hill toward the farm. When they got there the door was open to receive them.

"At last," he said, and with his lips pressed gently against the hollow of her throat, he carried her over the threshold.

# CONCLUSION

On a day in June 1910, Donna Trevarvas stood at her bedroom window, watching a woman walking down the drive toward the house, Polbreath. The figure was young, almost a girl's, and she carried a baby in her arms. Until she reached the steps the rigid black-clad form did not move, simply stared fixedly ahead, wondering if what she saw was true—if her own daughter had at last thought fit to invade her privacy. Donna's feelings were mixed; she had grown used to loneliness. Since Nicholas died she'd assumed an armor of defense as somber and uncompromising as the dead black she always wore. Not, she thought ironically, that her attire was in any way out of place at the moment. King Edward had died in May that same year, and many people were in mourning merely out of respect for him. There was a feeling life would never be the same again. He'd been a peacemaker, and opinion was growing—even in Cornwall—that war was slowly brewing throughout Europe. This might mean that even Jason could be taken from her in the not too far-off future.

William she supposed would be safe. But William was little comfort to her. He seemed determined on marrying Jet Connor once Charlotte divorced him, which at last she'd agreed to do. As for Andrew—what satisfaction could there be in having a son helping savages in faraway Africa? Matthew, William's son—there was no doubt of that anymore—was amusing and a force in the household. But when William built his new home near Penmartin, he, too, would be gone. So what would remain for her at Polbreath but memories and a sense of life squandered and gone sour?

A bitter expression crossed her face. She was still a good-looking woman, hardly a thread of gray showed in her black hair, her eyes were still of the same orange gold they'd been when she was a girl, her figure was erect and slender. But her perfect features had become fixed into a static mold without warmth or happiness.

Jason had been good to her; she was grateful. But she'd sensed, recently, that life at Polbreath was more of a duty than a pleasure to him, and the conviction was growing in her that she should insist he leave and at last go to Paris as he'd planned before his father's accident.

Then what?

How would she fill her days in that great place, eating her meals alone at an empty table? What would be left for her but to go visiting mining families in an effort to be of some use before she was too old—to spend her time searching for charitable causes that would take her mind off herself?

What kind of an existence would it be?

In a succession of fleeting questions the thoughts raced one upon the other through her mind, and her heart instinctively quickened as the girl below paused, lifting her head up to the window. A ray of afternoon sunlight caught the young face sideways, accentuating the well-remembered features framed by russet hair—the dimpled chin, and mouth that seemed always on the brink of laughter or tears.

Donna's first instinct was to pull the curtains in defiance of the emotion that threatened to overwhelm her. Juliet, her daughter. How dare she intrude now after so long? And how dare she, Donna, bear to face her?

She stood there motionless for minutes it seemed, until there was a knock on the door, followed by Beth's face poking round.

"It's—it's—there's someone to see you in the parlor, Mrs. Trevarvas, ma'am—" Beth said hesitantly. "She's got a baby with her."

Donna turned. "Oh?"

Beth's lips tightened. "I think you should go down."

"Do you?" Donna said coldly. "Why? Did she give her name?"

"She didn't have to. It's your daughter, Miss Juliet—Mrs. Connor, I should say; and if you ask me, it's time you two made it up."

"What you think is of no importance," Donna snapped. "Or your business either—" Then, relenting suddenly, she added quickly, "Oh, Beth! I'm sorry. I didn't mean it." She swept a hand across her forehead wearily.

"Of course you didn't, my love," the housekeeper assured her in the old friendly terms of years ago. "But don't you think the time's come for bygones to be bygones? The little boy, too—he's—well, if you had just a look at him—"

"What do you mean?"

Beth smiled knowingly. "You go and see for yourself," she said.

"Very well," Donna agreed abruptly. "You can tell her I'll be down."

Beth withdrew, leaving Donna to get her nerves properly under control before she faced what she knew would be a strained and difficult interview ahead.

But it wasn't.

When she went into the room, Juliet was standing at the window, pointing out a small bird on the windowsill to her young son. She looked round quickly as the door opened and snapped to again. Juliet, with the child in her arms, moved slowly toward the tall, too-thin figure.

"Hullo, mother," she said with a tentative nervous note in her voice. "This is—Nicholas. Nicky. Say hullo to your grandmama, Nicky."

Donna moved forward cautiously, almost with fear. The child lifted his face to hers, gazing at her solemnly. He had dark, very striking eyes in a face that already held an uncanny resemblance not to Trefyn his father but to one person only—Nicholas, his grandfather.

Juliet waited until her mother echoed, "*Nicholas. Nicky. Oh, Juliet—*" her voice trembled, and suddenly the little boy was close against her, in her arms, while Juliet just stood by, watching and waiting.

And in those few moments all that was best of the past was reborn again like a great golden phoenix rising from the ashes.

As Donna stared into the child's eyes she saw reflected all the moments of her life that had eternal meaning—her time with Nicholas, the love that had grown and spread through difficulties and a wealth of enriching experiences so its roots could thrive and blossom anew.

There was no end to it.

No death.

Only change of circumstance, which she knew now she had the strength to accept and welcome.

She glanced briefly at the window, and just for a second, as driven clouds passed the face of the sun, they seemed to assume the shape of a horseman riding—forever riding—against the afternoon sky.

# THE DARK HORSEMAN

## Marianne Harvey
### author of *The Proud Hunter*

Beautiful Donna Penroze had sworn to her dying father that she would save her sole legacy, the crumbling tin mines and the ancient, desolate estate *Trencobban*. But the mines were failing, and Donna had no one to turn to. No one except the mysterious Nicholas Trevarvas—rich, arrogant, commanding. Donna would do anything but surrender her pride, anything but admit her irresistible longing for *The Dark Horseman*.

### A Dell Book    $3.25